THE EARTHLY PARADISE

ARTS AND CRAFTS

BY WILLIAM MORRIS AND HIS CIRCLE

FROM CANADIAN COLLECTIONS

Edited by

Katharine A. Lochnan

Douglas E. Schoenherr

Carole Silver

ART GALLERY OF ONTARIO

KEY PORTER BOOKS LIMITED

1993

Financial assistance for this exhibition has been generously provided by the Museums Assistance Program of the Department of Communications, Ottawa.

The Art Gallery of Ontario is funded by the people of Ontario through the Ministry of Culture and Communications. Additional financial support is received from the Municipality of Metropolitan Toronto, Communications Canada, and The Canada Council.

Canadian Cataloguing in Publication Data

Main entry under title: The Earthly paradise : arts and crafts by William Morris and his circle
Published in conjunction with an exhibition held at the Art Gallery of Ontario in 1993.
Includes index.
ISBN 1-55013-450-7

1. Morris, William, 1834-1896. 2. Morris, William, 1834-1896 – Influence. 3. Arts and crafts movement. 4. Arts and crafts movement – Canada. 5. Decorative arts – England – History – 19th century. 6. Decorative arts – Canada – 19th century. I. Art Gallery of Ontario.

NK1140.E27 1992   745′.0971   C92-094587-2

Editor: Robert Stacey
Editorial coordination: Brenda Rix and Catherine Van Baren
French translation coordination: Lucie Chevalier
Design: Boyes and Connolly, Toronto
Composition: Archetype, Toronto
Printing and binding: Mandarin Offset Inc., Hong Kong

Front and back covers: NO. F: 2. JOHN HENRY DEARLE, *Partridge* (embroidered panel) detail. Designed about 1890

Endpapers: NO. E: 15(b). WILLIAM MORRIS, *Sunflower* (hand-block-printed wallpaper) detail, 1879

Frontispiece: NO. M: 7. FREDERICK HOLLYER, *Burne-Jones and Morris*, 1874

Facing last text page: NO. M: 15. FREDERICK HOLLYER, *Burne-Jones and Morris, Sunday Morning, The Grange Garden*, 27 July 1890

Note to the Reader

Items marked with an asterisk (*) were not included in any of the venues of the travelling exhibition *The Earthly Paradise*, of which this publication serves as the catalogue.

Abbreviations: AAM: Art Association of Montreal; AGO: Art Gallery of Ontario, Toronto; MMFA: Montreal Museum of Fine Arts; NGC: National Gallery of Canada, Ottawa; PRB: Pre-Raphaelite Brotherhood; ROM: Royal Ontario Museum, Toronto; U of T: University of Toronto; V & A: Victoria and Albert Museum, London.

Itinerary of the Exhibition

Art Gallery of Ontario, Toronto	25 Jun. – 6 Sept. 1993
National Gallery of Canada, Ottawa	22 Oct. 1993 – 16 Jan. 1994
Musée du Québec, Quebec City	16 Feb. – 15 May 1994
Winnipeg Art Gallery, Winnipeg	23 Jul. – 9 Oct. 1994

Key Porter Books Limited
70 The Esplanade
Toronto, Ontario
Canada M5E 1R2

CONTENTS

FOREWORD

William Morris (1834-1896), poet, artist, designer, utopian socialist, and visionary, was above all an astute businessman. It was this aspect of his character that transformed the scope of his work in less than two decades from the decoration of his own home in an apple orchard in Kent to far-flung corners of the British Empire. Along with a taste for his designs, his persuasive ideas spread to North America through travel, emigration, art periodicals, company catalogues, trade fairs in Philadelphia and Boston, an agent in New York, and Morris's own writings.

This is the first time that a wide range of works by Morris and his associates from Canadian collections have been brought together for discussion and display. While there have been many important exhibitions that have explored individual aspects of Morris's activity, this exhibition provides the most comprehensive overview to date of the different areas in which Morris & Co. were active. The catalogue documents, again often for the first time, the existence of works long isolated, unknown and unsung, which collectively bear witness through their provenance to a virtually unbroken enthusiasm for Morris & Co. in Canada from the mid-1870s to the present day.

On the eve of the centenary of his death, this enterprise is a fitting tribute by Canada to a man who is increasingly recognized as one of the greatest designers of all time, while also providing a solid base for future investigation into the evolution of the Canadian Arts and Crafts movement. As contemporary artists stretch the boundaries of exploration and expression, we are increasingly witnessing a breakdown between traditional definitions of media. This exhibition reflects the continuing interest of the Art Gallery of Ontario in the inter-relationship between the visual and decorative arts. It is not without precedent; earlier exhibitions have included *Bauhaus* (1969), *Charles Rennie Mackintosh* (1978), *The Arts of Italy in Toronto Collections* (1981) and the *Functional Sculpture Competition* (1992).

It is appropriate that the first major loan exhibition in the newly expanded Art Gallery of Ontario should be devoted to a man who exercised a formative influence on artistic vision and education in the young Dominion of Canada. It brings together material from over sixty lenders, public and private, from Victoria, British Columbia, to Halifax, Nova Scotia. In addition to being seen in Toronto, *The Earthly Paradise* will travel east and west, to the National Gallery of Canada, the Musée du Québec, and the Winnipeg Art Gallery.

This ambitious and complex undertaking would not have been possible without the enthusiastic support and generosity of lenders, sister institutions, and scholars, as well as generous financial assistance from the federal Department of Communications' Museums Assistance Programme. While many individuals on the staff of the AGO have contributed to the exhibition, I would like to recognize the key role of Dr. Katharine Lochnan, curator of prints and drawings, who initiated and developed the exhibition concept over a period of twenty years. In bringing it to fruition, she put together a team of fourteen scholars in three countries who have contributed to the catalogue, two of whom became members of her curatorial committee: Dr. Carole Silver, professor of English at Yeshiva University, New York, and Dr. Douglas Schoenherr, associate curator of prints and drawings at the National Gallery of Canada.

Fuelled by their enthusiasm for Morris, this triumvirate has been responsible for building up and vetting the imposing inventory of works by Morris and his circle in Canadian collections, selecting the contents of the exhibition, defining the theme, sharing information, determining the nature and scope of the catalogue, editing contributions, and working with the designers to plan the exhibition layout.

We have been greatly assisted by our colleagues at the National Gallery of Canada. I would especially like to thank Dr. Shirley Thomson, director, and Brydon Smith, assistant director, collections and research, who have permitted Douglas Schoenherr to bring his encyclopedic knowledge to bear on this endeavour, and to devote a great deal of time and energy to its realization.

This exhibition is a complex and exciting collaboration between private collectors, public institutions, curators and scholars across the land, as well as their friends in Britain and the United States.

Glenn D. Lowry
Director, Art Gallery of Ontario

PREFACE

Although Canada's major public museums and art colleges were founded by friends and adherents of William Morris and the Arts and Crafts movement, there is not a single public display devoted to William Morris, Pre-Raphaelite painting, or the Arts and Crafts movement in a Canadian museum. The Victoria and Albert Museum, London, with its incomparable William Morris room, remains the epicentre of pilgrimage for Morris scholars. In organizing this exhibition from Canadian sources, we hope to introduce Morris and his associates to a broader Canadian public, and dispel the myth that there is little or no Morris & Co. material of consequence in this country.

It was in the context of the left-wing intellectual "counter-culture" and the hippy movement that the Utopian ideology of William Morris and the Arts and Crafts movement was rediscovered by the generation that came of age in the 1960s. In 1969 Mario Amaya, then chief curator, brought to the Art Gallery of Ontario the extraordinary exhibition *The Sacred and Profane in Symbolist Art*, which included paintings by Dante Gabriel Rossetti, Edward Burne-Jones, John Everett Millais and Walter Crane. As the newly appointed curatorial assistant, I was asked to hang them; the paintings left an indelible impression.

This exhibition generated a level of controversy and excitement in Toronto art circles seldom produced by historical exhibitions before or since. Senior members of the fine art confraternity, raised to believe that British art was provincial, the term Victorian pejorative, and the Pre-Raphaelite movement its artistic nadir, debated the merits of its contents vigorously. Prof. Stephen Vickers, chairman of the Fine Art Department at the University of Toronto, maintained (with a characteristic twinkle in his eye) that he never expected to live to see the day when the Pre-Raphaelites would hang on the walls of the Art Gallery of Ontario. Upon his retirement, he arranged to lend to the Gallery Burne-Jones's austere *Portrait of Caroline Fitzgerald* (No. B: 2) and *Mercury and Love*. While the former enjoyed the honour of being on the wall of his office, the latter lived face to the wall for many years before being permanently banished to the hallway, where it afforded the faculty much amusement.

There were a few ardent supporters in Toronto. The indomitable Jerrold Morris showed Pre-Raphaelite drawings in his gallery on Prince Arthur Avenue, among them sheets by Burne-Jones (Nos. A: 19, 21, 38), and the splendid Morris cartoon for stained glass, *St. Agnes and St. Alban in Procession* (No. A: 6). As soon as I was entrusted with my first purchase funds, I rushed to the Morris Gallery to secure a long-coveted Burne-Jones, only to learn that it had been sold the day before! The MacMillan and Perrin Gallery, which opened in Yorkville in the mid-1970s (see Nos. A: 9, 37 and D: 4), also showed Pre-Raphaelite drawings, but rapidly escalating prices continually placed choice pieces beyond our reach.

In the early 1970s, knowledge of the interesting cache of drawings and watercolours that C.T. Currelly had deposited in the European Department of the Royal Ontario Museum, the Kelmscott Press books in the Metropolitan Toronto Library, and choice items in private collections planted the kernel of an idea for an exhibition of prints, drawings and books related to Morris and his circle. A catalytic reaction took place when I met the Morris literary scholar Carole Silver in London in the summer of 1975; on discovering our mutual enthusiasm for Morris, we decided to work together on the project. To the delight of the newly formed William Morris Society of Canada, the exhibition received approval in principle in the late 1970s. Carole was appointed guest curator. In 1984 the search began in earnest when we examined material in Toronto, Montreal, and Ottawa.

From the beginning, we were keen to adopt a holistic approach to Morris (whose multifaceted activities have given rise to a fragmented one), while simultaneously focusing on his achievements in different media. Carole kept the big picture continually in mind, and we recruited a team of specialists to contribute expertise in each area.

The project took a great leap forward when Douglas Schoenherr wrote to inform us of the depth of his involvement in this area. After visiting Douglas in Ottawa in 1984, we invited him to join the team. Douglas brought a new energy and commitment to the project and played an indispensable role by continuing the search, building up the inventory list, and helping to define the theme. The three of us joined forces in a curatorial committee, struck in 1990, to make final decisions regarding the exhibition contents and the component parts of the catalogue. The geographic spread posed a formidable challenge, but in the fall of 1990 Douglas and I travelled from Victoria to Halifax, following up every lead, and examining every piece in the original.

We have experienced the thrill of the chase. Carole and I will never forget our first glimpse of *The Partridge* (No. F: 2) as Lady Margaret Ayre (now deceased) gently extracted it from a plastic garbage bag and spread it out in all its glory on the green shag carpet in the lobby of the Chateau Versailles hotel in Montreal. I will never forget Douglas's excitement when he was finally able to see, and positively identify, the Morris & Co. stained glass window that had eluded A.C. Sewter, the leading expert on the subject, in Wilmot United Church in Fredericton. Nor will we forget the breathless scramble to secure the last-minute loan of the splendid Holland Park carpet from Peter Tolliday who, unaware of the exhibition, had consigned it to a London auction house (No. F: 30).

The items in this exhibition have all found their way to Canada at different times, their advent corresponding with recurring waves of enthusiasm from the mid-1870s to the present day. We hope that they will provide a clearer picture of the Morris movement on this side of the Atlantic, and that the handful of unique items, along with the many fine examples, will more than compensate for any limitations imposed by adopting a geographical frame of reference. This *omnium gatherum* is designed to provide a delightful glimpse of Morris's "earthly paradise," in which nature, art, and literature are united.

Katharine A. Lochnan
Chair, Curatorial Committee

ACKNOWLEDGEMENTS

The realization of this exhibition and the publication that accompanies it has involved a network of individuals in Canada, Britain and the United States, including the members of the curatorial committee, the curators and staff of lending institutions, catalogue contributors, and the William Morris Society of Canada. Many individuals have assisted in locating material and facilitating loans. We are especially grateful to Martha Cooke, The Very Rt. Rev. Dean Cruikshank, Marie Elwood, Conrad Graham, Valerie Greenfield, Jean Johnson and the William Morris Society of Canada, Walter Klinkhoff, John Morris, Steven Otto, Trudy Ramsey, The Rt. Rev. G.H. Parke-Taylor, the Rev. Ron Sykes, R.H.V. Tee & Son Ltd., and Simon Waegemakers.

There has been a groundswell of patriotic support for our effort not only to bring the material together but to ensure that it is seen in three regions of Canada. Our sixty-three lenders (see Lenders to the Exhibition) come from almost every province of the country. Their generosity, despite legitimate concerns about fragile and light-sensitive material, has been exemplary. We are especially indebted to the thirty-six private lenders to whom such loans cause inconvenience and the temporary foregoing of the joy they derive from their cherished objects. I would like to mention one individual in particular: Peter Tolliday, of Peter Tolliday Oriental Carpets, Vancouver, who went to a great deal of trouble to make his splendid Holland Park carpet available.

Institutional lenders have supported the venture from the outset, and curators, librarians, and clerics have provided assistance well beyond the call of duty, frequently drawing to our attention material in their area. A love of Morris and their concern to make their own holdings better known have fuelled their enthusiasm, resulting in the collaboration of fourteen art galleries and museums, eleven university libraries, two public libraries, and two churches.

We have brought to Canada a handful of items that were at one time in this country, or are thought to have been. Thanks are due to the International Museum of Photography, George Eastman House, in Rochester, New York, for lending photographs formerly in the Gordon Conn collection in Toronto, and to Arthur Sanderson & Son Ltd., England, for lending wallpaper samples and blocks through Arthur Sanderson Canada Inc. Although Morris wallpaper was installed in Montreal residences, very little, understandably, has survived.

The Earthly Paradise began with a very modest idea. As it expanded, more and more individuals became involved in turning vision into reality. I could not have seen it through without the full support of Douglas Schoenherr and Carole Silver, who brought their scholarly arsenals to bear on the topic, along with irrepressible enthusiasm and an unshakeable belief in the value of the exercise.

In putting together the exhibition and publication, we have depended heavily on the expertise of our thirteen catalogue contributors, all of whom have hectic schedules, and for whom participation has been largely a labour of love. They have worked closely with the curatorial committee, shortlisting works for inclusion and advising on packing and installation. While many of them have been able to inspect the works in the original, logistics have also necessitated the writing of entries on the basis of Polaroid photographs and secondary sources. Their good humour and team spirit, as well as their generosity in sharing information with each other, have been greatly appreciated.

A team of conservators has gone to work across the land preparing material for exhibition. Catherine Collins, Emrys Evans and Isabella Krasuski have provided valuable advice.

Leading London dealers have generously provided information gained from the unparalleled experience of discovering, handling, identifying and publishing Morris material. They include Richard Dennis, Jeremy Maas, Geoffrey Munn, and Michael Whiteway. In Toronto we were assisted by Ronald Fraleigh and Ellen Morris.

The authors are indebted to many other individuals in Canada, Britain, and the United States. Meredith Chilton particularly wishes to thank David McFadden, Susan Jefferies, Diane Wolfe, Barbara Ratigan, Carola Gascoyne, Dr. Timothy Dickenson, and Kathleen Campbell. Elizabeth Collard would like to thank Dr. R.V.V. Nicholls and Mrs. Lynn Miller. Rosalind Pepall is grateful to Anthony Adamson, Susan Wagg, and Martin Segger. K. Corey Keeble would like to thank Anne Pappart and the late Dr. Alice B. Hamilton. Douglas Schoenherr expresses his gratitude to colleagues at the National Gallery of Canada: Michael Pantazzi, Maria Conley, Julie Hodgson, Bonnie Bates, Maija Vilcins, and Catherine Jensen. Among the many who have assisted, he would especially like to thank Roger Boulet, Felicity Bradley,

Avril M. Broster, Howard Collinson, Peter Cormack, Linda Dornan, Jordan Elliott, Marie Elwood, Lydia Foy, Prof. William E. Fredeman, Norah Gillow, Julian Hartnoll, Doris and Edward Hollamby, Prof. Thomas Howarth, Ann Hutchison, Adam Karpowicz, Gemey Kelly, Marie Korey, Dr. Dennis T. Lanigan, Ian G. Lumsden, Micheline Moisan, John Morris, Peter Nahum, Daniel Perrin, Scott Robson, John Shearer, Tom Smart, Joseph M. Tanenbaum, Ian Thom, Stephen Wildman, Andrew Wilton, Bruce Wilson, and Anne Yandle. Robert Little would like to thank Clive Wainwright. I would like to thank Charlotte Gere, Geoffrey Munn, Judy Rudoe, Susan Stronge, Lesley Hoskins, Neville Bowers, and Stephen Astley.

This project could not have been realized without significant sponsorship from the Department of Communications' Museums Assistance Program. We have also received support from the British Council, Arthur Sanderson Canada Inc., and Robert Dirstein of Dirstein and Robertson.

We are grateful to graphic designers Kevin Connolly and Dennis Boyes for their elegant catalogue design and editor Robert Stacey, who worked with the authors to ensure that their connected prose is as coherent and consistent as possible.

Finally, I would like to thank Brenda Rix, who has taken on the daunting task of coordinating authors, lenders, and the many staff members at the Art Gallery of Ontario who have played a vital role in bringing the project to fruition. Her patience and organizational skills have inspired confidence in all who have had contact with her.

In closing I would like to thank Director Glenn D. Lowry and Chief Curator Roald Nasgaard for their support of this undertaking through thick and thin, ensuring its successful completion at a time of institutional crisis.

K.A.L.

LENDERS TO THE EXHIBITION

INSTITUTIONAL AND CORPORATE LENDERS

Archives and Special Collections, York University, Downsview, Ontario

Art Gallery of Ontario, Toronto, Ontario

Arthur Sanderson Canada Inc., Toronto, Ontario

Beaverbrook Art Gallery, Fredericton, New Brunswick

Bertrand Russell Archives, McMaster University Library, Hamilton, Ontario

Blacker-Wood Library of Biology, McGill University, Montreal, Quebec

Bruce Peel Special Collections Library, University of Alberta, Edmonton, Alberta

Centre Canadien d'Architecture/Canadian Centre for Architecture, Montreal, Quebec

Christ Church Cathedral, Vancouver, British Columbia

The Church of St. Andrew and St. Paul, Montreal, Quebec

Department of Archives and Special Collections, University of Manitoba Libraries, Winnipeg, Manitoba

Department of Rare Books and Special Collections, McGill University Libraries, Montreal, Quebec

The Edmonton Art Gallery, Edmonton, Alberta

Governing Council of the University of Toronto, Toronto, Ontario

International Museum of Photography, George Eastman House, Rochester, New York, U.S.A.

McCord Museum of Canadian History, Montreal, Quebec

Maltwood Art Museum and Gallery, University of Victoria, Victoria, British Columbia

Metropolitan Toronto Reference Library, Toronto, Ontario

The Montreal Museum of Fine Arts, Montreal, Quebec

The Museum for Textiles, Toronto, Ontario

National Gallery of Canada, Ottawa, Ontario

National Library of Canada Rare Book Collection, Ottawa, Ontario

Owens Art Gallery, Mount Allison University, Sackville, New Brunswick

Peter Tolliday Oriental Carpets, Vancouver, British Columbia

Robertson Davies Library, Massey College, University of Toronto, Toronto, Ontario

Royal Ontario Museum, Toronto, Ontario

Special Collections, Douglas Library, Queen's University, Kingston, Ontario

Thomas Fisher Rare Book Library, University of Toronto, Toronto, Ontario

University of British Columbia Library, Special Collections, Vancouver, British Columbia

Vancouver Art Gallery, Vancouver, British Columbia

Vancouver Museum, Vancouver, British Columbia

William Inglis Morse Collection, Special Collections, Dalhousie University Libraries, Halifax, Nova Scotia

Winnipeg Art Gallery, Winnipeg, Manitoba

PRIVATE LENDERS

The late Margaret I. Ayre

Virginia Berry

Conrad Biernacki

Elizabeth Collard

R. Fraser Elliott

Dr. and Mrs. Neville Elwood

Prof. John Ettlinger

Mrs. John Flemer

Prof. William E. Fredeman

Prof. Thomas Howarth

Ruth Jackson

Dr. Dennis Lanigan

Enid Maclachlan

Heather Maclachlan

Mrs. Graham McInnes

Simon McInnes

Mr. and Mrs. Jack Morris

Vivian Morris

H.A. Parker

Joan R. Randall

Dr. Harry and Barbara Rosenberg

Jules Samson

Mr. and Mrs. John D. Shearer

Joey and Toby Tanenbaum

Mary F. Williamson

Dennis Young

Four anonymous lenders

CONTRIBUTORS

Meredith Chilton: curator, George R. Gardiner Museum of Ceramic Art, Toronto

Elizabeth Collard: honorary curator of ceramics, McCord Museum of Canadian History, Montreal; consultant on ceramics, Canadian Museum of Civilization, Ottawa

K. Corey Keeble: associate curator, European Department, Royal Ontario Museum, Toronto

Richard Landon: director, Thomas Fisher Rare Book Library, University of Toronto

Robert Little: curator, Decorative Arts (non-Canadian), The Montreal Museum of Fine Arts, Montreal

Katharine A. Lochnan: curator, Prints and Drawings, Art Gallery of Ontario, Toronto

Brian Musselwhite: curatorial assistant, European Department, Royal Ontario Museum, Toronto

Linda Parry: deputy curator, Department of Textiles and Dress, Victoria and Albert Museum, London

Rosalind Pepall: curator, Canadian Decorative Arts, The Montreal Museum of Fine Arts, Montreal

Brenda Rix: guest curator and former assistant curator, Prints and Drawings, Art Gallery of Ontario, Toronto

Douglas E. Schoenherr: associate curator, European and American Prints and Drawings, National Gallery of Canada, Ottawa

Carole Silver: professor of English Literature and chair, Humanities Division, Yeshiva University, New York

Maia-Mari Sutnik: photographic coordinator, Art Gallery of Ontario, Toronto

BIBLIOGRAPHICAL NOTE

Space does not permit the inclusion of a bibliography of references cited in this publication. For these, the endnotes to each section should be consulted.

For virtually comprehensive bibliographies of publications by and related to William Morris and Morris & Co., see Gary L. Aho, *William Morris: A Reference Guide* (Boston: G.K. Hall and Co., 1985); David and Sheila Latham, *An Annotated Critical Bibliography of William Morris* (London: Harvest Wheatsheaf; New York: St. Martin's Press, 1991), and William S. Peterson, *A Bibliography of the Kelmscott Press* (Oxford: Clarendon Press, 1991). For works on the Pre-Raphaelites published prior to 1965, see William E. Fredeman, *Pre-Raphaelitism: A Bibliocritical Study* (Cambridge, Mass.: Harvard University Press, 1965).

David and Sheila Latham are based in Lethbridge, Alberta, and W.E. Fredeman in Vancouver.

SETTING THE CROOKED STRAIGHT: THE WORK OF WILLIAM MORRIS

Carole Silver

Dreamer of dreams, born out of my due time,
Why should I strive to set the crooked straight?
– William Morris, *The Earthly Paradise*

When William Morris died in 1896, at the age of sixty-two, his doctor noted that the cause of death was "simply being William Morris and having done more work than most ten men."[1] Poet, designer, translator, thinker, lecturer, fantasist, ecologist, preservationist, reformer, socialist, Morris produced enough in each sphere for a single lifetime. Always a "maker," he designed furniture, stained glass, tiles, wallpapers, woven textiles, printed textiles, tapestries, embroideries, carpets, type-fonts, and books and their bindings. He illuminated and calligraphed manuscripts and turned his hands permanently blue dyeing fabrics he had designed. In his later years he fought to prevent the destruction, disguised as "restoration," of historic buildings; he struggled to combat industrial pollution and to create better towns and cities; he battled to correct the abuses of Capital and Empire, and to change the world through education and revolution. Behind these seemingly disparate activities lay a powerful unifying impulse: the desire to make this earth, the only one we human beings possess, an earthly paradise for all.

Born in 1834 into a rising middle-class family, Morris was exposed to the upbringing and education typical of a Victorian gentleman. He was raised in affluence in Walthamstow (then rural rather than suburban), placed at Marlborough College in 1848, and, when a student riot interrupted his education in 1851, tutored privately at home. He entered Exeter College, Oxford, in 1853, travelled to Belgium and France during two long vacations, changed his career goals several times, and graduated from Oxford (without honours) in 1855. He had intended, in the aftermath of the religious fervour created by the Oxford Movement, to become a priest, but he had found a competing vocation in art, and decided upon a career in architecture.

Like other bright and lively undergraduates, Morris made close friends at university, among them Ned Jones of Birmingham (later famous as Sir Edward Coley Burne-Jones, Bt.) and Charles Faulkner (who would join him in the first Morris & Co.); with them and other lifelong comrades, Cormell (Crom) Price, R.W. Dixon, and William Fulford, he further explored the medieval world he so admired, and debated the issues of his own day, ago-nizing over the ravages wrought by the Industrial Revolution and seeking answers to the question of the "Condition of England."

For Morris and his friends had been born into an age of radical change and industrial and social upheaval. Because he was from Birmingham, Ned Jones had probably seen some of the problems created by the Industrial Rev-olution at first hand, but all the young men knew of the horrors caused by factories – the "dark Satanic mills" of Victorian reality and imagination – of increasing pollution and squalor, of the despoiling of the countryside, and of the hideous condition of the industrial landscape. Moreover, they recog-nized that urban industrialization had resulted in the dehumanizing of work-ers, in the turning of men and women into "hands," in the degradations of slum life including prostitution, incest, and infanticide, and in the building of grey and hideous Coketowns. To them, the condition of England seemed terminal – not one of technological advance and spiritual progress, but one of materialism, class warfare and aesthetic blight.

This group of idealistic young men first committed themselves to a "Crusade and Holy Warfare against the age"[2] by planning to establish a celibate, monastic community (not unlike that of John Henry Newman at Littlemore) and, slightly later, by forming another sort of brotherhood. The latter would encompass both the activism preached by such Christian Social-ists as Frederick Denison Maurice and Charles Kingsley and attention to lit-erary work and art. Later, Morris and Jones were to become involved with the second phase of yet another brotherhood, that of the Pre-Raphaelites.

Admiring the first volumes of *Modern Painters* and especially the famous chapter on "The Nature of Gothic" in *The Stones of Venice* of 1853 (see No. L: 17), Morris and Burne-Jones became personally acquainted with their author, John Ruskin (1819-1900), the arbiter of Victorian Gothic taste. Excited by Ruskin's protests against the disjunction between art and labour in the post-Renaissance world, and by his equation of good art and a good society, they found in him a hero for their generation. In part through Ruskin's praise of Pre-Raphaelitism, they became attracted to the new movement, with its attention to "truth to nature" and truth to imagina-tion, and its vision of an art untainted by Raphael and his followers or by the Royal Academy. They rapidly fell under the influence of one of the

NO. M: 2
ELLIOT & FRY, LONDON
Portrait of Ford Madox Brown,
c. 1878

founding members of the PRB, an experienced and productive painter and poet, Dante Gabriel Rossetti.

Even in these early years, Morris differed from others of his class and education in his passion for and knowledge of history, his half-conscious unconventionality, and his enormous energy. In 1856, at the age of twenty-two, he was already publishing a magazine, originally titled *The Brotherhood*, modeled on the *The Germ*, the journal created by the Pre-Raphaelite Brotherhood, and finally called *The Oxford and Cambridge Magazine*. It contained his own poems, tales, and critical essays, as well as those of his friends. He was studying architecture, as an apprentice to G.E. Street (1824-1881), designing furniture for the flat in London's Red Lion Square he shared with Burne-Jones, struggling to become a painter, and pledging himself to a Brotherhood of Art. Not unlike the young Bernard Shaw, Morris had a sense that there was something at which he could excel, but could not yet determine what that "something" was.

By 1858, he had fallen in love with Jane Burden, the Oxford hostler's daughter whose face, repeatedly depicted by Rossetti (see Nos. A: 43-44), became an archetype of Pre-Raphaelite beauty, and thoughts of brotherhood succumbed to thoughts of marriage. He published an important, if not critically successful, volume of poetry, *The Defence of Guenevere*. And, to celebrate his marriage to Jane Burden in 1859, he commissioned a friend from Street's office, Philip Webb, to design a home for himself and his bride, the

Red House at Upton, near Bexleyheath, Kent, not far from the ancient Pilgrim's Way of Chaucer's time.

It was as a direct result of the efforts to decorate this home that Morris, Marshall, Faulkner & Co. (the first Morris firm) was born. Morris, once again unable to find furnishings that suited him, decided with his friends to make his own. Thus, the band designed furniture and stained-glass; they painted ceilings, embroidered wall-hangings, and covered walls with murals. Rossetti's *Salutation of Beatrice* (No. B: 4) was originally part of a settle designed for the house. In April 1861 the group issued a prospectus advertising themselves as "Fine Art Workmen in Painting, Carving, Furniture and the Metals." The founding members were Ford Madox Brown, a painter associated with the PRB, who had already designed furniture and stained-glass for commercial firms; Edward Burne-Jones, Morris's lifelong colleague in design (also skilled at stained-glass design, he had taught a class in it at the Working Men's College); Charles Faulkner, a Fellow in Mathematics at Oxford and a contributor to *The Oxford and Cambridge Magazine*; P.P. Marshall, a friend of Brown's and an amateur painter as well as a professional surveyor and sanitary engineer; Dante Gabriel Rossetti (also adept at designing glass for commercial firms); Philip Webb, both a practising architect and a skilled designer of metalwork and glassware; and Morris himself. Each member held a single share in the firm, while Faulkner served as book-keeper and Morris as full-time manager.

The new firm's prospectus described its areas of expertise as mural decoration, carving, stained glass, metalwork, jewellery, furniture and embroidery. What it produced was not entirely new; in actuality, Morris and his friends could probably have found the furniture they desired among the pieces created by Augustus Welby Northmore Pugin (1812-1852) or by the Gothic Revival architect William Burges (1827-1881). Other designers, including Sir Henry Cole (1808-1882), Pugin, and Owen Jones (1809-1874), were already at work reviving the decorative arts. In 1847 Cole had established Summerly's Art Manufactures to encourage painters and sculptors to produce worthy designs for everyday articles and thus raise the low level of Industrial Art. Then, in the early 1850s, he had founded the South Kensington Museums (which became the Victoria and Albert Museum) to hold examples of fine workmanship in the applied arts; still later, he developed schools of design attached to the Museum. A.W.N. Pugin was not only the great apologist for the Victorian Gothic revival but had himself linked architecture and industrial design in his own workshop, designing jewellery, plate, furniture, fabrics and stained glass, while preaching the connections between the use of the Gothic and the improvement of society. Owen Jones had contributed to both the theory and the practice of the decorative arts; he argued that "No improvement can take place in the Art of the present generation

NO. M: 1
W. & D. DOWNEY,
*John Ruskin and Dante Gabriel
Rossetti in Cheyne Walk
Garden*, June 1863

until all classes, Artists, Manufacturers, and the Public, are better educated in Art" and thus recognize the "existence of general principles" of good design.[3] Although his main fame was as a pattern designer, Jones had successfully practised many of the applied arts.

The new element in Morris, Marshall, Faulkner & Co. was that its participants perceived themselves as a cooperative of artists; they intended to involve themselves in the actual production of the objects they designed, instead of merely leaving such labour to semi-skilled workers. Consciously or unconsciously, the scheme signalled their desire to recapture the spirit of the Middle Ages, a period in which (following Ruskin) they believed that there had been no distinction between "high art" and handicraft, an era when artists designed all sorts of decorative objects. Their plan constituted a protest against the fragmentation of work and of workers caused by the division of labour. Their essential drive was to reintegrate the arts.

Interestingly, the Firm was something of a family affair; Morris embroidered, teaching his wife and her sister, Elizabeth (Bessy), some of the fine points of the craft. Lucy and Kate Faulkner, Charles's sisters, painted tiles and pottery. After 1864, many of these ceramics were designed by the great designer and unofficial affiliate of the Firm, William Frend De Morgan (1839-1917). Georgiana Burne-Jones, Ned's wife and Morris's confidante, painted tiles and embroidered. Morris himself does not appear to have designed furniture for the company, although he probably assisted in the decorating of a few of the large, imposing "State" or public pieces. But he tried his hand at almost all the other crafts.

Contrary to expectations, the Firm's first important commissions were not primarily domestic. Instead, they were for ecclesiastical furnishings, especially stained-glass windows: windows for the new Gothic churches G.E. Street and G.F. Bodley (1827-1907) were building or for the older ones they were renovating. The windows, which competitors accused the Firm of "faking" rather than making – insisting that they were pieces of medieval glass restored – reveal Morris's knowledge of history and sense of technology. For Morris controlled the colour and layout and designed the backgrounds for much of the glass; contrary to the myth that he could not effectively draw human figures, he created some 150 subject-designs. Yet it was when he began to design flat patterns, wallpapers and hangings that he found his true *métier*.

By the end of 1862, the Firm was established in earnest, greatly helped by the displays organized and produced for the International Exhibition at South Kensington earlier that year. Its two stalls in the "Mediaeval Court" of the Exhibition, one containing stained glass, the other, "decorated furniture, tapestries [actually, embroideries], etc.,"[4] received considerable attention from both the trade and the public. The jury awarded the company two medals and, equally important, almost £150-worth of goods were sold. Thus, Red House and the dream of a communal life shared with friends, especially the Burne-Joneses, had to be renounced, and Morris literally became "the Firm." The business side was taken over by the astute and careful Warington Taylor, until his death in 1870. And two important commissions were received: the decoration of the Green Dining Room in what is now the V & A, and the decoration of a suite of rooms at St. James's Palace – the first of several prestigious royal commissions.

Yet Morris still found time to write. He had not stopped after the mainly unfavourable reception of his first brilliant, eccentric, and cacophonous volume, *The Defence of Guenevere* (1858); instead, he had changed genres. Rather than writing intense lyrics and dramatic monologues whose themes were drawn from Malory's *Morte D'Arthur* or Froissart's *Chronicles* or from the world of folklore, he had turned, first, to depicting "Scenes From the Fall of

Troy" with which – in the form of murals by Burne-Jones – he had intended to decorate the staircase walls of Red House (neither the powerful set of poems about a Homeric society gone bad nor the wall-paintings were ever finished), and secondly, to a series of long verse narratives drawn from Greek mythology, medieval romance, and folklore that were to comprise *The Earthly Paradise*. One of these tales, *The Life and Death of Jason*, a book-length retelling of the *Argonautica* of Apollonius of Rhodes, published separately in 1867, made him famous. His reputation was secured by *The Earthly Paradise* (1868-70), twenty-four tales in verse prefaced by a "Wanderers' Pro-logue" which set the time of telling in the plague years of the fourteenth century and explained the reasons for the quest for a terrestrial Eden. Vic-torian audiences loved the work's medievalized Greek and Norse myths as well as its renderings of the lore and legend of the Middle Ages. Perfect for family reading, with its beautiful descriptive passages, muted sensuality, and ruminations on love, fate, and death, *The Earthly Paradise* was repeatedly republished during the period. But the poem meant something more to Morris than to much of his audience; it contained his vision of an alter-native world, his dream of a place without "six counties overhung with smoke", a realm where contentment, simplicity and communality of life were possible. The verse tales, too, were connected to Morris's work in design. In their utilization of verbal and motival patterns and of complex substructures of variation and repetition, they are not unlike designs for chintz or wallpaper; their posing of figures, especially those of women centred icon-like in landscapes, is strikingly similar to the single-figured tapestries and stained-glass panels Morris was simultaneously creating.

But while the late 1860s brought poetic fame to Morris, they also brought the fading of his marriage. Jane Morris became the favourite model and the beloved of Dante Gabriel Rossetti, and Morris, perhaps to compen-sate for her loss, began an intensive study of the Icelandic language and of Norse mythology and history. He turned increasingly to Georgiana Burne-Jones for support and consolation, perhaps even for romantic love. In Kelm-scott Manor, in Lechlade, Oxfordshire, he found a house to love, "a heaven on earth," as he described it to his friend Faulkner in a letter of 1871. Joint tenant with Rossetti in the Elizabethan stone house, Morris often left Jane and their two daughters there, finding his own solace in intensified work for the Firm, in manuscript illumination – like embroidery, a popular Vic-torian pastime for both men and women – and in two momentous trips to Iceland in 1871 and 1873.

Iceland, a mixture of the historic, the awesome, and the ordinary (of Reykjavik Morris wrote, "the town itself might be in Canada"), came to rep-resent an important conceptual and symbolic structure in his life. While some critics have explored the connections between the Icelandic journeys and the

lessons of simplicity and stoic fortitude they provided, and others have discussed Morris's growing realization that even grinding poverty was less evil than class inequality, no one has examined the relations between Iceland and Morris's decorative art. Did Iceland engender the more austere and formalist turn of Morris's patterns in the late 1870s? Did his Icelandic experiences begin the gradual process that changed his taste from a love for what Jack Lindsay describes as the dark richness of Red House[5] to the lighter, simpler white-walled decor he created in the 1880s? (Descriptions of Icelandic interiors in his journals of 1871 and 1873 lend some validity to this idea.) Did Iceland, at the least, cause him to look more carefully at the patterns and designs of cultures other than his own?

Clearly, Iceland did turn Morris from introspection to action in one sphere. By the end of 1874, he had decided to reconstitute the Firm – in effect, to free himself from Rossetti. His reasons were partially economic; in 1874, England entered a long economic recession and, with effective competition coming from American and German industry, the British were discovering that they were not the only serious manufacturers in the world. In addition, Morris was having personal financial problems; when the value of the mining shares that constituted his legacy fell in the late 1860s, he was nearly bankrupt, and he was regularly short of funds in the early 1870s. Most important, from Morris's point of view, was the fact that Marshall, Brown, and Rossetti had been "sleeping partners" for a number of years. Though Brown and Rossetti contributed fine work to the Firm (see, for example, Brown's splendid cartoon for a stained-glass window executed by the Firm, *The Finding of Moses*, No. A: 8), they were paid for their individual designs. The Firm really consisted of Morris, Burne-Jones and Philip Webb. In the strife that followed, Burne-Jones and Webb supported Morris, while Brown, backed by Rossetti and Marshall, resisted the plan for a "buy-out" and demanded a sizeable compensation for his share. A compromise figure, £1,000 to each member, was arrived at in 1875, and the Firm was dissolved. The bad feelings that resulted left Brown and Morris estranged for the next ten years, while the rift between Rossetti (who allocated his share of the money to Mrs. Morris) and Morris never healed. However, the change created a new Morris & Co. and left Morris its sole manager and policy maker.

From 1875 on, textiles were the new company's most popular products. Morris became extraordinarily productive as a fabric and wallpaper designer, creating at least twenty-two chintzes and eleven papers between 1876 and 1883. With the help of Thomas Wardle, he began to experiment with dye-stuffs, learning from old herbals and attempting to recapture the lost art of vegetable dyeing – not for esoteric reasons, but because he found modern aniline dyes either too ugly to look at or too fugitive to be useful. (Colours for wallpapers were apparently no problem and the papers continued to be

Kelmscott Manor: from the Orchard   Frederick H. Evans 1897.Spring.

printed by Jeffrey and Co. until after Morris's death.)

At the same time, serving as an adviser to the Science and Art Department of the South Kensington Museums, Morris began the serious study of textiles and woven goods from other cultures; he became interested in the textiles of medieval Spain and Sicily, in Flemish and Burgundian tapestries, and in Persian carpets. His own designs, never merely archeological, reflect not only a synthesis of formalism and naturalism but his increasingly historical and multi-cultural awareness. Such popular chintzes as *Strawberry Thief* and *Brother Rabbit*, and the great woolen woven hangings like *Peacock and Dragon* (No. F: 20) are inspired by the medieval woven silks of Sicily and northern Italy. Persian rugs provided motifs not only for Morris & Co.'s own carpets but for ceiling papers; Indian fabric designs contributed richly to such fabrics and papers as *Snakeshead* and *Bluebell* and *Evenlode* (Nos. F: 8, 15).

So successful was the new company that by 1877 Morris could afford to open a fashionable showroom on Oxford Street (fig. 1). There one could buy everything needed to furnish an elegant home. In addition to "Morris" chairs and other furniture, there were "painted glass windows," fabrics, wallpapers, curtains and carpets, embroideries, upholstery and tiles, while, under the rubric of "general house decorations," one could purchase the silver, metalwork, glass, and ceramics of Morris friends and associates, such as William De Morgan, as well as imported wares from Italy and India.

Morris's growing historicism and fascination with foreign cultures was expressed in other ways as well. Preoccupied with translating the saga literature of the North, he published in 1877 the poem he thought his best, a version of the Icelandic *Volsunga Saga* (which he had translated in 1869), *The Story of Sigurd the Volsung*. The same fascination with history and its impact on his society led him to social activism in the areas of preservation and of politics. In 1877, together with Carlyle, Ruskin, Burne-Jones and Webb, Morris became a founder of the Society for the Protection of Ancient Buildings, and its secretary. "Anti-Scrape," as it was jocularly called, stemmed directly from restorations being made to Tewkesbury Abbey, but its real impetus was the awareness that ancient buildings were being destroyed or mutilated in the name of mechanical, unhistorical renovation. For example, architects demolished a twelfth-century tower at Canterbury because it differed in style from the fifteenth-century building that had evolved beside it. From 1877 on, Morris & Co. would reject commissions to provide new windows for old churches, hence forfeiting highly lucrative business on the grounds of principle.

The same year, 1877, marked Morris's first public lecture on the decorative arts and his first foray into politics, through the Eastern Question Association. The Association had been founded at the end of 1876 in a specific attempt to persuade the British against intervention in a Russo-Turkish

FIG. 1
Morris & Co.'s shop on Oxford
Street, London

conflict over the Balkans, but in general to protest against England's growing colonial aspirations and conquests. As jingoism increased, Morris published a manifesto, "Unjust War: To the Working-men of England." Its very title indicates the unusual nature of this document; an attack on British imperialism, it was written for the working class. Becoming aware of British colonialist foreign policy, Morris argued against intervening against Russia in Bulgaria and against the Afghan campaign (also directed against Russia) and opposed Britain's conflicts with the Boers in the Transvaal and with the "Kaffirs" and the Zulus. From the late 1870s until his death, he wrote and lectured against imperialism in all its forms, whether that of the Irish Coercion Bill or the British acquisition of part of Cyprus or the occupation of Egypt and the Sudan. Morris even disapproved of the Imperial Federation League; he saw it as a group of opportunists "trying to persuade themselves that Australia and Canada will consider themselves one country with each other and with England so as to give weight to any attempts at Burglary which it may be convenient for us [the British] to make."[6]

As Morris became increasingly aware of the political impact of British imperialism, he also became cognisant of its cultural impact, of how colonial rule was destroying the handicrafts of the East, "once beautiful, orderly, living…and above all, popular."[7] Always linking craftswork and the struggle for a better world, he was angered at what colonial policies were doing to the cultures Britain dominated. He knew, for example, that the mass-produced cheap prints spread by the textile manufacturers of Lancashire and Scotland were driving Indian cotton weavers and their beautiful native designs out of the market. He noted the irony that, while increasing interest in the decorative arts had led pattern designers – himself among them – to look East for inspiration, the very art they admired was being destroyed by Western conquest and commerce. He argued that all the Victorian science, commerce, technology, and thought around him – the fruits of ostensibly glorious "progress" – could not successfully reproduce the handiwork "of a wandering Kurdish shepherd" or that "of a skin-and-bone, oppressed Indian ryot."[8] He passionately proclaimed that imperialism and the "commercial war" it propagated destroyed every culture it touched:

> no country is safe from its ravages: the traditions of a thousand years fall before it in a month;…the Indian or Javanese craftsman may no longer ply his craft leisurely, working a few hours a day, in producing a maze of strange beauty on a piece of cloth: a steam-engine is set a-going in Manchester, and that victory over Nature…is used for the base work of producing a sort of plaster of china-clay and shoddy, and the Asiatic worker, if he is not starved to death outright…is driven himself into a factory to lower the wages of his Manchester brother worker, and nothing of character is left him except…an accumulation of fear and hatred of… his English master.[9]

Morris recognized that the problem was not solely that "the conquered races in their hopelessness are everywhere giving up the genuine practice of their own arts";[10] it was that colonialism killed the spirit necessary to produce worthwhile art, for it destroyed man's joy in labour. Morris knew that he was seeking to sell to a divided world the wares he felt an integrated society would, as a matter of course, naturally produce. Perhaps he feared, too, that his designs would displace or stunt the growth of a colony's "native" manufactures; perhaps he worried about "cannibalizing" Eastern cultures as he borrowed from them. Yet, until 1883, he did not have an ideology with which to frame his fears and discontents.

In the few intervening years before his discovery of Marxist thought, Morris moved to yet another dwelling, Kelmscott House in Hammersmith, and, in 1879, became the treasurer of yet another political organization, the National Liberal League. A natural successor to the EQA, the League attempted to connect trade unionists, representatives of London's radical and workers' clubs, and middle-class sympathizers for limited democratic reforms. But Morris was soon disillusioned with Liberalism and with Gladstone, who had betrayed the anti-imperialist promise of "Peace, Retrenchment, Reform." As he spent more and more time lecturing and writing on the connections between the applied arts and social change (the volume of lectures called *Hopes and Fears for Art* was published in 1882), he became increasingly politicized.

Almost magically, however, Morris was also highly productive in design and business. Some of his most famous textile and paper patterns date from the early 1880s, during which Morris & Co. began a period of increasing expansion. Ironically, the company needed to rely more and more on commercial manufacturers and processes. By the early 1880s, the Firm, now widely known to the general public, had become an influence on popular taste; no longer was it the almost exclusive territory of the design community and the rich *cognoscenti*. Morris's dictum, *"Have nothing in your houses which you do not know to be useful or believe to be beautiful"*,[11] began to have an impact on the English world. Moreover, not all Morris & Co. products were too expensive for the ordinary purchaser; the popular Sussex rush chairs (Nos. G: 2-3, 5) were not costly and such items as embroidery kits (No. F: 2) cost only one pound. The need to expand, specifically to gain more space for making tapestries, woven fabrics and carpets, led to the moving of some of the facilities to Merton Abbey, on the River Wandle, south of Wimbledon, in 1881.

In 1883 Morris found the ideology that would link his visions of what both the crafts and the world should be. That ideology was Marxism, or "scientific socialism" as it was then often called. Morris shared with Karl Marx the view that the division of labour and commodity production had caused the alienation of the human being from both self- and social realization. Marxism reaffirmed Morris's medievalism (Marx and Engels had both praised the pre-capitalist Middle Ages) and enriched his historicism (it constituted an organizing principle that could explain the flow of history); Marxism spoke to Morris's concern for the working person, for the havoc wreaked by colonialism, for the destruction to the environment and those who inhabit it wrought by nineteenth-century capitalism. Just as Morris needed to shape raw experience into poetry and to organize the world of nature into patterns, so he needed to discover an order in which he could believe. His earliest fiction, the romances he had contributed to *The Oxford and Cambridge Magazine*, had lauded "fellowship," the yielding of the individual's desires to the communal good, and, in scientific Socialism, he found a way of applying this idea to life itself. In the "withering away of the state" and the Golden Age to follow, he found the promise of an earthly paradise that he could help create and in which he could have faith.[12]

In the process of becoming a practising Marxist (and it must be remembered that Morris was the only eminent Victorian who actually participated in the struggle), he lost much of his status and some of his friends; only Webb and Faulkner embraced the "Cause." Burne-Jones remained a Liberal (though his friendship with Morris never faltered); Jane Morris heartily disliked her husband's socialist cohorts, and friends in the middle-class and artistic communities merely snickered. Morris did make new friends in the Cause, including Walter Crane, Emery Walker and T.J. Cobden-Sanderson, but he felt alienated from the very working class whose struggle he had embraced, sadly accepting the fact that, despite the simple, undecorated, utilitarian nature of his socialist lectures, pamphlets and articles, he could not fully communicate. Nevertheless, he wrestled with Marx's economic theory, studied his copies of *Capital* and clearly meant his statement that he stood with Marx *contra mundum*.

Morris joined the Democratic Federation in 1883; helped launch and support the first socialist weekly paper, *Justice*; he founded the Socialist League in 1884; took over and began writing and editing for *Commonweal* in 1885; and actively travelled, lectured and wrote for the Cause during these years. Yet, despite this busy and pressured life of political activity, he continued his creative work both for the Firm and in literature. While his younger daughter, May, and his assistant, John Henry Dearle, became increasingly active as designers of fabrics and papers, Morris's own work did not cease. Almost revitalized by his conversion to Marxism, he produced translations and original poems, including "The Pilgrims of Hope" (one of the few literary pieces he set in his own century), continued to design splendid patterns, and began to study the art of typography.

Morris vented his creativity in further ways in the period from 1886 to

1890, for he produced his two great socialist romances, *The Dream of John Ball* (1886) and *News From Nowhere* (1890), as well as the first of his late prose romances – fusions of Marxist historicism and fantasy – *The House of the Wolfings* (1888) and *The Roots of the Mountains* (1889). Somehow, he found the hours to translate and publish *The Aeneid of Virgil* (1876) and *The Odyssey* (1887) and to continue lecturing and writing on socialism and on the relations between it and the arts (*Signs of Change*, his collection of essays on these subjects, was published in 1888), all while designing for and expanding Morris & Co.

However, by 1890, personal and political tensions had begun to disrupt the unanimity of those working for the Cause, forcing the withdrawal of the Hammersmith Branch, with Morris at its head, from the now anarchist-dominated Socialist League. Withdrawing slightly from the day-to-day struggles of the movement, Morris launched his last and perhaps most culturally significant new ventures. *News From Nowhere*, his Utopian vision of a Marxist Golden Age to come, fostered the timeless, archetypal romances of the 1890s, including *The Story of the Glittering Plain* (1890), *The Wood Beyond the World* (1894), *The Well at the World's End* (1895), and the posthumously published *Water of the Wondrous Isles* and *The Sundering Flood* (1897). Derided by some, these works profoundly influenced such writers as William Butler Yeats, C.S. Lewis and J.R.R. Tolkien and are considered major progenitors of modern fantasy literature. In addition, Morris's longheld conviction about the need for good design in all areas of life, his realization that printing, too, was an art in decay, bore fruit in the Kelmscott Press, founded by him in 1891.

Emery Walker, Morris's neighbour at Hammersmith and a pioneer in process engraving and fine printing, had developed Morris's interest in printing through a lecture he gave at the first Arts and Crafts exhibition in 1888. Morris began to design his own fonts of type (he had already supervised the typography, layout and decorative title-pages of the Chiswick Press editions of his two historical romances), and in 1891 the first Kelmscott Press book, *The Glittering Plain*, saw the light of day. Illustrations for the Kelmscott volumes that followed were mainly provided by Burne-Jones, but also by Charles Gere, Arthur Gaskin and Walter Crane, while Morris himself contributed vast numbers of decorative borders, initial capitals, marginal ornaments, and title-pages (see Nos. A: 27-30). Through both its elegantly simple small books, like Ruskin's *On the Nature of Gothic* (which sold for only half a crown), and its richly decorated masterpieces, like the *Chaucer* (No. L: 30) – considered one of the great jewels of modern book collectors – Kelmscott became the inspiration for much of the private press movement. Morris's very idea of changing and improving book design, of rethinking how a volume should look and feel, has had a major impact upon hand-press and high-quality commercial printing alike. Although the Kelmscott Press survived its creator by only two years, its sixty-eight books have greatly appreciated in value and its influence has never waned.

Morris & Co. had a longer life, surviving its founder by some forty-four years. At Morris's demise, his share of the business, valued at almost £30,000, was purchased by his junior partners, Frank and Robert Smith, who promoted John Henry Dearle to the position of art director. The death of Burne-Jones in 1898 represented a further loss to the world of design, but work continued for a number of years under Dearle's artistic eye, much as it had under Morris's. In 1905, nine years after Morris's death, the company name was changed to Morris & Co. Decorators Ltd.; that same year, the Smiths, needing money, relinquished full control of the company and added new members to the board of directors. Much of the new funding came from Henry Curry Marillier, known more for his essays on Rossetti, Morris, and the Arts and Crafts Movement than for his business acumen. Much of the skill in design came from his partner in another art company, W.A.S. Benson. Despite a tendency merely to adapt and recycle old designs rather than create new ones, the company continued to be both fashionable and profitable until 1914, obtaining such prestigious commissions as the providing of embroidered cloths and thrones for the coronation of King George V. The outbreak of the First World War deprived the Firm of both workers and work, but business soon intensified at the close of the war.

In 1925, renamed Morris & Company Art Workers Ltd., the business further diversified into pottery, glass and ironwork. Yet, ironically, by ignoring the impact on design of trends Morris himself is credited with influencing – such styles as Bauhaus and Art Déco – it became increasingly old-fashioned. By 1929 and the collapse of the British economy, it was in decline and, with the death of Dearle in 1932, stagnation set in. When the Second World War began, the Firm succumbed to its impact; it was liquidated in May 1940. Deprived of the vision, flexibility and aesthetic energy of Morris and his earlier associates, it could not survive.

Thus, it is not hyperbole to suggest – as that anonymous doctor did – that, in his lifetime, Morris produced the work of at least ten other men. He learned and practised virtually every craft his company utilized. He created more than six-hundred designs; he wrote more than twenty-four volumes of poetry, romance and nonfiction. He influenced countless members of his generation and of the eras to follow. A life spent in attempting to create a world of beauty, joyful work and fellowship – in striving to build paradise on earth, to "set the crooked straight" – is not a life to be forgotten. This exhibition and the publication that accompanies it celebrate that life and all it wrought.

ENDNOTES

1. Quoted in Ian Bradley, *William Morris and His World* (London, 1978), p. 108.

2. Edward Burne-Jones, quoted in J.W. Mackail, *The Life of William Morris*, vol. 1 (London, 1899; reprinted New York, 1968), p. 63.

3. Quoted in Bradley, *William Morris and His World*, p. 32.

4. Mackail, *The Life of William Morris*, vol. 1, p. 154.

5. Jack Lindsay, *William Morris: His Life and Work* (London, 1975), pp. 108-10.

6. *The Unpublished Lectures of William Morris*, ed. Eugene D. Lemire (Detroit, 1969), p. 128.

7. *The Collected Works of William Morris*, ed. May Morris, vol. 22 (London, 1914; reprinted New York, 1966), p. 35.

8. *Ibid.*, p. 180.

9. *Ibid.*, vol. 23, pp. 8-9.

10. *Ibid.*, vol. 22, p. 36.

11. *Ibid.*, p. 77.

12. For more on this issue, see the introduction to Carole Silver, *The Romance of William Morris* (Ohio, 1982).

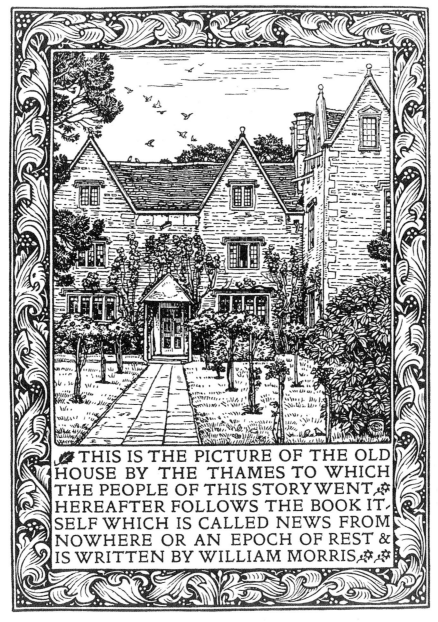

NO. L: 21. WILLIAM MORRIS, *News from Nowhere*, Hammersmith: Kelmscott Press, 24 March 1893

TO THE GLORY OF GOD | AND IN MEMORY OF | ANDREW ALLAN 1902

UNDER THE SPELL OF MORRIS: A CANADIAN PERSPECTIVE

Rosalind Pepall

In 1888 a small, eclectic Quebec review, *Le Chercheur*, carried one of William Morris's most frequently cited quotations from his first public lecture in 1877, which was published under the title "The Lesser Arts." The *Le Chercheur* article, entitled "L'Art pour tous," began with Morris's words, as rendered in French: "Je ne veux pas d'un art pour le petit nombre, non plus que d'une éducation pour le petit nombre ni d'une liberté pour le petit nombre."[1]

In the pages of an 1898 issue of *The Canadian Architect and Builder*, W.H. Elliott, of Toronto's foremost decorating firm, deplored the ugly pictures Canadians hung on their walls and urged instead the use of "one of Morris's or Crane's or Shand Kydd's bold designs."[2]

Through the 1880s and 1890s, references to William Morris and his followers appeared in Canadian journals, which closely followed cultural developments in England and were certainly aware of Morris and his influence on the Arts and Crafts movement in Europe and North America. Even though Morris devoted much of his later career to Socialist politics, and in 1892 was considered for the vacant position of Poet Laureate in England, at his death, contemporary accounts emphasized above all his achievements as a designer and reformer of the arts.[3] It is in this role that his impact was most strongly felt in Canada. Morris wallpapers, textiles and stained-glass windows were admired by Canadian artists and clients for their beauty and quality. But it was Morris's writings, above all, and his efforts to improve the standards of design, that most inspired Canadians who came under the spell of his ideas.

William Morris wanted the craftsman to be regarded as an artist, and he considered the decorative arts (or what he called the "lesser arts") as important as the fine arts of painting, sculpture and architecture. The integration of all the arts was a major concern of Morris and the promoters of the Arts and Crafts movement in England. Painters and architects connected with

FIG. 3. MORRIS & CO. Stained-glass window in the Church of St. Andrew and St. Paul, Montreal (1903)

the movement involved themselves with every aspect of design, from wallpapers to metalwork and from furniture to decorative mural panels. Not only William Morris, but artists and architects such as Walter Crane, Dante Gabriel Rossetti, Edward Burne-Jones, C.R. Ashbee and Philip Webb, set an example for Canadians in the fields of art and architecture.

With missionary fervour, Morris attempted to reform design and the working conditions of the craftsman/worker, and wrote numerous articles and delivered lectures on his beliefs. His writings ranged from detailed accounts of the technical aspects of the handcrafted arts to his influential novel *News from Nowhere* (1890), in which he put forth his utopian ideal of a worker's life. In this way Morris's success was due not only to his own example as a craftsman/designer but also to his ability to write convincingly of his aims for art.

During Morris's lifetime, and even after his death in 1896, his ideas were well publicized in newspapers and magazines. Through these articles, Canadians became aware of his work and the principles that drove him to create with such energy in so many spheres of art. Canadians would have been able to read about Morris in such British magazines as *The Builder*, *The Art Journal*, and *The Studio*. From its inception in 1893, *The Studio* was the major review of British Arts and Crafts design, and its pages carried many illustrations of interiors decorated with William Morris fabrics and wall coverings. Canadians acquired much of their knowledge of British decorative arts from *The Studio*, which occasionally had references to Canadian work.[4]

American magazines were readily accessible as well, and Canadian patrons could well have seen such articles as "A Day in Surrey with William Morris," published in *Century Illustrated Magazine* in July 1886, or the two issues of the Arts and Crafts review *Craftsman* in 1901, which were devoted to Ruskin and William Morris's work. As is pointed out above, Canadian journals published excerpts from Morris's writings or commented on the activities of members of his circle, such as Edward Burne-Jones or Walter Crane.[5] In the years 1883-85 the "Literary Gossip" columns in the Toronto review *The Week* included mentions of Morris's writings.[6] An anonymous writer in the Montreal cultural magazine *Arcadia* discussed England's "Painter-poets" in an 1892 issue, and noted that "Mr. Morris like Mr. [Dante Gabriel] Rossetti should have a study to himself for he too is a leader of men."[7]

Because of Canada's social and political ties with England, the Canadian art community closely followed the developments in art and architecture in the "mother country," not only through magazines and newspapers but through trips to England as well. In London, those visitors interested in the arts could see examples of William Morris's work and that of his followers in the Arts and Crafts Exhibition Society's shows, which took place annually for three years from 1888 and then sporadically afterwards. Or prospective clients from Canada could visit the Morris & Co.'s retail shop and showroom on Oxford street (located after 1917 at Hanover Square).[8] Another likely stopover for a Canadian visitor with an interest in art and design would have been the South Kensington Museums (now the Victoria and Albert Museum), the Green Dining Room of which had been decorated by Morris, Marshall, Faulkner & Co. in 1866.

MONTREAL PATRONS

Recorded examples of Morris & Co.'s work owned by Canadians during Morris's lifetime or just after are difficult to trace. However, notable works by the Firm were owned by a group of Montreal patrons of Morris who had in common their active participation in the running of the Art Association of Montreal (now called the Montreal Museum of Fine Arts). The earliest Canadian commission for a stained-glass window from Morris & Co. came from a museum councillor, David Allan Poe Watt (1830-1917), of Montreal. According to A.C. Sewter, the Firm's catalogue of designs records a stained-glass panel of Timothy and Eunice made for "Montreal" in 1878 (No. D: 2). This was for Mr. Watt, who in 1882 ordered directly from the Firm two more windows depicting "Minstrel Angels" (No. D: 3).[9]

Watt emigrated to Canada from Scotland at the age of sixteen and carried on a prosperous career as a shipping and exporting merchant. His biography tells us that "Mr. W. takes his recreation in both science and art. He is an old time life member of the Natural History Society and was for a while editor of its journal *The Canadian Naturalist*."[10] Perhaps his interest in William Morris designs came from his love of plants, for Watt collected ferns and was considered an authority on the subject. A loyal and active life-member of the Art Association of Montreal, Watt was one of its original subscribers in 1864 and sat almost continuously as a councillor from 1879 until his death.[11] Throughout the 1880s and 1890s he also sat on the Council's Standing Committee of Industrial and Decorative Art, usually in the position of chairman. In addition to the stained-glass windows, Watt's house (demolished) on Stanley Street in Montreal's "Square Mile" was decorated with William Morris wallpaper and the Firm's wool and cotton fabrics (see Nos. E: 11, 15, F: 1, 4). Watt also admired William De Morgan ceramics and owned a sales catalogue of De Morgan pottery published in 1880.[12] At the time of Watt's death in 1917, each of his three daughters inherited a William Morris window.[13] The 1882 windows were given to the Montreal Museum of Fine Arts in 1918 by two Watt sisters, and the third window was passed down through the family of the third daughter, with whom it still remains.

Another active member of the Art Association of Montreal who had an interest in the work of Morris & Co. was the architect Alexander D.

Steele (1841-1890), a native of England who spent nearly twenty years in Montreal; his name first appears in Montreal city directories in 1872-73.[14] Two or three years later, he went into partnership with another architect, Alexander C. Hutchison. Their most noteworthy building was the Redpath Museum (1882), on the campus of McGill University. Steele was a member of the AAM Council continuously from 1881 until 1890, when he returned to England because of ill health. Just before his departure, Steele opened his house at 19 Essex Avenue to the public prior to selling the contents. A *Montreal Gazette* reporter was on the spot and was able to comment on "a petite type of an old English home, ... with a charming picturesqueness pervading all...." In a description of the furnishings on view, among the armour, rapiers and Venetian glass, the journalist remarked that "In curtains and wall hangings and carpets we have some good examples of William Morris' art, all in admirable preservation."[15]

David A.P. Watt and Alexander Steele worked together on committees of the AAM and shared their interest in British art and design with other members of the museum's Council. Two councillors, James Ross and Sir George Drummond, who were among Canada's most important art collectors of the period, owned paintings by Morris's friends and collaborators, the Pre-Raphaelite artists Edward Burne-Jones and Dante Gabriel Rossetti. Burne-Jones's work was known to Montrealers because, in an 1889 exhibition of paintings from England at the AAM gallery, the artist's *Danae: The Tower of Brass* occupied "the post of honour" on one of the walls.[16] A few years later, James Ross acquired two important watercolours by Edward Burne-Jones, entitled *Day* and *Night* respectively, both dated 1870 (fig. 1). Included in the composition of each work is a *trompe l'oeil* parchment on which is inscribed a short quotation from William Morris.[17] Ross also owned two works by Dante Gabriel Rossetti, an undated watercolour, *Figure with Passion Flowers*, and an oil painting, *La Ghirlandata* (1873), both of which were exhibited at the AAM's gallery.[18]

The influential art collector and president of the Bank of Montreal, Sir George Drummond, acquired his Rossetti drawing, entitled *Pandora* (1878), sometime after 1888.[19] It was hung in the Council Room of the AAM's new gallery on Sherbrooke Street in 1913. Other Pre-Raphaelite paintings are not recorded in Montreal collections, but two other AAM councillors and art collectors, Richard B. Angus and Edward B. Greenshields, owned a number of important William De Morgan ceramics.[20] Two of Greenshields's pieces have found their way into museum collections in Montreal (Nos. H: 12, 13).[21]

Another artist of Morris's circle who was a favourite with Montreal patrons was Walter Crane. When the AAM Councillors heard that the Boston Museum of Fine Arts had organized a travelling exhibition of Crane's work

for 1891, the members got in touch with Crane directly to make sure that the show would travel to Montreal. It arrived in 1892 and met with enthusiastic approval.[22]

The designs of both Crane and Morris were popular in North American cities, especially after their wallpapers were displayed at the Centennial Exhibition of 1876 in Philadelphia.[23] Montreal's prominent businessmen were in constant touch with their U.S. colleagues, and like them built grand mansions decorated in the latest fashion. For example, Charles Hosmer, who made his fortune with the Canadian Pacific Railway, built his red-stone mansion on Drummond Street in 1901-02, each room of which was richly decorated and ornamented in a different style.[24] William Morris wall-coverings were frequently recommended for "aesthetic" interiors in the many decorating books published at the end of the nineteenth century. In keeping with the fashion, Charles Hosmer had his dining-room walls hung with Morris's *Peacock and Dragon* blue woven-wool fabric, which went well with the rich tones of the decoratively carved mahogany panelling and the chandeliers of hand-wrought "old steel" with Gothic motifs (fig. 2).[25] As well, the account books of Edward Maxwell, the architect of the house, record that $848.23 was paid to Morris & Co. for carpets in 1901-02.[26]

None of the records for the house indicate who, between Charles Hosmer and his architect, Edward Maxwell (1867-1923), proposed the Morris furnishings, but there is no doubt that Maxwell was interested in Morris's ideas and work, because in 1898 he had acquired a copy of the Aymer Vallance biography of the designer.[27] Maxwell noted on the back flyleaf of the book the specific pages referring to Morris's statements on restoration and on architecture.

In many of the houses built by Edward Maxwell and his brother, William Maxwell, their appreciation for handcrafted work and Arts and Crafts design is evident. Both architects had spent three to four years of training in Boston, which was a centre of North American interest in William Morris and his followers.[28] Edward had worked for the firm of Shepley, Rutan and Coolidge, successors to the office of the eminent American architect Henry Hobson Richardson (1838-1886). Richardson had met William Morris and frequently decorated his buildings with Morris wallpapers, textiles and stained-glass.[29] Edward Maxwell, in turn, was very much influenced by the work of Richardson, whom he greatly admired and emulated in his early career.[30]

Although the only direct reference to Morris & Co. in the Maxwell firm's existing account books is for Charles Hosmer's carpets, the brothers frequently ordered wallpapers or furnishings from W. Scott & Sons, who advertised themselves as the "Canadian agents for Morris & Co., the leading silk and tapestry merchants in London."[31] Another reference to William

FIG. 2
Dining-room, Charles Hosmer
house, Montreal, 1911

Morris among the Edward and W.S. Maxwell archives is an undated floor-plan for the arrangement of furniture in the H. Vincent Meredith House, built in 1894. This plan has been stamped with the Morris & Co. mark and address at 449 Oxford St., London.[32] Unfortunately, there are few records or photographs of the interior of the Meredith house to indicate what furnishings, if any, the Firm supplied.

Edward and W.S. Maxwell were very much a part of the inner circle running the AAM, as they were the architects of its new art gallery, opened in 1912. A fellow architect and another active member of the Association from the time of his arrival in Canada was Percy E. Nobbs (1875-1964), one of the chief exponents of the Arts and Crafts philosophy in architecture and the decorative arts in Canada.[33] Born in Scotland, Nobbs had articled in Edinburgh with the noted Arts and Crafts architect Robert Lorimer, and had spent two years in London before emigrating to Canada in 1903, at the age of twenty-eight, to take up his appointment as Macdonald Professor of Architecture at McGill University.

The Arts and Crafts ideals that Percy Nobbs had absorbed during his training were reflected in his teaching and architecture in Canada. He offered these principles as a basis for the development of a truly Canadian architecture, which he believed could grow from the study and understanding of the French and English traditions in early Canadian buildings. In an address, "On the Value of the Study of Old Work", Nobbs told his students that Canada's pioneer architects, who responded to the requirements of climate and function in a simple yet appealing way, would have been admired by Morris:

> The beautiful words of William Morris in appreciating the vernacular art of England are as appropriate to the work we find here around us, and I feel sure if he were familiar with the charm and quaintness of the old Quebec farms and seigneuries he would have written something very similar about it.[34]

Although Nobbs's own buildings were not elaborately ornamented, he was drawn to the decorative aspect of architecture. In his own Montreal house, built in 1914, Nobbs had William Morris wallpaper and William De Morgan fireplace tiles.[35] He was a talented draughtsman and often designed the ironwork, plaster decoration and stained glass in his own buildings. True to Ruskin's and Morris's philosophy that the artist should be his own "grinder of colours," Nobbs studied the techniques of forged metal and decorative plasterwork.

In Montreal, interest in William Morris was evident in the 1880s and 1890s among art and architecture enthusiasts who usually had a close connection with the AAM. Also, the first commission from a Canadian church for a Morris & Co. stained-glass window was given by St. Paul's church in Montreal.[36] The window, ordered in 1885, was dedicated to the wife of Andrew Allan, of the prominent Montreal shipping family. Another window for this church was ordered in 1903 (fig. 3), at the time of Allan's death.[37] Two other Montreal churches also ordered memorial stained-glass windows from the Firm in these years: Crescent Street Presbyterian Church (demolished), in 1901, and Christ Church Cathedral, in 1902 (see p. 122).

THE TORONTO CIRCLE

In Montreal, patrons of William Morris and his followers met together at the Art Association. Similarly, in Toronto, awareness and interest in Morris and the Arts and Crafts movement grew out of a group of friends and associates who worked together on the same committees and belonged to the same art societies. A pivotal figure in the group of Morris followers in Toronto was James Mavor (1854-1925), a Scottish immigrant who brought with him a knowledge of and direct link with recent British developments in art and design. A native of Glasgow, Mavor came to Canada in 1892 to take the chair of Political Economy and Constitutional History at the University of Toronto. In Scotland, Mavor had been involved in Socialist politics and was a member of the Socialist League, founded by William Morris in 1884. Morris went often to Scotland to address the Glasgow branch of the League, and so was in frequent contact with Mavor. Among Mavor's papers are a few letters from Morris concerning his lectures in Scotland and *The Commonweal*, the journal of the Socialist League.[38] In one undated letter from Kelmscott House, Morris chides Mavor for trying to arrange cheap furniture for workers. In it, Morris sums up perfectly the dilemma he felt as a designer of crafted furnishings which were too expensive for the worker whose lot he was hoping to improve by promoting handcrafted work:

> Here's the point – whatever is cheap is made by machinery and in huge quantities. A special design for a piece of furniture means at the least trebling its cost more likely 10 folding it. The cheapest chair that we can sell costs about 7 s/0 (and they are made 4 or 5 dozen at a time too)[;] a workman can get a chair for 1 s/6, and as you very well know he must buy them as cheap as he can. I beg you to dismiss from your mind the idea that the workman can afford any art of any sort whatever in the teeth of the "Iron Law". The workman's two rooms at Manchester (which by the by were pretty dismal) could only be attained to by a *jolly* workman, a foreman at £5 per week. So here's 3 cheers for the Social Revolution! For till it comes art must be in the hands of the Monopolists and their parasites – whereof I am one – Yours be truly, William Morris.[39]

Knowledgeable in both art and literature, Mavor for a brief period in 1889 had been editor of the *Scottish Art Review*, which carried articles on the revival of the arts and crafts, among other features.[40] Having established himself in Toronto, Mavor continued to write and lecture on art. On 12 January 1897 he gave an address to the Women's Art Association on William Morris, "Poet and Socialist", in which he reminisced about his friendship with Morris.[41] At various times before his emigration to Canada he had travelled with Morris, and on one occasion, en route from Edinburgh to Glasgow in 1889, the company included Walter Crane, Emery Walker, and T.J. Cobden Sanderson. "All very merry – Morris telling stories and in high boyish humour," Mavor commented. Mavor maintained his friendship with Morris until the designer's death and devoted a whole chapter to his old friend in his published memoirs.[42]

Morris's daughter May corresponded with Mavor in 1910, while she was on a tour of the United States to promote the publication of her father's collected writings. According to a letter of 1 March, she was to travel also to Montreal and Toronto.[43]

In Canada, James Mavor was quick to join efforts with those in Toronto who wanted to encourage the appreciation of art and to build an art museum for the city. At the centre of this group was the Canadian painter and teacher George A. Reid (1860-1947), who became a good friend of Mavor's. Throughout his distinguished career, in his roles as president of the Ontario Society of Artists and the Royal Canadian Academy, as principal of the Ontario College of Art, as a director of the Toronto Art Museum, as a founder-member of the Society of Mural Decorators, and as a member of the advisory board of the Toronto Guild of Civic Art, Reid promoted the union of the various arts. The ideas he presented in his lectures and writings on the need for the integration of the arts and for reform in design derived directly from the teachings of William Morris, and his interest in Morris would no doubt have been strengthened by his friendship with Mavor.

Reid was the driving force behind a group of like-minded artists who formed the Arts and Crafts Society of Canada in 1903. The members acknowledged their debt to William Morris and his belief in the value of handcrafted work. In their first exhibition in April 1904, artists and architects displayed their designs for furniture and decorative panels, along with other exhibits by metal-craftsmen, potters and stained-glass designers, all in the spirit of the Arts and Crafts ideal of uniting the fine and decorative arts.[44] In this inaugural show, George Reid, a founding partner and vice-president of the Society, included among his exhibits a simple, upright piano of stained oak decorated with painted allegorical landscape scenes (fig. 4). He was no doubt inspired by the furniture embellished by the Pre-Raphaelite artists in the early days of the Morris firm. Edward Burne-Jones, in particular, set the example with his decorations on a grand piano for William Graham in 1879-80.[45]

Working with Reid to promote the Arts and Crafts Society was its president, Mabel Adamson (1871-1943).[46] Before the founding of the society, she had spent a number of months in 1902-03 at C.R. Ashbee's Guild of Handicrafts, which had recently moved from East London to the the quaint Cotswold village of Chipping Camden, in Gloucestershire. She complained to her husband that she could not even get a bath at the Guild,[47] but she was willing to give up such luxuries in order to work on her enamelling and metalwork, crafts for which the Guild's artisans were especially noted.[48] Imbued with the spirit of the Arts and Crafts ideals from her months of training with one of the major designers of the movement, Adamson returned to Toronto with her husband in 1903 and with him set up a decorating business, the Thornton-Smith Co.

George Reid was at the centre of another community of friends who

FIG. 4
Piano designed and decorated
by George A. Reid, 1900
National Gallery of Canada,
Ottawa (acc. no. 30050.1-2)

shared similar interests in art and architecture. This was in an area of Toronto called Wychwood Park, which, with its pond, meandering paths and wild vegetation, had attracted a number of artists, architects, writers and academics to establish a cultural enclave. The land forming the park had originally belonged to the artist Marmaduke Matthews (1837-1913), who made plans to develop it into an artists' community in the 1890s. The park was called after Matthew's house, Wychwood, a name inspired by the area of Oxfordshire in which he grew up, near the Wychwood Forest, not far from William Morris's country retreat, Kelmscott Manor.[49]

In 1905 Reid moved to Wychwood Park, where he built his own English Arts and Crafts-style house, complete with inglenook, musicians' gallery and decorative murals. Among Reid's friends in Wychwood Park was the architect Eden Smith (1858-1949), a fellow committee member of the Arts and Crafts Society of Canada. Smith had come to Canada from England in 1885. Largely self-taught as an architect, he became a respected member of the Ontario Society of Architects and most sought-after by clients who wished to have an English "cottage-style" home with an Arts and Crafts flavour. Smith, who purposely kept the details of his English background unclear, does not seem to have had James Mavor's direct links to Morris; however,

Smith's "conscious marketing of his Englishness" contributed to his success.[50] The houses designed by Smith in Wychwood Park represent some of his best work in the English cottage manner.[51]

Included in this interrelated group of artists and friends in Wychwood Park was another of Reid's colleagues, Dr. Charles T. Currelly (1875-1957), who was a close neighbour from 1911. Currelly, for many years a professor of archaeology at the University of Toronto, worked unceasingly to establish the Royal Ontario Museum, of which he was the first director.[52] Currelly was frequently in London, seeking out art works and artifacts for his new museum and visiting his artist friends. One of these was the Pre-Raphaelite painter William Holman Hunt (1827-1910), whom he had met through the English archaeologist Sir Flinders Petrie.[53]

On his London visits, Currelly also had the opportunity to meet Mrs. Margaret Mackail, the daughter of Edward Burne-Jones and the wife of William Morris's biographer, J.W. Mackail. Currelly was able to acquire ten Burne-Jones watercolours and drawings from Mrs. Mackail for the Royal Ontario Museum in 1926 (Nos. A: 20 b., 25 a.-b.). Among the other early acquisitions for the Museum purchased in London by Currelly were some William De Morgan tiles, bought from Thomas Sutton (Nos. H: 32, 44, 46), a Pilkington vase designed by Walter Crane (No. H: 17), and Henry Holiday's *Opus Sectile* (No. C: 2).

ACROSS CANADA

Enthusiasm for the work and ideas of William Morris was not confined to the major Canadian cities of Montreal and Toronto. The influence of Morris and the Arts and Crafts movement was also felt in western cities, such as Vancouver, and especially in Victoria. The architect Samuel Maclure (1860-1929), who had offices in both cities, became the most prolific builder of Arts and Crafts-inspired houses in British Columbia in the first decade of the twentieth century.

Born in Westminster, B.C., Maclure was basically self-trained, having studied art for only one year, 1884-85, at the Spring Garden Institute in Philadelphia.[54] Through reading British and American journals, Maclure became familiar with the work of English Arts and Crafts architects, and kept abreast of developments in the United States. In fact, Maclure's own work was featured in the widely read American Arts and Crafts magazine, *Craftsman*, in 1908, and in *The Studio* of 1911.

The Alex Martin house (1904), presented in *The Craftsman*, was constructed out of local materials and displayed typical Arts and Crafts features, such as half-timbering, beamed ceilings, natural wood panelling, practical and simple oak furniture, crafted ironwork, and intimate, cosy spaces. Its

Arts and Crafts nature was further enhanced by interior furnishings designed by the British architect M.H. Baillie Scott (1865-1945), whose work was frequently featured in *The Studio* and *Country Life* magazines.[55]

The closest link that Samuel Maclure had with the British movement was through his Vancouver partner, Cecil C. Fox (1879-1916). Maclure opened a Vancouver office in 1903 and hired Fox, his former draughtsman, to run it. Fox had emigrated to Canada in 1898 after having worked for about two years under Charles F.A. Voysey, a major figure in British Arts and Crafts architecture.[56] This direct tie was evident in the houses designed by Maclure and Fox, in which Maclure's partner played a major role.[57] The A. Edward Tulk house, designed by the firm between 1913 and 1915, especially reflected the British Arts and Crafts tradition and still contains its original William Morris wallpapers and textiles.[58]

Samuel Maclure was also a founder of one of the many Arts and Crafts societies that were formed in various Canadian cities as a result of the British movement. In Victoria the Island Arts and Crafts Society was organized in 1909 to present lectures and exhibitions of interest to its members.[59] Founded with similar ideals as their Toronto and Victoria counterparts were Arts and Crafts associations in Hamilton, Ontario (1894) and Vancouver (1900), and the Canadian Handicrafts Guild in Montreal (1906).[60] Organized by local artists and architects and inspired by William Morris's ideals, these groups across Canada aimed to bring together designers of both the fine and the decorative arts.

This collaboration is demonstrated visually on the certificate designed for the Ontario Association of Architects (fig. 5) by the Canadian painter and teacher J.E.H. MacDonald (1873-1932), who in his early career as a commercial artist was especially inspired by the designs that William Morris created for his Kelmscott Press. The composition and scrolled-leaf decoration on the certificate, issued in 1920, are modelled closely after similar works by Morris. The design, which incorporates figures symbolizing sculpture, painting, crafts and engineering allied to architecture, aptly represents the integration of the fine and applied arts that Morris strove to encourage and which Canadians took to heart.

Canadian members of the art community were also impressed by William Morris's efforts to improve the standards of design in England. He was not the first to look askance at British design in the nineteenth century; earlier, Sir Henry Cole set about to improve the training of the applied arts, and the establishment of the South Kensington Design Schools was a major step which members of the Arts and Crafts movement carried forward. Many of the Canadian schools founded at the turn of the century – for example, the Central Ontario School of Art and Design in Toronto, and the Nova Scotia College of Art in Halifax – had roots in the British reform

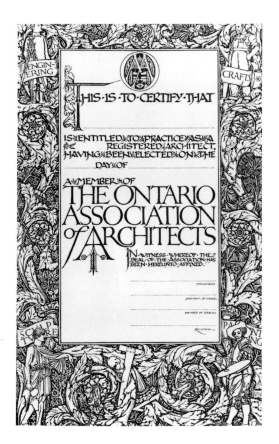

movement, and often derived their methods of instruction or their curricula from the South Kensington example.

Interest in the ideas of William Morris continued in Canada well after his work ceased to be fashionable. British immigrants who brought their knowledge of Morris with them kept arriving in Canada,[61] and word of Morris continued to come through American channels. The firm of Morris & Co. carried on its operations under various names until 1940, and Morris furnishings continued to be available to a Canadian clientèle. It was not his designs, however, that contributed to his wide and lasting appeal into the twentieth century. Rather, it was William Morris's approach to art, as Alfred Boe has stated:

> To Morris art was not a thing to be restricted within the frame of a picture and stuck on the wall, but a force allied to the very urge of life itself – something like a fundamental will to harmony, health, and beauty. Therefore, his concern was not primarily with books, or paintings, or architecture, or politics, or even design, his themes were "The Beauty of Life" and "Art and the Beauty of the Earth."[62]

To cultivate a taste and appreciation for art and to make art a part of everyday life was a common goal among the Canadian followers of William Morris and his circle. Inspired by their example, Canadian artists, architects, craftsmen and patrons worked together through art societies, guilds and schools to improve standards of design and to unite the arts.

ENDNOTES

1. *Le Chercheur* 1 (11 October 1888): 52.

   In the original, Morris's words read as: "I do not want art for a few, any more than education for a few, or freedom for a few."

2. *Canadian Architect and Builder* (November 1898): 188.

   Elliott repeated this recommendation in the June 1901 issue (pp. 116-17).

3. In her book *William Morris Textiles* (London, 1982; New York, 1983; p. 130), Linda Parry points this out and quotes from Morris's obituary notices from the *Globe* and the *Daily Telegraph* in 1896.

4. The reading room of the Montreal Museum of Fine Arts, for example, always had copies of the latest art magazines from London and New York, such as *The Art Journal*, *The Decorator and Furnisher*, *The Century* and later *The Studio*, for members to consult. The museum was given the first twelve volumes of *The Studio* in 1942 by the Sir Herbert Holt estate. (See the Art Association of Montreal's annual report for 1890, p. 8.)

5. See Hardy George, ed., *Art Index to Nineteenth-Century Canadian Periodicals* (Montreal, 1981).

6. *Ibid.*, p. 175.

7. *Arcadia* 1 (1 October 1892): 217.

8. A number of Morris's textile fragments, given to the MMFA by Mrs. J. Kippen, were purchased by her from Morris & Co.'s Hanover Square shop. See Robert Little, *The Work of William Morris from the Collection of the Montreal Museum of Fine Arts* (Montreal, 1991), pp. 29-31.

9. A.C. Sewter, *The Stained Glass of William Morris and his Circle* (New Haven and London, 1975), pp. 215, 216.

10. Henry James Morgan, ed., *Canadian Men and Women of the Time* (Toronto, 1898), pp. 1062-63.

11. Watt is listed among the "original subscribers" in *Art Association of Montreal: The Act of Incorporation and the City By-Laws* (Montreal, 1864), p. 20. I am grateful to Juanita Toupin for bringing this information to my attention.

12. The MMFA received this catalogue, entitled *The Painted Tiles to be had of William De Morgan at Orange House Pottery, Chelsea, London, 1880*, from the Watt estate. Some of Watt's textiles and wallpaper were given to the Maltwood Museum, Victoria, B.C.

13. Communication with the great-granddaughter of David A.P. Watt.

14. I am grateful to Robert Hill for this information.

15. "An Artistic Mansion", *Montreal Gazette*, 22 September 1890; clipping in the MMFA Archives, Scrapbook 2, p. 69. See also "Remarkable Auction Sale", *Montreal Gazette*, 28 September 1890. Steele's house has been demolished.

16. *The Montreal Daily Herald*, 7 December 1889; clipping in the MMFA Archives, Scrapbook 3, p. 117.

17. Janet M. Brooke, *Discerning Tastes: Montreal Collectors, 1880-1920* (Montreal, 1989), p. 130.

   These watercolours were exhibited at the AAM in 1902, 1912 and 1915 (p. 225).

18. *Ibid.*, pp. 225-26.

19. *Ibid.*, p. 225.

   This work is now in the collection of the Lady Lever Art Gallery, Port Sunlight, England.

20. Elizabeth Collard, *Nineteenth-Century Pottery and Porcelain in Canada* (Montreal, 1967), pp. 157-58.

21. The De Morgan vase in the collection of the McCord Museum was a gift from the estate of Mrs. Graham Drinkwater, the daughter of E.B. Greenshields, and a De Morgan dish was given to the MMFA by Mrs. Drinkwater's husband.

22. See, in particular, "A Visit to the Art Gallery: The Walter Crane Exhibition", *Montreal Weekly Witness*, 1 October 1892; clipping in the MMFA Archives, Scrapbook 4, p. 5.

23. See *In Pursuit of Beauty: Americans and the Aesthetic Movement* (New York, 1986), pp. 69-76.

   Morris & Co.'s main American agent in 1878 was Messrs. Cowtan & Tout, Madison Ave., New York, but the Firm also had agents in other cities such as Boston and Philadelphia.

24. For a description of the Hosmer house, see *The Architecture of Edward & W.S. Maxwell* (Montreal, 1991), pp. 121-25.

25. "Montreal Residence in Renaissance Design by E. and W.S. Maxwell", *Construction* (August 1911): 55.

26. Maxwell Work Costs Book F, Maxwell Archive, Canadian Architecture Collection, Blackader-Lauterman Library, McGill University, Montreal, p. 46.

27. Aymer Vallance, *William Morris: His Art, His Writings, and His Public Life*, 2nd ed. (London, 1898).

   Edward Maxwell had signed and dated the flyleaf, 1898. (See Irena Murray, ed., *The Libraries of Edward and W.S. Maxwell* [Montreal, 1991], p. 45).

28. William Maxwell gave the MMFA a pair of William De Morgan tiles from his collection (No. H: 33).

29. Richard Guy Wilson, "American Arts and Crafts Architecture", in Wendy Kaplan, *"The Art That is Life": The*

Arts and Crafts Movement in America, 1875-1920 (Boston, 1987), p. 111.

Worth noting here is William Morris's respect for H.H. Richardson. In his memoirs, James Mavor states, "William Morris used to speak of Richardson as the only American architect, and one of the few modern architects anywhere, who have produced a distinctively original style" (*My Windows on the Streets of the World*, vol. 1 [London and Toronto, 1923], p. 193).

30. See *The Architecture of Edward & W.S. Maxwell*, pp. 25-6.

31. Ernest T. Chambers, ed., *The Book of Montreal* (Montreal, 1903), p. 155.

32. It is interesting to note that around 1931-32 H.V. Meredith's wife, Lady Isobel Meredith, commissioned from Morris & Co. the tapestry (No. F: 31) for the Church of St. Andrew and St. Paul, Montreal, where two Morris & Co. windows were dedicated to her parents, the Andrew Allans.

33. Nobbs's life and work are examined in Susan Wagg, *Percy Erskine Nobbs: Architect, Artist and Craftsman* (Kingston and Montreal, 1982).

34. Address to the Sketching Club of the Province of Quebec Association of Architects, published in *Canadian Architect and Builder* 18 (May 1905): 75.

35. Wagg, *Percy Erskine Nobbs...*, pp. 23-4.
    The tiles are still in place in his residence.

36. A.C. Sewter, *The Stained Glass of William Morris and His Circle: A Catalogue* (New Haven, 1975), p. 215.

37. St. Paul's Church joined with the congregation of St. Andrew's Church in 1918. The two Morris & Co. windows were moved to the Church of St. Andrew and St. Paul's new building when it was constructed in 1931-32.

38. James Mavor Papers, Thomas Fisher Rare Book Library, University of Toronto, box 13, files 16, 17.

39. James Mavor Papers, box 13, file 16.

40. *The Scottish Art Review* of November 1889 (vol. 2) featured a review of the Arts and Crafts Exhibition Society's annual exhibition, in which Morris & Co. were included (see pp. 174-75).

41. The lecture was announced in *Toronto Saturday Night* (26 December 1896), p. 9. An undated draft of a lecture on Morris, in the James Mavor Papers, Box 56, files 2-3, is very likely the one he delivered in 1897.

42. *My Windows on the Street of the World*, vol. 1, pp. 99-104.

43. Letter dated 1 March 1910, James Mavor Papers, Box 13, file 15.

44. *The Arts and Crafts Society of Canada: Catalogue of the First Exhibition* (Toronto, 1904). Among the exhibitors were the architects Frank Darling and Eden Smith and the artists Frederick S. Challener, E. Wyly Grier and Gustav Hahn.

45. *The Paintings, Graphic and Decorative Work of Sir Edward Burne-Jones 1833-1898* (London, 1975), cat. no. 208, p. 71.

Alan Crawford, in his study of C.R. Ashbee, who also decorated pianos, refers to the interest in "artistic" pianos: piano "cases along Burne-Jones's lines were made by Broadwoods and decorated, sometimes by Morris & Company, sometimes by other artists..." (*C.R. Ashbee* [New Haven and London, 1985], p. 288).

46. Sandra Gwyn writes about Mabel Adamson's marriage and life with Agar Adamson in her book *The Private Capital* (Toronto, 1984), pp. 343-70. The present author also interviewed Anthony Adamson, the architect son of Mabel and Agar Adamson, in Toronto in June 1990.

47. Letter dated 20 November 1902, Anthony Adamson collection, Toronto.

48. The Guild of Handicrafts' metalwork was exhibited at the English Arts and Crafts exhibitions in the 1890s. Crawford states in *C.R. Ashbee* (p. 324) that the years 1896-1902 marked the flowering of Guild metalwork.

49. Albert W. Fulton and Keith M. Miller, *The Art of Wychwood*, a privately published catalogue on the history of Wychwood Park, prepared for the 100th anniversary of the original plan for the subdivision of the park (Toronto, 1988), pp. 94-5.

50. Annmarie Adams pointed this out in "Eden Smith and the Canadian Domestic Revival", an unpublished paper delivered at the Society of Architectural Historians, Montreal, April 1989. See also Carolyn Neal, *Eden Smith: Architect 1858-1949* (Toronto, 1976). I am indebted to Annmarie Adams for lending me her paper and directing me to additional Smith material.

51. One of the more notable houses by Smith was built in 1910 for Michael Chapman. His wife had been raised in England and was the adopted daughter of the Victorian painter and sculptor George Frederick Watts, whose work was prominently displayed in the house. See Fulton and Miller, *The Art of Wychwood*, p. 59. See also "Wychwood Park Heritage Conservation District Study, Inventory of Buildings", unpublished manuscript prepared by Harold D. Kalman, 1982.

Eden Smith also designed a Toronto house in 1904 for the British-born silversmith William Herbert Reid, who shared with him an interest in the Arts and Crafts movement.

52. Currelly tells the story of his efforts to establish the museum and its first collections in *I Brought the Ages Home* (Toronto, 1946, reprinted 1967).

53. Katharine A. Lochnan discusses Currelly's connection with Holman Hunt in "The Walker Journals: Reminiscences of John Lavery and William Holman Hunt," *RACAR* 9 (1982): 57-63.

54. The architecture of Samuel Maclure is examined in Martin Segger's *The Buildings of Samuel Maclure* (Victoria, B.C., 1986).

55. *Ibid.*, p. 105.

56. *Ibid.*, p. 163; and Janet Bingham, *Samuel Maclure: Architect* (Ganges, B.C., 1985), pp. 73-5.

57. Segger, *The Buildings of Samuel Maclure*, p. 174.

58. Bingham, *Samuel Maclure…*, p. 84.

59. The aims set out in a pamphlet by the Island Arts and Crafts Society are reprinted in the appendix of the master's thesis, "The Crease Family and the Arts in Victoria, British Columbia", by Christina Betts Johnson-Dean, University of Victoria, 1980, p. 462.

60. *Canadian Architect and Builder* (February 1894): 22; *Canadian Architect and Builder* (December 1900): 234-36.

61. The British-trained artist John Kyle (1871-1958) emigrated from Vancouver in 1906 and was appointed Organizer of Technical Education for British Columbia in 1914. He lectured on "William Morris" and "The Designs of Crafts for Industry" in Victoria in 1921 and 1922 as part of his efforts to improve industrial design. (See Geoffrey Hodder, *John Kyle: Artist and Educator: 1871-1958* [Victoria, 1984].)

    The artist Katharine Maltwood (1878-1961), who had been immersed in the Arts and Crafts movement in England, settled in Victoria in 1935. She brought with her a thorough knowledge of the movement and its principles. (See Rosemary A. Brown, *Katharine Emma Maltwood: Artist, 1878-1961* [Victoria, 1981].)

62. Alfred Boe, *From Gothic Revival to Functional Form: A Study in Victorian Theories of Design* (Oslo, 1957), p. 29.

    The titles are from two lectures William Morris gave in 1880 and 1881 respectively.

D R A W I N G S

D o u g l a s   E .   S c h o e n h e r r

Drawing was the foundation of William Morris's art and the basis upon which the achievement of Morris & Co. rested. Before there could be a stained-glass window, an embroidery, a wallpaper, a tile, or a font of type, there had to be a drawing. Just as the autograph manuscript was the vehicle for recording Morris's verbal thoughts, so the drawing, made in many instances with the same materials, was the vehicle for recording his visual ideas. Following Ruskin, he felt very strongly, however, that not only artists but everybody ought to be taught to draw, just as everybody ought to be taught to read and write.

From his first years at Oxford to the last days of his life, Morris was engaged in drawing, producing an amazing number of designs – 174 cartoons for stained glass, for example, and 644 designs for the Kelmscott Press – an achievement as a draughtsman that has scarcely been recognized. Although we read of Morris with his twin saucers of black and white effortlessly creating decorations for the Kelmscott Press, the image of him before his easel or sketchbook is a much less familiar one, but he was often to be found working in this way, usually muttering lines of a newly minted poem under his breath at the same time as he stroked a new design into existence.

One of the central cruxes of Morris the draughtsman is the notion, very long-lived and difficult to dislodge, that he could not draw. This idea derives overwhelmingly from his own diffidence concerning life drawing, a misgiving that may reflect his lack of confidence in his own body and in his physical relationships with women. The emphasis he placed on life drawing is surprising. From his evenings at Leigh's Life School, which he attended with Burne-Jones when he first settled in London, to his hiring of professional models in the mid-1870s, he struggled to master the contours of the human form. The 1860s were really his high point as a figure draughtsman, when he produced such cartoons as the *St. Agnes and St. Alban in Procession*, which convincingly demonstrates a command of the human

NO. A: 6. WILLIAM MORRIS, *St. Agnes and St. Alban in Procession*, c. 1864

37

figure particularly suited to the bold simplicity of stained glass (No. A: 6).

There was a profound connection between Morris's painful slogging away at life drawing and his design work that he articulated in his very first public lecture in 1877:

> As to the kind of drawing that should be taught to men engaged in ornamental work, there is only *one best* way of teaching drawing, and that is teaching the scholar to draw the human figure: both because the lines of a man's body are much more subtle than anything else, and because you can more surely be found out and set right if you go wrong.[1]

Even his biographer, J.W. Mackail, who was responsible for taking Morris at his word and perpetuating the myth that he could not draw, detected "a greater breadth and decisiveness of design in his decoration" as a result of his life drawing.[2] No one has ever questioned Morris's supreme genius as a designer of pattern, although the fact that each design began as a drawing has not been sufficiently studied. His mastery of execution is superbly demonstrated in his drawings for the Kelmscott Press, especially the full-page borders of the Kelmscott *Chaucer* (No. A: 28).

If Morris's drawings have been unjustly denigrated and neglected, those by Edward Burne-Jones have been almost universally admired from his day to ours. Having begun sketching as a small child, he discovered at an early age that drawing was his characteristic occupation and it remained throughout his life a necessary means of expression. Unlike Morris, who could pen words with the same facility that he could draw flowers, Burne-Jones recognized that he was predominantly visual rather than verbal: "I naturally draw when I've a pen in my hand."[3] Although he created many drawings in preparation for his paintings, such as the fine studies for *The Golden Stairs* (No. A: 38), a large part of his huge graphic output consists of his design work, from cartoons for stained glass and studies for domestic and ecclesiastical wall-decoration to designs for tapestries and painted pianos. *Fides* (No. A: 14), a large watercolour, illustrates how Burne-Jones's design work nourished and cross-fertilized his easel art. He was also a gifted caricaturist whose cartoons of the rotund Morris reveal a talent for humour that was treasured by his close friends and family.

All design drawings are *working* drawings, which may be a familiar idea to us, but was unfamiliar to the Victorian public. In a contribution to an Arts and Crafts Exhibition Society publication, Lewis F. Day was at pains to describe what a working drawing was: "A workman intent on his design will sacrifice his drawing to it – harden it, as I said, for the sake of emphasis, annotate it, patch it, cut it up into pieces to prove it, if need be do anything to make his meaning clear to the workman who comes after him."[4]

If Victorians expected the high finish of an academic show-piece, we

NO. A: 14
EDWARD BURNE-JONES,
Fides, 1872

today can appreciate these drawings as the initial steps in the creative process leading to the all-important finished product. The folds, the inscriptions, the fingerprints, the trial brush-marks, all reveal the signs of the workshop and the birth of an idea made concrete for the first time. Without the drawings that embodied their visions, the arts and crafts of Morris and his associates would never have existed to give joy to their makers and users as Morris so ardently intended.

NO. A: 43. DANTE GABRIEL ROSSETTI, *The Roseleaf*, 1870

No. A: 1

JOHN EVERETT MILLAIS

The Return of the Dove to the Ark 1851
Brush and pen with black and grey ink over traces of
   graphite, with scraping out, on wove paper with
   border in gold paint
23.4 x 12.9 cm (trimmed to arch at top)
Inscribed by the artist, lower-right, in brushpoint and
   black ink: *1851 JEM* (in monogram)
Provenance: Juliet Pritchett; her sale, Sotheby's, London,
   15 July 1964, lot 35; J.S. Maas & Co., London;
   purchased 1964
National Gallery of Canada, Ottawa (acc. no. 14661)

When Morris and Burne-Jones went up to Oxford in 1853,
neither of them had heard of the Pre-Raphaelites. They
had already discovered Ruskin, however, and Burne-Jones
recounts how one morning Morris ran into his rooms with
Ruskin's newly published *Lectures on Architecture and Painting* (issued in April 1854), and immediately read it aloud
to him, a custom with favourite books that lasted for the
rest of their lives. In the fourth lecture they learned about
the Pre-Raphaelite Brotherhood and saw the name of Dante
Gabriel Rossetti for the first time. Shortly thereafter, the
friends finally saw their first PRB picture, John Everett
Millais's *The Return of the Dove to the Ark*, which was on
display at the shop of the Oxford art dealer James Wyatt,
at 115 High Street. The picture of the two girls with the
dove (described as the daughters of Noah or the wives of
the sons of Noah) was one of the major epiphanies of their
art education: "and then," Burne-Jones said, "we knew."
The painting belonged to Thomas Combe, Superintendent of the Clarendon Press, committed High Churchman,
friend and patron of Millais, and one of the staunchest early
collectors of Pre-Raphaelite paintings and drawings.

   Millais's painting, for which this drawing is the final
preparatory study, made a profound impression on Burne-
Jones. Scriptural typology, or the method of finding anticipations of Christ in Old Testament persons and events, was
a fundamental device of Victorian literature and art, particularly of the Pre-Raphaelites. In working on his *Return
of the Dove to the Ark*, Millais evidently came to realize that
the motif could be interpreted as a typological prefigura-

NO. A: 1

tion of the Annunciation. Not only was the cast of characters similar, but also the theme of hope and imminent
salvation was central to both events. That Millais was
thinking of an Annunciation subtext for his *Return of the
Dove to the Ark* is suggested by the change in costume of
the girl on the right that he made between this final study
and the finished picture. Instead of the vaguely medieval
smocks that both girls wear in the Ottawa drawing, in the
painting he gave the girl kissing the dove a white ecclesiastical surplice, like a nun's scapular, which he borrowed
from the Angel Gabriel in Rossetti's famous Annunciation
picture, *Ecce Ancilla Domini!* (Tate Gallery, London). If the
figure on the right has associations with the Angel Gabriel,
the principal figure on the left, holding the dove to her
breast, evokes the Virgin Annunciate.

   That contemporary viewers understood the Annunciation imagery in Millais's dove picture is confirmed by an early watercolour and stained-glass design by Burne-Jones himself. His watercolour of *The Annunciation*, begun in 1859 and finished in 1861 (Birmingham), shows the Virgin on the left pressing the dove to her breast, while Gabriel in an ecclesiastical vestment approaches from the right. The motif of the Virgin with the clasped dove, which quite obviously derives from Millais's picture, was repeated in Burne-Jones's highly original Annunciation design (c. 1860, before the founding of Morris, Marshall, Faulkner & Co.) for a Lavers and Barraud window commissioned for St. Columba's, Topcliffe, Yorkshire, by the architect William Butterfield. The unorthodox and sensual gesture of the Virgin so offended Butterfield that when Burne-Jones refused to change it, the remaining windows were taken away from him and awarded to Michael Frederick Halliday.

DESIGN FOR THE DECORATION OF RED HOUSE

No. A: 2

EDWARD BURNE-JONES

Study for "The Wedding Feast of Sire Degrevaunt" 1860
Watercolour and gouache over graphite with scraping out,
    heightened with gum arabic, on cream wove paper
26.2 x 29.5 cm
Inscribed by the artist, upper left, in brush and brown
    watercolour: *EBJ / to / FEHB*
Provenance: anonymous sale, Sotheby's, London, 15 June
    1982, lot 100; Virginia Surtees; Maas Gallery,
    London; purchased 1989
Private collection

When Morris and his bride moved into the Red House towards the end of the summer of 1860, it became the laboratory for experiments in decorating by their friends. Embroideries were begun for the bedroom and dining-room, and during the summer and autumn of that year, Burne-Jones undertook a series of wall-paintings in the principal room, the drawing-room on the upper floor. On the walls around the celebrated settle, for which Rossetti painted the cupboard doors (see No. B: 4), he began to paint scenes from the English medieval romance *Sire Degrevaunt*, which was a favourite Arthurian story of his and Morris's. Out of this burst of artistic activity was born the idea of Morris, Marshall, Faulkner & Co. the following year.

Although seven scenes were apparently designed, only three were executed (in bright colours in tempera and gold) and still survive *in situ*: the wedding ceremony on a short wall just inside the door, and the wedding procession and the wedding banquet to the left and right of the settle, all these scenes representing the very end of the story. The sources for the latter two were, appropriately enough, the frescos by Giotto of the wedding procession of the Virgin and the marriage at Cana in the Arena Chapel. Since Burne-Jones had not yet visited Padua, his knowledge of these compositions derived from a portfolio of woodcut reproductions, published by the Arundel Society in 1853-60, with an explanatory text by Ruskin. The stripes between the two figures in the present drawing are copied from the wall-hanging behind the table in Giotto's *Marriage at Cana*, but a gold hanging was substituted in the finished Red House picture.

For the wedding feast, Burne-Jones made several drawings, a general compositional study in pen and ink and wash (now in the Yale Center for British Art, New Haven) and several figure studies from life in watercolour, such as this sheet and another of wedding guests (Fitzwilliam Museum, Cambridge). Fanny Cornforth, Rossetti's housekeeper and mistress, is said to have posed for the figure of the serving wench in the present drawing, while it seems probable that the red-haired Algernon Charles Swinburne, crowned with laurel, was the model for the seated man absorbed in his book. When one realizes that this figure is in fact the anonymous minstrel-bard who composed *Sire Degrevaunt* around 1400, studying, indeed singing his composition from a richly illuminated manuscript that con-

NO. A: 2

tains in the finished picture both lines of text and music, one understands the appropriateness of the young poet posing for this character. In the finished mural, all reference to Swinburne has however disappeared, the bard becoming a Dantesque figure in red and black with a headdress very similar to the one worn by the poet in the Rossetti shutter on the nearby settle. Through Burne-Jones's fancy, the minstrel-bard is allowed to participate in the very last episode of his story. In the preliminary studies, as indeed in the wedding ceremony and procession murals, the bride and groom are young unidentifiable Pre-Raphaelite types. In the final picture, however, Burne-Jones very appropriately represented Morris and Janey as Sire Degrevaunt and his bride Melidor at their wedding feast, although the sudden change in their appearance from the wedding procession is somewhat disconcerting.

This drawing was presented by the artist to "FEHB", a group of initials that have evaded decoding.[5] At the very end of his career, Burne-Jones provided an illustration for the Kelmscott Press edition of *Sire Degrevaunt* (No. L: 34).

DESIGNS FOR STAINED GLASS

ST. MARTIN'S-ON-THE-HILL, SCARBOROUGH

No. A: 3

DANTE GABRIEL ROSSETTI

Devil Carrying a Damned Soul to Hell c. 1861
Watercolour, heightened with gum arabic, on cream wove
    paper, inset into decorative border in pen and brown
    and black ink and watercolour on buff cardboard
6.9 cm (diameter, irregular; image); 13.5 cm (diameter,
    irregular; sheet with border)
Provenance: the artist's sale, Christie's, London, 12 May
    1883, part of lot 96(c); bought Brough; Sir Thomas
    Wardle, Leek, Staffordshire;[6] (?) his sale, Leek, May
    1909; Janet Camp Troxell, New Haven, Conn.; her
    sale, Christie's, London, 21 February 1989, part of lot
    100; bought Abbot & Holder, London; purchased
    1989 through Julian Hartnoll
Private collection, Ottawa

When Morris, Marshall, Faulkner & Co. was founded in 1861, the two senior members of the partnership were Dante Gabriel Rossetti and Ford Madox Brown. On the basis of their already established reputations as designers of the decorative arts, the young firm received its first com-

NO. A: 3

missions for stained glass from such Gothic Revival architects as G.E. Street, with whom both Webb and Morris had worked, and G.F. Bodley. Among the company's earliest commissions were windows and other decorative schemes in the latter's church, St. Martin's-on-the-Hill, Scarborough. Most of the artists in the Firm participated in the project and work continued into the early 1870s, making the church a veritable museum of Morris glass.

Around 1861, when Rossetti was designing the Parable of the Vineyard for the east window of St. Martin's, he executed nine small watercolours of saved and damned souls for a Last Judgement. Although they were never executed, it seems clear that they were intended for the western rose that surmounts the twin lancets with Ford Madox Brown's Adam and Eve. *The Builder* for 25 July 1863 reported that "it is proposed to fill the great rose window at the west end with the subject of the Last Judgment."[7] A design for the large circular light showing Christ in Majesty (Berger Collection, Carmel, California) was apparently the original idea for the centre, around which the nine lobes by Rossetti were to form the petals of the rose. Into his conception Rossetti also incorporated the Wheel of Fortune motif, as found in such medieval rose windows as that at S. Etienne, Beauvais, visited by Morris and Burne-Jones on their 1855 tour of France.

For the bottom lobe, Rossetti designed a St. Michael weighing a saved and a damned soul in a balance. The four lobes on the left were each to contain flying angels in white carrying saved souls, all depicted as beautiful blonde-haired girls, upwards towards heaven, symbolized by the deep blue backgrounds. In contrast, as the wheel turns past the top, the four lobes on the right were to contain green devils carrying damned souls, all depicted as men in ochre smocks, downward to hell, suggested by the red backgrounds. The present design was intended to occupy the lobe at the one o'clock position, the first one beginning the downward descent. In it the damned soul is a clearly recognizable portrait of William Morris, being dragged kicking to hell by – what else? – his hair! Just to rub the joke in, Rossetti also cast him as the minute damned soul in St. Michael's scale, found too light, though overweight, for Paradise. This sort of in-joke was typical of the Firm in its early days, Morris being cast as the heavy or the villain in a number of other windows, including Rossetti's Vineyard at Scarborough.[8]

For whatever reason, the Last Judgement theme was rejected and replaced by an Annunciation that Burne-Jones had originally designed as a tile panel, surrounded by half-length music-making angels by Burne-Jones and Morris that are more legible than Rossetti's small figures would have been. Rossetti's designs were never executed elsewhere, remaining in his possession until his death. They were subsequently owned by Thomas Wardle of Leek, the cloth manufacturer who dyed Morris's fabrics before his own vats were set up at Merton Abbey, passing into the hands of the distinguished Rossetti scholar and collector Janet Camp Troxell.

No. A: 4 a.-b.

FORD MADOX BROWN

a. *The Charity of St. Martin of Tours* 1864
Brush and grey and black wash over graphite with
    scraping out on cream wove paper
Verso, upside down, in graphite: preliminary study for
    the composition
75.7 x 55.1 cm (sheet, irregular); 73.7 x 50.8 cm (image)
Provenance: (?)artist's estate sale, London, 29-31 May
    1894, lot 254 ("St. Martin Catechumen");[9] W.R.
    Lethaby by 1925; bought by Dr. A.B. Alexander for
    Lord Beaverbrook

b. *The Reward of St. Martin of Tours* 1864
Brush and grey and black wash with graphite, black
    chalk and some scraping out on cream wove paper;
    flowers added in graphite by William Morris
79.9 x 54.5 cm (sheet, irregular, including 3.3 cm strip
    added at bottom); 76.1 x 50.8 cm (image)
Provenance: artist's estate sale, London, 29-31 May 1894,

lot 270; bought Harold Rathbone; W.R. Lethaby by 1925; bought by Dr. A.B. Alexander for Lord Beaverbrook
Beaverbrook Art Gallery, Fredericton, gifts of the Second Beaverbrook Foundation, 1960 (acc. nos. 59.379 & 59.378)

Long before the Firm had been founded, Ford Madox Brown had been active as a designer. He had done a Transfiguration window for Powell's in 1857 and had submitted furniture designs to the Hogarth Club summer exhibition in 1859. When he came to organize his own *Exhibition of WORK and Other Paintings* in 1865, nineteen cartoons for Morris & Co. stained glass were included, indicating the importance he attached to this sphere of his work. His notes in the catalogue stated the three qualities he required in a good stained-glass design: "invention, expression and good dramatic action", all to be found in abundance in his own work. Since fine colour was also imperative, Brown

FIG. A: 1. St. Martin window, St. Martin's-on-the-Hill, Scarborough, England

NO. A: 4 a.-b.

went on to explain why the cartoons for this firm were never coloured: Morris, "the manager," established the colour by selecting the glass during the manufacturing process.

Among other important designs for St. Martin's-on-the-Hill, Ford Madox Brown contributed this two-lancet window, dedicated to the patron saint of the church. Executed in Brown's typically rough, almost caricatural style, these cartoons narrate two episodes in the story of the Roman soldier Martin, who shared his cloak with a freezing beggar during a severely cold winter at Amiens. That night in a dream, Christ appeared to him wearing the half-cloak and announced that He had been the beggar. As a result, Martin was immediately baptized. In his first cartoon Madox Brown had given this twist of plot away by giving the beggar a cruciform halo, but it was suppressed in the final window. As it was Morris's task to interpret the cartoons to the glass-painters, he inscribed extensive instructions on these two. In an area of scrubby wash in *The Charity* he wrote sarcastically: "This is not a snow storm", and a landscape background of bare and leafy trees was added in the window. He was also careful to devise a distinctive "halfpenny" pattern for the saint's cloak, which figures as such an important prop in the story and must be immediately recognizable in the second episode. Morris often designed backgrounds or foregrounds to the figure compositions by others; in *The Reward* cartoon he added in pencil the lovely carpet of flowers that is so reminiscent of his early wallpaper designs, such as *Daisy* (No. E: 6).

Unlike the other designers in the Firm, Brown retained his original cartoons as his own property, usually inscribing them with the warning that copyright only for stained glass had been granted to Morris & Co., as on *The Charity* cartoon. When the artist's sale occurred after his death, a large number of Brown's stained-glass cartoons were on the market for the first time. In a blurb for Rathbone's portfolio of reproductions, which included *The Reward*, Morris expressed his admiration for his colleague's work: "I think it would be a great pity if some public body were not to secure the Brown Cartoons now they are to be had, being such characteristic work of such a characteristic master. Yours very truly, WILLIAM MORRIS."[10]

NO. A: 5 a.-b.

No. A: 5 a.-b.

EDWARD BURNE-JONES

a. *St. Stephen* 1873
Brush and brown wash with opaque white over traces of
    graphite on cream wove paper, laid down to card-
    board; strip (10.7 x 49.2 cm) cut off along top, now
    separately preserved
63.8 x 49.2 cm

b. *Daniel* 1873
Brush and brown wash with opaque white over traces
    of graphite, with details added in graphite, on
    cream wove paper, laid down to cardboard; strip
    (10.6 x 50.1 cm) cut off along top, now separately
    preserved
63.7 x 49.3 cm

Provenance: Laurence W. Hodson, Compton Hall, near
    Wolverhampton; his sale, Christie, Manson & Woods,
    London, 25 June 1906, lot 43; bought Sampson; anon-
    ymous sale, Christie's, London, 9 November 1976, lot
    127; P. & D. Colnaghi, London; purchased 1978
Private collection, Ottawa

Work continued at St. Martin's-on-the-Hill for over a decade. For two unusually shaped lights in the south and
north aisles respectively, Burne-Jones designed these cartoons of St. Stephen and Daniel, entering them in his
account books between 1 January and 1 April 1873 and
charging the Firm £8 for each of the designs. (The fees
the designer received from the company increased according to the size and complexity of the designs required.) In
both configurations the central lights were flanked by
taller lancets and surmounted by an attractive small rose.
St. Stephen the Protomartyr was flanked by standing
figures of St. Peter and St. Paul, both from stock cartoons
that Burne-Jones had already designed for other locations,
but a royalty was paid by the Firm whenever cartoons were
re-used. Daniel was flanked by the standing Old Testament
prophets Isaiah, an old design by Morris, and Ezekiel,
another earlier design by Burne-Jones. A large repertoire
of standing figures was gradually built up that could be
reused as required, or varied by being reversed, as was the
case with the Ezekiel, but the squat, bottle-shaped lights
in the centre obviously had to be custom-designed.

In order to maintain the same scale for the central figure
as for the standing ones on either side, Burne-Jones hit on

the idea of the kneeling pose. With each head touching the curved window top and locked in place by the halo, the figures were designed as two-dimensional patterns and expertly composed to fit into the unusual space. The rocks on the ground serve to identify Stephen, but no particular attribute was given for Daniel, who is often represented as kneeling in prayer in the lions' den. For the final windows, Morris chose the colours of the glass, as was his custom, and probably also supplied the scrolled pattern-work that filled up the backgrounds.

Burne-Jones conceived of the two figures as twin exercises in expressive drapery: St. Stephen's dalmatic seems heavy and earth-bound, dragging the martyr down to his death, while Daniel's draperies flutter with an ecstatic shiver that runs like an electric current from his toes to his decorative locks. The drawings were boldly executed in brown wash probably during the evenings and by lamplight, as was Burne-Jones's custom, the daylight hours being reserved for his painting. The evident drips, and the imprint of the artist's fingers to define the clasp at the side of Stephen's dalmatic, indicate the speed with which these cartoons were knocked off, while he listened to Georgie reading or to music or to the chatter of visitors.

Executed together, the drawings have always remained as a pair, first in the collection of Laurence Hodson of Compton Hall, which was decorated by Morris & Co. in the 1890s and for which the "Compton" wallpaper and chintz was originally designed. Although the cartoons were entered into the Figure Portfolios of the company and still bear their classification numbers, they were never re-used, undoubtedly because of their unusual shape, and were therefore sold to Hodson probably at the time his house was decorated.

ALL SAINTS, MIDDLETON CHENEY

No. A:6

WILLIAM MORRIS

St. Agnes and St. Alban in Procession c. 1864
Brush and brown and black wash with graphite, black
    chalk and scraping out over black chalk (?) under-
    drawing, on wove paper, laid down to fabric backing
72.5 x 46.3 cm
Provenance: Morris & Co, dispersal sale, London 1940
    (according to S. & K. Morris); anonymous sale,
    Christie's, London, 23 July 1974, lot 82, pl. 8; bought

S. & K. Morris, Stratford-upon-Avon; Morris
    Gallery, Toronto; purchased 1976
Private collection, Toronto

In 1865 Morris, Marshall, Faulkner & Co. completed the great east window in the chancel of All Saints, Middleton Cheney, Northamptonshire, that has been hailed as "a triumphant success, a masterpiece, and one of the most splendid achievements in all English stained glass."[11] The window is all the more remarkable in that it is the result of team-work involving no less than five artists, pulled together and harmonized into a unified whole by the coordinating talents of Morris and Philip Webb. The subject of the large window, composed of four lancets with tracery above, is appropriately a procession of All Saints, both

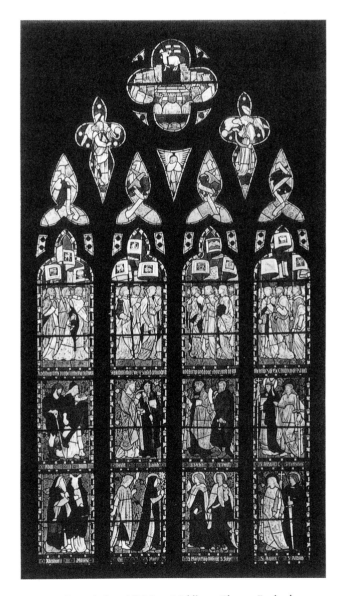

FIG. A: 2. East window, All Saints, Middleton Cheney, England

Old and New Testament characters, arranged in three tiers across the four lights. The top tier depicts a congregation of saints and martyrs, designed by Simeon Solomon, advancing from left and right and holding banners of the twelve tribes of Israel, designed by Philip Webb, that effectively fill the pointed tops of the lancets.[12] This is the only Morris window for which Solomon, who was a close friend of Burne-Jones at this time, created designs. In the lower two tiers, each light contains a pair of figures that are again advancing from left to right to meet in the centre, designed by Brown, Solomon and Morris, who drew the present cartoon for St. Agnes and St. Alban in the lower right corner.

It is something of a surprise to discover that after Burne-Jones, who contributed an amazing 682 cartoons for stained glass to the Firm, Morris himself was the next most prolific designer, creating an impressive 174 cartoons, compared to the 150 made by Ford Madox Brown and the mere thirty-six by Rossetti. In point of fact, Morris's designs were some of the most popular and most often repeated. In the words of Lewis F. Day, "his cartoons for glass were in some respects more severely appropriate to the methods of the glazier than those of his friend [Burne-Jones]."[13] The figures in the present cartoon are typical of Morris's best work in their quiet monumentality, dignity and amplitude of form, combined with his true genius for pattern work.

Since Morris is known to have made preliminary drapery studies for his St. Peter and St. Catherine in this window (Berger Collection, Carmel, California), it is quite possible that similar studies from the model were made for the present pair of figures. The artist started by blocking in his forms with a quick sketch in black chalk or graphite, and one can still see beneath the profile head of St. Alban a pentimento showing his face turned more fully towards us. Once the figures had been established, Morris boldly marked the lead-lines with black wash, indicating others lightly in black chalk within the figures, for example diagonally across the chest of Agnes or on her left arm. In brown wash he added the circular flower patterns to the lining of Agnes's sleeve, the decoration around her neckline and the diapering in the lining of her skirt which she shows by lifting her draperies with her right hand. A beautiful pattern of flowers and leaves is delicately drawn in graphite on her dress, which anticipates in a remarkable way the undulating, diagonal "branch" patterns that Morris would design two decades later for such chintzes in the "Thames Tributaries" series as *Evenlode* (No. F: 15). The designs on Agnes's dress were all exe-cuted in silver stain on white glass, which when fired produces a range of yellows, making her figure a glorious one of gold and white, played against the dark blue and green of St. Alban's cloak and gown.

St. Agnes's luxuriant knee-length hair is not merely the typical Pre-Raphaelite hair-fetishism, but in this case is iconographically significant. In *The Golden Legend*, which Morris knew well and later reprinted at the Kelmscott Press, it is explained that when St. Agnes refused to sacrifice to pagan idols, she was taken to a brothel to be deflowered, "but anon as she was unclothed god gaf to her suche grace that the heeris of her heed bycam so longe that they covered all her body to her feet, so that her body was not seen."[14]

To all of his co-designers' pairs of figures Morris added, as was his usual practice, a unifying foreground of grass and flowers and a background of apple, pomegranate, oak or rose, that was executed in a striking blue-green glass. For Agnes and Alban, Morris composed a background of pomegranate leaves decoratively punctuated here and there with fruit. That the window emerged as a unified work of art is due particularly to Morris's genius for colour. The lower portion of the window is coloured in a rich, heavy way, appropriate for the majesty of the figures, and accentuated by the richly patterned backgrounds. As the eye moves upward from this slow and dignified procession, the colour lightens into the predominantly gold and white of the top tier, becoming more transparent and ethereal as it reaches the heavenly vision at the very top of the tracery.

HOLY TRINITY, MEOLE BRACE

No. A: 7

FORD MADOX BROWN

The Expulsion from Paradise 1869
Brush and grey and black wash with scraping out over traces of underdrawing in black chalk (?) on wove paper
99.7 x 53.0 cm (sheet, irregular); 99.0 x 51.4 cm (image)
Provenance: Catherine Hueffer, the artist's daughter; by descent to anonymous sale, Christie's, London, 16 October 1981, lot 38; anonymous sale, Christie's, London, 19 July 1988, lot 112; bought by George J. Rosengarten, Montreal
Beaverbrook Art Gallery, Fredericton, gift of Mr. George J. Rosengarten, Montreal, 1990 (acc. no. 90.10)

The winter of 1868-69 was an anxious time for Brown, as he had not received a commission for twelve months. On 11 February 1869, however, he wrote to his friend Frederick Shields: "I have been arousing the Firm, and have extracted some cartoon work from it",[15] an indication of how important income from the Firm was to its partners. One of the major commissions he received at that time was for panels in an Old Testament window in the apse of Holy Trinity, Meole Brace, near Shrewsbury.

This composition of *The Expulsion* was to occupy the most prominent position in the three-lancet window: top of the centre lancet. The subject of Adam and Eve had a very personal significance for the artist throughout his career. The year after his St. Martin windows (No. A: 4), Brown had designed a monumental Adam and Eve with animals for the west window of St. Martin's-on-the-Hill, Scarborough, in which he rather curiously cast himself and his second wife, Emma, as the progenitors of mankind.[16] When he came to design the present *Expulsion*, Brown again cast himself as Adam and his wife Emma as Eve in what may be called *The Last of Paradise*, echoing his celebrated painting *The Last of England*, in which they had appeared as the immigrant couple.

Apparently to maintain the symmetry of its position, Brown introduced the rather unusual iconography of the two avenging angels who flank the fallen couple and point

FIG. A: 3. Old Testament window, Holy Trinity, Meole Brace, England

NO. A: 7

to the flaming sword in the very centre of the composition. The two angels are in fact Brown's daughters, quite recognizable in the cartoon: the elder, Lucy, on the right and the younger, Catherine, on the left. While it was quite common, especially in the early days of the Firm, to introduce recognizable portraits within the stained-glass window designs, sometimes with tongue-in-cheek results (see No. A: 3), it was much less usual to find self-portraits, let alone family portraits in the windows. That the *Expulsion* cartoon had personal significance is indicated further by the fact that, at the time it was illustrated in Ford Madox Hueffer's monograph on his grandfather, the cartoon was the property of his mother, Catherine, who had posed for one of the angels. In the finished window, a brick wall has been introduced in the background, indicating forcibly the irrevocable banishment of the couple.

No. A: 8

FORD MADOX BROWN

The Finding of Moses 1869
Brush and grey wash over graphite with extensive
    scraping out on ivory wove paper
66.2 x 53.7 cm (sheet); 64.2 x 51.6 cm (image)
Provenance: anonymous sale, Sotheby's, Belgravia, 28
    November 1972, lot 38; bought Hartnoll & Eyre,
    London; Fine Art Society, London; Julian Hartnoll,
    London; purchased 1979
Private collection, Ottawa

This cartoon is the design for another panel in the same Old Testament window at Meole Brace. Since the Victorians were fond of interpreting the Bible typologically, it is very likely that Brown intended the present composition to evoke the birth of Christ.

Of the principal designers that worked on early Morris & Co. stained glass, Brown was the most pictorial in his approach, subsequently turning many of his cartoons into oil paintings or watercolours. This is particularly apparent in the present cartoon, with its deep perspective and its realistic details such as the reeds, which would have been very difficult to translate into stained glass. In fact, the resulting window is almost entirely painted, since it was impossible to interpret the design as a mosaic of pieces of coloured glass.[17] Although Burne-Jones was the more skilful designer of stained glass, Brown has his own distinctive qualities of drama and eccentric story-telling, which are very evident in this work.

NO. A: 8

By 1869, Victorian artists were quite capable of archaeological accuracy in the depiction of ancient Egypt. One has just to compare Edward John Poynter's impressive painting *Israel in Egypt* (1867, Guildhall Art Gallery, London) with Brown's present cartoon to realize how whimsical the latter's treatment of ancient Egypt is. The jelly mould serving as a picturesque hat on the umbrella-bearer is a particularly endearing touch that is typical of the very idiosyncratic work of this artist.

JESUS COLLEGE CHAPEL, CAMBRIDGE

No. A: 9

EDWARD BURNE-JONES

The Trinity 1875
Graphite over traces of brownish chalk or charcoal on
    ivory wove paper; brown wash border
59.7 x 48.5 cm (sheet); 52.7 x 42.9 cm (image)
Provenance: Laurence W. Hodson, Compton Hall, near
    Wolverhampton; his sale, Christie's, London, 25 June

1906, part of lot 47; A.C. Sewter; Bill Waters; Ian Hodgkins; Fine Art Society, London; Julian Hartnoll, London; MacMillan and Perrin, Toronto; Sotheby's, London, 16 June 1982, lot 291, bought in; MacMillan and Perrin sale, Christie's, London, 1 March 1983, lot 106; purchased at the sale
Private collection, Ottawa

When the architect G.F. Bodley was appointed to oversee an extensive restoration of Jesus College Chapel in Cambridge, he strongly advocated that Morris & Co. work with him as collaborators. As a result of his recommendations, the Firm contributed painted ceilings to the structure, as well as a spectacular series of windows that make the church one of the greatest collections of Morris glass. Beginning with the ceilings in 1866, the work on the windows continued until 1878.

Dominated by the stupendous Angelic Hierarchy in the great south window, the south transept contains on its east and west walls the windows of the four Evangelists, powerful Michelangelesque figures by Burne-Jones, each flanked by pairs of equally imposing Sibyls. Below these monumental figures runs a continuous band of predella panels telling the essence of the Christian story from the

FIG. A: 4. DIDRON, *Iconographie chrétienne: Histoire de Dieu* (1843)

Nativity scenes, designed by Burne-Jones, to the Passion, assigned to Ford Madox Brown. In the final predella sequence in the St. John window, three apocalyptic scenes were contributed by Burne-Jones: the Ascension, the Worship of the Lamb, and the very last panel in the sequence, this conception of the Trinity, which the artist entered in his account book on 9 April 1875, charging £10 for the cartoon.

If Burne-Jones had never lifted a paintbrush, he would have earned a high place in Victorian art history just for his superb design work for Morris & Co. stained glass, inventing and reinventing the whole gamut of Christian iconography. Very little attention has been given, however, to the sources behind his designs. While it would be a mistake to think that every window had a specific source from which he worked, many of them did, including this very interesting Trinity. We know from the artist's conversations in the spring of 1874, recorded by his studio assistant T.M. Rooke, that Burne-Jones owned and used the iconographical studies of Adolphe-Napoléon Didron, whose *Iconographie chrétienne: Histoire de Dieu* was published in

NO. A: 9

Paris in 1843.[18] It seems quite understandable that in commencing his one and only design of the Trinity, Burne-Jones would have turned to the relevant chapter in Didron. There, on page 562, he found an illustration of a sixteenth-century manuscript illumination from the Bibliothèque Sainte-Geneviève that he used as the basis for his design (fig. A: 4).[19] Since the two figures of God the Father and God the Son are virtually identical in Didron, Burne-Jones decided to turn the figure holding the orb into Christ by making him young and clean-shaven, with a crown of thorns around his papal tiara. (In the source illustration, Christ is actually the figure on the left, i.e., on the right hand of God the Father.) The rather striking conception of the Dove of the Holy Spirit inspiring the two other persons of the Trinity by linking their mouths with his wings, was changed by Burne-Jones, who cleverly wove the wings of the dove into the plates of the halos, emphasizing the unity of the Trinity. The rainbow on which the figures sit is found in other illustrations of the Trinity on following pages of Didron, and appears regularly in images of Christ in Majesty, including those by Burne-Jones. In translating his source into the cartoon, Burne-Jones also seems to have recollected the God the Father in Van Eyck's Ghent altarpiece, a tribute to one of Morris's favourite artists.

With its richness of surface-pattern that flows from the wavy heavens at the bottom through the undulating draperies to the curls of the beard and the stars in the sky, this cartoon epitomizes the decorative sophistication that Burne-Jones brought to his design work. Re-used only once for the top tracery light in the Ascension window, south aisle, All Hallows, Allerton (1882), the Trinity cartoon was sold to Laurence Hodson, who had no less than five predella cartoons for Jesus College in his collection. As the colour notations in the margin indicate, God the Father was given a deep ruby robe, while Christ's is a medium blue. The cloak that effectively unites the figures is white, to which a gold pattern in silver stain has been added.

ST. JOHN OF BEVERLEY, WHATTON

No. A: 10

EDWARD BURNE-JONES

The Raising of Lazarus 1877
Graphite and coloured chalks on buff wove paper; brown wash border
59.5 x 56.8 cm

Provenance: apparently Sir Philip Burne-Jones, the artist's son; his sale, Christie, Manson & Woods, London, 5 June 1919, part of lot 95 ("Raising of Lazarus" pastel); anonymous sale, Christie's, London, 4 February 1986, lot 252, bought in; purchased after the sale by the present owner
Private collection

In contrast to St. Martin's-on-the-Hill and Jesus College Chapel, which are treasure-houses filled with Morris & Co. windows, the church of St. John of Beverley in Whatton, Nottinghamshire, is graced with only one: a three-light window with standing figures of St. Peter, Salvator Mundi and St. John the Evangelist with predella panels beneath and angels in the tracery. The present cartoon is a design for the predella panel underneath the central figure of Christ and illustrates one of his most astonishing miracles. Burne-Jones entered the design in his account books between 1 July and 9 November 1877, charging £12 for each of the three Whatton predella designs.

From the very beginning of his career, Burne-Jones drew inspiration from the work of Giotto, basing his early *Sire Degrevaunt* murals in the Red House on scenes from the Arena Chapel in Padua (No. A: 2). For this first attempt at designing the Lazarus subject, he turned once again to the Arena Chapel, which he had seen during his second trip to Italy with Ruskin in 1862. In Giotto's fresco, the scene is set in the same rocky landscape with Christ on the left, gesturing with a similar command towards Lazarus on the right, wrapped in his funeral shroud and rising from his tomb. Between the two major figures is a compressed group of huddled heads which Burne-Jones translated into the similar group of women. The two-dimensional patterns of the rocks and especially of the wonderful draperies have been orchestrated into a masterful design for stained glass.

Morris & Co. cartoons for stained glass were never coloured. Burne-Jones, however, sometimes turned his cartoons into independent works of art by adding colour to them. This is apparently what has happened with this work, for the colours added in pastel are not related to the actual colours of the window. The cartoon having been returned to the artist for colouring, some sort of copy or tracing must have been kept within the Firm's portfolios, for this design was re-used twice afterwards. Although the coloured cartoons were undoubtedly intended for re-sale to collectors, this Lazarus apparently remained with the artist, probably being the pastel that appeared in Sir Philip Burne-Jones's sale in 1919.

NO. A: 10

HILLHEAD CHURCH, GLASGOW

No. A: 11

EDWARD BURNE-JONES

Christ Blessing the Little Children 1892
Black and white chalk with graphite border on brown
    paper, laid down on canvas on stretcher; squared
    in graphite
162.2 x 61.0 cm
Provenance: the artist's sale, Christie's, London, 16-18
    July 1898, part of lot 178; bought Agnew; The
    Ruskin Gallery, Birmingham, proprietor John Gibbons
    (from small label on bottom centre of stretcher); the
    Parochial Church Council of St. Mary's Church,
    Selly Park; their sale, Christie's, London, 18 October
    1977, lot 207; Sotheby's, Belgravia, 18 April 1978,
    lot 50; Christie's, London, 20 July 1979, lot 180;
    purchased 1979
Joey and Toby Tanenbaum, Toronto

Beginning in the early 1880s, Burne-Jones's stained-glass
designs changed into what may be called his late style:
extremely elongated figures, often in a continuous pictorial field that unifies several lancets of a single window
into one large picture. These traits are to be seen in the
four cartoons for a window for Hillhead Church, Glasgow,
which the artist entered in his account books in Septem-

ber 1892, charging the large sum of £100 for them. The
two narrow lancets are divided into two horizontal regis-
ters, for which the artist designed compositions that ran
across both lancets. In the top register, he composed a scene
of Christ blessing the little children, with the present
design appearing in the left-hand light. In the right-hand
light are found a group of three mothers bringing their
children to Christ. The two cartoons forming a continuous scene were sold together in the artist's studio sale in
1898 and remained together until quite recently.[20] Beneath
the top scene, which was further unified with a continuous background of foliage, runs the lower register, composed of two angels holding a scroll between them that
again extends across both lights. The cartoons for the
angels were formerly in the collection of Harold Rathbone.[21] By the end of his long career as a designer for
stained glass, Burne-Jones had acquired an amazing facility
of execution, favouring coloured chalks on brown paper
for many of his cartoons. Burne-Jones actually designed six
versions of Christ blessing the children, including one for
Speldhurst in 1874[22] that was re-used for the late Morris
& Co. tapestry now in the Church of St. Andrew and St.
Paul in Montreal (No. F: 31).

PRELIMINARY STUDIES FOR STAINED GLASS

No. A: 12

HENRY HOLIDAY

The Magdalene Anointing Christ's Feet c. 1860
Verso: Academic study of a male nude
Graphite on wove paper
25.3 x 35.4 cm
Provenance: the artist's studio; Walker's Art Gallery,
    London; Moss Galleries, London; purchased 1988
Private collection

At the age of thirteen, Holiday was taught drawing by
William Cave Thomas, an associate of the Pre-Raphaelites,
and received encouragement for his youthful efforts from
Ford Madox Brown. In 1855 he began his studies at the
Royal Academy Schools, where he formed a sketching club
with Marcus Stone, Simeon Solomon and Albert Moore.
Four years later, while still continuing his studies at the
RA, he joined the Artists' Volunteer Corps, whose mem-
bers included William Morris and Dante Gabriel Rossetti.
He was introduced to Burne-Jones by Simeon Solomon in

NO. A: 11

FIG. A: 5. *Christ Blessing the Little Children*, right-hand cartoon for
Hillhead Church, Glasgow

1860, becoming a frequent visitor to his studio. One can see from this brief summary that Holiday had rejected the academic principles that were being taught him at the Royal Academy and had enthusiastically embraced Pre-Raphaelitism at an early age.

In 1860, his last year as an RA student, he was admitted to the Life School and studied anatomy at King's College, University of London. It was probably at this time that he made the academic nude study on the *verso* of the present sheet, which in its painful truth to nature is the opposite of heroic idealization. The compositional study of *The Magdalene Anointing Christ's Feet* is not known to relate to any painting which Holiday undertook at this time, but is very Pre-Raphaelite in feeling. What is even more interesting is that the head of Christ bears a striking resemblance to that of William Morris. The profile with its delicate mouth and beginning moustache and beard seems quite close to Rossetti's well-known portrait of Morris for the Llandaff altarpiece,[23] which is of approximately the same date. Only the hair on the Holiday Christ, thick as it is, does not seem quite right for Morris. It was very characteristic of the early Pre-Raphaelites to use each other as models; just as Rossetti cast Morris as David in his triptych, so Holiday may have modelled his Christ on Morris, paying the ultimate tribute to one of his heroes. There is only a slight connection between the present composition and the circular window of the same subject that Holiday designed in 1865 for St. Lawrence Jewry, Guildhall, London, and the windows at Westerham, Mere, Headington and elsewhere. The present drawing may perhaps be best understood as an early preliminary study, traces of which were carried over into the later designs.

NO. A: 12

When Burne-Jones left James Powell & Sons' stained-glass firm to work exclusively for the newly founded Morris, Marshall, Faulkner & Co., Holiday was engaged as their principal designer. He went on to become one of the best of the progressive stained-glass designers of the Victorian period, rejecting an excessive medievalism for aesthetic goals similar to those of Morris and Burne-Jones, with whom he remained friends. In 1880 he provided illustrations for Morris's poem "Riding Together" in an anthology called *British Ballads*. In 1891 he opened his own stained-glass works in Hampstead and went on to produce some notable windows all over the world, including Canada.

HOUSEHOLD SCIENCES BUILDING,
UNIVERSITY OF TORONTO

No. A: 13 a.-c.

HENRY HOLIDAY

Designs for the Stained-glass window "Domestic Arts in Ancient Egypt" c. 1914
a. *Left Panel: Preparing Food*
Watercolour and gouache over graphite with opaque white, brown gouache border, on cream wove paper
42.6 x 26.0 cm (sheet); 26.2 x 17.4 cm (border);
 19.9 x 11.0 cm (image)

b. *Centre Panel: Weaving and Spinning*
Watercolour and gouache over graphite with opaque white, brown gouache border, on cream wove paper (two sheets joined horizontally below frieze separating the upper register of the scene from the lower)
42.8 x 25.8 cm (sheet); 26.3 x 17.5 cm (border);
 19.9 x 11.0 cm (image)

c. *Right Panel: Beating Flax and Storing Cloth*
Watercolour and gouache over graphite with opaque white, brown gouache border, on cream wove paper
42.8 x 26.3 cm (sheet); 26.3 x 17.5 cm (border);
 19.9 x 11.0 cm (image)
Provenance: by descent to the artist's daughter, Winifred Holiday
Royal Ontario Museum, Toronto, gift of Winifred Holiday, 1927 (acc. nos. 1927.114.3, 1927.114.2, 1927.114.1)

In 1913 the Household Sciences Building of the University of Toronto opened on Queen's Park across from the Royal Ontario Museum of Archaeology. A stained-glass window having been proposed for the staircase landing, Lillian Massey-Treble, who funded the building, turned for advice to her husband's first cousin, C.T. Currelly, a founder and the first director of the ROM. In 1902 Currelly had gone to England, where his interest in ancient Egypt brought him into contact with the famous archaeologist Flinders Petrie. At this time Henry Holiday was seriously studying Egyptian art in order to produce convincing illustrations of the story of Joseph. Currelly visited his studio and they became friends. Hearing that the artist wished to go to Egypt, Currelly invited Holiday and his studio assistant, Miss Jessie Mothersole, to visit him there during the winter of 1907.[24] After the deaths of Morris and Burne-Jones, Holiday was generally considered to be the best stained-glass artist in Britain, so that it is no surprise that Currelly chose him for the Lillian Massey-Treble Building window. Having visited Canada in 1890, Holiday had already produced two windows there, one for the Hospital for Sick Children in Toronto in 1891 and another for the University of Winnipeg in 1893.

Domestic science was naturally to be the subject of the window, but because the building was classical in design, Currelly originally had proposed setting the scenes in ancient Greece. In his reply of 7 May 1913,[25] Holiday suggested ancient Egypt instead, arguing that Egypt would provide the earliest known examples of domestic skills for which a pictorial tradition existed in wall-paintings and reliefs. The artist, who had become quite famous for his Egyptian windows, must have known that Currelly would find the idea irresistible and so work began on the Egyptian window. The stained glass arrived in Montreal by ship on 3 August 1915 and was installed by October. On 3 November Mrs. Massey-Treble died in Santa Barbara, California, apparently never having seen the window for which she had paid £539. According to the Latin inscription in the three small lights above it, the Holiday window was in honour of Mrs. Massey-Treble's mother, Elissa Phelps Massey, and "of all other good women who adorned their homes with their domestic abilities, of which adornments they themselves were the greatest part." Holiday wrote to Currelly on 19 May 1916 to express how pleased he was "to know that the windows are liked so much."

In designing this large window, Holiday first divided his composition into two tiers cleverly representing the upper and lower floors of an Egyptian house, which extend through the three vertical lights into which the window was further divided according to subject. On the left he depicted the preparation of food, with women making

FIG. A: 6. *Domestic Arts in Ancient Egypt*, Office of the Ontario Ombudsman (formerly Household Sciences Building, University of Toronto)

  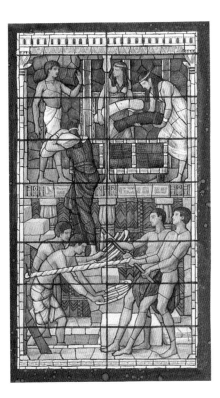

NO. A: 13 a.-c.

bread upstairs, while men are roasting and boiling meat in the foreground. In the centre, three women work at an upright loom,[26] while three graceful women spin below them. To the right, slaves are engaged in beating flax and carrying bales of cloth to a chest in the upper chamber.

The present three *modelli* are the finished designs, to a one-inch scale, that Holiday habitually prepared for his windows. As was the practice also with Morris & Co., these watercolour designs remained the property of Holiday's stained-glass firm and were only given to the ROM in 1927 by the artist's daughter, Winifred. At this point in his career, Holiday no longer made finished cartoons, only full-scale outline drawings that could be traced by the glass painters. Details and shading were taken from the many separate studies that the artist drew. At the end of a very prolific career spanning over sixty-five years, Holiday had produced an incredible body of work: 330 coloured designs, between 2,000-3,000 cartoons, and 1,882 studies. In comparing the watercolour designs to the finished window, one discovers that the artist reversed the composition for the right panel, and all the men were turned into Nubians by giving them a dark skin that contrasts effectively with the lighter flesh-tints of the women. Numerous small details were changed, as was the general disposition of the colour, which in the window is a glorious jewel-like medley of predominant greens and blues with effective

accents of bright red. The remarkable effect of the nude female bodies daringly revealed beneath the see-through draperies must have attracted hordes of goggle-eyed male undergraduates for decades. Times have changed. Household Sciences are now as extinct as life in ancient Egypt, good women are no longer the chief adornments of the home, and the Household Sciences Building now provides offices for the Ontario Ombudsman. But Holiday's window remains, one of the most absurdly splendid achievements of the art of stained glass in Canada.

INDEPENDENT WORKS BASED ON STAINED-GLASS DESIGNS

No. A: 14

EDWARD BURNE-JONES

Fides 1872
Watercolour and gouache heightened with gum arabic and gold paint on wove paper, laid down on paper; in original frame
178.1 x 63.2 cm
Inscribed by the artist, lower right on base of pilaster, in brown paint: *E.B.J. / MDCCCLXXI.*; bottom centre, in white paint: *FIDES*[27]
Provenance: Commissioned by F.S. Ellis; his sale,

Christie's, London, 16 May 1885, lot 93; bought
John Graham, Skelmorlie Castle, Ayrshire; his sale,
Christie's, London, 30 April 1887, lot 88; bought
Agnew; Sir Alexander Henderson (Lord Faringdon),
by 1898; his sale, Sotheby's, London, 13 June 1934,
lot 101; purchased by Sir Charles Holmes for
Harold Athelstan Stone, one of the Founders of the
Vancouver Art Gallery
Vancouver Art Gallery, Founders Fund, 1934
(acc. no. 34.16)

In 1870-71 Burne-Jones designed figures of the three theo-logical Virtues, Faith, Hope and Charity, for a window in Christ Church, Oxford. The result was a classic of Morris & Co. stained glass that was repeated again and again all over the world. With different colours and different back-grounds, as was customary with such repetitions, a ver-

FIG. A: 7. Morris & Co., stained-glass window in the Church of
St. Andrew and St. Paul, Montreal (1885)

sion was made in 1885 for St. Paul's, Montreal, a fine window that is now in the Church of St. Andrew and St. Paul. The artist was obviously pleased with his designs and proposed to turn them into independent paintings. The painted series of Virtues was commissioned by F.S. Ellis, a bookseller who published Morris's *The Earthly Paradise*, edited numerous publications of the Kelmscott Press, and acted as one of Morris's executors after his death. The first Virtue Burne-Jones undertook for Ellis was a *Caritas* (Charity), in progress by 1870 and based on an earlier design for stained glass at Greenock. The second was the present *Fides* (Faith), which, despite the date of 1871 in-scribed on it, appears to have been completed in 1872,[28] followed by *Temperantia* (Temperance), making a set of three, but not the traditional three theological Virtues of the original Oxford Window. Around the same time a *Spes* (Hope) was begun, which was also offered to Ellis, but the artist jokingly suggested that he might prefer "a figure of 'Drink' or 'Polygamy'… after so much virtue."[29] Behind the series is probably the recollection of the Vir-tues and Vices in Giotto's Arena Chapel, sketches of which Burne-Jones had made during his visit in 1862. As Ruskin perceptively commented in his Oxford lecture on Burne-Jones in 1883, "his essential gift and habit of thought is in personification…."[30]

Inspiration from his trip to Italy in the fall of 1871 may be clearly seen in the artist's conception of *Fides*, shown standing in a Renaissance niche with bronze putti hold-ing strings of beads from the capitals of the pilasters, motifs that are found frequently in the work of one of Burne-Jones's favourite artists, Mantegna. The figure is loaded with props that symbolically convey its allegorical mean-ing. In her right hand she holds the lamp, a traditional symbol of faith, while around her left hand curls the ser-pent of Divine Wisdom. Underfoot she tramples on the dragon of Doubt, which writhes amidst flames. Having filled the composition with a rather personal and esoteric collection of symbols, including the wreath of jasmine on her head and the branch of myrtle in her hand, the artist was dismayed when "a rumour once reached him that there was a mystic intention in the number of beads that are threaded on a string held by *bambini* in the background of 'Fides.'"[31] The implication is that they had no specific meaning, but commentators like Fortunée de Lisle and Dennis Wheeler have been determined to decipher them.[32]

Throughout the 1860s and '70s, Burne-Jones followed Rossetti's lead and did not choose to exhibit much of his work publicly, preferring to sell direct to a select group of patrons and collectors. This practice changed dramatically in 1877 when the artist agreed to exhibit at Sir Coutts Lindsay's newly opened Grosvenor Gallery on Bond Street, a smart contra-salon set up in opposition to the Royal Academy. Burne-Jones sent eight pictures to the first show: three major pictures hung on the line, *The Days of Creation*, *The Mirror of Venus*, and *The Beguiling of Merlin*, with five large single figures above, including *Spes*, *Temperantia* and *Fides*. Overnight he became one of the leading artists in Britain and a hero of the Aesthetic Movement, continuing to be a star attraction for a decade before he transferred his allegiance to the New Gallery. As Sidney Colvin said of the first Grosvenor Gallery exhibition: "The genius of Mr. Burne-Jones will on these walls become a reality to those to whom it had hitherto been only a report."[33]

One might be excused for thinking that the present work, with its monumental scale and brilliant colours, was an oil painting instead of a watercolour on paper, for Burne-Jones's use of the latter medium fooled a lot of people, including Ruskin. So unorthodox was his watercolour technique, again derived from the practice of Rossetti, that the artist's studio assistant T.M. Rooke was asked to write a note on it for the 1933 Burne-Jones centenary exhibition at the Tate Gallery. Rooke explained that Burne-Jones favoured the newly invented moist watercolours in tubes and cakes, applying them with hog-hair brushes made for oils: "Whether he painted in oil or water colour he liked the same result, one like fresco and egg tempera, so he has puzzled people about his medium's identity."[34]

This superb *Fides*, which still remains in its original frame, was acquired by Harold Athelstan Stone in 1934 for the recently founded Vancouver Art Gallery. Sets of large allegorical single figures were favourite subjects with the artist, as for example in his six pictures of *Day* and *Night*, *Spring*, *Summer*, *Autumn* and *Winter*, painted for Frederick Leyland in 1869-71 and shown at the second Grosvenor Gallery exhibition in 1878; the former pair were later owned by the important Montreal collector James Ross, while the magnificent Seasons were with the MacMillan and Perrin Gallery in Vancouver in the late 1970s.

No. A: 15

EDWARD BURNE-JONES

Saint Michael the Archangel 1896
Gouache with gold, copper and silver paint on card
  prepared with purple gouache
35.2 x 25.0 cm

Provenance: gift of the artist to Laura Alma-Tadema, the
  wife of Sir Lawrence Alma-Tadema;[35] anonymous
  sale, Christie's, London, 1 March 1946, lot 38; bought
  by Dr. A.B. Alexander for Lord Beaverbrook
Owens Art Gallery, Sackville, New Brunswick, gift of
  Lord Beaverbrook, c. 1949 (acc. no. 49.3)

For Burne-Jones, whose work was a combination of the decorative and the spiritual in equal measure, angels were the quintessential subject. Some of his most beautiful angelic creations appeared in his stained-glass designs, which obviously provided great scope for their decorative proliferation. This particular St. Michael was originally designed in 1886 for a window in the English Church of St. George in Berlin.[36] A similar figure of St. Michael, standing, as in the present work, on the ramparts of heaven, was designed by Burne-Jones for the apse mosaics in the American Church in Rome. It was probably these mosaic designs, with their glittering golds, that inspired the artist in the 1890s to create a series of drawings in metallic paints on black or dark-brown paper that are among the most stunning, most unusual and most Symbolist of his entire career. Such drawings "in tints of gold on coloured grounds" are noted as having been made at Rottingdean in 1896 in the artist's autograph work records. This taste for metallic paint and iridescent effects may go back to his early memory of a woman in Warwick painting bronze colour on a butterfly for an album.[37]

As the inscription reveals, this precious object was given by the artist and his wife, Georgie, to Laura Alma-Tadema, the second wife of the painter (later Sir) Lawrence Alma-Tadema, on 8 January 1896, the laurel boughs surrounding the dedication undoubtedly being in this case a flattering reference to the recipient's name. The day was, in fact, the birthday of her husband, but the gift was no doubt meant to be a gracious offering to both husband and wife. In the *Memorials*, Georgie recorded the close friendship of the two families that developed particularly after 1881. Although Alma-Tadema's art could not be further removed from Burne-Jones's, being for the most part microscopically elaborate recreations of life in ancient Greece and Rome, the two artists became close friends and enjoyed the company of each other's families.

Accompanying the drawing was a letter from the artist that was found behind the work when the frame was opened c. 1975. The letter, which unfortunately has since disappeared, was partially transcribed:

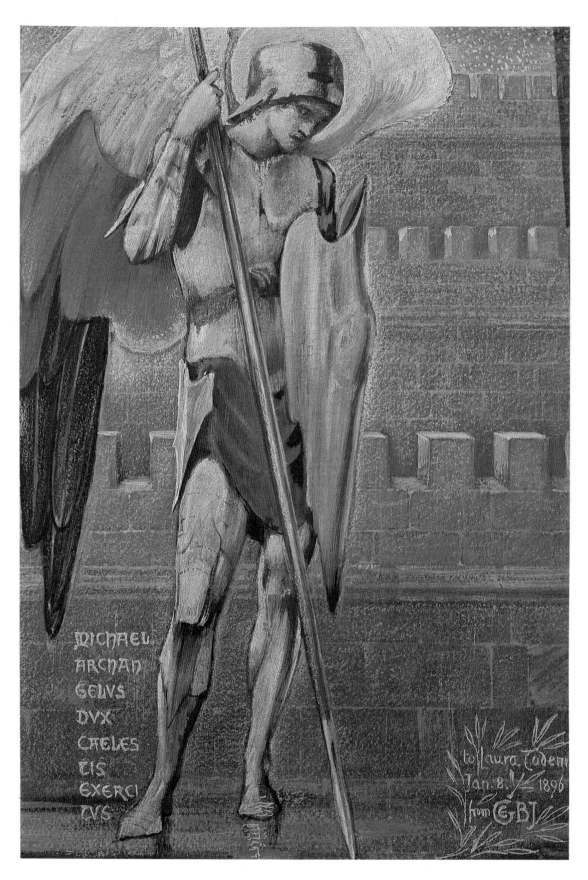

MICHAEL
ARCHAN
GELVS
DVX
CAELES
TIS
EXERCI
TVS

to Laura Tadem
Jan. 8. 1896
from E.B.J

NO. A: 15. EDWARD BURNE-JONES, *Saint Michael the Archangel*, 1896

Here is a little gold sort-of-thing which I have made o' purpose for you.... I only wish it was prettier, and that the gold would shine more – but if you will accept it as coming from loving and lasting friends, its purpose will be accomplished. This evening we come, but after dinner please, I am a bit ailing these days – eyes troubling me and feeling tired and weak....[38]

A preliminary study for this drawing in gouache and coloured chalks is known;[39] its provenance was at one time confused with that of the present work.

DESIGNS FOR CHURCH DECORATION

ST. JOHN'S, TORQUAY

No. A: 16

EDWARD BURNE-JONES

Study for "The King and the Shepherd" c. 1887-88
Watercolour, gouache, pastel and metallic paint over
    charcoal, heightened with gum arabic, on brown
    wove paper, laid down to canvas and stretcher
40.1 x 61.1 cm
Provenance: by descent to the artist's daughter, Margaret
    Mackail; her sale, Christie's, London, 3 December
    1954, part of lot 27; bought Cevat; anonymous sale,
    Sotheby's Belgravia, 24 October 1978, lot 7, bought
    in; The Curzon Gallery, Boca Raton, Florida (as
    "School of Gustave Moreau"); purchased 1991
Mr. and Mrs. John D. Shearer

The church of St. John's, Torquay, was built between 1864 and 1871 to the designs of G.E. Street, who undoubtedly secured for Morris, Marshall, Faulkner & Co. the commission for the great east window, completed in 1865. The two side-walls of the chancel were originally intended for mosaic decoration, but in 1887-88 Burne-Jones was asked to provide monumental painted murals instead, which were executed largely by an assistant. Having studied and admired the mosaics in Ravenna and being occupied at that very time with an ambitious scheme of mosaic decoration for Street's American Episcopal Church in Rome, the artist designed his wall decorations for Torquay in a flat decorative style with gold backgrounds that clearly evoke that ancient art form. For the south wall he produced a *Nativity* that is closely related to the huge *Star of Bethlehem* watercolour he was then undertaking for Birmingham. The subject of the north wall was somewhat unusual, representing two angels leading a Magus and a Shepherd by two different paths towards the manger on the other side of the sanctuary, the King symbolizing the rich and the Shepherd the poor of the world, who are both being led to Christ as their saviour. Burne-Jones explained to the vicar of the church the significance of the gestures of the angels, who are both placing a finger to their lips: the angel leading the King "is holding his fingers in a manner which betokens the sealing of *his own* lips and demonstrates his own reverence, whilst the other angel extends his fingers towards the Shepherd, enjoining silence upon him."[40]

It would seem that this rarely encountered subject is intentionally related to the east window overhead, which Burne-Jones had designed over twenty years before. There, in the two outside panels of the lower tier of figures, one sees on the left an angel leading a woman by the hand and on the right an angel leading a man by the hand towards the Heavenly Jerusalem that is depicted as a turreted golden city across the top of the lights. This idea of angels ministering to humanity was apparently taken up again and further elaborated in the wall paintings.

In preparation for the paintings, the artist made colour studies in pastel, the present one for *The King and the Shepherd* and two for the *Nativity*, one of which, in the Walsall Museum and Art Gallery, bears the inscription (evidently not by the artist): "Done at Rottingdean in April 1887 by Sir Ed. Burne-Jones...." The other pastel for the *Nativity*, along with thirteen more (mostly chalk) studies for the Torquay murals, is presently in the Whitworth Art Gallery, Manchester. If the artist executed one of the colour studies at his sea-side house in 1887, it is possible that he did the present pendant at the same time, but it should be noted that the artist himself listed the pictures, both their design and execution, in his work records under 1888. Typical of Burne-Jones's late Symbolist style at its most austere and expressionistic, this study was recently sold with an attribution to the School of Gustave Moreau, which is not as far-fetched as it may seem, for in 1922 Léonce Bénédite bracketed these two artists together in a chapter of his book *Notre art, nos maîtres*, underscoring the important place that was assigned to Burne-Jones among the Symbolists in France.

In order to heighten the parallelism between the two figures, Burne-Jones changed the King's robe from the deep blue in the colour study to the same rosy pink as the Shepherd's cloak in the finished painting. The frame on the present work is its original one, being virtually iden-

NO. A: 16

tical with that on the pastel study for *Love Leading the Pilgrim*, which has also some similarities in iconography with *The King and the Shepherd*.[41] The artist's son reported that his father intended to paint two large easel pictures of these subjects, but he only got as far as blocking in the figures in monochrome.[42] It is sad to report that the two mural paintings, "perhaps the greatest treasures which St. John's possesses", in the words of the vicar who commissioned them, were recently removed from the church and sold.[43]

EATON HALL CHAPEL, NEAR CHESTER

No. A: 17 a.-d.

JOHN HENRY DEARLE

The Symbols of the Four Evangelists 1893 or 1894
a. *The Winged Man of St. Matthew*
Brush and brown wash with watercolour and gouache, heightened with opaque white, over graphite on light-brown wove paper
46.3 x 38.4 cm (sheet, irregular); 39.7 x 35.1 cm (image)

b. *The Winged Lion of St. Mark*
Brush and brown wash with watercolour and gouache over graphite on light-brown wove paper; two vertical ruled lines in red pencil
45.6 x 38.9 cm (sheet, irregular); 40.0 x 35.1 cm (image)

c. *The Winged Ox of St. Luke*
Brush and brown wash with watercolour and gouache, heightened with opaque white, over graphite on light-brown wove paper
45.0 x 39.6 cm (sheet, irregular); 39.6 x 35.3 cm (image)

d. *The Eagle of St. John*
Brush and brown wash with watercolour and gouache, heightened with opaque white, over graphite on light-brown wove paper
48.7 x 43.7 cm (sheet, irregular); 39.7 x 35.1 cm (image)
Provenance: by descent in the Dearle family; unidentified auction sale; Julian Hartnoll, London; purchased 1979
Private collection, Ottawa

In the same letter of 2 February 1883 in which Ruskin inquired about the progress of the *Proserpine* picture he had commissioned from Burne-Jones (see No. A: 39), he also asked his friend if he would design some stained-glass windows for the chapel at Whitelands, an Anglican girls' training college on the King's Road in Chelsea, in which Ruskin took a deep interest through his friend the Rev. John Faunthorpe, its principal. Morris & Co. eventually supplied at cost all the windows of the chapel, dedicated to Ruskin's favourite saint, Ursula, and went on to pro-

NO. A: 17 a.-d.

vide extensive interior decoration. When the east window was installed in 1886, it was decided that the sanctuary should be further enriched with a Morris & Co. reredos, a panelled screen directly behind the altar. When Morris submitted his sketch of a grid of spiralling acanthus leaves, Rev. Faunthorpe objected that he would like a little bit of Christianity in the design. Morris replied in a letter of 22 October 1886: "I think if I were you I would be satisfied with the emblems of the 4 evangelists & the sheaf of arrows for Ursula: I could alter the designs to suit these...."[44]

The suggestion was accepted and Kate Faulkner executed the reredos in gesso relief, which was then silvered all over and coloured with transparent glazes to produce a brilliant, jewel-like effect, similar to that of the decorated pianos she produced for Morris & Co. The designs for the Four Evangelists, which were simply inserted into the grid in two pairs to the right and left of the altar, were by Philip Webb, who was usually responsible for animal iconography of this sort in the Firm's stained glass, as was most of the ornament.[45] The reredos, together with almost all of the original Morris stained glass, was reinstalled in the new chapel by Sir Giles Gilbert Scott when Whitelands College moved to West Hill, Putney, in the early 1930s. The archives there contain all the correspondence between Faunthorpe and Morris & Co., constituting a fascinating case-study of the relationship between the Firm and a client over a considerable period of time.[46]

The Whitelands reredos was such a success that the Duke of Westminster, a patron of that institution, ordered his own version for the chapel at Eaton Hall, part of a complex of buildings near Chester recently constructed by the architect Alfred Waterhouse (1830-1905). An estimate of 4 January 1893 submitted by Morris & Co. to the Duke explained that "the general effect of color will be similar to that at 'Whitelands' which we understand you have seen." The work was completed and installed by 6 November 1894, when an invoice was submitted for payment of £345, £5 less than the original estimate.[47]

Probably because a different size of grid was required, Dearle produced these new cartoons, to be inserted together with panels of acanthus, lilies and other decorative flowers in three blind arcades to the right and left of the altar. The exquisitely modelled gesso reliefs, silvered, gilded and lacquered, were undoubtedly again the work of Kate Faulkner, who followed Dearle's cartoons very closely, but changed the colour of the dramatic acanthus fronds to a delicate silvery green, and the little flowers in the secondary pattern in the background to red.

Although 1860 is usually given as his date of birth, Dearle was in fact born on 22 August 1859 at 27 Queen Street, Camden Town.[48] He joined Morris & Co. as a young man in 1878, being the first to be taught high-warp tapestry weaving. He spent the rest of his life with the company, playing a considerable role in the tapestry and stained-glass departments and rising to become art director of the Firm after Morris's death. Lewis F. Day recorded that he had "learnt to work so like him [Morris] that the design of the pupil may well be mistaken, even by the experienced in design, for that of the master."[49] That this was so is demonstrated by the fact that two of the classic "Morris" chintzes, *Daffodil* and *Compton*, were until quite recently considered to be the work of Morris himself, when they are in reality the creation of the self-effacing Dearle, who deserves more recognition for his contribution to the Firm than he has so far received. He died on 15 January 1932 at his house, called Kelmscott, at Graycott Green-lane, Purley, Surrey, leaving an estate of £10,794 8s 10d. His son, Duncan William Dearle, bought the stained-glass department when Morris & Co. closed down in 1940, and went on to supply a number of windows in Canada (see "Stained Glass" chapter of this book).

DECORATIVE PROJECTS INSPIRED BY MORRIS'S *THE EARTHLY PARADISE*

THE GRAHAM PIANO

No. A: 18 a.-d.

EDWARD BURNE-JONES

Four Designs for the Story of "Orpheus and Eurydice" c. 1872

a. *Orpheus with his Lyre*
Brown and white gouache on cream wove paper prepared with brown gouache
22.9 x 22.4 cm (round image)

b. *Eurydice Bitten by a Snake*
Brown and white gouache on cream wove paper prepared with brown gouache
22.7 x 22.8 cm (round image)

c. *Orpheus and Eurydice Embracing*
Brown and white gouache over an underdrawing of white chalk (?) on cream wove paper prepared with brown gouache

22.8 x 22.8 cm (round image)

d. *Orpheus Pursued by the Furies*
Brown and white gouache on cream wove paper prepared
   with brown gouache
22.8 x 22.8 cm (round image)
Provenance: Margaret Mackail, the artist's daughter; from
   whom purchased by the father of the present owner
Dr. and Mrs. Neville Elwood

In the mid-1860s, when Morris was planning and beginning to write his long narrative poem *The Earthly Paradise*,
it was decided that the work would be lavishly illustrated
with several hundred wood-engravings after the designs of

Burne-Jones. Although only the wood-blocks for "Cupid
and Psyche" were actually cut (see Nos. K: 6-8), Burne-
Jones designed many other illustrations. Among the first of
the stories to be completed was "Orpheus and Eurydice",
which Mackail says Morris wrote in 1866. For this poem,
which was finally excluded from the published version of
The Earthly Paradise, Burne-Jones made a large number of
designs. The group of five drawings of Orpheus, formerly
in the Sir John Witt collection and now in a private Canadian collection,[50] are probably among Burne-Jones's earliest sketches of the subject.

Although they were never used as intended, Burne-
Jones's designs for *The Earthly Paradise* illustrations became

NO. A: 18 a.-d.

a rich source for his own future artistic work. The Orpheus story was taken up in 1872, according to the artist's autograph work-record in the Fitzwilliam Museum, Cambridge, and it is likely that the present four gouaches (and two unfinished ones of related subjects in the Elwood collection) date from that year. When Burne-Jones's friend and patron William Graham commissioned a decorated piano for his daughter Frances in 1879, Burne-Jones resurrected his Orpheus designs as being highly appropriate embellishments for a musical instrument.

So great was the mania for painted furniture within the Morris circle that pianos did not escape such enhancement. As soon as he received a very modest upright as a wedding present in 1860, Burne-Jones set about painting it. From the decoration of pianos, he progressed to the actual designing of the cases in collaboration with W.A.S. Benson, substituting the chaste lines of earlier harpsichords for the objectionable bulges and curves of the Victorian instruments that were, he said, the very altars of the home. On the newly designed case that Broadwood had executed for him, he painted in roundels the story of Orpheus and Eurydice, based on a series of finished drawings that are now in the Fitzwilliam Museum, which had evolved in their turn from the earlier gouaches.[51] Morris & Co. went on to supply a number of lavishly ornamented pianos, executed in gesso by Kate Faulkner, to such clients as Alexander Ionides and W.K. D'Arcy as part of the comprehensive decoration of their houses.

Other round gouaches from the same series are in the Fitzwilliam Museum and the Tate Gallery, and are known from an album of Hollyer photographs in the possession of Peter Nahum, London, and in the Witt photograph files at the Courtauld Institute. Boldly conceived and freely executed, they are good examples of the great influence that Morris's *The Earthly Paradise* had on the whole subsequent career of his artist-friend.

THE BALFOUR MUSIC ROOM

No. A: 19

EDWARD BURNE-JONES

Study of Perseus for "Perseus and the Graiae" c. 1880
Black, red and white chalk on brick-red wove paper
22.7 x 30.2 cm
Provenance: anonymous sale, Sotheby's Belgravia,
    19 October 1971, lot 68; bought Hartnoll & Eyre,

NO. A: 19

London; Morris Gallery, Toronto; purchased 1974
R. Fraser Elliott

In 1875 A.J. Balfour, the future prime minister, commissioned Burne-Jones to create a set of pictures to decorate his music room at 4 Carlton Gardens, London. The subject matter having been left to the artist's choice, Burne-Jones once again returned to studies he had originally made in the 1860s to illustrate Morris's *The Earthly Paradise*. In this case, he chose the Perseus story, which Morris had treated in his poem "The Doom of King Acrisius", twenty-eight episodes of which had originally been identified for the illustration project. Three drawings of c. 1875 in the Tate Gallery represent the initial proposal for the decoration, showing pictures by Burne-Jones, some to be painted and some to be executed in gilt and silvered gesso on oak, framed by panels of swirling acanthus, obviously designed by Morris and very similar to his *Acanthus* wallpaper of that year.

Although the subject of Perseus rescuing Andromeda from the sea monster was common enough in European art, some of the episodes, such as the second in the series, showing Perseus and the Graiae, had rarely if ever been depicted. In order to discover the whereabouts of the sea-nymphs who would arm him for his encounter with Medusa, Perseus first sought out the Graiae and by snatching the single eye they shared between them – the action of the present study – gained the information he required. Before the definitive oil painting (now in Stuttgart), Burne-Jones executed three other versions: one in gesso relief, according to the original scheme, which he called the "Golden Graiae" and which received severe criticism when it was exhibited at the Grosvenor Gallery in 1878, causing the artist to abandon the idea of the gesso reliefs; the full-scale gouache cartoon; and a small panel picture of 1882. The final oil, finished in 1893, is one of the most striking, indeed most Wagnerian of Burne-Jones's pictures, with its strange grey figures crouching in a grey lunar landscape. A large number of preparatory drawings exist, including a beautiful nude study for the present figure in a sketchbook in the Fogg Museum, Cambridge, Mass., and another nude study that appeared at Sotheby's, London, 27 June 1984, lot 29.

No. A: 20 a.-b.

EDWARD BURNE-JONES

a. *Study of Medusa for "The Finding of Medusa"* c. 1875
Two types of graphite on cream wove paper
26.4 x 17.5 cm

Provenance: by descent to the artist's son, Sir Philip
  Burne-Jones; his sale, Christie's, London, 5 June 1919,
  part of lot 53; bought Gooden & Fox, London;
  William Hesketh Lever, Viscount Leverhulme for the
  Lady Lever Art Gallery, Port Sunlight; their sale,
  Christie's, London, 6 June 1958, part of lot 25; bought
  Brown for Lord Beaverbrook
Beaverbrook Art Gallery, Fredericton, gift of the Second
  Beaverbrook Foundation, 1960 (acc. no. 59.320)

b. *Study of Medusa for "The Finding of Medusa"* c. 1890
Black, blue and white chalk on cream laid paper
33.4 x 25.0 cm
Provenance: by descent to the artist's daughter, Margaret
  Mackail; purchased October 1926
Royal Ontario Museum, Toronto (acc. no. 926.48.6)

These two sheets are more studies for the Perseus cycle for the Balfour music room, discussed in the preceding entry. After receiving armour from the sea-nymphs (third pic-

NO. A: 20 a.-b.

ture), Perseus approached Medusa with the help of his magic mirror in the fourth episode, *The Finding of Medusa.* Burne-Jones took great pains with the figure of Medusa, who raises a hand in apprehension to her head as it is about to be struck off by the invisible Perseus. The present two drawings demonstrate a fascinating contrast of approaches to the study of the same figure. In the sheet from the Beaverbrook Art Gallery, the artist has concentrated on the linear elaboration of the folds of Medusa's gown, which he has drawn in graphite with great decorative effect. Comparable drawings are to be found in a sketchbook in Birmingham and in the Lady Lever Art Gallery, Port Sunlight. In the later study in the Royal Ontario Museum, Burne-Jones has applied the coloured chalks almost expressionistically to create a stark, brooding silhouette against the blank page. The final painting of *The Finding of Medusa* was never executed, the artist having completed only the full-scale gouache cartoon of c. 1882 (now in Southampton) and another full-scale cartoon of 1890 in gouache and chalk (now in Stuttgart). It would appear that the Royal Ontario Museum study was prepared for the latter version. It was acquired by C.T. Currelly for the ROM from the artist's daughter in 1926.

DESIGNS FOR SCULPTURAL RELIEFS

No. A: 21 a.-b.

EDWARD BURNE-JONES

a. *Sea Nymph* 1878
Watercolour and gouache on brown (or brown prepared?)
    paper, mounted on canvas and stretcher
61.1 x 62.0 cm (sight)

b. *Wood Nymph* 1878
Watercolour and gouache on brown (or brown prepared?)
    paper, mounted on canvas and stretcher
64.1 x 62.9 cm (sight)
Provenance: Private collection, Holmbury St. Mary,
    Surrey; anonymous sale, Christie's, London, 17 June
    1975, lot 150; The Morris Gallery, Toronto
Vivian Morris

Under the year 1878, Burne-Jones entered in his autograph work record: "designed three panels for low relief of wood nymph, water nymph & Hesperides." Derived from a sketch originally made in the 1860s to illustrate Morris's poem *The Life and Death of Jason,*[52] the *Garden of the Hesperides* design was executed as a painted gesso relief

in two versions: an overmantel for Lady Lewis's dining-room at Ashley Cottage, Walton-on-Thames, 1882 (now in the Victoria and Albert Museum) and a cassone front for Frances Graham, Lady Horner, in 1888 (now in the Birmingham City Museums and Art Gallery, on loan to Wightwick Manor).

The fact that the *Wood Nymph* and the *Sea Nymph* were listed together with the *Hesperides* would suggest that they were all originally conceived for some ensemble. Being the same height as the cartoon for the *Hesperides,*[53] the present cartoons would appear to have been designed as the square sides of a cassone that was intended to have the garden composition on the front, an idea that was suggested in the 1975 sale catalogue, where these drawings were described as designs "for gesso panels for a chest." At least one of them appears to have been executed as an independent gesso relief, for in 1889, when Burne-Jones bought the little house beside his own at Rottingdean, he turned the kitchen of the former into his beloved pot-house room and "above the fireplace...he put up a painted bas-relief of a mermaid sporting in the waves, from which he called the place 'The Merry Mermaid.' "[54] His seaside life at Rottingdean inspired a whole series of mermaids and merbabies from 1882 to 1892. Although Burne-Jones is known to have made a number of gesso reliefs himself, some projects, such as the Horner cassone, were executed by assistants and then painted by the artist.[55]

The motif of the mermaid with fish in her hands goes back to a design for woven stuffs that Burne-Jones listed under 1875 in his work record, where an identical figure is combined with swirls of leaves and flowers apparently by Morris (now in the William Morris Gallery, Walthamstow). As was so often the case with Burne-Jones's design work, his cartoons for the Sea and Wood Nymphs were turned into oil paintings double the size of the drawings, which the artist listed under 1879 and 1880 in his work record. Harmonies in monochromatic green and blue, the pictures were criticized because the highly modelled and finished figures were not integrated with the conventionalized backgrounds, a dichotomy of approach that was avoided in the purely decorative cartoons.[56] The oil *Wood Nymph*, dated 1883, is now in the South African Cultural History Museum, Cape Town. A watercolour version of the *Wood Nymph* was also executed, with the addition of two delightful rabbits, which the artist's daughter lent to the Burne-Jones centenary exhibition at the Tate Gallery in 1933 (no. 67); it is now in the Burne-Jones family collection, Toronto.

NO. A: 21 a.-b.

With their marvellous patterns of leaves and waves, effectively repeated in the undulating hair of the nymphs, these drawings represent Burne-Jones's genius for two-dimensional design at its most assured and attractive and look forward to the linear extravaganzas of Art Nouveau at the turn of the century.

DESIGNS FOR WALLPAPER

No. A: 22

WALTER CRANE

Design for "Fairy Garden" Wallpaper c. 1890
Watercolour and gouache over graphite, heightened with
    opaque white, on cream wove paper; squared for
    transfer in graphite
59.1 x 63.4 cm
Provenance: purchased from the artist through the
    Women's Art Association of Canada, Toronto, 1909
National Gallery of Canada, Ottawa (acc. no. 189)

Although Walter Crane was never officially a member of Morris & Co., he had very close connections with the Firm and with Morris personally, designing occasional stained-glass windows, the cartoon for the first tapestry containing figures, and illustrations for the Kelmscott Press (No. L: 23), as well as enthusiastically supporting Morris in his Socialist causes. For his own part, Morris evidently thought

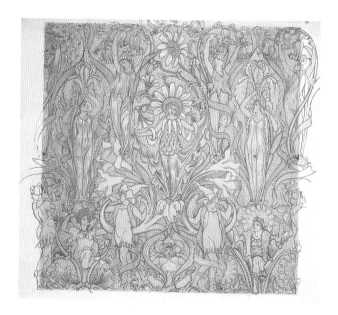

NO. A: 22

highly of Crane's work, considering it to be "worth looking at" when the idea of the Arts and Crafts Exhibition Society was mooted.[57] Crane was active for three decades as a designer of wallpapers for both nursery and general use, but for the most part his work was quite different in character from Morris's.

There is a definite interrelationship between Crane's illustrated Toy Books and his wallpaper designs. As a result of the great success that he enjoyed as an illustrator of delightfully coloured children's books from 1865 onwards, he was commissioned by Metford Warner, proprietor of Jeffrey & Co., to design his first nursery paper in 1874. Warner was well known for his artistic wallpapers, employing leading artists on a freelance basis to provide the designs, and was meticulous in executing them, so meticulous in fact that Morris, who usually had to do it himself to get the quality he wanted, was content to let Jeffrey & Co. print all of his wallpapers. Unlike his wallpapers for general use which were hand-printed, Crane's nursery papers were machine-printed, probably because the limited market for such items would not bear the very high cost of hand-printing. Crane's wallpapers were available in Canada through Elliott & Son in Toronto and through Scotts Interior Decorations House in Montreal, both of which also sold Morris papers.[58]

In 1890 Crane published this nursery paper, called *Fairy Garden*, which was specifically intended to capitalize on the success of *Flora's Feast*, one of his most attractive illustrated books that had appeared the year before. The enchanting fairy personifications of flowers were mostly inspired by the plates in the book. Unlike Morris, Crane often introduced the human figure into his wallpaper and fabric designs, although one surviving design by Burne-Jones and Morris, called *Mermaid*, which was never executed, indicates that they at least considered the possibilities of a semi-human figure in a flat repeating pattern (see No. A: 21).

This and three other designs (Nos. A: 23, 32, 36) were part of a group of seventeen Crane drawings that the National Gallery of Canada purchased in Toronto in 1909 from the artist's travelling exhibition; they were among the first European drawings to enter the national collection.[59]

No. A: 23

WALTER CRANE

Design for "Lion and Dove Frieze" 1900
Gouache with graphite and white chalk on grey laid
    paper (enlarged by two horizontal strips added along

NO. A: 23

the top), originally laid down on canvas on wooden strainer

62.4 x 108.0 cm

Inscribed by the artist, lower left, in red gouache, cropped along lower edge: *Walter Crane 1900* (?)

Provenance: purchased from the artist through the Women's Art Association of Canada, Toronto, 1909

National Gallery of Canada, Ottawa (acc. no. 186)

Such books as Charles Eastlake's *Hints on Household Taste* (1868) recommended that, in decorating a wall, the tasteful Victorian should divide it into three distinct horizontal units: a dado along the floor, a frieze below the ceiling, and in between, the filling. In all of their grander decorative schemes, Morris & Co. followed this prevailing fashion, as for example in the Green Dining Room at the South Kensington Museums (now the V & A). The Firm's official position on the matter of friezes and dados was articulated in the Morris & Co. brochure for the 1883-84 Boston Foreign Fair: "It will be understood from this that Morris and Company do not print distinctive frieze-patterns.... Our wall-papers therefore are simple fillings; they imitate no architectural features, neither dados, friezes, nor panellings."[60] Walter Crane, however, regularly designed com-

plementary sets of wallpapers, including dados, fillings and friezes, which were hand-printed and sold by Jeffrey & Co.

The present design for the *Lion and Dove Frieze* was published in 1900 to complement a filling called *Rose Bush*, which depicts clumps of roses on vertical trunks in a manner very reminiscent of the work of Charles Rennie Mackintosh in Glasgow. The matching papers were shown with great success at the Paris Universal Exposition that year. Just as he often introduced human beings into his wallpaper designs, so Crane often turned his walls into books by incorporating quotations of one kind or another. The Bible-reading Victorians would have had no difficulty identifying the inscription "The wilderness shall blossom as the rose", for it comes from Isaiah 35:1: "The wilderness and the solitary place shall be glad for them; and the desert shall rejoice, and blossom as the rose". This particular text of Isaiah describes the joyful flourishing of Christ's kingdom to come and continues: "No lion shall be there, nor any ravenous beast shall go up thereon, it shall not be found there; but the redeemed shall walk there" (verse 9). Taking his cue from this prophecy of a peaceable kingdom, Crane has shown the warlike British Lion tamed by the Dove of Peace. It is quite likely that Crane's image of

FIG. A: 8. *The Arming and Departure of the Knights*, tapestry, 1895-96, Birmingham City Museum and Art Gallery

hoped-for peace refers to topical events of the day, for the Boer War had broken out the year before he executed this frieze. Crane was one of the small minority in Britain who actively opposed that war, designing a printed textile *Pax* in 1902 to celebrate its conclusion, the original cartoon for which is now also in the collection of the National Gallery of Canada. Unlike Morris, Crane was therefore willing to introduce his private political convictions into such public design work as wallpaper or chintz designs.

Crane's frieze, moreover, may be interpreted as a tribute to Morris & Co. Not only does the background bring to mind Burne-Jones's *Briar Rose* paintings, now at Buscot, but the entire idea seems to derive from *The Forest* tapestry woven in 1887, which is a long, frieze-like composition with a procession of animals designed by Philip Webb in a garden setting, including a majestic lion facing a large black crow, while a scroll of text by Morris floats overhead (V & A). Although Crane's wallpapers tended to be quite different in feeling from Morris's, being opulent, showy and Italianate for the most part, when he came to design his first paper for general use in 1876, he based it on Morris's perennial favourite, *Daisy*, but gave it a smart French elegance that matches its inscription: *Si Douce est La Margarete*. Altogether, Crane designed more than sixty papers for Jeffrey & Co., including flocked or embossed examples, and luxurious gilded, lacquered and hand-painted ranges that simulated stamped leather. His work was considered too advanced for any taste but the most aesthetically rarefied – it would take considerable nerve to install this frieze of lions around one's room – and his hand-printed papers, like Morris's, were so expensive, costing up to 15s a roll, that they were to be found only in the drawing-rooms of the most affluent.

DESIGNS FOR TAPESTRY

No. A: 24

EDWARD BURNE-JONES

Study for "The Arming and Departure of the Knights" 1893
Black chalk and graphite on off white laid paper, laid down to thin wove paper backing
33.1 x 16.3 cm
Inscribed by the artist, lower left, in graphite: *E B-J / 1863* [*sic*]...
Provenance: Georgiana Burne-Jones, the artist's widow;[61] Mrs. M. Wade, Vancouver; Muse Antiques and Art Galleries (G. Mayer), Vancouver; Mr. & Mrs. Ernest E. Poole, Edmonton; Ernest E. Poole Foundation; on loan to the Edmonton Art Gallery, 1968-75
The Edmonton Art Gallery Collection, gift of the Ernest E. Poole Foundation, 1975 (acc. no. 68.6.11)

The Holy Grail Tapestries represent the summit of Morris's attempts to resurrect the art of high-warp weaving in England. Commissioned in 1890 to provide sumptuous decoration for several rooms in William Knox D'Arcy's house, Stanmore Hall, Morris pulled out all the stops for the dining-room, for which a series of six narrative tapestries with verdure panels underneath were created. The subject was the search and discovery of the Holy Grail by the Knights of the Round Table, as described in Malory's *Morte D'Arthur*, the single most important book for both Morris and Burne-Jones. Having begun their careers in the visual arts by painting episodes from that work on the walls of the Oxford Union in 1857, the two friends must have found it highly gratifying to be able to return to the same subject for one of their last creations together. The achievement of the tapestries make up somewhat for the lavish Kelmscott Malory that was planned but never realized. The success of these tapestries, as Morris rightly acknowledged, depended on the stupendous design talents of Burne-Jones, who was then at the height of his powers. Burne-Jones's account books (Fitzwilliam Museum) reveal that he was paid the then-enormous sum of £1,000 for the Stanmore tapestry designs.

After the basic composition for each scene had been established, the artist made many detailed studies for individual figures. The woman holding the helmet in the present sheet is a study for one of the two maidens helping Guenevere to arm Lancelot outside the gates of Camelot in the second episode of the series, *The Arming and Departure of the Knights*. The position of her head, as well as her costume and the helmet, was changed in the final tapestry, but she is still quite recognizable. After these individual figure studies had been completed, the artist integrated them all into rather small *modelli* in coloured chalks that established the definitive composition for the weavers as well as the overall colour scheme.[62] The coloured-chalk *modello* was then blown up photographically to produce

the full-size cartoon, which Burne-Jones would rework until he was satisfied with it.[63] Because the designs were generalized and lacking in minute detail, the weavers were allowed considerable freedom in executing them on the loom, John Henry Dearle being responsible for a great deal of the decorative details, such as the *mille fleurs* foregrounds in which the figures stand. The Stanmore Hall tapestries were completed by 1895, and other repetitions were subsequently woven. They are now divided between the Duke of Westminster and a private collector, the latter owning *The Arming and Departure of the Knights*.

The misdating of the present sheet by the artist himself has a curious explanation. In preparation for an exhibition of his drawings at the Fine Art Society in April 1896, in which this sheet figured as part of no. 144, Burne-Jones reviewed hundreds of his works, adding titles and dates when necessary. So numbing was the exercise that many errors were committed, as the artist explained: "I am so dazed and tired as to have forgotten how to spell – how do you spell *resurrection*?"[64] In this case, his spelling is correct, but he accidentally inscribed a *6* for a *9* in the date. The drawing, however, dates from the 1890s and not the 1860s, and is part of a large recognizable group with the 1893 date.[65]

No. A: 25 a.-b.

EDWARD BURNE-JONES

a. *Nude Study of Sir Lancelot for "The Failure of Lancelot"* c. 1894
Black and white chalk with stumping on green wove paper, partially squared in white chalk
31.2 x 47.9 cm

b. *Study of Sir Lancelot in Armour for "The Failure of Lancelot"* c. 1894
Graphite with black and blue chalk on cream laid paper
28.1 x 45.2 cm
Provenance: by descent to the artist's daughter, Margaret Mackail; purchased October 1926
Royal Ontario Museum, Toronto (acc. nos. 926.48.4, 926.48.7)

As was so often the case in Burne-Jones's career, his design work on the Holy Grail tapestries nourished his easel painting. Having designed *The Failure of Lancelot* as the fourth tapestry in the series, the artist decided to turn the composition into a painting, which he accounted among his favourite works (1896; Southampton Art Gallery).[66] The subject, showing Lancelot asleep before the chapel of the Holy Grail and forbidden to enter because of his adulterous relationship with Guenevere, obviously had a personal significance for Burne-Jones, since he himself had posed almost forty years before for the figure of Lancelot in Rossetti's version of the same scene on the walls of the Oxford Union. Rossetti's well-known study in Birmingham shows the youthful Burne-Jones asleep with his legs crossed, a motif that the latter borrowed for his reprise of Lancelot. The artist's wife recognized the connection between her husband's later work and Rossetti's earlier one, believing that Burne-Jones's version may have had a commemorative significance for him.[67] The picture may also allude obliquely to the painter's adulterous relationship with Maria Zambaco.

Although the painting is very similar to the tapestry, separate studies incorporating subtle changes were made in preparation for it. For example, in the tapestry the knight's head is shown in strict profile, while in the painting it is shown almost full-face, leaning towards the viewer;

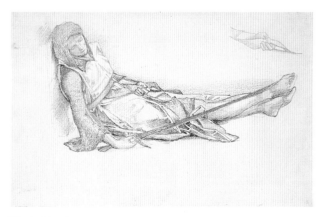

NO. A: 25 a.-b.

the position of Lancelot's sword has also been changed, from lying flat on the ground in the tapestry to lying diagonally across his legs in the painting. The positions of the head and the sword in the present two drawings would seem to indicate that they were made in preparation for the later painting rather than for the tapestry. When, in 1926, the director of the Royal Ontario Museum, C.T. Currelly (see No. A: 20 b), wrote to Burne-Jones's daughter, Mrs. Margaret Mackail, requesting to purchase "twenty to thirty pounds" worth of her father's drawings, she answered enthusiastically, offering ten drawings. Explaining why she chose this particular pair, she wrote: "I send these two to illustrate his invariable habit of drawing a figure undraped first."[68] Interestingly enough, an identical pair of studies, nude and clothed, for the Lancelot in the tapestry are now preserved together in the Bradford Art Gallery.

DESIGNS FOR BOOK DECORATIONS AND ILLUSTRATIONS

DESIGN FOR A MORRIS ILLUMINATED MANUSCRIPT

No. A: 26

EDWARD BURNE-JONES

The Burning of the Ships c. 1874
Two types of graphite on ivory wove paper
25.2 x 17.7 cm (sheet); 14.2 x 14.6 cm (image)
Provenance: Phillips, London, 28 April 1986, lot 117; purchased at the sale
Private collection

Always a passionate admirer of medieval manuscript illumination (see No. A: 34), Morris is reported to have tried it himself as early as his Oxford days. Certainly calligraphy and manuscript decoration were one of his major concerns during the period 1869-75, when he executed over 1,500 pages of finely penned text. A splendid manuscript of Virgil's *Aeneid* on vellum was begun in 1874 and became, as Morris intended, his calligraphic masterpiece. Burne-Jones was naturally recruited to design twelve half-page illustrations, one for each of the twelve books. Towards the end of 1874 he wrote: "Every Sunday morning you may think of Morris and me together – he reads a book to me and I make drawings for a big Virgil he is writing – it is to be wonderful and put an end to printing."[69] Of flame-like energy, this drawing is a preparatory study for the

NO. A: 26

finished version in the Fitzwilliam Museum, Cambridge, dated 1874. Charles Fairfax Murray executed the miniature in Morris's manuscript, where it is featured at the opening for Book V. The scene shows a group of three Trojan women, expanded to six in the finished version, rushing at the instigation of Juno to burn the fleet about to convey Aeneas to Italy. In the preparatory study we see one of the artist's characteristic ships at the far right, a detail which he unfortunately eliminated from the final composition.

Morris also designed a series of twenty-two large initials for the margins, for which Burne-Jones produced historiated decorations. The ambitious undertaking was never finished by Morris, who completed about half the book in his fine Roman hand. The manuscript was acquired by Fairfax Murray, who commissioned Graily Hewitt and Louise Powell to work on it. Even with their contributions, the manuscript remains incomplete, yet is nevertheless one of the masterpieces of its kind. It was later owned by the California collector Estelle Doheny, who gave it to the St. John's Seminary, Camarillo. That collection was sold in 1989, the *Aeneid* passing to Andrew Lloyd Webber, a great Morris and Pre-Raphaelite collector.

DESIGNS FOR THE KELMSCOTT PRESS

No. A: 27 a.-d.

WILLIAM MORRIS

a. *Designs for Decorated Letters "I" and "N"* c. 1891-92
Brush and black ink with opaque white over graphite on cream wove paper, pasted by Sydney Cockerell to folio 2 of William Morris's *A Dream of John Ball* (London: Kelmscott Press, 1892)
5.2 x 10.8 cm (sheet); 4.7 x 4.7 cm (design of "I"); 4.7 x 4.5 cm (design of "N")

b. *Designs for Decorated Letters "T" and "A"* c. 1891-92
Brush and black ink with opaque white over graphite on cream wove paper, pasted by Sydney Cockerell into book below previous drawing
5.5 x 10.9 cm (sheet); 4.7 x 4.8 cm (design of "T" and "A")
Provenance: gift of the artist to Sydney Cockerell; his sale, Sotheby's, London, 10 December 1956, lot 8; Alan G. Thomas, Bournemouth; purchased 1958
Department of Rare Books and Special Collections, McGill University Library, Montreal

c. *Design for a Decorated Letter "N"* c. 1895
Brush and black ink with opaque white over graphite on wove(?) paper, pasted by Sydney Cockerell to inside front cover of William Morris's translation of *Of the Friendship of Amis and Amile* (London: Kelmscott Press, 1894)
5.2 x 3.7 cm (sheet); 2.7 x 2.7 cm (design of "N")
Provenance: gift of the artist to Sydney Cockerell; his sale, Sotheby's, London, 10 December 1956, lot 26; probably Bertram Rota, London; bought by Robertson Davies for the Massey College Library, c. 1960-63
Robertson Davies Library, Massey College, University of Toronto, gift of Robertson Davies

d. *Designs for Decorated Letters "W", "O" and "T"* 1896
Brush and black ink with opaque white over graphite on wove(?) paper, pasted by Sydney Cockerell to inside front cover of J.W. Mackail's version of the *Biblia Innocentium* (London: Kelmscott Press, 1892)
11.7 x 8.9 cm (sheet, bottom right corner cut out); 2.7 x 2.7 cm (design of "O" and "T"); 2.7 x 3.0 cm (design of "W")
Inscribed by the artist(?), upper left, in graphite: *Jan 1st* (stroked out) *Feb 8 1896*
Provenance: gift of the artist to Sydney Cockerell; his sale, Sotheby's, London, 10 December 1956, lot 11; probably Bertram Rota, London; bought by Robertson Davies for the Massey College Library, c. 1960-63
Robertson Davies Library, Massey College, University of Toronto, gift of Robertson Davies

In addition to creating the two fonts of type for the Kelmscott Press, William Morris also designed a profusion of decorations for these books, which he regarded first and foremost as works of art. In seven years he produced no less than 644 typographical decorations: decorated initials, full-page borders, marginal ornaments, frames for illustrations, title-pages, initial words, line-endings and printers' marks. In addition to these designs that were actually used in his books, there were many others that he drew but then for some reason rejected.

Decorated letters, which Morris humorously called "bloomers," i.e., initials that under his hand had sprung into leaf and bloom, were an important element in his page design, marking according to their size such important subdivisions of the text as the beginning of books, chapters or paragraphs. Their sizes were established according to the number of lines of text that they occupied: three-line, six-line and ten-line bloomers were the usual sizes, but four-line and eight-line ones are also found, as well as odd letters, in five-line, thirteen-line and even twenty-line formats. The total number of decorated initials used in the Kelmscott Press is an amazing 384, evidence of Morris's seemingly effortless and endless powers of invention.

Morris would first quickly sketch in his idea for a decorated letter in graphite, and then with two fine brushes,

one in a saucer of black and one in a saucer of white, would proceed to produce the finished design, using the white to make corrections or add delicate details over the black. The drawings were then photographed onto woodblocks by Emery Walker, and a team of wood engravers, led by William Harcourt Hooper, proceeded to engrave them. Several initials or ornaments were often engraved on each block and were not cut off into separate pieces for printing, because Walker had convinced an at first sceptical Morris that electrotypes would produce a printed impression equal in quality to that from an engraved block. Once an initial had been engraved and a proof printed, Morris mounted it in his "Bloomer Book", giving each consecutive version of a letter its own identification number. When he came to design a page, he had only to indicate to the printers which number of which letter he wished to use. As the years progressed, an ever-increasing repertoire of decorations was built up, but Morris quickly discarded some of his earliest designs, often favouring in his current books the new versions that he had just created.

The four ten-line bloomers, "I", "N", "T" and "A", that Cockerell pasted into his copy of *A Dream of John Ball* (No. 27 a.-b.) were never engraved. With their sometimes very elaborate plant interlacings, which thread their way through the pierced forms of the letters themselves, they resemble the sort of letters Morris designed in the early 1890s for *The Golden Legend*. The "T", with its too-slender and sparse decoration, was executed almost entirely in black, with only touches of opaque white along two branches. The "I", on the other hand, is executed almost entirely in opaque white against a black background.

The "N", which Cockerell pasted into his copy of *Of the Friendship of Amis and Amile* (No. A: 27 c.), is a six-line bloomer that was engraved and used in Kelmscott books. As its inscription indicates, it was the twelfth "N" Morris had designed, being N12 in the Bloomer Book; it made its first appearance on page 62 of vol. 1 of *Child Christopher and Goldilind the Fair* (published in 1895). For a considerable length of time, all the bloomers in Kelmscott Press books were designed as white letters and ornament on black backgrounds, to contrast with the black letterpress. Gradually, however, Morris began to introduce a few black-on-white bloomers, such as the three-line ones in *The Order of Chivalry*, *The History of Godefrey of Boloyne*, and *Utopia* (all 1893), or the four-line ones in *Gothic Architecture* (also 1893). It was not until Rossetti's *Sonnets and Lyrical Poems* was published in 1894, however, that black six-line bloomers first appeared. In his later bloomers, such as the present "N", Morris rejected his extravagant earlier interlacing and piercing for bolder, more monumental letters, set in this case against an effective swirl of acanthus leaves.

The three white-letter, six-line bloomers decorated with leaves, flowers and grapes that Cockerell pasted into his copy of the *Biblia Innocentium* (No. A: 27 d.), also late designs apparently made in 1896 according to the inscription, were first used in Morris's *The Earthly Paradise*, the "T" appearing on page 181 of vol. 1 to embellish "The Man Born to be King", the "W" on page 40 of vol. 2 to enhance "The Doom of King Acrisius", and the "O" on page 86 of vol. 3 to decorate "The Story of Cupid and Psyche", all published in 1896. As Cockerell indicated, the "W" was the twentieth one Morris designed, the "O" the eighteenth, and the "T" the thirty-first, out of a total of thirty-four "T"s in the Bloomer Book.

Morris regarded his drawings as a means to an end. Once the ornaments had been engraved, he had no further use for them and was indifferent to their fate, often giving them in presentation copies to his friends. Most of the original Kelmscott Press designs in this section come from Sydney Cockerell, the second secretary of the Kelmscott Press, who either picked up discarded scraps, like the present initials, and rather confusingly pasted them into books with which they have no connection, or was given other more important designs by Morris, like that for the title-page for *Child Christopher* (No. A: 30). That a wealth of preparatory material survives from the Kelmscott Press is due entirely to the energy and foresight of this man, who recognized its importance for posterity.

No. A: 28

WILLIAM MORRIS

Design for a Full-Page Border for the Kelmscott "Chaucer" c. 1893
Brush and black ink with opaque white over graphite on cream wove paper
45.9 x 34.0 cm (sheet); 39.1 x 26.8 cm (image)
Provenance: (?) Sydney Cockerell; (?) Alice Millard, Pasadena; Estelle Doheny, Los Angeles, by June 1937;[70] gift of the latter to the Edward Laurence Doheny Memorial Library, St. John's Seminary, Camarillo, California; their sale, Christie's, New York, 19 May 1989, lot 2336; purchased at the sale
National Gallery of Canada, Ottawa (acc. no. 30238)

For the very first book of the Kelmscott Press, *The Story*

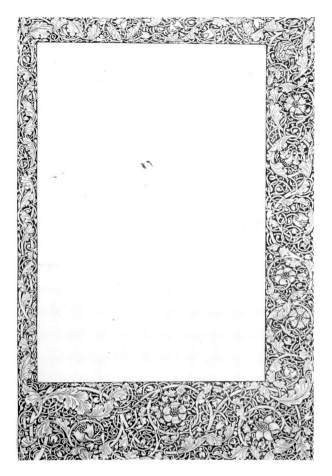

NO. A: 28

of the Glittering Plain (No. L: 15), Morris designed a full-page border that frames the first page of text, balanced rather strangely by the blank margin surrounding the "Table of the Chapters" on the facing page. The concept of the double-page opening as a single design unit having been quickly established, Morris then developed his full-page borders in pairs, a *recto* balancing a *verso*. In all, Morris designed some fifty-seven borders for his private press. By far the largest and best were the seven pairs of full-page borders for the *Chaucer*, on which Morris worked over a period of several years (see No. L: 30).

We get a glimpse of his progress from the diaries of Sydney Cockerell. On 1 February 1893 Morris began his first Chaucer border around a page proof of the double-column text, but he was dissatisfied with it and abandoned it in an uncompleted state (Pierpont Morgan Library, New York). Undeterred, three days later he began the vine border for the first page of text, working at it on the 6th and completing it on the 11th, one week after he started it (also Pierpont Morgan Library, New York). On 20 February he was at work on the second border, apparently the one with the large swirling acanthus leaves that appeared on page 9. The present design is for the third border, which was probably drawn shortly after the second. It was first used on page 15 to surround the second illustration to the "Knight's Tale", full-page borders appearing to mark the beginning of important subdivisions of the text and also to decorate every page with a Burne-Jones illustration. On 3 April 1894 Morris finished the first *verso* border: "He has taken a fortnight over this & a border of the same character, of course doing much other work besides."[71] A year later, on 4 April 1895, work on the borders was finally coming to an end, Morris having begun the *verso* design of the *Chaucer* border no. 6.

Although he usually designed his decorations around page proofs, sometimes with impressions of the wood-engraved illustrations pasted in place, by the time that he came to design the Ottawa border, he was confident enough to compose it straight onto a blank sheet of paper. Over the slightest indications in pencil, he evolved a design of great complexity by alternately drawing with his two fine brushes and twin saucers of black ink and Chinese white, using the margins to make trial strokes with the black brush. Perfectly balanced and adjusted to the different sizes of each side – the margins in Kelmscott Press books increased successively by twenty percent from the inner margin that was always the narrowest, to the top, the outer and finally bottom that was the widest – the design is a completely asymmetrical *tour de force*. Beginning in the lower left corner, one group of stems twists its way up the left border and across the top, while the other spirals along the lower border and up the right side, pulsating with the *élan vital* of Nature itself. A combination of close natural observation with an almost Celtic intricacy and energy, the beautifully controlled tangle of stylized stems, leaves and flowers appears effortless and inevitable. Although inspired by prototypes in early books and manuscripts, the resulting border is no dry archaeological reconstruction, but the quintessence of Morris's originality and genius for design.

When the drawing was completed, it was photographed by Emery Walker and printed on a wood-block. While Morris always worked to full scale, it is interesting to note that the size of this border was slightly reduced from the drawing (39.1 x 26.8 cm) to the final engraved version (37.7 x 26.2 cm), perhaps indicating that a slightly larger page-size was at first considered. The two points marked "join" on the drawing indicate the seam in the woodblock, several pieces of wood having to be joined to make

a block big enough for the border.[72] The present border was used thirteen times throughout the volume, appearing with its matching *verso* for the first time on pages 22-23.

Although fourteen full-page border-designs were made for the *Chaucer*, only a few of the original drawings are known today. Besides the first rejected design and the drawing for the first page in New York, one border drawing is in the V & A, two are in the William Andrews Clark Memorial Library, Los Angeles, and one is in the Stanford University Library.[73] Other designs are known from the Cockerell sale, two accompanying his vellum *Chaucer*,[74] and from a Charles Fairfax Murray/Sir Philip Burne-Jones sale that also included as "the Property of a Gentleman" a folio border for the *Chaucer*.[75] But it is clear that Cockerell originally owned more, for he sold one of the attractive designs for a rose border to Maggs on 31 October 1944. Quite likely the present drawing also went from Cockerell – it is unclear, however, whether his inscription on the sheet indicates that he owned it or that he merely inscribed it for documentary purposes – to the California dealer Alice Millard, from whom Estelle Doheny acquired considerable material. From her Frank Lloyd Wright house in Pasadena called "La Miniatura," Alice Millard "continued to exercise what amounted to a near American monopoly on special works and documents of the Kelmscott and Doves Presses through her friendship with Sydney Cockerell, May Morris, and T.J. Cobden-Sanderson and his family."[77]

No. A: 29

WILLIAM MORRIS

Design for a Half-Border for "The Well at the World's End" c. 1892

Brush and black ink with opaque white over graphite on ivory laid Kelmscott "Flower" paper (page proof of *The Well at the World's End*); inserted with three other original border-designs into a presentation copy to W.H. Hooper of Morris's *The Well at the World's End* (London: Kelmscott Press, 1896)

28.7 x 20.5 cm

Provenance: gift of the artist to W.H. Hooper; The Petersfield Bookshop, Petersfield, Hampshire (List 32/84, no. 52); purchased 1984

Private collection, Ottawa

The first Kelmscott Press book to contain a marginal ornament other than a full-page border was the fifth publication, *The Defence of Guenevere*, which has a half-border. Two more were included in the preface to *The Golden Legend* of the same year, 1892. Eventually the decorations, ranging from simple flowers to elaborate three-quarter borders, became a regular feature of the Kelmscott Press, 108 different ones having been designed by Morris and engraved on wood. For these partial borders, which Morris called "weepers," it seems clear that he took his inspiration from those in Johann Zainer's *Historia Griseldis* or *De Claris Mulieribus* (both Ulm, 1473), where very similar marginal decorations are found, the latter book being the first important purchase Morris made from F.S. Ellis. The present border of grapes and vine, one of Morris's perennially favourite motifs, was drawn for his *The Well at the World's End*, begun in 1892 but only published immediately before the *Chaucer* in 1896 and one of the handsomest of Kelmscott books, with a profusion of borders, marginal ornaments and four illustrations by Burne-Jones. It was the first book of the press to be printed in the double-column format, for which Morris designed special ornaments that snake down between the columns.

A man who knew the Kelmscott Press and some of the

NO. A: 29

workers there thought it was appropriate that grapes and vine figure prominently in its decorations, because he recognized that "our old hand printing presses are adaptations of the old wine presses."[78] Although Morris was something of an oenophile, it is doubtful that his grape borders had any such secret meaning for him, the motif being a traditional one that appears in almost all of his design work from wallpapers to stained glass. When their purpose had been served, Morris was generous in giving away his designs, often in presentation copies of the finished volumes. This and three other intercolumnar border-designs were inserted in a presentation copy dated 21 July 1896 to W.H. Hooper, who had very likely engraved them on wood (see No. L: 29). Another border-design for the same book was included in a presentation copy to Swinburne, now in the Pierpont Morgan Library, New York.

In all, twenty-six different marginal ornaments were designed for this book, some used only once or twice, but others repeated up to eleven and thirteen times. The present border first appeared on page 90 (not 80, as was originally planned according to the inscription) to mark the opening of Book 1, Chapter 19, and was repeated three more times throughout the book, as well as in such subsequent books as the *Laudes Beatae Mariae Virginis* and *The Water of the Wondrous Isles*. As was Morris's usual practice, the design was made on a page proof of the book to be decorated, which in this case is not only different typographically from the final published page (i.e., different lineation and different bloomers), but it also differs textually.

No. A: 30

WILLIAM MORRIS

Design for the Title-Page of "Child Christopher and Goldilind the Fair" c. 1894
Brush and black ink with opaque white over traces of graphite on wove(?) paper, pasted by Sydney Cockerell to inside front cover of *Child Christopher and Goldilind the Fair*, vol. 1 (London: Kelmscott Press, 1895)
10.8 x 7.3 cm (sheet); 8.2 x 6.0 cm (design area)
Provenance: gift of the artist to Sydney Cockerell; his sale, Sotheby's, London, 10 December 1956, lot 38; probably Bertram Rota, London; bought by Robertson Davies for the Massey College Library, c. 1960-63
Robertson Davies Library, Massey College, University of Toronto, gift of Robertson Davies

NO. A: 30

same volume. When the wood-engraved title-page was printed within its border, a perfect balance between the two had been miraculously achieved through the unerring eye and hand of the master.

DESIGNS FOR BOOKS INFLUENCED
BY THE KELMSCOTT PRESS

No. A: 31

A U B R E Y   B E A R D S L E Y

Chapter Heading for "Le Morte Darthur" c. 1894
Pen, brush and black ink over graphite on wove paper
13.8 x 8.3 cm
Provenance: Pickford Waller, the designer and friend of
    Whistler; by descent to his daughter, Sybil Waller;
    her sale, Christie's, London, 12 November 1965, lot
    45; bought J.S. Maas & Co., London; purchased 1966
National Gallery of Canada, Ottawa (acc. no. 15220)

The crowning glory of a Kelmscott Press book is often the decorated title-page, with its special lettering and surrounding ornamentation, that Morris designed for twenty-eight volumes. The first wood-engraved title-page appeared in 1892 in *The Golden Legend*. In the earliest examples, Morris favoured the positive-negative effect of a black-on-white title-page contrasted against the white-on-black decoration of the surrounding borders, but he gradually came to prefer, in certain instances, white letters and vine decoration against a black background, as in the present example or in the glorious title-page for the Kelmscott *Chaucer* (see L: 30). In the present design, the title in Gothic letters, complementing the Chaucer type used throughout the book, has been skilfully integrated into an asymmetrical but balanced arrangement of vines, leaves and flowers that curl around, over, under and even through the letters. The result is a rich pattern of black and white, like the arabesques of the Persian carpets Morris loved so much. Often Morris designed his title-pages within a proof impression of the border with which he intended to surround it, but in this instance he simply drew the design on a blank sheet of paper. The drawing for the surrounding border, dated "Nov. 1894," was also done on a separate sheet, which Cockerell glued onto folio 1 *verso* of the

With the appearance of the revolutionary Kelmscott Press in the early 1890s, many publishers sought to incorporate features of Morris's work into their own productions. Two monumental projects that sought to translate some of the Kelmscott Press's ideals into machine-printed volumes for the general market were J.M. Dent's *Morte Darthur*, with Aubrey Beardsley's provocative illustrations, and George Allen's edition of Spenser's *Faerie Queene*, illustrated by Walter Crane (No. A: 32). Both projects sought a Kelmscott Press "look," but used photomechanical means, instead of expensive and time-consuming wood-engravings, to reproduce the illustrations.

As a Brighton schoolboy, Beardsley regularly knelt before the Morris & Co. east window in the Church of the Annunciation, designed by Burne-Jones in 1866. It is therefore not surprising that the latter artist became the dominant influence on his early work. Beardsley even ventured to pay him a visit on a Sunday afternoon and received warm encouragement and advice from the man he then considered "the greatest living artist in Europe."[79] When Beardsley was working as a clerk in a London insurance office, he often spent his lunch hours in the bookshop of the photographer Frederick Evans, who took an interest in his work (see Nos. M: 23-26). Through Evans, Beardsley received the commission from J.M. Dent to illustrate Malory's *Morte Darthur* at the end of the summer of 1892. On receiving the £250 fee, Beardsley left his job to become a professional artist and create his first masterpiece.

While the Kelmscott Press and Burne-Jones were Beardsley's prime models, he also added other ingredients to produce a thoroughly idiosyncratic result: Whistler and Japanese art, the masters of the Italian Quattrocento, continental Art Nouveau *via* Toulouse-Lautrec, and even Blake, as well as a taste for the erotic, the decadent and the evil that was all his own. Aymer Vallance had introduced Beardsley to Morris with the hope that the latter would use a Beardsley drawing for the frontispiece to the Kelmscott Press edition of *Sidonia the Sorceress*, but the master was not impressed with the young man's specimen drawing and ventured to criticise it, thus earning Beardsley's eternal contempt. That Beardsley himself had no qualms about his approach to the task is attested to in a letter of c. 15 February 1893 to G.F. Scotson-Clark, in which he boasted:

> The work I have already done for Dent has simply made my name. Subscribers crowd from all parts. William Morris has sworn a terrible oath against me for daring to bring out a book in his manner. The truth is that, while *his* work is a mere imitation of the old stuff, mine is fresh and original. Anyhow all the good critics are on my side, but I expect there will be more rows when the book appears (June).[80]

This prediction was soon borne out. When Vallance brought some of the first *Morte Darthur* drawings to Kelmscott House, Morris was in a rage: it was "an act of usurpation", he declared. "A man ought to do his own work."[81]

The problem was no doubt exacerbated by the fact that Beardsley had dared to illustrate Malory, a text that Morris and Burne-Jones had long venerated as almost sacred writ. They had intended to produce an edition themselves at the Kelmscott Press, but the project never got off the ground. The day Beardsley's obituary appeared in the *Times*, Burne-Jones told his studio assistant Rooke about the young artist's last, and unwelcome, visit to The Grange:

> I asked him how he was getting on with the book he was decorating – King Arthur that was – and he said he'd be precious glad when it was done, he hated it so.... He hated the story and he hated all medieval things – and I said, how could it be successful work then. I never saw such a pitiful exhibition of vanity in my life.[82]

In his own copy of Beardsley's *Morte Darthur*, George Bernard Shaw wrote an account of how Morris reacted to the publication:

> ...Morris, never jealous on his own account, was blindly and fiercely so on that of Burne-Jones, whom Beardsley had dared to imitate (not without success), and this, too, in a book full of bad typesetting. He had already spotted the boy's talent and cast him out forever. He would not listen to my plea....[83]

In response to Shaw's favourable comments about Beardsley, Morris stated his opinion in a letter dated 11 October 1894: "Beardsley – hm – I can only say that the illustrations to the M.D.A. which *I* saw were quite below contempt: absolutely *nothing* in them, except an obvious desire to be done with the job – But he *may* have got better since – though I don't think it."[84]

In all, Beardsley produced some 350 designs for the Malory book, which was issued in parts from June 1893 to mid-1894. At first the illustrations and borders had a medieval flavour appropriate to the text, but as the work dragged on over eighteen months and the delights of *The Yellow Book* and *Salomé* beckoned, Beardsley gave up any attempt to illustrate the story with appropriate images.

NO. A: 31

Pictures of contemporary life appeared, such as the present chapter-heading for Book XVIII, Chapter XXI, which had nothing whatever to do with the nominal story: "Of Great Jousts Done All Christmas, and of a Great Jousts and Tourney Ordained by King Arthur; and of Sir Lancelot." Beardsley has given us one of his New Women, a Modern Eve leaning casually against the Tree of Knowledge and about to sin again with the forbidden fruits all about her. The double meaning and the sly scriptural allusion are both typical.

Although Beardsley railed that Morris was old-fashioned to use wood-engraving and that he himself was modern and looking to the future in using photomechanical processes such as the line-block to reproduce his drawings, the older artist did in fact use the same process for A.J. Gaskin's illustrations in his Kelmscott Press *Shepheardes Calender* (No. L: 33). But while Gaskin's drawings were deliberately made to resemble wood-engravings, and several commentators have been fooled, Beardsley used the line blocks in a new way, with areas of solid black balancing asymmetrical areas of white and areas of pattern, derived from wood-engraving, such as the leaves in the present example, mediating between them.

No. A: 32

WALTER CRANE

Illustration to Spenser's "Faerie Queene" c. 1896
Pen and brush and black (India) ink over graphite,
    corrected with opaque white, on heavy wove paper
28.5 x 22.5 cm (sheet); 24.4 x 19.6 cm (image)
Provenance: purchased from the artist through the
    Women's Art Association of Canada, Toronto, 1909
National Gallery of Canada, Ottawa (acc. no. 187.3)

Around the time that Beardsley's *Morte Darthur* was completed, Walter Crane undertook for the publisher George Allen a large number of illustrations and decorations for a multi-volume edition of Spenser's *Faerie Queene*, which occupied him for the years 1894-97. The idea once again was to introduce some of the features of the Kelmscott Press into a commercial publication with photomechanically reproduced illustrations.

Compared to Crane's delightful children's books, the ponderous six volumes of the *Faerie Queene* must be counted something of a bore, but there is still much to admire in this massive undertaking. Crane claimed that it had been a dream of his to illustrate the book, "as the antique form,

the beauty and chivalric romance, with the vivid allegory, and fine sense of decorative detail of Spenser's poetry were extremely alluring."[85] From the twelve original illustrations that the National Gallery of Canada acquired from the artist in 1909, this drawing for the Fifth Book, Canto 2, has been selected because it shows how very different Crane's ideas about book illustration were from those of Burne-Jones and Morris at the Kelmscott Press. Morris's borders were meant to be decoration pure and simple, and only rarely have a symbolic content or meaning that refers to the picture or text which they frame (rose borders for the *Romaunt de la Rose* or heraldic shields for Froissart). Some of Crane's borders for the *Faerie Queene* are in the tradition of Morris's decorations – flowers and leaves curling in graceful patterns around the central image – but they lack Morris's Celtic energy in their intricate elaboration and growth. Often, however, Crane introduced elements of the story very successfully into the surrounding border decoration, as for example in the present full-page illustration. In his publication *Of the Decorative Illustration of Books Old and New*, Crane explained the source for this idea: "...the full-page designs are all treated as panels of figure design, and are enclosed in fanciful borders, in which subsidiary incidents of [*sic*, or?] characters in the

NO. A: 32

poem are introduced or suggested, somewhat on the plan of medieval tapestries."[86]

In the main picture Crane has drawn the fierce combat of the knight Artegall on the right with the pagan saracen on the left. The clash of swords amid the swirling river has been captured with great dramatic energy that contrasts with the almost soporific mood of dream-like stasis that pervades most of Burne-Jones's illustrations. Crane's fight takes place near a stone bridge which arches above the two combatants to close the composition at the top. In an open linear style that contrasts with the blacker central image, Crane has wittily extended the "real" bridge in the illustration into a "story-book" bridge in the upper margin, where two jousting knights are seen about to clash. The sides of the border also contain narrative elements, that on the right being turned into a castle wall with a woman at a window and a man at a door beneath her. The pen-and-ink style of the drawing is meant to evoke the style of wood-engraving, but the whole page was printed with a photomechanical line block.

No. A: 33

WALTER CRANE

Design for the Title-Page of "William Morris to Whistler" c. 1911
Pen and brush and black (India) ink over graphite, corrected with opaque white, on cream art-board
24.0 x 30.5 cm
Provenance: Edward D. Nudelman, Seattle, Washington (Catalogue 14, no. 160); purchased 1990
Private collection

Walter Crane's great concern to educate, convert and improve took active form in his teaching career, which began when he became part-time Director of Design at the Manchester School of Art (1893-96) and culminated with his appointment as Principal of the Royal College of Art in 1898. Closely related to his teaching were his activities as lecturer and author, which allowed him to reach a wider audience beyond the walls of the classroom or studio. Among his notable publications are *The Claims of Decorative Art* (1892), *The Bases of Design* (1898), *Line and Form* (1900), *Ideals in Art* (1905) and *An Artist's Reminiscences* (1907). Since Morris was one of his greatest heroes, many of his books and articles discuss the master's ideas and life, among them *William Morris to Whistler*, for which the present drawing was a preparatory study for the typography and decoration of the title-page.

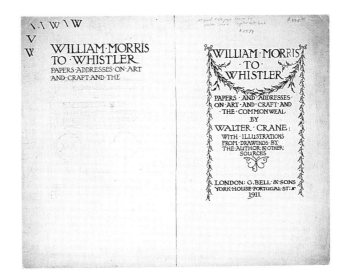

NO. A: 33

The opening essay on Morris was based on a lecture Crane had given at the Art Workers' Guild, together with two articles he had published in *The Progressive Review* and *The Century Magazine*. Combining a character sketch with a summary of Morris's achievements, Crane was at pains to stress Morris's Socialist commitment, which he felt had been neglected in favour of his more palatable activities in poetry and design. The book contains an assortment of essays "on Art and Craft and the Commonweal", as the subtitle describes it, and ends with "The Apotheosis of 'The Butterfly'", hence its title, *William Morris to Whistler*. It is doubtful, however, that Morris would have been pleased to be linked in this way with the creator of visual Nocturnes and Symphonies, for which he had little sympathy. In the published volume, issued in 1911 by G. Bell & Sons, a more elaborate border of intertwining roses was used on the title-page, but the layout for the typography of the title is retained from the arrangement on the left. The Whistlerian butterfly with the poisonous dart in its tail, not found on the published title-page, was used as part of the blocked cover decoration.

PAGE FROM MORRIS'S COLLECTION OF ILLUMINATED MANUSCRIPTS

No. A: 34

UNKNOWN ARTIST
(ITALIAN OR FRENCH, 15TH CENTURY)

Nine Famous Men: Elisha, Lycurgus, Azariah, Sardanapalus, Amos, Hosea, Joel, Obadiah, and Jonah c. 1450 (?)

NO. A: 34

Pen and brown ink and watercolour, heightened with
    opaque white (oxidized), on vellum
31.6 x 20.1 cm
Provenance: old French collection (?); Bernard Quaritch,
    London; William Morris, London 1894; traded to
    Charles Fairfax Murray; his sale, Sotheby's, London,
    18 July 1919, lot 50 (whole book); Sir Sydney
    Cockerell; his sale, Sotheby's, London, 2 July 1958,
    lot 18; Dr. and Mrs. Francis Springell; their sale,
    Sotheby's, London, lot 5; purchased at the sale
    through A.E. Popham
National Gallery of Canada, Ottawa (acc. no. 9896)

From his undergraduate days in Oxford, William Morris
was interested in medieval illuminated manuscripts, enthusiastically studying the examples in the Bodleian Library
and later those in the British Museum. Since he practised
illuminating at an early date, and most especially from
1869 to 1875, it is not surprising that he would wish to own

some historic examples for himself, but it was not until
the 1890s that he had both the inclination and the money to
collect such manuscripts on a grand scale. In notes Morris
made about his library for a projected Kelmscott Press catalogue, he reveals his overwhelming interest in the design
elements of his collection. He was particularly interested
in the way the earlier illuminated manuscripts contributed
to the evolution of the first printed books.

Morris already had a very impressive collection of illuminated manuscripts when he purchased the fragment of
a picture chronicle from which the present vellum leaf
comes. Since it was a Thursday, he brought his latest treasure, as was his custom, to the committee meeting of the
Society for the Protection of Ancient Buildings, which was
held regularly on that afternoon in Buckingham Street.
After the meeting, he adjourned with his inner circle of
friends to Gatti's, across the Strand, for tea or supper.
Here, the latest acquisitions or the latest designs for the
Kelmscott Press were passed around the table. Suffering a
severe case of hero-worship, young Sydney Cockerell was
there as Morris's Boswell to record in his diary the doings
of the Great Man. We find the following entry for Thursday, 20 December 1894: "W.M. bought a very beautiful
fragment of a book containing Italian drawings to illustrate a Chronicle (from B.Q. [Bernard Quaritch] £5 !)
Antiscrape Com.... Tea afterwards with W.M., Webb &
Lethaby."[87] In a typed extract, Cockerell wrote under the
same date: "W.M. at SPAB & Gatti's. He had with him a
very beautiful fragment of a book containing Italian drawings to illustrate a chronicle. (afterwards mine)."[88]

Quaritch was a major source of Morris's manuscripts,
and this one Cockerell evidently considered a bargain at
£5. Being works of the Italian Renaissance, the eight leaves
were somewhat unusual in Morris's collection, which eventually totalled 112 manuscripts, but he did have other
Italian humanist manuscripts of the same period. His main
interest definitely lay with medieval illuminations, however, and it is understandable that he was soon to trade
this Renaissance fragment for four leaves from an English
thirteenth-century Psalter that belonged to his friend, fellow designer and collector, Charles Fairfax Murray. When
exactly this trade occurred – 1894 or 1896 – is uncertain.[89]
If it was traded in 1894, Morris owned it for all of eleven
days or less! At any rate, by 8 June 1896 the trade had been
completed, for on that date an exhibition of English medieval paintings and illuminated manuscripts opened at the
Society of Antiquaries at Burlington House, to which
Morris had lent five manuscripts and the Fairfax Murray

leaves from his own library. When Morris and Burne-Jones arrived to view the exhibition, they were astonished to discover that Morris's leaves were originally part of a magnificent psalter then owned by Lord Aldenham, which was exhibited beside his fragment. Instead of ceding his leaves to Lord Aldenham, Morris offered him the very large sum of £1,000 for the whole manuscript and was accepted. Morris thus acquired his last and most important illuminated manuscript, the celebrated "Windmill Psalter," which he so named from a prominent windmill on the most lavishly decorated page. This treasure is now in the Pierpont Morgan Library in New York, which holds the largest surviving remains of Morris's library, and was displayed in Ottawa in the National Gallery of Canada's *Art and the Courts* exhibition in 1972.

The present drawing therefore played a small part in the acquisition of Morris's greatest manuscript. But it is easy to see why Morris was attracted to the Quattrocento drawings in the first place: they were of very high quality, they were cheap and, from the designer's point of view, they seemed to address a problem he was familiar with from his stained-glass work. He may even have connected them with the great east window in Holy Trinity, Sloane Street, which contains no less than forty-eight standing figures in four rows and which was in production at the very time he bought this manuscript. The challenges of varying the figures in pose and colour from row to row in the largest window ever executed by Morris & Co. had also been successfully met by the fifteenth-century artist who composed row after row of figures in the picture chronicle.

In the Fairfax Murray sale, Morris's eight leaves passed to Sydney Cockerell, who had admired them at Gatti's on that first exciting afternoon, and the book became known as the "Cockerell Chronicle." It depicts rows of "Uomini famosi" or "Famous Men" from Adam to Tamerlane, derived from frescos by Masolino in the Orsini Palace in Rome that were completed before 1432 and probably destroyed in the 1480s. The figures in the Morris-Cockerell chronicle were not copied directly from the frescos, however, but from an earlier illuminated manuscript by Leonardo da Besozzo (Crespi collection, Milan). Morris obviously thought that his drawings were Italian, as did Berenson, who ascribed them to the School of Fra Angelico, but current scholarship has suggested a French artist visiting Italy as the copyist of the Crespi chronicle. The names of Jean Fouquet and most recently Barthélemy d'Eyck have been proposed. The other seven leaves of Morris's fragment are now dispersed among the drawing

collections of the world, and a ninth leaf from the same chronicle was discovered in England and is now in Berlin.

DESIGN FOR MONOGRAM

No. A: 35

DANTE GABRIEL ROSSETTI

Designs for Monograms of Jane Morris c. 1865-72
Graphite on laid paper
7.0 x 9.8 cm
Provenance: the artist's brother William Michael Rossetti; by descent through his family; gift to the present owner
Private collection, Vancouver

Inspired by the practice of such early artists as Albrecht Dürer (1471-1528), who was vastly admired, most of the Pre-Raphaelites designed their own personal monograms. Rossetti's various combinations of DGR within a circle are well known from his paintings and drawings, such as *Study for the Figure of Love* and *The Roseleaf* (Nos. A: 37, 43). His monogram was also used from 1862 as part of the engraved letterhead on his stationery for 16 Cheyne Walk, Chelsea. During the period of the Morrises' residence at 26 Queen Square, 1865-72, Rossetti designed these versions of Jane's monogram for her stationery, which was apparently never engraved. While the circular motif was well suited to his own initials, it must be admitted that the JM sits uneasily inside the ring of feeble flowers and foliage. If it was not for William Michael Rossetti's "G" on its *verso* indicating Gabriel's authorship, one might be tempted to think that

NO. A: 35

it had been drawn by Jane herself, for she is known to have attempted such designs. In a Christmas keepsake book that she compiled and bound, she drew her monogram within a framework of a leaf or flower, possibly a pansy, which she and Rossetti had chosen as her emblem in the 1870s.[90] Other similar books also contain her initials as decoration. One can understand why Rossetti might design Jane's monogram, but it comes as something of a surprise that he provided the service for others, such as those, again circular, for John Ferguson MacLennan. Rossetti's comments in a letter to him give some indication of the artist's ideas on designing monograms: "I have found your monogram specially difficult to manage considering as I do that clearness is essential.... Combining the lines [evidently of the initials in ligature] I found not practicable in this case. It has a hopeful bank-note look which is cheery."[91]

NO. A: 36

COSTUME DESIGN

No. A: 36

WALTER CRANE

Design for the Armour of Trueheart 1899
Watercolour and gouache on dark brown wove paper
39.0 x 44.8 cm
Provenance: purchased from the artist through the
   Women's Art Association of Canada, Toronto, 1909
National Gallery of Canada, Ottawa (acc. no. 185)

As a direct result of Morris's revival of many handicrafts that had flourished in the Middle Ages, but had reached near extinction in the industrialized Britain of the nineteenth century, the Arts and Crafts movement was born. Groups such as A.H. Mackmurdo's Century Guild and the Art Workers' Guild sprang up in the early 1880s to further the cause of hand-made decorative arts, a cause that was often closely allied to the same political and social goals that Morris was championing. Crane became one of the leading members of the Art Workers' Guild, founded in 1884 and deliberately patterned on the medieval guilds that had formerly supported the crafts and provided a corporate solidarity for their advancement. William Morris became a member of the Art Workers' Guild and was very active, with Crane, in its splinter group, the Arts and Crafts Exhibition Society, founded two years later. To this day, the laurel-crowned bust of Morris has pride of place in the niche above the Master's chair in the Hall of the Art

Workers' Guild on Queen Square, the very location having strong associations with Morris & Co.

Since the medieval guilds regularly presented civic pageants and masques, Crane got the idea that the AWG should produce a modern equivalent. Called *Beauty's Awakening; A Masque of Winter and of Spring*, the whole affair, absurd and noble at the same time, was a cooperative effort of the entire membership, a group of designers including Crane, Henry Holiday, William Strang and Selwyn Image undertaking the lavish sets, costumes and props that were the most notable aspects of the pageant. The present drawing is a costume design, obviously in the Burne-Jones style of his Perseus armour, for the leading character, Trueheart. The story was based on the Sleeping Beauty legend, given an allegorical and Socialist twist that would not have been appreciated by the Lord Mayor and his Council when they witnessed the production on 28 June 1899 in London's Guildhall.

Beauty and her attendants were discovered asleep, bewitched by the evil Malebodea. Trueheart defeats her dragon, but then must contend with her seven demons who hold London in thrall: Philistinus, Bogus, Scampinus, Cupiditas, Ignoramus, Bumble-beadalus, Slumdum and Jerrybuiltus. How the spirit of William Morris must have cheered at the rout of all his enemies! With the awakening of Beauty, London takes her rightful place among the great art-producing cities of the world, each represented by historical personages. The role of Trueheart was taken by the stained-glass designer and book illustrator Paul Woodroffe, and the rest of the amateur cast was a virtual Who's Who of the Arts and Crafts movement, including Morris's daughter May as St. Helena, representing Byzantium, and Crane himself as Albrecht Dürer of Nuremberg. A second sheet of costume designs for Freedom and Commerce is also in the collection of the National Gallery of Canada.[92] The masque was published in the 1899 summer issue of *The Studio*, which contains a reproduction of a Crane pen-and-ink drawing of Trueheart in his armour similar to the present gouache, as well as a design for his shield.

STUDIES FOR PAINTINGS

No. A: 37

DANTE GABRIEL ROSSETTI

Study of the Figure of Love for "Dante's Dream at the Time of the Death of Beatrice" 1874

Black, red, brown and grey chalk on pale grey-green wove paper

59.0 x 42.3 cm

Inscribed by the artist, lower right, in black and red chalk: *DGR* (in monogram, in circle) / *1874*

Provenance: Charles Augustus Howell; possibly C.H. Dancocks, 22 St. Mary Abbot's Terrace, Kensington; possibly his sale, 28 November 1908, lot 18 (Study of a Figure for "Dante at the Bier of Beatrice", red chalk, dated 1874, 22½ x 16½ in.);[93] bought Sampson; Espace Co. Ltd., Japan; Julian Hartnoll, London; Fine Art Society, London; Sotheby's Belgravia, London, 17 June 1980, lot 21, bought in; MacMillan and Perrin Gallery, Toronto; their sale, Christie's, London, 1 March 1983, lot 96, bought in; purchased 1983

Private collection

Themes from Dante formed an important part of Rossetti's art, especially subjects from the *Vita Nuova* concerning Dante himself and his beloved Beatrice, which had a deeply personal meaning for the artist named after him. This is especially true of *The Salutation of Beatrice*, which Rossetti painted on the Red House settle (No. B: 4). Another major work on a similar subject was *Dante's Dream at the Time of the Death of Beatrice*, which Rossetti first created as a watercolour of 1856. A large oil version, the largest of Rossetti's works, was begun in 1869 and finished in 1871 (Walker Art Gallery, Liverpool). While he was working on this huge canvas in 1870, Rossetti entered into an agreement with Charles Augustus Howell, his factotum and agent (and also, he was convinced, his forger), to sell him a group

of eight preparatory drawings for the picture for £140. Since these preparatory drawings were unfinished, in some cases only drapery studies without heads or hands, additional work was necessary on them before they could be considered saleable. A further thirty pounds was apparently promised by Howell when the artist delivered the completed sheets. Between 1873 and 1875, a series of letters between artist and agent documents the repercussions of this transaction in excruciating detail, Howell making accusations and Rossetti responding with counter-accusations that went on and on for months and years. Finally, on 31 December 1874, Rossetti announced that he was adding three more drawings to the group: "1 figure at foot of bed (now at Kelmscott), 1 Love, 1 Love and Beatrice. The last two are here [16 Cheyne Walk] and I have now nearly finished working them up at odd times since I saw you."[94] The *Love* referred to is apparently the present drawing, dated 1874. On 28 January 1875 and again on 14 May 1875, Rossetti mentioned "Another Love" full-length, that he was finishing,[95] this second study being the Wyndham

NO. A: 37

drawing with the arrow omitted, dated 1875.[96] An old photograph shows this drawing hanging in Madeline Wyndham's boudoir, a Morris & Co. interior in Philip Webb's masterpiece, Clouds.[97]

Because Rossetti made a somewhat smaller version of the very large picture of *Dante's Dream*, begun in 1878 and finished in 1880, Surtees and others have assumed that the Howell drawings were preparatory for it, since they bear dates between the two pictures, but they are more properly to be understood as preparatory studies for the first large oil that Rossetti finished and dated some years later. They would have been no help to the artist in making his second painting, since they had all been handed over to Howell by 1875 and dispersed. When excerpted from the whole composition, the pose of the present figure of Love appears rather odd; in reality, he is holding hands with Dante with his right hand, hence the extended arm, while bending forward to kiss the corpse of Beatrice. The figure gave Rossetti difficulties and he was sufficiently dissatisfied with it to repaint it in the 1871 version before beginning the smaller replica in 1878. Jane Morris modelled for the dead Beatrice, while the young Johnston Forbes Robertson, later to become one of the leading actors of his day, posed for the figure of Love.

No. A: 38

EDWARD BURNE-JONES

Nude Studies for "The Golden Stairs" 1875
Metalpoint, brush and opaque white with scraping out
    on wove paper with a prepared reddish-brown ground
25.2 x 15.0 cm
Inscribed by the artist, lower right, in graphite: *EBJ /*
    Studies for / GOLDEN STAIRS / 1875
Provenance: by descent to the artist's son, Sir Philip
    Burne-Jones; his sale, Christie's, London, 5 June 1919,
    part of lot 131; William Hesketh Lever, Viscount
    Leverhulme, for the Lady Lever Art Gallery, Port
    Sunlight; their sale, Christie's, London, 6 June 1958,
    part of lot 19; bought Agnew; Sotheby's Belgravia,
    14 June 1977, lot 11; bought Agnew; Morris Gallery,
    Toronto; purchased 1979
R. Fraser Elliott

One of Burne-Jones's most celebrated pictures, *The Golden Stairs* (Tate Gallery) is a subjectless and almost colourless composition of graceful maidens descending a curved staircase with musical instruments. Its genesis, progress and changing title may be followed in the artist's autograph work accounts. It makes its first appearance under the year 1872, where Burne-Jones wrote, "designed and made studies for the procession of girls coming down a flight of steps." Under 1876 he continued: "Began the picture of the King's Wedding, that is a tall picture with girls coming down steps about 10 feet high." Finally it was completed for the 1880 exhibition at the Grosvenor Gallery: "Music on the stairs – called afterwards, The Golden Stairs". When it was exhibited, it aroused considerable controversy because of its lack of a specific subject. With its almost cinematic treatment of movement, it has sometimes been seen as a prefiguration of Marcel Duchamps's *Nude Descending a Staircase*, but it is doubtful that Burne-Jones would have been pleased with the comparison.

The professional model Antonia Caiva is known to have posed for some of the nude studies for the picture and perhaps also for the present sheet. Although the artist's daughter Margaret, Morris's daughter May, and other young women are supposed to have sat for the heads, in the final picture they all emerge as more Burne-Jones types than actual women of flesh and blood. Among the finest drawings the artist ever made, these nude studies for *The Golden Stairs* are very old-masterish in their technique of metalpoint and white gouache on a prepared coloured ground. Italian drawings of the fifteenth century in similar media were among the favourites of the artist, who collected large albums of photographs of such works. The present sheet was part of a group of four that belonged to the artist's family and remained together until 1958. How they were originally framed together can be seen in an installation shot of the 1910 Japan British exhibition in London, where we find the four studies matted horizontally, with the present drawing, the only one to depict two figures instead of one, on the extreme left.[98]

No. A: 39

EDWARD BURNE-JONES

Study for "The Rape of Proserpine" c. 1884
Graphite on cream wove paper
25.4 x 36.2 cm (sheet); 21.5 x 36.2 cm (image)
Provenance: John Ruskin, Brantwood, Coniston; his sale,
    Sotheby's, London, 20 May 1931, part of lot 21;[99]
    bought Danielson; Mr. & Mrs. F.J. Berryman, Great
    Chesterton, Essex
The Montreal Museum of Fine Arts, gift of Mr. & Mrs.
    F.J. Berryman, England, 1938 (acc. no. 1938.44)

NO. A: 38

Ruskin's ideas on art, particularly the importance of the decorative arts and the social conditions under which they could flourish, had a very fundamental influence on William Morris's thought. For Burne-Jones, Ruskin was mentor, patron and sometimes exasperating friend, for whom numerous projects from embroidery designs to book illustrations were undertaken over the years, although many of them, like the present scheme, never saw completion. On Candlemas (2 February) 1883, Ruskin wrote to his "Darling Ned" inquiring about their current project: "Also, if my Proserpine isn't begun, *please* begin it; and if it is stopped, go on again; and if it is going on again, do a nice little bit as the Spring comes."[100] Concerning the status of this commission, Burne-Jones replied: "Proserpine bides, my dear, I haven't begun her yet, I am practising my art; one day I mean to paint a picture."[101] Over a year later, Proserpine's turn had come, and the artist wrote to Ruskin:

> I have designed what should look beautiful and awful if it were well done, Pluto going down with Proserpine into the earth, and a nice garden, a real one, all broken to bits, and fire breaking out amongst the anemones; and Pluto is an awful thing, shadowy and beautiful.[102]

The artist's wife goes on to say that "a very careful pencil drawing of this exists, but the picture was never painted."

At the time of the commission, Ruskin was engaged in his botanical study of wild flowers that he titled *Proserpina* (1875-86). While this book may have had something to do with the proposed picture, it seems more likely that it was intended as a memorial to Rose La Touche, the young Irish girl who had rejected Ruskin's proposal of marriage and died in 1875 at the age of twenty-seven, leaving him shattered. Proserpine was one of his nicknames for her, which he specifically used in a letter to Burne-Jones in the spring of 1866.[103] On another occasion he explained that in spelling *Proserpina* to himself, he always omitted the first *P* and the second *r*, leaving *Rose*pina.[104] The rape of Proserpine by Pluto would therefore have been a very appropriate subject to commemorate Rose's sudden death, but the legend also contained hope, because Proserpine was allowed to return to the earth each year, bringing the spring and the renewed crops. Ruskin alluded to this very familiar idea in mentioning the advent of spring in his 1883 letter to Burne-Jones.[105]

The very careful pencil drawing that Georgie knew was one that remained in the artist's family and appeared in some of the early exhibitions of Burne-Jones's work (now

NO. A: 39

in Birmingham). Though more highly finished, it is very similar to the present drawing, which was apparently all that Ruskin received from the commission. A colour study in a bold experimental style is also known.[106] One of the sources for the composition was a fifteenth-century picture-chronicle, then attributed to Maso Finiguerra, that Ruskin had bought at Burne-Jones's recommendation and that was well known to the artist, who made copies of the *Rape of Proserpine* in the book. Now in the British Museum, a facsimile of the picture-chronicle was published by Sidney Colvin just after Burne-Jones's death and was dedicated to him. One is struck by the proto-Art Nouveau character of Burne-Jones's work, which seems more related to his earlier book illustration than to his easel painting, and which looks forward to the linear extravaganzas of Toorop at the turn of the century. For a famous version of *Proserpine* by Rossetti, see No. A: 44.

PORTRAITS AND CARICATURES

No. A: 40

DANTE GABRIEL ROSSETTI

Self-Portrait with William Michael Rossetti c. 1853
Pen and brown ink with brown wash on cream laid paper
17.1 x 19.7 cm (sight)
Provenance: the artist's brother William Michael Rossetti; his daughter Mrs. Helen Rossetti Angeli; her daughter Mrs. Geoffrey Dennis; gift of the latter to the present owner, 1972
Private collection, Vancouver

Soon after Burne-Jones came down from Oxford in 1856, he caught a glimpse of Rossetti at a meeting of the Working Men's College and met him a few nights later at Vernon Lushington's rooms, where his brother William Michael was also present. Through Burne-Jones, Morris was quickly introduced to the hero who would loom so large, for good and ill, in both their lives. Under the spell of his magnetic personality, something of which is captured in this brooding self-portrait, the two young men both decided to become painters, an ambition that only one of them realized. The celebrated episode of the Oxford Union murals followed the next year with Rossetti clearly in command of the second generation of Pre-Raphaelite artists. Rossetti had, of course, been one of the original Pre-Raphaelite Brotherhood, as had his non-artist brother William Michael, who also became a friend of Morris and Burne-Jones.

Rossetti's caricatures of everything from wombats to

NO. A: 40

"stunners," including wickedly funny ones skewering Morris, were well known among his circle, inspiring Burne-Jones's own exercises in the same genre. In this connection it is instructive to compare the present self-caricature with Burne-Jones's later send-up of Rossetti's pretensions to sartorial splendour (No. A: 42). Although the present sketch is only mildly caricatured, the artist has skilfully captured the contrasting personalities of the two very different brothers, turning the prematurely balding William Michael into "a funeral mute."[107] William Michael has left us some interesting comments on this drawing:

> It represents him [Dante Gabriel] at full-length, carrying a walking-stick, and in his right hand a wide-awake hat. The facial angle is substantially the same as in the photograph [by Mark Anthony of 1853] and in Hunt's drawing [made for Woolner the same year]; the eyes large, the expression rather grim and sarcastic; the attitude slouching, with legs firmly planted apart and shoulders high and narrow – a point which, if true at all, must be here much exaggerated. The sketch is like him in a way, but has a certain Jewish aspect which was alien to him. On the same piece of paper (my property) is a similar but independent sketch of myself.[108]

No. A: 41

EDWARD BURNE-JONES

William Morris at his Desk c. 1865
Graphite on wove paper, pasted to the half-title page of William Morris's *The Earthly Paradise: A Poem*, vol. 1 (London: F.S. Ellis, 1868)

7.5 x 7.4 cm
Provenance: The Times Bookshop, London; purchased
    c. 1960
Private collection, Vancouver

Burne-Jones had an unusual sense of humour that mani-
fested itself in his conversation and letters, but especially
in his caricatures. Although he had produced comic drawings from an early age, the impetus, as with so much of
his art, seems to have come from Rossetti, who was celebrated for his cartoons. Since Burne-Jones was thin and
frail, he had a particular aversion to corpulence, which he
mocked in the form of his famous fat ladies and also in the
shape of the rotund Morris. While his humour was usually good-natured, he did enjoy ribbing the overweight
Morris at any opportunity; behind the good fun was very
likely a real concern for his friend's health and well-being.

Pasted into the first volume of Morris's *The Earthly
Paradise*, this compelling image of the young poet shows
him undoubtedly composing further volumes of that very
long work. Morris had great facility for writing verse and
could produce reams of it seemingly effortlessly. Having
written a mountain of pages, Morris would treat his friends
to a reading, a scene Burne-Jones burlesqued in another
caricature. When Morris and Burne-Jones were undergraduates at Oxford, the current bestseller was Harriet
Beecher Stowe's *Uncle Tom's Cabin*, which contained a
character with wild hair named Topsy. Since Morris's hair

was "unnaturally and unnecessarily curly" in the words
of his friend Ned, Morris was immediately nicknamed
Topsy, often shortened to Top, which stuck for the rest
of his life. The curly mop was an essential component of
the caricatures.

It is sometimes said that Burne-Jones added a decorative
laurel branch to those drawings which he considered most
successful, but in this case the laurel boughs are doubly
appropriate as a tribute to the poet himself. Burne-Jones
has supplied a caption to this vignette by inscribing "page
158, line 20" below the drawing, which refers to the following lines from "The Man Born to be King": "For he was
round-paunched, short of limb, / Red-faced...." Morris's
own poetry is therefore delightfully turned against him.

No. A: 42

EDWARD BURNE-JONES

*Caricatures of William Morris, Dante Gabriel Rossetti and
    the Artist Himself* c. 1866
Graphite on pp. 50-51 of W.M. Rossetti's *Swinburne's
    Poems and Ballads: A Criticism* (London: John
    Camden Hotten, 1866)
17.1 x 10.7 cm (each page)
Provenance: Norman Colbeck, Bournemouth; presented
    by him to the University of British Columbia in 1966
Special Collections, University of British Columbia
    Library, Vancouver

William Michael Rossetti published as his first book a
defense of Swinburne's poems, this copy of which he presented "with the author's compliments" to an unknown
recipient, possibly either Burne-Jones or Morris. On pages
50-51, William Michael discusses other writers and artists
working in the same vein as Swinburne, mentioning Morris, Dante Gabriel Rossetti and Burne-Jones. The latter
could not refrain from embellishing the margins with some
charming caricatures to complement the text.

Opposite the discussion of Morris, described as "by far
the most genially and subtly chivalrous and medieval of
all modern English poets", we see the curly-haired man
himself, his workman's smock stretched tightly across his
ample belly, his arms behind his back and his legs "strad-
dling out like the portraits of Henry VIII," as Mackail
described the little figures of Morris that were painted in
odd corners of the Oxford Union ceiling. The helmet
refers specifically to the one Morris had made by the local
blacksmith at the time of the Oxford murals in 1857 and in

NO. A: 41

which he became stuck on one memorable occasion, when he roared to the great delight of all his laughing friends. (The original basinet is now in the collection of the William Morris Gallery, Walthamstow.) The joke was pushed even further against Morris. On the *verso* of the half-title, Burne-Jones has written an erratum for page 50, referring to this sentence: "A page of Morris is as rich as a painted window…and as dreamily sonorous as the choral chant from the further end of the cathedral". Instead of "end of the cathedral", Burne-Jones wickedly says, read "knave."

Opposite the mention of D.G. Rossetti, Burne-Jones has drawn a mock full-length portrait of his friend as a respectable Victorian gentleman, posing with cane and top hat against a background of drapery swags and classical column, the conventions of the grand portrait tradition of Sir Joshua (alias Sir Sloshua) Reynolds, which Rossetti and his circle abominated. Opposite mention of his own name, Burne-Jones has depicted himself as a prematurely forlorn old man, one of his standing jokes, with his hands diffidently stuck in his pockets. On the other side of the page he has sketched his easel with a pathetic stick figure on the canvas, a comic admission of his inability to draw.

No. A: 43

DANTE GABRIEL ROSSETTI

The Roseleaf 1870
Two types of graphite on wove paper
39.0 x 35.2 cm
Inscribed by the artist, centre left, in graphite: *DGR*
(in monogram, in a circle) / *1870*
Provenance: the artist's sale, Christie's, London, 12 May
1883, lot 189; bought McLean; J.F. Swann, Oak-
field, Wimbledon Common, S.W.; his sale, Christie's,
London, 15 May 1925, lot 41; bought at the sale
through P. & D. Colnaghi, London
National Gallery of Canada, Ottawa (acc. no. 3202)

In 1865, after the Morrises were forced to abandon the Red House and return to London, Rossetti posed Jane for a series of extraordinary photographs taken in his Chelsea garden by John R. Parsons (see Nos. M: 3-4). *The Roseleaf* is one of several works based directly on these photographs. By 1868, Jane had begun to sit regularly for Rossetti and her marriage to Morris had broken down. Many of Rossetti's images of her at this time contain hidden references to her entrapment in a loveless marriage, a meaning that became even more apparent in his versions of *Proserpine*

(No. A: 44). The year of this drawing, 1870, was a turning-point in the relationship of artist and model. Two of Rossetti's love letters of that year are the most passionate demonstrations of his devotion to Jane that survive. The volume of his *Poems* published that year contains fifty newly written sonnets celebrating his love – poor Morris had to review it! – and for the first time the lovers were alone together at Scalands. The experiment of a country retreat, ostensibly for their health, was so successful that it led the following year to the joint tenancy of Kelmscott Manor in remote Oxfordshire by Rossetti and Morris, who suffered by his wife's defection, but felt she had the right to seek personal happiness away from her legal mate.

For Rossetti the rose was always the flower of physical passion, the roseleaf signifying in Victorian language-of-flowers manuals "You may hope." The present portrait therefore has a meaning close to Rossetti's *Pandora*, where Mrs. Morris holds the closed box containing hope – a version of which was formerly in the collection of Sir George Drummond in Montreal.[109] The artist liked the present drawing so much that he kept it for himself until his death. Executed in a cool silvery graphite, the portrait exudes a gentle melancholy, a mood of vulnerability and alienation that is enhanced by the turn of the back towards the spectator. The pale rectangle of light falling on the wall to the right of the head enhances the feeling of imprisonment and looks forward to the re-use of the same motif in *Proserpine*. *The Roseleaf* is one of Rossetti's most poignant portraits of the woman who came to dominate his art and his life for the last two decades of his career. As W. Graham Robertson said, "Hers is one of the few World Faces…."[110]

No. A: 44

DANTE GABRIEL ROSSETTI

Cartoon for "Proserpine" c. 1871
Graphite on wove paper, laid down; squared for transfer
in graphite
93.8 x 47.4 cm
Provenance: the artist's brother W.M. Rossetti; by descent
to his granddaughter Mrs. Geoffrey Dennis; purchased from her by an unidentified collector; who
sold it to S. & K. Morris, Stratford-upon-Avon;
Morris Gallery, Toronto; purchased 1980
Dr. Harry and Barbara Rosenberg

Proserpine became Jane Morris's most memorable role in Rossetti's painting: the Goddess of Hades, allowed out of

NO. A: 44

her husband's dark and dreary kingdom for only brief moments of bliss, because she had tasted one seed of the pomegranate. The idea for the picture, which was eventually undertaken in no less than eight versions, germinated in 1871, apparently during the first months of Rossetti's and Jane's occupancy together of Kelmscott Manor. At first, the subject was to be an Eve, but was soon changed to Proserpine, both women having fallen by tasting of a fatal fruit. It is possible that a trace of this original idea, an apple instead of a pomegranate, survives in this cartoon for the first version, a pastel and black chalk drawing dated 1871. The latter obviously had some personal significance,

since the artist bequeathed it to Mrs. Morris at his death. The present cartoon, squared for transfer, corresponds in size and details, such as the fall of the drapery over the foreground ledge, with the pastel version, which May Morris left to the Ashmolean Museum in Oxford. In the paintings, which all derive from the pastel, Rossetti added such symbolic accessories as the ivy, the incense-burner and the scroll with the poem, turning what was originally a portrait of Jane into a more saleable allegorical picture. The earliest and best surviving painting, begun in 1873 and finished in 1877, is the one formerly in the collection of the English painter L.S. Lowry.[111]

ENDNOTES

1. *Hopes and Fears for Art: Five Lectures Delivered in Birming-ham, London and Nottingham, 1878-1881*, 5th ed. (London: 1898), p. 27.

2. *The Life of William Morris*, vol. 1 (London: 1899; reprinted New York, 1968), p. 301.

3. Quoted in Georgiana Burne-Jones, *Memorials of Edward Burne-Jones*, vol. 1 (London, 1904; reprinted New York, 1971), p. 62.

4. "Of Designs and Working Drawings", *Arts and Crafts Essays by Members of the Arts and Crafts Exhibition Society* (London: 1893), pp. 258.

5. Could it have been a gift to "Ford [and] Emma Hill Brown", Hill being Emma's maiden name? The Browns had been very kind to the Burne-Joneses that year. Indeed, Georgie had even stayed with them before her marriage to Ned, and Emma became almost an elder sister to both her and Janey in their new stations. It would have been appropriate for Burne-Jones to give them such a tribute as the present drawing.

6. He lent it to a *City of Bradford Exhibition* in 1904 (no. 453).

7. "Church-Building News", *The Builder* (25 July 1863): 537.

8. The iconography of Morris as a damned soul also includes Rossetti's cartoon *Rupes Topseia* (British Museum), punning on the *rupes Tarpeia*, from which traitors were hurled in ancient Rome; it shows Morris heading straight for the flames and pitchforks of Hell (a comment, apparently, on the events leading up to the dissolution of the Firm in 1875). Another such work is Burne-Jones's caricature of Morris as a stained-glass *Judas Damnatus*, clutching a money-bag against the flames of Hell, in the first volume of the artist's account

books in the Fitzwilliam Museum.

9. This would seem to be an odd title for the present work, but Brown is not known to have made any other St. Martin designs besides the present two.

10. Ford Madox Hueffer, *Ford Madox Brown: A Record of his Life and Work* (London, 1896), advertisement following p. 459.

11. A. Charles Sewter, *The Stained Glass of William Morris and his Circle* (New Haven and London, 1974), p. 29.

12. Originally designed for embroidery, these banners were remembered by Burne-Jones many years later and were incorporated into his first, rejected design for *The Arming and Departure of the Knights* in the Holy Grail tapestry series (Christie's, London, 4 July 1967, lot 61).

13. "A Disciple of William Morris", *The Art Journal* 67 (March 1905): 87.

14. *The Golden Legend*, vol. 1 (Hammersmith, 1892), p. 347.

15. Quoted in Hueffer, *Ford Madox Brown...*, p. 252.

16. May Morris confirmed that "the heads are those of Madox Brown himself and his wife – very like my remembrance of them." [*William Morris: Artist, Writer, Socialist*, vol. 1 (Oxford, 1936; reprinted New York, 1966], p. 22.)

17. It is instructive to compare Brown's *Finding of Moses* with Burne-Jones's 1879 cartoon of the same subject for All Hallows, Allerton (Sewter, *The Stained Glass of William Morris...*, fig. 544; cartoon in the Tate Gallery). The composition has been reduced to three main figures which are larger than Brown's and much more two-dimensional, the reeds being interpreted decoratively as a leafy halo around Moses' sister, who occupies the same lower right-hand corner.

18. Mary Lago, ed., *Burne-Jones Talking* (London, 1982), p. 28; and R.W. Lightbown, "The Inspiration of Christian Art", *Influences in Victorian Art and Architecture*, ed. S. Macready and F.H. Thompson, The Society of Antiquaries Occasional Paper (New Series) 7 (London, 1985), pp. 30, 36.

19. An English translation of Didron was published under the title of *Christian Iconography*, the first volume appearing in 1851, the second in 1886. Since the present illustration of the Trinity only appeared in the second volume of the English translation, Burne-Jones must have been using the original French volume in 1875.

20. The right-hand portion was last seen with the dealer Peter Nahum in London (*Burne-Jones, the Pre-Raphaelites and their Century*, vol. 2 [London, 1989], pl. 51).

21. See Aymer Vallance, "The Decorative Art of Sir Edward Burne-Jones, Baronet", *The Easter Art Annual* (extra number of *The Art Journal*) (1900): 9, fig. 12.

22. See Sewter, *The Stained Glass of William Morris...*, fig. 449, cartoon in the Leeds City Art Gallery.

23. Virginia Surtees, *The Paintings and Drawings of Dante Gabriel Rossetti (1828-1882): A Catalogue Raisonné* (Oxford, 1971), no. 105 J.

24. Holiday's autobiography contains an interesting account of his month at Currelly's camp at Deir-el-Bahari. (*Reminiscences of My Life* [London, 1914], pp. 414-20.)

25. Registration Department, Royal Ontario Museum, Toronto.

26. Currelly having challenged the archaeological accuracy of the upright loom, Holiday was at pains to defend it in his letter of 19 May 1916.

27. *Verso*, lower centre on label: *This Picture, being painted in WATER / COLOUR, would be injured by the slight- / est moisture / Great care must be used whenever / it is removed from the Frame. / Edward Burne-Jones*

28. Artist's work record, Fitzwilliam Museum, Cambridge, and Malcolm Bell, *Edward Burne-Jones: A Record and Review* (London and New York, 1892), p. 109.

29. Quoted in G. Burne-Jones, *Memorials...*, vol. 2, p. 41.

30. *The Complete Works of John Ruskin*, ed. E.T. Cooke and A. Wedderburn, vol. 33 (London, 1908), p. 292.

31. Quoted in G. Burne-Jones, *Memorials...*, vol. 1, p. 297.

32. According to De Lisle, the infants with beads symbolized "the many forms of religion with which the children of men occupy themselves, and the great current of faith which runs through and unites them all" (*Burne-Jones*, 2nd ed. [London, 1906], p. 104). In an unpublished paper on the iconography of *Fides*, Wheeler has proposed reading both the numbers and the colours of the beads according to Christian numerology and colour symbolism ("The Iconography of Sir Edward Burne-Jones' *Fides* and Related Works", unpublished MS, Vancouver Art Gallery, 1971, p. 9).

33. Sidney Colvin, "The Grosvenor Gallery", *Fortnightly Review* 27 (June 1877), reprinted in *Victorian Painting: Essays and Reviews* 3 (1861-1880), ed. by John Charles Olmsted (New York and London, 1985), p. 438.

34. *Centenary Exhibition of Paintings and Drawings by Sir Edward Burne-Jones, Bart.* (London, 1933), pp. 8-9.

Despite the warning labels that he placed on the backs of his large watercolours, including this one, disaster struck in 1893 when his watercolour *Love Among the Ruins* was sent to Paris to be reproduced in photogravure. Thinking it was an oil painting, a technician washed it over with something like white of egg to heighten it and completely destroyed it.

35. Lent to the Burne-Jones commemorative exhibition, New Gallery, London, 1898-99, no. 161.

36. Although the window itself was destroyed in the Second World War, the cartoon for it is now at Brantwood, Ruskin's home on Coniston Water.

37. G. Burne-Jones, *Memorials...*, vol. 1, p. 9.

38. *European Drawings from Canadian Collections, 1500-1900* (Ottawa, 1976), p. 118.

39. *Burne-Jones: The Paintings, Graphic and Decorative Work of Sir Edward Burne-Jones, 1833-1898* (London, 1975), no. 331.

40. Basil Reginald Airy, *A Brief History of S. John's, Torquay* (Torquay, 1902), p. 14.

41. *Burne-Jones: The Paintings...*, no. 188; photograph in the Witt Library, London.

42. Philip Burne-Jones, "Notes on Some Unfinished Works of Sir Edward Burne-Jones, Bt.", *The Magazine of Art* (1900): 164.

The present design was exhibited posthumously in the Garden Studio of The Grange in 1899-1900 (no. 30).

43. Sotheby's, London, 21 November 1989, lots 30 and 31.

44. Whitelands Archives, Putney; see Malcolm Cole, *Whitelands College: The Chapel*, Whitelands College Monographs No. 3 (Putney, 1985), p. 16.

45. W.R. Lethaby, *Philip Webb and his Work* (London, 1979), p. 190.

46. These letters have not been included in Norman Kelvin's on-going edition of Morris's complete correspondence.

47. Archives of Eaton Hall, near Chester, England.

48. In the birth register (St. Catherine's House, London), his mother is listed as Sarah Louisa, née Palmer, and his father is given as William, a mechanical draughtsman.

49. "William Morris and His Art", *The Easter Art Annual* (extra number of *The Art Journal*) (1899): 30.

50. Sotheby's, London, 19 February 1987, lot 175.

51. The celebrated Graham piano is now in the collection of the Earl of Oxford and Asquith, a descendant of the original owner.

52. Sotheby's Belgravia, 12 December 1978, lot 49.

53. Artist's sale, Christie's, London, 16 July 1898, lot 50 (25 x 55 in.). A painting of the *Garden of the Hesperides*, described as "tempera on panel" (63.5 x 149.9 cm; 25 x 59 in.), is in the collection of the Owens Art Gallery, Sackville, N.B.

54. G. Burne-Jones, *Memorials...*, vol. 2, p. 196.

55. John Christian, "Burne-Jones and Sculpture", *Pre-Raphaelite Sculpture: Nature and Imagination in British Sculpture, 1848-1914*, ed. Benedict Read and Joanna Barnes (London, 1991), pp. 84, 89.

56. Malcolm Bell, *Edward Burne-Jones, A Record and Review* (London and New York, 1892), p. 58.

57. *The Collected Letters of William Morris*, ed. Norman Kelvin, vol. 2 (Princeton, 1987), no. 1440, p. 730.

58. Felicity L. Leung, *Wallpaper in Canada: 1660s-1930s*, vol. 1, Parks Canada Microfiche Report Series ([Ottawa], 1983), pp. 194, 227.

59. The present design was exhibited in the artist's show at the Fine Art Society, London, in 1891 (no. 61).

60. [George Wardle?], *The Morris Exhibit at the Foreign Fair, Boston, 1883-1884* (Boston, 1883), pp. 18, 23.

61. She lent it to the Second Annual Free Picture Exhibition at the Hampshire House Social Club (no. 213), according to a label on the frame backing.

62. In the *modello* for the present tapestry, last seen at the Christie's, London, auction of 4 July 1967 (lot 62), the woman holding the helmet prominently appears almost in the centre of the composition.

63. The cartoon for *The Arming* is in the William Morris Gallery, Walthamstow.

64. G. Burne-Jones, *Memorials...*, vol. 2, p. 281.

65. A nude study for the figure of a knight on horseback, apparently preparatory for this same tapestry (black and white chalk on brick-red wove paper, inscribed on the *verso* "Study for Sir Galahad"), is now in the collection of Red Deer College in Alberta.

66. A smaller gouache version is also known, owned by Lance Thirkell and on loan to Leighton House in 1971.

67. G. Burne-Jones, *Memorials...*, vol. 2, p. 258.

68. Letter dated 5 September 1926, Registration Department, Royal Ontario Museum, Toronto.

69. Quoted in Joseph Dunlap, "William Morris: Calligrapher", *William Morris and the Art of the Book* (New York, 1976), p. 66.

70. All of Mrs. Doheny's designs for the Kelmscott Press, including the Ottawa one, were originally mounted in an album inscribed on the spine "Original Drawings of William Morris / Certificates, Announcements etc. Printed at the Kelmscott Press" (lot 2358 of her sale, with the drawings removed). The album was "bound by Rivière for Mrs. Doheny June 1937", indicating that she had purchased her drawings by that date.

71. Cockerell Papers, British Library, Add. Ms. 52631.

72. In the famous photograph of Morris's library at Kelmscott House, taken around the time of his death (repro-

duced in *William Morris and the Art of the Book*, no. 8), one sees on the table in the foreground, beside the Windmill Psalter on the lectern, a large uncut woodblock with a full-page border-design printed on it, possibly one of the borders for *Sigurd the Volsung*.

73. William S. Peterson, *A Bibliography of the Kelmscott Press* (Oxford, 1984), p. 112.

74. Sotheby's, London, 10 December 1956, lot 43.

75. Sotheby's, London, 7 July 1919, lot 238.

76. Cockerell Papers, British Library, Add. Ms. 52773.

77. Robert Rosenthal, "Los Angeles & Chicago: Two Cities, Two Bibliophiles", *A Bibliophile's Los Angeles* (Los Angeles, 1985), p. 13.

78. Frank Colebrook, *William Morris: Master Printer*, ed. W.S. Peterson (Council Bluffs, Iowa, 1989), p. 32.

79. *The Letters of Aubrey Beardsley*, ed. Henry Maas, J.L. Duncan and W.G. Good (London, 1970), p. 22.

80. *Ibid*, p. 44.

81. Quoted in Stanley Weintraub, *Beardsley*, Pelican Biographies (Harmondsworth, Middlesex, 1972), p. 60.

82. Lago, ed., *Burne-Jones Talking*, pp. 174-75.

83. Quoted in *Flyleaves*, ed. Dan Laurence and Daniel Leary (Austin, Texas, 1977), p. 27.

84. Quoted in John Y. Le Bourgeois, "William Morris to George Bernard Shaw", *Durham University Journal*, n.s., 34 (March 1973): 210.

85. "The Work of Walter Crane", *The Easter Art Annual* (extra number of *The Art Journal*) (1898): 12.

86. *Of the Decorative Illustration of Books Old and New* (London, 1896; reprinted London, 1984), p. 222.

87. Cockerell Papers, British Library, Add. Mss. 52631, vol. 9, p. 63.

88. Cockerell Papers, British Library, Add. Mss. 52772, p. 36. Words in brackets added in pencil.

89. Paul Needham, in "William Morris: Book Collector", *William Morris and the Art of the Book* (New York, 1976; p. 42), states 1894; Mackail, in *The Life of William Morris*, vol. 2 (p. 328), states 1896.

90. British Library, Add. Ms. 45-351-A; see *1839 Jane Morris 1914: A Biographical Exhibition* (Walthamstow, 1986), p. 23.

91. William E. Fredeman, ed., "A Rossetti Cabinet: A Portfolio of Drawings by Dante Gabriel Rossetti Hitherto Unpublished, Unrecorded or Undocumented…", *The Journal of Pre-Raphaelite and Aesthetic Studies* 2 (Fall 1989; published 1991): 9, no. and pl. 69a.

92. Other Crane designs for *Beauty's Awakening* are in the William Morris Gallery, Walthamstow, the Victoria and Albert Museum, the Art Workers' Guild and the Royal Borough of Kensington and Chelsea Library and Arts Service, which owns another version of Trueheart asleep.

93. No other known drawing fits this description as well as the present work; no drawing is listed in Surtees with a Dancocks provenance.

94. C.L. Cline, ed., *The Owl and the Rossettis: Letters of Charles A. Howell and Dante Gabriel, Christina and William Michael Rossetti* (University Park, Pennsylvania, and London, 1978), letter 407.

95. *Ibid.*, letters 408, 416.

96. Surtees, *The Paintings and Drawings of Dante Gabriel Rossetti…* (Oxford, 1971), Appendix no. 9.

97. Jane Abdy and Charlotte Gere, *The Souls* (London, 1984), p. 89, bottom fig.

98. *Official Report of the Japan British Exhibition 1910 at the Great White City, Shepherd's Bush, London* (London and Woking, Surrey, 1911), p. 330.

The drawings were also exhibited at the Burlington Fine Arts Club, 1899 (no. 94).

99. The drawing is inscribed on the *verso*: *From the Ruskin Coll.*

100. *The Complete Works of John Ruskin*, vol. 37 (London, 1909), p. 437.

101. G. Burne-Jones, *Memorials…*, vol. 2, p. 129.

102. *Ibid.*

103. *Ibid.*, vol. 1, pp. 299-300.

104. *The Brantwood Diary of John Ruskin*, ed. Helen Gill Viljoen (New Haven and London, 1971), p. 110.

105. Given the very strong connection between Proserpine and Rose La Touche, one wonders if "a design of Proserpine", listed in Burne-Jones's autograph work-record in the Fitzwilliam Museum under 1875, the year of her death, might not have had some connection with Ruskin and his lost beloved.

106. *Burne-Jones: The Painting…*, no. 324.

107. H.C. Marillier, *Dante Gabriel Rossetti: An Illustrated Memorial of his Art and Life* (London, 1899), p. 217.

108. William Michael Rossetti, "The Portraits of Dante Gabriel Rossetti", *The Magazine of Art* (1889): 58.

109. Surtees, *The Paintings and Drawings of Dante Gabriel Rossetti…*, no. 224 R. I.A.

110. *Time Was* (London, 1931), p. 95.

111. Christie's, London, 27 November 1987, lot 140.

PAINTINGS

Douglas E. Schoenherr

Under the influence of Dante Gabriel Rossetti, William Morris not only started painting but began collecting paintings, one of his first purchases being Arthur Hughes's *April Love* (see No. B: 3 for a related work). But he was not destined to be a painter – only one picture survives from his hand, the so-called *Guenevere* of 1858 (Tate Gallery, London) – any more than he was destined to be a collector of pictures. In the period 1856-62, he was a pioneer in the development of painted Neo-Gothic furniture, where almost every blank area was an invitation to be filled with painting. When the famous Red Lion Square settle, his most notorious exercise in furniture design, was moved to the Red House, Rossetti painted the three cupboard doors with a Dante subject, which partly survive as *The Salutation of Beatrice on Earth and in Eden* (No. B: 4). Its gold ground and bright colours emphasize its debt to late-medieval panel-paintings of the type the Morris group admired.

After the early days, Morris never bought a picture, and his first purchases were quickly disposed of. With beautiful furniture, wall-coverings, and artifacts like Chinese ceramics or Persian rugs, the Morris room needed no pictures to complete the decorative effect. Besides the family portraits that he always kept and hung, his houses were almost "pictureless," in the words of J.W. Mackail.[1]

Although he revered Fra Angelico, Van Eyck and Holbein, Morris did not visit picture galleries or exhibitions very frequently, the only contemporary painting of deep interest to him being that of his close friend Edward Burne-Jones (see Nos. B: 1-2). In addition to his highly successful career as a designer, Burne-Jones was also one of the leading painters of his day, enjoying an international reputation. The two paintings by which he is represented in this publication illustrate different facets of his pictorial accomplishments. *Hero Lighting the Beacon for Leander* reveals how his design

NO. B: 1. EDWARD BURNE-JONES, *Hero Lighting the Beacon for Leander*, 1875-77

work nourished his easel painting, while his *Portrait of Caroline FitzGerald* is a little-known picture of a hitherto mysterious subject.

In spite of his apparent indifference to most contemporary painting, Morris was persuaded to write a review of the Royal Academy exhibition in 1884. He signed it "By a Rare Visitor", and found some workmanlike skill, but no decorative beauty of form or colour on the crowded walls. Having never lost his interest in Pre-Raphaelite painting, he gave an address at the opening of an exhibition at Birmingham in 1891 that remains his most formal discourse on the art of painting. A beautiful house or a fine book continued, however, to rank higher in Morris's hierarchy of values than any painting.

NO. B: 4

No. B: 1

E D W A R D   B U R N E - J O N E S

Hero Lighting the Beacon for Leander 1875-77

Oil on canvas

54.3 x 54.5 cm (circular)

Inscribed by the artist, bottom, in paint: *E.B.J.*; by the
artist (?), verso on lining, upper right, in black paint:
E. Burne-Jones / 1877.

Provenance: Lord Hillglade;[2] Lord Beaverbrook

Owens Art Gallery, Sackville, New Brunswick, gift of
Lord Beaverbrook, in or before 1949 (acc. no. 49.1)

This beautiful picture is a good example of how Burne-
Jones's easel painting was inspired and nourished by his
design work. In 1861-63, during the early days of the Firm,
the artist designed a considerable number of tiles and tile
panels depicting fairy-tale and classical subjects (see No. H:
20). The two tile designs of Hero, executed in blue wash
and black chalk, that were lent to the 1933 Burne-Jones
centenary exhibition at the Tate Gallery by William Roth-
enstein,[3] together with a third one called *Luna*, were drawn
c. 1868 for Murray Marks, who intended to have them
made in Holland – hence the blue and white – but they
were never executed.[4] Hero is shown lighting a beacon to
guide Leander, who swam nightly across the Hellespont
to be with her. When he drowned in a storm one night,
she threw herself into the sea in despair. One of these
designs, showing Hero in a dramatic chiaroscuro crouching to the left of the fire, was the inspiration for this tondo,
which reverses the composition.

Progress on the painting is recorded in Burne-Jones's
work record (Fitzwilliam Museum, Cambridge) under
1875: "worked at circular picture of Hero", and 1876:
"small sitting figure of Hero lighting the signal, a round
picture in oil". The work was probably completed only
in 1877, as the inscription on the back of the canvas indicates. It has recently been claimed that the present picture
was originally purchased by William Graham, the friend
of Burne-Jones and a great collector of the Pre-Raphaelites,
who also commissioned the decorated piano from him (see
No. A: 18).[5] The painting of Hero that Graham owned
was, however, another one, lent to the Burne-Jones exhibition at the New Gallery by his widow in 1898 and
described as follows in the catalogue: "Full-length figure
of Hero, in white drapery, bending to right, and thrusting
a branch into a fire, a signal to Leander. Oil, 28½ x 30½ in.
Painted in 1875...."[6] The present whereabouts of the Gra-

ham picture is unknown. A technical examination of the
Owens tondo reveals that considerable changes were made
during its execution. The canvas is formed of two vertically joined pieces, and the original painted background
was covered with a new white ground all around the figure
and subsequently repainted. A pentimento is visible in
Hero's right hand.

No. B: 2

E D W A R D   B U R N E - J O N E S

Portrait of Caroline FitzGerald 1884

Oil on canvas

82.9 x 52.1 cm

Provenance: apparently commissioned by the sitter's
father, William John FitzGerald; his widow; their
son, Augustine FitzGerald; his widow Mrs FitzGerald,
19 Princes Gate, London; gift of the latter to the
University of Toronto, 1932

Art Gallery of Ontario, Toronto, on extended loan from
the Governing Council of the University of Toronto
since 1976

The gravely beautiful young woman who is the subject of
this haunting portrait has only recently emerged for a few
seconds from the mists of time and then slipped back again
into oblivion. Caroline FitzGerald (1865-1911) was the
only daughter of William John (sometimes given as James)
FitzGerald, who came of distinguished Irish lineage. At
an early age he came to Toronto, entering Upper Canada
College on 4 January 1830 among the first class of students;
in the Register of Admissions, his guardian is given as
I. Chewett of York and no birth date is recorded. He was
a day student and left the College at Christmas 1835, being
at that time head boy. His education continued at Trinity
College, Dublin, ending with law school. He later practised law in Toronto, probably being the "W.J. Fitzgerald"
that is listed in the Directory for 1850-51 as a partner in
"Fitzgibbon & Fitzgerald", his residence being on Wellington Street near York and his office at 43 King Street
West. His years in Toronto evidently meant much to him,
as we shall see.

Sometime in the 1860s he moved to New York and married Mary A. White, the daughter of Eli White, an exceedingly rich New York merchant. Caroline was their eldest
child, with two younger brothers, Augustine and Edward,
the former becoming an artist in Paris, the latter, a famous
explorer. As a young woman, Caroline was well-known

in New York society, especially in literary circles, as a poet, classical scholar and linguist, having studied Sanskrit under Professor Whitney of Yale College. She was also an active member of the American Oriental Society.

The family appears to have spent much time abroad, where their London base was 19 Rutland Gate. Caroline FitzGerald, who was not only oriental in her literary tendencies, but also in her style of dress, was soon as well known in London social circles as she had been in New York. In July of 1884, according to the Burne-Jones's work accounts (Fitzwilliam Museum, Cambridge), the nineteen-year-old girl sat to him for her portrait, unfortunately not in one of her oriental outfits, but rather in a simple black dress. We do not know how Burne-Jones had met her – they certainly had many mutual acquaintances in high and artistic society – but he obviously knew her quite well by 1884 and was sufficiently charmed by the gifted and wealthy blue-stocking to agree to paint her portrait, his aversion to portraits in general, and to society portraits in particular, being well known. Although Caroline's portrait is usually dated 1884, it is interesting to note that the artist wrote in his work record under 1887: "finished a portrait of an American girl". A preliminary study may also have been made, for we find reference to a drawing of "A Yankee wench" in the artist's enumeration of his sketchbooks.[7] Like other Burne-Jones portraits of female sitters, Caroline's is based on Renaissance protoypes, with a touch of Mannerist influence to be detected in the elongation of the figure and the extremely restrained palette of colours.

In 1889 Caroline published a volume of poetry with the very Ruskinian title *Venetia Victrix and Other Poems*, dedicated "to my friend Robert Browning." On 10 July of that same year the *New York Times* announced, under the headline "TO WED A LORD", her engagement to Lord Edmond Fitzmaurice, the younger brother of the fifth Marquess of Lansdowne; at the time of Burne-Jones's portrait the latter was Governor-General of Canada. On 23 November 1889 the forty-three-year-old aristocrat married the twenty-four-year-old heiress at St. Peter's, Eaton Square, with a veritable Who's Who of London society in attendance. Even if he had been invited, it is unlikely that Burne-Jones would have graced such an event, but in the list of wedding gifts we find mention of Sidney Colvin and also of Sir George and Lady Trevelyan, who gave the couple Venetian drawings by Ruskin. These might be the very persons who had brought Burne-Jones into contact with the FitzGeralds in the first place.

NO. B: 2

Caroline's story-book romance now veers towards tragedy. According to documents preserved at Somerset House, London, on 7 August 1894, some five years after the wedding, Caroline, now Lady Edmond Fitzmaurice, filed a petition for Wife's Nullity in the High Court of Justice, Divorce Division, on the grounds of non-consummation. Lord Edmond denied the allegations, but apparently withdrew his defence, for Caroline received unopposed a Decree Nisi for Nullity of Marriage on 29 October 1894, the Decree Absolute being pronounced on 6 May 1895. With this very traumatic event, Caroline's brief and eventful history comes almost to a stop, as far as we are concerned. Her father died in London in 1899, but her mother apparently continued to live there, for she lent the portrait of Caroline, discreetly titled "A Portrait", to the Burne-Jones retrospective at the New Gallery in 1898-99 (no. 114). She also lent a crayon "Portrait of Edward FitzGerald, Esq" (signed and dated 1896; no. 199), apparently a portrait of Caroline's younger brother, indicating that Burne-Jones continued his connection with the family for many years after completing her portrait.[8]

In 1932 Augustine FitzGerald's widow, then residing at 19 Princes Gate, London, gave to the University of Toronto a group of books and paintings in memory of her late husband and especially of her husband's father, William FitzGerald. Among the books were many early editions of classical texts that must have originally belonged to Caroline and that Morris would have admired from a typographical point of view. Although Burne-Jones favoured an open book as an attribute in his portraits, the volume in Caroline's hand obviously had a special significance, referring to her accomplishments as a scholar and linguist and to her own very impressive library. The laurel leaves in the background are a conventional tribute to her talents as a poet. The pink rosebud at her neck undoubtedly refers to her youth – that of a gifted girl about to blossom into a mature woman.

As part of Mrs. Augustine FitzGerald's gift, there was also a copy of *The Oxford and Cambridge Magazine* of 1856, hinting at a possible connection between Caroline and Morris himself.[9] The fact that her brother Augustine had her portrait after her death would seem to indicate that Caroline did not remarry and go on to have a family of her own, as Effie Ruskin did in similar circumstances. Whatever happened to Caroline? The wistful countenance looks back at us, but does not answer. Her story is worthy of Henry James.

No. B: 3

ARTHUR HUGHES

The Lady with the Lilacs 1863
Oil on panel
44.5 x 22.5 cm (arched top)
Inscribed by the artist, lower right, in red paint:
    ARTHUR HUGHES
Provenance: painted for Charles Lutwidge Dodgson (Lewis Carroll) in 1863; on his death presumably to his sister, Mary Collingwood; on her death presumably to her son, Bertram Collingwood; on his death presumably to his wife, Grace Collingwood; sold Christie's, London, 16 July 1965, lot 89; bought Thos. Agnew & Sons, London; purchased in 1965
Art Gallery of Ontario, Toronto, presented in Memory of Frances Baines, Membership Secretary (1951-64) by Members of Council, the Women's Committee and Staff of the Art Gallery of Toronto, 1966 (acc. no. 65/29)

Strongly under the spell of Rossetti, Morris in 1856 had decided to become a painter, Rossetti's doctrine being that everyone ought to be a painter. But if you were rich enough, as Morris was, you were also required to buy pictures. So while Morris was still articling with the architect G.E. Street in Oxford, he started to buy Pre-Raphaelite paintings. At the Royal Academy's exhibition he had been greatly delighted by Arthur Hughes's magnificent *April Love*, showing the aftermath of a lovers' quarrel in a garden pavilion engulfed in the acidic greens of a wet spring (Tate Gallery, London). After brooding on the subject for a few days, Morris decided to buy it, writing to Burne-Jones from Oxford on 17 May: "Will you do me a great favour, viz. go and nobble that picture called 'April Love,' as soon as possible lest anybody else should buy it."[10] There was indeed some competition for it, Ruskin having tried to persuade his father to buy it, but Burne-Jones was successful. Many years later, Hughes remembered Burne-Jones arriving at his house with Morris's cheque for £30: "My chief feeling then was surprise at an Oxford student buying pictures."[11] Hughes became a good friend of Morris and Burne-Jones, his name appearing as a partner in the first prospectus for Morris, Marshall, Faulkner & Co. in 1861, but he withdrew before it was formally registered on the grounds that he lived in the country too far outside London to make attending meetings practical. His letter of resignation crossed one from Morris asking him to design a portion of a window and that design, *The Birth of Tristram*, for Walter Dunlop of Harden Grange, remains his only contribution to the Firm.

The present picture, with its lilacs repeated from *April Love*, was painted for Charles Lutwidge Dodgson, the Oxford don who under the pen-name of Lewis Carroll wrote *Alice's Adventures in Wonderland*. *The Lady with the Lilacs* is in fact a charming excerpt from a larger painting that Hughes was working on at the same time, *Silver and Gold*,[12] showing two women in Elizabethan dress, an old lady in black "Silver" and a young girl in red "Gold," walking together in a grand formal garden with a peacock, sun-dial and immaculate hedges in the background. Shakespearean subjects figure largely in Hughes's early work, and even the contemporary theme of *The Long Engagement* is known to have been commenced as a scene from *As You*

Like It. Anyone who knows *All's Well that Ends Well* will be struck by the fact that Hughes's *Silver and Gold* appears to illustrate a scene in it. The two ladies in Elizabethan costumes could well be Shakespeare's Old Lady, the Countess, walking in the garden of Rousillon with her ward Helena, who has just confided her love of Bertram, the Old Lady's son, to her (Act I, scene iii).

When Dodgson moved into his elegant suite of rooms overlooking St. Aldates in 1868, he hung Hughes's *The Lady with the Lilacs* in his sitting room. An old photograph survives, showing it hanging in its present frame to the right of the fireplace. According to his diary for 4 March 1887, Dodgson "called on Mr. William de [*sic*] Morgan and chose a set of red tiles for the large fireplace", which we see in place in the photograph. When children visited his rooms, he would interpret De Morgan's delightful birds and monsters as the Lory, the Dodo, the Fawn, the Eaglet and the Gryphon from *Alice in Wonderland*. Happily, the tiles survive in the form of a fire-screen. It has been claimed, moreover, that Hughes's painting inspired Dodgson's own illustrations of Alice, which he drew the year after acquiring the picture.

No. B: 4

DANTE GABRIEL ROSSETTI

The Salutation of Beatrice on Earth and in Eden 1859
Oil and gold leaf on two pine panels, gilded frame
    painted by the artist in 1863
101.0 x 202.0 cm (including frame); 75.9 x 80.9 cm
    (left panel); 75.6 x 80.9 cm (right panel)
Inscribed by the artist, left panel, lower right, in brown
    paint: *DGR* (in monogram) / *June 16-25 / 1859*;
    right panel, lower left, in paint: *DGR* (in monogram)
    1859[13]
Provenance: gift of the artist to William and Jane Morris;
    returned to the artist who sold it to the London
    dealer Ernest Gambart, c. 10 August 1863; sold to the
    London dealer E.F. White, 27 October 1863, for
    £367.10.0; Sir Frederick Burton; sold to James
    Leathart, Newcastle upon Tyne, 18 January 1868, for
    £367.10.0; by 30 March 1896,[14] sold to F.J. Tennant;
    Michael Tennant; Christie's, London, 23 November
    1956, lot 47; Leger Galleries, London; purchased 1957
National Gallery of Canada, Ottawa (acc. no. 6750)

When Morris and Burne-Jones moved into Rossetti's former quarters at 17 Red Lion Square at the end of Novem-ber 1856, they were faced with the prospect of bare rooms and no commercially available furniture that suited them. Morris immediately set to work designing pieces that were to be constructed by a neighbourhood carpenter. By mid-December, Rossetti could report to William Allingham:

> Morris is rather doing the magnificent there [Red Lion Square], and is having some intensely mediaeval furniture made – tables and chairs like incubi and succubi. He and I have painted the back of a chair with figures and inscriptions in gules and vert and azure, and we are all three going to cover a cabinet with pictures.[15]

The "cabinet" referred to is undoubtedly Morris's *pièce de résistance* of furniture design, a massive cupboard-settle that blocked the stairway on arrival and took up one-third of the studio space when properly installed. Rossetti laughed when he saw it, "but approved". The neighbour-hood carpenter who constructed it was the cabinet-maker Henry Price, who worked for Tommy Baker of Christopher Street, Hatton Garden, not far from Red Lion Square. He has left a fascinating (if ill-spelled) description of it in his diary:

> Oak, Walnut, Pitch, Pine, Lime Tree and Mahogany all went into the job. A large Cabinet about 7ft high and as long, a seat forming a bunk, with arms each end Carv to represent Fishes. Three Cupboards The Doors with fantastic ironwork hinges, representing Birds, fishes and Flowers Bolted on, and gilt coloured.[16]

This is almost certainly the famous large settle, described as having "a long seat below, and above, three cupboards with great swing doors."[17]

Although Rossetti intended to help with the decoration of the settle, nothing had been done by the time Morris married on 26 April 1859 and vacated Red Lion Square, taking furnished rooms at 41 Great Ormond Street. Burne-Jones left at this time as well, and a Mr. Swan moved into their Red Lion Square quarters. What happened to the settle in the meantime? Just a few days after the Morrises returned from their honeymoon, Rossetti began the present two paintings of *The Salutation of Beatrice* on two of the three cupboard doors, dating the first June 16-25, 1859. "I have done a whole picture in a week on one of Topsy's doors", he wrote to Ford Madox Brown on 22 June 1859.[18] In the years to come, Rossetti referred to the panels as sketches, wishing to create a replica (which he finally did in watercolour) that would have the proper finish. It would appear that they were painted as his wedding present to the young couple, just as Philip Webb had designed and Burne-Jones had painted the *Prioress's Tale* wardrobe as their gift. Since the settle had probably been dismantled for storage, the two outer cupboard doors, made of pine planks in three layers, were now separated from it. The two iron hinges that had been bolted across the outside of each door had been removed, leaving two rows of five holes that were filled with plugs before Rossetti commenced his paintings. These small plugs can now be clearly seen with the naked eye in two horizontal rows on each panel.[19] That the doors were separated from the furniture at this point is proven by the fact that the *Salutation of Beatrice in Eden* was shown at the Hogarth Club in March of 1860, where James Smetham saw and greatly admired it. It is therefore evident from this chronology that Rossetti's painted doors were never on the settle when it was at Red Lion Square, as is sometimes stated.

In the meantime, Philip Webb's new house for the Morrises, the Red House in Bexleyheath, had been started in May 1859 and was not ready to receive the owners until the late summer of 1860. The settle in some form or other was moved to the Red House and in its renovated state installed at the end of the drawing-room, where it still stands, with Rossetti's two doors on the two outer cupboards, the centre cupboard remaining either open shelving or closed with an unpainted door. Rossetti quickly got the idea of turning his diptych into a triptych by painting the centre door with the crucial episode that takes place between the two salutations: the death of Beatrice on 9 June 1290. That Dante's love for Beatrice was taken very seriously within the Morris circle is indicated by the fact that Georgiana and Edward Burne-Jones became engaged deliberately on 9 June 1856 and married deliberately on 9 June four years later.

Rossetti married Lizzie Siddal on 23 May 1860, and in October of that year, when she was visiting the Red House, he went up to join her because "I have a panel to paint there."[20] This panel was very probably the *Dantis Amor* that he painted on a solid piece of mahogany for the centre cupboard, which cannot have been one of the original doors, because it does not have the plugs from the former hinges. Other than Mackail's claim, there is no further evidence that Rossetti also painted panels on "the sides of the settle".[21]

To what remained of the Red Lion settle Philip Webb added a minstrels' gallery across the top, and one may be justified in thinking that he almost completely redesigned

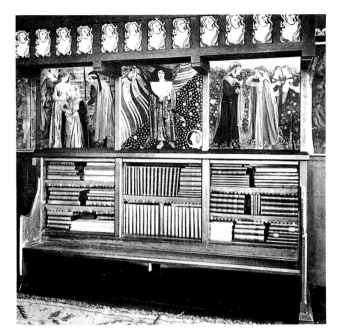

FIG. B: 1. Reconstruction of the Red House settle.

the piece, because all the carving has disappeared. Two small sketches of the settle with the minstrels' gallery and the three upper cupboard doors clearly indicated may be seen on No. 1 and No. 2 of his original plans for the Red House, now in the Victoria and Albert Museum, London. Sometime in the 1920s the settle was painted with white enamel, but that was certainly not its original colour. In the earliest known photograph of it, reproduced in vol. 1 (1904) of Hermann Muthesius's enormously influential *Das Englische Haus* (p. 106, fig. 70), we see a dark settle, as we also do in Gerald Crow's later book, presumably reproducing an old photograph.[22] If one climbs up to the minstrels' gallery today, one discovers that its inside, unseen from the floor below, remains a dark red-brown, just that shade of Dragon's Blood stain that Morris favoured for Webb's dresser in the dining-room and for the inside of the settle in the hall. Rossetti's pictures, with their bright colours and gold leaf, would have looked particularly stunning in a setting of Dragon's Blood. A photographic reconstruction using the plate in Crow (fig. B: 1) gives some idea of how splendid it looked, with Burne-Jones's *Sire Degrevaunt* murals flanking it (see No. A: 2).

One will recall from Rossetti's earliest mention of the cabinet that "all three" friends intended to take a hand in painting it. In fact, Burne-Jones did begin his part of the decoration: "I began a picture from the Niebelungen Lied on the inside of one of the shutters of this settle...." Georgiana Burne-Jones goes on to explain:

The Niebelungen Lied design of which Edward speaks was never finished, and if it was begun upon the back of either of the beautiful "Salutations of Beatrice" which Rossetti painted on the outside of the doors of the big settle, it may perhaps still remain there.[23]

In fact, it appears to have remained on the back of the left panel, the *Salutation of Beatrice on Earth*, covered with a layer of black paint but recognizable as some sort of design, until 1964, when the National Gallery's conservation department chiselled off the lower two layers of pine boards in order to stabilize the top panel on which Rossetti's picture was painted. With it, they removed what may well have been the beginnings of Burne-Jones's Niebelungen Lied design, three arches of which can clearly be seen in the photograph that was taken to document the condition before the treatment was undertaken.[24]

The works of Dante were of major importance to Rossetti, who not only painted numerous subjects, especially of Dante's ideal love, Beatrice, but also published translations of the poet after whom he had been named. For his settle doors, the artist went back to one of his own earlier designs, a pen-and-ink diptych of 1849-50 showing Beatrice's two salutations to Dante, first on a street in Florence and then in heaven after her death (Fogg Art Museum, Cambridge, Mass.). Although Lizzie Siddal is associated overwhelmingly with the role of Beatrice in Rossetti's art, now and then other models were used. As a flattering compliment to the bride, with whom he was very likely in love, Rossetti cast Jane Morris as the Beatrice on earth, flanked by his housekeeper (and mistress) Fanny Cornforth in front and Red Lion Mary, Morris's and Burne-Jones's former maid at Red Lion Square, behind. The intriguing composition shows a series of steps filling almost all of the picture area. Because Red Lion Mary was plain, she was rarely invited to sit as a model, but on this occasion Rossetti immortalized her, giving her the top position on the highest step and allowing her to tower over the tall Jane Morris, the joke being that Red Lion Mary was also too short to be an effective model. What can only be called – although the phrase was not yet coined – a magnificent "Arts and Crafts" ironwork balustrade separates the descending Beloved from the ascending Lover, with its dull iron lilies, symbols of Florence, echoing the glorious real lilies to be seen in the Eden pendant. The rose trellis, alive with exotic birds in the golden-skied Paradise, would appear to be the prototype for the famous rose trellises that closed the well-quadrangle at the Red House, which in turn inspired Morris's

first wallpaper design, *Trellis* (No. E: 8). For the meeting in Paradise, Rossetti reversed the composition, the two Dantes, colour-coded in easily recognizable red and black, being shown back-to-back. Beatrice and her ladies, however, appear to have turned into different women. Although her hair is partially covered with a white veil, the Beatrice in Eden has deep-red hair that is not at all like the dark-brown wavy locks that characterize Mrs. Morris. William Michael Rossetti clarified the problem by pointing out that his brother depicted Jane Morris in "the first compartment of 'Salutatio Beatricis' ", but "his wife [i.e., Elizabeth Siddal] in the second compartment."[25] Being very likely in love with Janey but about to marry Lizzie, Rossetti resolved his dual loyalties with breath-taking audacity by casting the former as his Beatrice on Earth and the latter as his Beatrice in Heaven.

A feminist critic has recently pointed out that Lizzie's "own death was the unwitting consummation of her Beatrice role", an event that occurred on 11 February 1862 from a overdose of laudanum.[26] Rossetti's painting on the settle had literally come true: Lizzie had become indeed his Beatrice in Heaven. We know that he was so racked with guilt and remorse at his wife's death that he buried the manuscript of his poems in her grave. It is possible that Lizzie's death had something to do with the sudden removal of the Salutation pictures from the settle by early August 1863, long before there was any thought of the Morrises leaving Red House, the reason that is usually given for their removal. The two outer panels were taken down and enclosed within a new painted and gilded frame reproducing the symbolic death of Beatrice on the central bar, and offered to the dealer Gambart in the format they retain today. The centre panel of *Dantis Amor* was sold separately (now in the Tate Gallery). The fact remains that the pictures that were ostensibly wedding presents to Morris and Jane were returned to the artist, who sold them to the dealer Gambart around the middle of August 1863. When Webb's and Burne-Jones's painted wardrobe remained a focal-point of the Morrises's drawing-room for the rest of their lives, why was Rossetti's wedding gift returned to him? It can only be because he asked for it back, the reminder of his Beatrice in Heaven being possibly too much for him to view with equanimity on Morris's settle for the rest of their lives together, for at this point everyone concerned would have thought that the settle and the Morrises would remain in the Red House indefinitely. It is also possible that Morris was not unhappy to see the paintings go, for one can only wonder what the young husband thought of seeing Janey every day presented as the beloved of Dante the poet, but also the beloved of Dante the painter, who would soon become her lover and something less than his former friend.

ENDNOTES

1. *The Life of William Morris*, vol. 2 (London: 1899; reprinted New York, 1968), p. 274.

2. Remains of labels on frame: *The Property of Lord Hillglade / Framer: Leggatt Brothers....*

3. Sold Sotheby's, Belgravia, 14 February 1978, lot 45.

4. See Aymer Vallance, "The Decorative Art of Sir Edward Burne-Jones, Baronet", *The Easter Art Annual* (extra number of *The Art Journal*) (1900): 9, 11, fig. 13.

5. John Christian, *Burne-Jones and his Followers* (Tokyo, 1987), p. 67.

6. *Exhibition of the Works of Sir Edward Burne-Jones, Bart.* (London, 1898-99), no. 46.

7. Vol. 6, p. 57, Fitzwilliam Museum, Cambridge.

8. According to the entry on Lord Edmond Fitzmaurice in *The Dictionary of National Biography*, Caroline died in 1911, in her forty-sixth year – not exactly a ripe old age. Even as late as 1928, the FitzGerald family continued to be interested in Burne-Jones's work, buying his *Mercury and Love* at Christie's on 17-18 May (lot 183).

9. Among the other pictures were Turner's large watercolour of *Pembroke Castle* and Burne-Jones's *Mercury and Love* (largely the work of a studio assistant), both now on loan to the Art Gallery of Ontario, as well as a Boucher drawing, and oils by Monticelli, Delacroix, Fantin Latour and Augustine FitzGerald.

10. Quoted in Georgiana Burne-Jones, *Memorials of Edward Burne-Jones*, vol. 1 (London, 1904; reprinted New York, 1971), p. 132.

11. *Pall Mall Gazette*, 13 July 1912.

12. Sold Christie's, London, 25 October 1991, lot 50.

13. The inscription continues in the upper left and upper right, on scrolls, in paint: *hortus Eden*, upper left, by Dante, in paint: *POETA / DANTES DE ALIGhERIIS / DE FLORENTIA*, upper centre, above Beatrice, in paint: *BEATA / BEATRIX*, on frame, above centre bar, in paint: *SALVTATIO / BEATRICIS*, below centre bar: *IN TERRA / ET / IN EDEN*, centre bar above angel: *9 JVN: 1290*, centre bar below angel: *QVOMODO SEDET SOLA CIVITAS!* ("How doth the city sit solitary!" [from Jeremiah])....

14. A letter from Charles Fairfax Murray to William Michael Rossetti of that date states, "I have also lately purchased ...the 'Christmas Carol' that belonged to Leathart. I much regret that I was unable to purchase the fine double picture of the meeting of Beatrice and Dante." (Angeli-Dennis Papers, Special Collections, Library, University of British Columbia, Vancouver). Although the work had apparently already been sold to F.J. Tennant, it did appear in the Leathart exhibition at the Goupil Gallery in June and July 1896.

15. *Letters of Dante Gabriel Rossetti*, ed. Oswald Doughty and John Robert Wahl, vol. 1 (Oxford, 1965-67), no. 254, p. 312.

16. Quoted in Pat Kirkham, "William Morris's Early Furniture", *The Journal of the William Morris Society* 4 (Summer 1981): 26.

17. Mackail, *The Life of William Morris*, vol. 1, p. 113.

18. Rossetti, *Letters...*, vol. 1, no. 310, p. 352.

19. That the present hinges on the cupboards of the settle have nothing to do with the original ones is indicated by the fact that they are bolted on with seven screws, not five as was originally the case.

20. Rossetti, *Letters...*, vol. 1, no. 347, p. 379.

21. Mackail, *The Life of William Morris*, vol. 1, pp. 113-14.

22. "William Morris: Designer", *The Special Winter Number of The Studio* (London and New York, 1934): facing p. 40.

    The surviving heraldic shields and helmets that are stencilled in gold on the recessed panels across the front of the minstrels' gallery appear to have been added around the turn of the century, together with similar gold stencilwork along the tops of Burne-Jones's *Sire Degrevaunt* murals, which has subsequently been removed.

23. *Memorials...*, vol. 1, pp. 209, 211.

24. It may be this project that Burne-Jones mistakenly entered in his manuscript work-record under 1856: "a background of a city for the Niblungen Lied never finished, painted in oil."

25. "Notes on Rossetti and His Works", *The Art Journal* (1884): 167.

26. Lynne Pearce, *Women/ Image/ Text: Readings in Pre-Raphaelite Art and Literature* (Toronto and Buffalo, 1991), p. 51.

GLASS

Brian Musselwhite

Among the glass displays at the Great Exhibition of 1851, Ralph Nicholson Wornum noted that Apsley Pellatt & Co. exhibited "curious imitations of Venetian frosted and gilt glass" which "though...a revival of an old taste, is now only a novelty." He also mentioned that Sharpus & Cullum "exhibit... wine-glasses...after the taste of the old Dutch glass" and that "some curious Venetian glass is exhibited by P. Bigaglia."[1]

Although older styles of glass were dutifully mentioned in the exhibition's catalogues, the most admired feature of English glass at the time was not its styling but its clarity. To emphasize this aspect, Apsley Pellatt & Co. displayed glass models of diamonds, including the Koh-i-noor. Wornum claimed that the models were "nothing inferior in brilliancy to the original."[2]

It was this aspect of glass that John Ruskin condemned when he wrote "Our modern glass is exquisitely clear...We ought to be ashamed of it." He found "old Venice glass", which was "muddy" and "inaccurate in all its forms", more acceptable, but only because he felt that each Venetian glassmaker "invented a new design for every glass he made." He believed that the two chief characteristics of glass were "its ductility when heated and its transparency when cold." If the glass did not display those qualities, it should not be made. "Consequently, all cut glass is barbarous for the cutting conceals its ductility and confuses it with crystal."[3] William Morris championed the thoughts of Ruskin on glass by going even further:

> Never till our own day [he wrote] has an ugly or stupid glass vessel been made.... [I]f I were setting about getting good glasses made I would get some good workmen together, tell them the height and capacity of the vessels I wanted, and perhaps some general idea as to shape, and then let them do their best.[4]

NO. C: 2. HENRY HOLIDAY, *Angel*, c. 1890-1900

He believed that moulded and cut glass had no artistic value and only glass blown and worked by hand was acceptable. He also felt that the glass needed slight tints and imperfections to make its form visible. Rationalizing his moral and aesthetic beliefs with his business practices, he concluded by stating that the Venetians would have been contented with an even thicker and rougher body if they had needed to maximize production and minimize breakage.

NO. C: 1

No. C: 1

SIR THOMAS GRAHAM JACKSON, R.A.
DESIGNED FOR JAMES POWELL & SONS, WHITEFRIARS, LONDON

Goblet 1880s-c. 1908
Sap-green lead glass, minute air bubbles; tiny chip to footrim
Height: 15 cm; diameter of foot: 6.3 cm
Provenance: originally from a set of 12, English collection; purchased from Jeanette Hayhurst Fine Glass, London, 1990; two from set in Victoria and Albert Museum and two in British Museum
Royal Ontario Museum, Museum purchase, gift of Mrs. Richard Gilbert (acc. no. 990.76.1)

Morris did not design for glass himself, but commissioned Philip Webb to design the first set of glassware for the Red House in 1859. This large service, produced by James Powell & Sons in medieval Germanic shapes, with Venetian enamelled decoration, has since disappeared.[5] However, Webb soon began producing numerous designs for Powell's that were sold by Morris, Marshall, Faulkner & Co. The glass proved so popular that Powell's commissioned the architect T.G. Jackson in 1874 to produce similarly inspired shapes in green glass.

In *Victorian Table Glass and Ornaments*, Barbara Morris states that the designs of the first set by Philip Webb are in the Victoria and Albert Museum, London.[6]

– Brian Musselwhite

No. C: 2

HENRY HOLIDAY

Angel c. 1890-1900
65.5 cm (diameter)
Opus sectile tondo: ceramic or opaque glass base cut into sections, painted and fired like glass and cemented

Provenance: sold to the Royal Ontario Museum of
    Archaeology in 1927 by Winifred Holiday
Royal Ontario Museum, Toronto (acc. no. 927.114.4)

Henry Holiday, who has been described as "the earliest follower of Burne-Jones as a stained glass designer,"[7] was also
an expert sculptor, enameller and mosaicist. His work in
mosaic was complemented by that in *opus sectile*, a method
of making permanent decorations in which tiles are cut
into the required shapes, painted and fired, like glass, and
fixed to the wall by bedding in cement.[8]

The date of this tondo is not recorded, but it is probably contemporary with the *opus sectile* decorations Holiday
designed in 1898 for St. Chad's Church, Kirkby, near
Liverpool, or the Charity panel at Bethnal Green of 1903.[9]
The draperies, modelling and painting of the head and
limbs and the treatment of the hair of the angel are close
in style and detail to features of Holiday's glass designs of
the 1890s, and are comparable to those in Holiday's 1892
Theology window in the Library stairway of the University of Winnipeg.[10]

Documentation concerning this work forms part of
the extensive correspondence carried on in 1927 between
the ROM's founding director, Charles T. Currelly, and
Winifred Holiday, the artist's daughter. Currelly negoti-
ated the acquisition of five Holiday cartoons for stained
glass (now unlocated) and this *opus sectile* panel. All had
arrived in Toronto by 23 September 1927. A letter from
Winifred Holiday to Currelly dated 17 June 1927 notes that
the *opus sectile* panel had been in the drawing-room of the
Holiday house in London. Further letters reveal that the
stained-glass cartoons (two for Lincoln Cathedral, three
for Southwark Cathedral) were among 2,000-3,000 cartoons and many small designs spanning Holiday's career
of over sixty years, but make no reference to this panel or
its relation to specific Holiday commissions. After its

acquisition, it was photographed and published in colour,
with a gold border and a brief text describing it as "opaque
glass," by Rous and Mann Ltd. of Toronto.

– K. Corey Keeble

ENDNOTES

1. "The Exhibition as a Lesson in Taste", *The Crystal Palace
   Exhibition Illustrated Catalogue* (London, 1851), p. xvii.
       R.N. Wornum (1812-1877), an art critic and author,
   joined the staff of *The Art Journal* in 1846 and won the
   competition of writing the essay "The Exhibition as a
   Lesson in Taste", to accompany the illustrated catalogue. He was also the author of *Analysis of Ornament*.
2. *Ibid*.
3. *The Stones of Venice*, vol. 2 (London, 1853), p. 168.
       While old Venetian glass is slightly tinted and imper-
   fect, it is not muddy or inaccurate. Ruskin was more interested in the moral issue of the glassmaker as designer
   and maker than in the aesthetic qualities of the glass.
4. "The Lesser Arts of Life" (lecture delivered in 1882),
   The Collected Works of William Morris, ed. May Morris,
   vol. 22 (London: 1914).
5. Barbara Morris, *Venetian Table Glass and Ornaments*
   (London, 1978), p. 176.
6. *Ibid.*, p. 175.
7. Martin Harrison, *Victorian Stained Glass* (London, Mel-
   bourne, Sydney, Auckland, Johannesburg, 1980), p. 44.
8. A.L. Baldry, "Henry Holiday", *Walker's Quarterly* (London, 1930), nos. 31-32.
9. *Ibid.*, pp. 29, 74.
10. Alice Hamilton, *Manitoba Stained Glass* (Winnipeg,
    1970), p. 253.

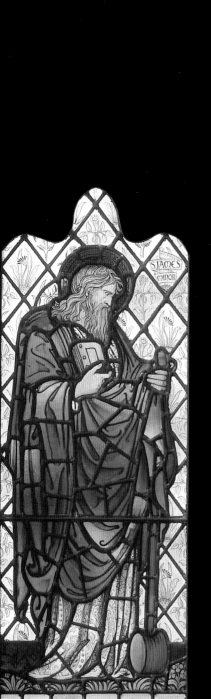

STAINED GLASS

K. Corey Keeble

The revival of stained glass in the 1800s was part of the revitalization of decorative art that took place against the background of the Gothic Revival, the Arts and Crafts movement, and the Industrial Revolution. Antiquarianism contributed to the reintroduction of the "true mosaic principle," in which lead-lines became an important aesthetic linear adjunct to glass-design.

The revival was international, its spread facilitated by improved communication, global colonization and trade. It is wrong to associate stained glass mainly with commissions for churches; domestic work was of equal importance. Further, the revival had important implications for hand-craftsmanship. The design and assembly of stained glass is essentially hand-work, requiring skilled, individual control of drawing, painting, glass-cutting and leading. In its stained glass, Morris & Co. not only followed procedures similar to those of the Middle Ages; other Victorian studios worked along similar lines, and the same basic operation and division of labour continues to the present day.

From the inception of Morris, Marshall, Faulkner & Co. in 1861 at Red Lion Square, London, stained glass was a major part of its operations; glass and tiles were the first items produced in April 1861. The stained-glass department benefitted from the revival of the art within the general context of the Gothic Revival. The "true mosaic principle" had been enunciated by scholars like Charles Winston, and glass technology was advanced and refined by Powell & Sons of Whitefriars, London, and Chance, of Birmingham. There were already dozens of stained-glass studios in Britain alone, and Morris was able to avail himself of their expertise in setting up his own operation. Ford Madox Brown and Edward Burne-Jones, both of whom provided designs for Morris stained glass, had prior experience with Powell & Sons, and Morris's first foreman, George Campfield, came to him from Heaton, Butler, and Bayne, one of the most respected stained-glass studios of its day, though he had also studied at the Working Men's College in Great Ormond

NO. D: 4. EDWARD BURNE-JONES and WILLIAM MORRIS, *SS James-the-Less, Andrew, and Bartholomew,* 1905

113

Street. At the beginning, according to A. Charles Sewter, the Red Lion Square premises were staffed by a dozen men and boys – the boys recruited from a home in the Euston Road.[1] The success of the Firm's early efforts was demonstrated at the International Exhibition of 1862 in London, when rivals falsely accused it of presenting examples of made-over medieval glass.[2]

Stained glass came from all the locations of the Morris firm – Red Lion Square (1861-65), 26 Queen Square, Bloomsbury (1865-77), 449 Oxford Street (1877-81), and Merton Abbey (from 1881 onwards). Glass-painters and other workers were recruited from the trade, sometimes on an intermittent basis, as with the painter Pozzi. Stained-glass workers habitually moved from studio to studio as the need arose. Some came to Morris from other firms; others who had benefitted from training and experience with him also went on to other companies.

The incunabula of Morris stained glass includes windows for Red House, and for G.F. Bodley's church of St. Michael, Brighton. Bodley's support in commissioning work for his churches guaranteed the early success of Morris stained glass.

Initially, Morris used the combined talents of several artists who produced stained-glass designs for him. Ford Madox Brown was an important designer up to 1874. The distinctive style of Morris stained glass, as it evolved from the 1860s into the 1870s, however, was more properly the concern of Philip Webb, Morris himself, and Edward Burne-Jones.

The Firm's early designs were more closely in harmony with the Gothic Revival, and with the legacy of fifteenth-century Late Gothic art, than were its later ones. Following the custom of his medieval precursors, Webb introduced simulated Gothic architectural canopies to frame the figures in some Morris glass, though they were never a major part of the company style. He produced figure designs as well as ornament. His involvement as a stained-glass designer, however, was over by c. 1875.

When Morris, Marshall, Faulkner & Co. was reorganized as Morris & Co. in 1874, stained-glass design devolved principally upon Edward Burne-Jones. Morris, who had designed figures, supervised the selection of colours for windows, and designed much of the ornament for the Firm's earlier stained glass, gradually withdrew from this side of the company's operations. However, he left an important legacy in the lush, scrolling foliage surrounds which increasingly became evident in Morris glass through the 1870s and 1880s, and which survived into the 1900s. Another legacy was his reluctance to install modern stained glass in historic buildings. As a founder, in 1877, of the Society for the Protection of Ancient Buildings (established to protect historic monuments from excessive restoration and modernization), he was prepared to refuse stained-glass commissions for "monuments of Ancient Art" and to concentrate instead on contemporary buildings.

NO. D: 2
EDWARD BURNE-JONES,
Timothy and Eunice, 1878

Burne-Jones dominated Morris glass design from the 1870s and built up a repository of designs and cartoons from which subsequent chief designers extensively drew. In the 1870s he made, on average, nearly forty designs or cartoons a year.[3] His style varied: Morris designs, regardless of their Gothic influences, were never merely imitative and always had a refreshing originality which set them apart from those of other firms. In the 1870s Burne-Jones moved away from the Gothic Revival and designed glass influenced by Florentine Quattrocento art. By the mid-1870s some of his designs included fluttering draperies and ribbons, which appear as precursors of Art Nouveau. In the 1870s he also shifted to Michelangelesque forms, evocative of the Cinquecento. In the 1880s his draperies tightened and his figures became Lysippan – elongated, with small heads. The influence of his work spread through the Arts and Crafts Movement, lasting well beyond his death in 1898. Parallels with his work appear in stained glass by Henry Holiday, and evocations of prognathous-profiled Burne-Jones figures continued to appear in stained glass by *retardataire* Arts and Crafts studios into the 1920s and '30s.

MORRIS GLASS *IN SITU* IN CANADA

Some Morris stained glass was made for clients outside Great Britain. However, exports, in comparison with those of the major commercial studios of the period, were comparatively few in number. Isolated commissions are recorded for English churches in Europe prior to Morris's death in 1896 and Burne-Jones's in 1898. More are recorded for Australia, India, the United

States, and Canada, but the greater number of commissions for Morris glass abroad came after 1900.

Canada had its own stained-glass studios. The earliest, like McCausland in Toronto and Spence in Montreal, originated in the 1850s. No Morris glass was commissioned for Toronto, its absence from which is partly explained by the dominance of local glass studios – principally McCausland and N.T. Lyon. Interestingly, Toronto patrons gave important commissions for windows in Gothic style to English firms like Clayton & Bell, and the German firm of Mayer of Munich.

The earliest Morris glass in Canada was made for David Allan Poe Watt and Andrew Allan, both of Montreal, between 1878 and 1885, slightly later than the earliest Morris glass in the United States (1874). The 1885 Allan window, in memory of his wife Isabella Anne Smith, with personifications of *Faith, Hope, and Charity*, originally in St. Paul's Church, is now in the church of St. Andrew and St. Paul on Sherbrooke Street. The most ambitious Morris work for a Canadian patron before 1900, it features re-workings of subjects Burne-Jones used in 1870-71 for Christ Church Cathedral, Oxford,[4] and in 1883 for All Saints' Church, Harrow Weald, Middlesex.[5] The Montreal window includes six rondels of the Acts of Mercy, relating to subjects in an 1883 window for St. Stephen's church, Gateacre, Lancashire.[6] Rondels and figures in the Montreal window are surrounded by classic Morris scrolling foliage. The figure of *Hope* has fluttering, swirling draperies. Similar draperies occurred in Canadian stained glass into the early 1900s. *Faith*, a lamp in her right hand, was paraphrased by Canadian studios in their own designs (see No. A: 14).

Burne-Jones was succeeded as chief designer of Morris stained glass by John Henry Dearle, one of the painters of the 1885 Montreal window. Dearle acted as chief designer until his death in 1932, re-using existing Burne-Jones designs and adapting them for new work. During his tenure, the number of Canadian commissions increased, the earliest of these being for Montreal. A 1901 window for Crescent Street Church was lost in a fire, but other Montreal windows survive. The chapel glass in Royal Victoria Hospital, dating from 1902, is made of figures and patterned quarries after Burne-Jones cartoons which are reminiscent of the *Minstrel* panels made for the Watt house. Typical of Dearle are the lead-lines, forming bands of quadrilaterals over the draperies or breaking them into tesserae-like sections.

A window in Christ Church Cathedral, Montreal, of *Eunice, Dorcas, and Priscilla*, with lead-lines like those in the Royal Victoria Hospital glass, also dates from 1902. In the tracery, an angel with a dulcimer is based on designs dating back to the 1870s. Dearle's re-use of earlier cartoons shows in the 1903 Andrew Allan window, formerly from the church of St. Paul and now in that of St. Andrew and St. Paul, also in Montreal. Its six figures, arranged in two rows, derive from Burne-Jones designs for St. Stephen's, Gateacre (1883); Albion Congregational church, at Ashton-under-Lyne, Lancashire (1893);[7] and Holy Trinity Church, Sloane Street, Chelsea, London (1894-95).[8] In re-using designs, Dearle and his associates simplified them. The 1903 Allan window is effective in this regard, being balanced in colour and line, and harmonious in the relationship of its individual parts.

The re-use and simplication, under Dearle, of Burne-Jones and Morris cartoons are also seen in a 1911 window in Christ Church Cathedral, and the re-discovered 1912 window in Wilmot United Church, Fredericton, commissioned by Sen. F.B. Thompson in memory of his wife, which has the same subjects: *Clothing the Naked*, and *Feeding the Hungry*. Both derive from the same cartoons and are in the same colours. Around them is simplified, traditional scrolling Morris foliage, the colours of which are reduced in number and intensity, with the brushwork for toning and shading muted, flattening the forms into two-dimensional bands of colour and line.

After 1912, no Morris glass was made for Canada until the 1920s, beginning with windows for All Saints Church, Winnipeg, in 1927 and 1928. In 1931, a year before Dearle's death, Morris & Co. made the glass copy of Frank Dicksee's *Harmony*, now in the Vancouver Art Gallery. Many stained-glass studios of the 1800s and 1900s made copies of paintings, the best example of this tendency being Holman Hunt's *Light of the World*, which was copied by studios in Britain, the U.S. and Canada. Traditionally, Morris & Co. eschewed academic copies and the Dicksee copy was an exception to its usual practice.

J.H. Dearle was succeeded in 1932 by W.H. Knight. In 1940, when Morris & Co. closed, the stained-glass department was purchased by Duncan W. Dearle, J.H. Dearle's son, and operated independently by him until 1954. While most Morris windows in Canada date from the period of John Henry Dearle and W.H. Knight, Duncan Dearle, who had been active with Morris & Co. before his father's death, made a significant number of windows perpetuating the Morris style for Canadian clients in Winnipeg and Vancouver between 1950 and 1954.

Windows designed under Knight are found in Winnipeg, Calgary and Caulfield, British Columbia, and one commission for 1939 is recorded for Newfoundland. In these last Morris & Co. windows before 1940, Burne-Jones's cartoons remained in use, though simplified. The reduction of painterly effects was the result of two factors: the tendency to simplify designs as they became further removed in time and spirit from the personalities and ethos that made them, and the slow, indirect penetration of influences from the modern movement. To the end, however, Morris & Co. continued to base its figures and ornament on the traditions established by Morris and Burne-Jones themselves.

NO. D: 1

STAINED GLASS

No. D: 1

PHILIP WEBB

Panel of painted and leaded glass quarries in a wooden frame c. 1861-62

Six quarries, each: 16.5 x 16.5 cm of alternating "white" (i.e., clear) and greenish glass in two rows with a narrow border of white and green glass above and below; the white quarries are painted in enamels with bird motifs; the greenish quarries have a stylized painted floral repeat

Provenance: from the nursery or nursery-passage at Red House, Bexleyheath, Kent; acquired by a Mrs McLean of the Isle of Mull, Scotland, from Morris & Co.

apparently before 1940; the Fine Art Society, London, by 1979; Haslam and Whiteway, London; purchased 1990

Private collection, Ottawa

Webb designed quarries and borders for the Morris firm from its inception in 1861 until c. 1874. The panel from Red House anticipates the range of decorative borders found in early Morris glass. Sewter dated quarry designs "with birds and formalized flowering plants" at Red House to c. 1861. He considered them as "certainly from designs by P[hilip]W[ebb]."[9] The floral motif in the present panel, thrice repeated, has the delicacy of line seen in early designs from the Morris studio, and is reminiscent of the *Daisy* wallpapers and tiles produced by the firm in the early 1860s (see Nos. E: 6, H: 18). Both the floral pattern and the birds are influenced by late-Gothic glass of the fifteenth and early sixteenth centuries. The birds in particular recall painted designs on late-Gothic quarries in the Victoria and Albert Museum, which derive in part from windows in Westminster Abbey and the College of St. Mark at Audley End, Essex.

The Red House quarries are arranged in a horizontal and vertical grid of lead-lines. The medieval ones were normally set diagonally in lozenge or diamond patterns. Quarry glass had two advantages: it allowed a maximum of light to enter an interior, and was amenable to the use of stencils for repeating standard patterns. It formed an important component in the production of all major Victorian stained-glass studios, whose work may often be recognized by the specific patterns used on the quarries themselves.

Other quarries from Red House with similar hand-painted floral and animal designs are in the Fitzwilliam Museum, Cambridge.

No. D: 2

EDWARD BURNE-JONES

Timothy and Eunice 1878
Stained-glass panel, leaded and painted; border of
    greenish round glass; curved top
69.5 x 83.0 cm
Provenance: commissioned by David A.P. Watt of
    Montreal, and passed by descent to the present owner
Private collection, British Columbia

The subject derives from 2 Timothy 1:5, where St. Paul recalls the faith of his disciple Timothy and that of his mother, Eunice. It was a popular one during the Victorian era, and is represented in stained glass by other firms. Sewter records two variants of the subject, both attributed to Burne-Jones.[10] This panel is the second variant, with Eunice seated and Timothy before her, hands held behind his back. The earliest example of the second variant cited by Sewter was made in 1876.[11] Others cited by Sewter, all for churches, date from 1878 or 1879, and 1888.[12] There are similarities between the head of Eunice and heads in cartoons for rondels with quarry glass surrounds dating back to the 1860s, such as the V & A's *Penelope* of 1863. There is an obvious kinship between the present Timothy and the infant Samuel in the Samuel and Eli panel of the 1872-73 Vyner window in Christ Church Cathedral, Oxford. The Samuel figure, however, is in left profile, here Timothy is in three-quarter view from the back, and is more illu-sionistically three-dimensional than Burne-Jones's Samuel of 1872-73.

Borders of round glass, as seen in the present example, are rare in Morris designs, but occur in glass panels of c. 1868 made for Burne-Jones's house The Grange and later moved to North End House, Rottingdean, Sussex, and in glass made in and around 1878, such as the Lazarus, and Rachel and Jacob windows in St. Etheldreda's church, Guilsborough, Northamptonshire.

Marilyn Ibach[13] identifies the subject as *Mary Instructing Jesus*; Sewter, however, specifically identifies it as *Timothy and Eunice*.

No. D: 3

WILLIAM MORRIS

Two Stained-Glass Panels of Minstrel Figures 1882
Composed of square quarries of greenish glass with
    floral repeats enclosing figures in red and blue glass,
    the whole leaded within wooden frames; each panel
    depicts two musicians, one showing harp and pipe,
    the other, portative organ and mandolin
64.7 x 78.7 cm (each panel)
Provenance: made in 1882 for David A.P. Watt, and
    donated to the Montreal Museum of Fine Arts in his
    memory in 1919 by his daughters
The Montreal Museum of Fine Arts (Inv. 19 Dg. 6-7)

The above-described *Timothy and Eunice* and the Montreal musician panels were probably all made for the Watt house in Montreal. Sewter records the Montreal musician figures as having been painted by Pozzi, the quarries by Single-ton. They relate to figures Morris designed in 1876 for Sidmouth Manor, Devon, to angel musicians dating back to the 1860s for church windows, and to the glass panels of c. 1868 made for Burne-Jones's The Grange (see No. M: 19) and later transferred to North End House, Rotting-dean, Sussex. Musician figures were adapted as minstrels or angels by adding or subtracting wings and haloes, depending on whether they were for church or house interiors, and are all variations on the same prototypes. Parallels to the Watt panels occur in glass of c. 1868 for Burne-Jones's house, and occur in poets and minstrels of c. 1872-74 in the V & A, with a similar arrangement of quarries with styl-ized floral repeats. As designs for domestic glass, the minstrels are also extensions of the draped female figures of Garland Weavers in the V & A's Green Dining Room of 1866-68, and the *Four Seasons* of c. 1867 in the Birmingham City Art Gallery.

NO. D: 3 a.-b. WILLIAM MORRIS, *Two Stained-Glass Panels of Minstrel Figures*, 1882

EDWARD BURNE-JONES
AND WILLIAM MORRIS

SS James-the-Less, Andrew, and Bartholomew 1905
Three stained-glass panels, leaded and painted, arranged
 as a three-light window in a modern wooden frame.
 From left to right, with books and the instruments of
 their martyrdom: St. James, with mallet; St. Andrew,
 with a saltire cross of branches; St. Bartholomew,
 with knife. Each figure is surrounded by diamond
 quarries with floral repeats of two patterns (flower
 with petals in profile, flower of trumpet shape). Above
 and to the right of each panel, the saint's name
102.0 x 38.0 cm (each window)
Provenance: formerly in the church of St. John,
 Cloughfold, Rawtenstall, Lancashire; Haslam and
 Whiteway, London; MacMillan and Perrin, Vancouver;
 purchased from the latter
Christ Church Cathedral, Vancouver (St. Andrew and
 St. Barthomolmew), and the Vancouver Museum
 (St. James-the-Less)

These three panels formerly comprised parts of a series of
six two-light windows in the north and south aisles of the
church of St. John, at Cloughfold, Rawtenstall, Lancashire,
all three having been in the windows of the north aisle.
Subsequently, the SS Andrew and Bartholomew panels
were acquired by Christ Church Cathedral, Vancouver.
The Vancouver Museum acquired the St. James, lending
it to the cathedral in 1985 when the three were repaired,
re-leaded, and subsequently combined as a three-light window for the Burrard Street entrance to the cathedral.

The panels are typical of Morris glass done after the
death of Edward Burne-Jones, when J.H. Dearle became
chief designer. As usual, they are based on Burne-Jones and
Morris cartoons, with simplification in detail and an overall softening and flattening of form. The St. Bartholomew
panel derives from a Morris design of 1865: one of the
figures in the lancets of the East window of the church of
St. Stephen, Guernsey. The same composition was re-used
in later windows, including the great East window of
1894-95 for Holy Trinity, Sloane Street, Chelsea. In the
1905 Cloughfold design, the head of St. Bartholomew still
retains a distinctly 1860s hairstyle and beard, but with
modifications in shading and in the painting of the individual strands of hair.

The St. Andrew panel, perhaps the most satisfactory
of the three figures in colour and detail, belongs to the
third of a series of four Morris studio interpretations of
the subject. It derives from a Burne-Jones design dating
back to 1876, but is more immediately related to the St.
Andrew figure in the window at Holy Trinity, Chelsea.
The small head and lush, flowing beard have close parallels in the Old Testament prophets depicted in a window
of 1897 in King's College Chapel, Aberdeen. The strong
linear patterning of the strands of the beard and of the draperies are typical of the re-working of Burne-Jones designs
under Dearle in the first decade of the twentieth century.

The St. James belongs to the fifth of five variations on
the subject recognized by Sewter. The earliest version of
the composition is Burne-Jones's 1875 design for the par-
ish church at Coatbridge, Lanarkshire, which he himself
deplored. The cartoon served as the basis for yet another
of the figures at Holy Trinity, Chelsea in 1894-95. The
ample draperies and the somewhat small head are features
found in numerous Burne-Jones compositions of the 1870s,
and are in marked contrast to the more tightly wrapped
draperies with narrow folds that he also designed in the
1870s and '80s.

The quarry grounds of the glass from Cloughfold, simply and pleasingly rendered, derive from types dating back
to the 1860s and 1870s. The quarries with small petalled
flowers are traceable in Morris glass back to the lower border of the St. Philip window of c. 1872 in St. Michael's
Church, Waterford, Hertfordshire, while the plant with
trumpet-shaped flowers makes an early appearance in the
quarries of the chancel south window of 1868 in All Saints'
church, Middleton Cheney, Northamptonshire. The glass
from Cloughfold shows leading across the figures, breaking them up into mosaic-like quadrilaterals. This is a distinctive feature of late Morris glass, particularly evident
in glass from the 1880s and 1890s onwards. The technique
is controlled in the glass from Cloughfold, but in some
designs of the early 1900s it looks decidedly aberrant, the
leads and cutlines intruding excessively into the designs.

According to Sewter, the St. James and St. Andrew were
painted by Bowman, the St. Bartholomew by Titcomb.[14]

MORRIS STAINED GLASS *IN SITU* IN CANADA

Alice Hamilton lists Morris glass in Winnipeg.[15] Sewter
lists all the Morris glass he was able to find in Canada.[16]
His 1975 list has been supplemented by Marilyn Ibach,
with her initial list, 1984 update, and subsequent revised
list of 1985. Based on Hamilton, Ibach, and Sewter, Mor-

ris glass up to 1940 has been recorded (alphabetically by province and city) as follows:

CALGARY, ALBERTA

Cathedral Church of the Redeemer
1935 2-light window
Sewter gives the subjects as St. Alban and St. Martha; Ibach as St. Cyprian and St. Martha.

FREDERICTON, NEW BRUNSWICK

Wilmot United Church
1912 2-light window: SS Gabriel and Raphael (above); Clothing the Naked, Feeding the Hungry (below)
Cited in Sewter under "Ottawa," but with the note that the window is probably in Fredericton, where indeed it is.[17] Ibach cited the window for Fredericton,[18] but did not know of its location in Wilmot United Church. It is not included in her 1985 list of Morris windows in Canada. The Fredericton window was commissioned by Sen. F.B. Thompson in memory of his wife, who had died in 1906, and was dedicated in 1913. The commission from a member of the Canadian Senate explains the references to Ottawa in the Morris records. The order for the window was recorded on July 3, 1912. The craftsmen who worked on the lights were Titcomb, Stokes and Watson. A related drawing is in the Sanford and Berger Collection, California.

MONTREAL, QUEBEC

Montreal Museum of Fine Arts
1882 2 panels of minstrel figures (see No. D: 3)

Church of St. Andrew and St. Paul
1885 3-light window: Hope, Charity, Faith with Six
 Acts of Mercy
1903 3-light window: St. Martin, Prudence, Christ as
 Love, Justice, St. George, Humility

Crescent Street Church
1901 6-light window (destroyed by fire)

Royal Victoria Hospital
1902 5-light window: Faith, Charity, Christ as Love

Christ Church Cathedral
1902 3-light window: Eunice, Dorcas, and Priscilla
1911 2-light window: Clothing the Naked, Feeding
 the Hungry

NEWFOUNDLAND

1939 3-light window: St. Mary the Virgin, St. Mary,
 Christ on the Cross, and St. John (the Evangelist)

FIG. D: 1. *SS Gabriel and Raphael* (above); *Clothing the Naked, Feeding the Hungry* (below), two-light window, Wilmot United Church, 1912

The precise location of the church is given by neither Sewter nor Ibach.

OTTAWA, ONTARIO

c. 1861-62 Panel of painted and leaded glass in a wooden
 frame (see No. D: 1)
Private collection, Ottawa
Designed by Philip Webb for Red House, Bexleyheath, Kent.

VANCOUVER, BRITISH COLUMBIA

Christ Church Cathedral
1905 3-light window: SS James Minor, Andrew, and
 Bartholomew, from Cloughfold, Rawtenstall,
 Lancashire (see No. D: 4)

The Cloughfold glass was installed in its present form in Christ Church Cathedral in 1985. One of the three panels, the St. James Minor, is on loan to the cathedral from the Vancouver Museum. When Sewter published his 1975 catalogue, the glass was listed in his entry under Cloughfold.

Vancouver Art Gallery
1931 1-light window: Harmony, after Frank Dicksee
On permanent loan to the West Vancouver Public Library

St. Andrew's Wesley United Church
1936-37 6-light window: Sermon on the Mount
Duncan Dearle was apparently responsible for the design, which includes accompanying saints.

1936-37 5-light window: Ascension
The composition was by Duncan Dearle, after an earlier design by his father.

1937-38 3-light window: Christ Blessing Children
The composition was by Duncan Dearle, further glass by whom was designed for St. Andrew's after 1948. Sewter's catalogue also lists Ryerson United Church, Vancouver. This is by Duncan Dearle and dates from 1953-54.

VICTORIA, BRITISH COLUMBIA

1878 Timothy and Eunice
Private collection, British Columbia (see No. D: 1)
Commissioned in 1878 for David A.P. Watt of Montreal, and recorded by Sewter under his entries for Montreal and for Victoria (1975), this window is cited by Ibach as *Mary Instructing Jesus*.

WEST VANCOUVER, BRITISH COLUMBIA

St. Francis-in-the-Wood
1935 1-light window: Christ in Glory
    2-light window: Landscape
Sewter records the St. Francis-in-the-Wood windows in Caulfield, B.C. They were probably designed by Duncan Dearle. Sewter gives the dates of the St. Francis glass as 1935 and 1938, but information supplied by Carolyn M. Nicholson of West Vancouver gives the date of all three panels at St. Francis-in-the-Wood as 1935. Ibach gives the date as 1935, but confirms that Dearle was working on sketches for the windows in 1932.[19]

WINNIPEG, MANITOBA

All Saints Church
1927 1-light window: St. Cecilia

1928 3-light window: Crucifixion with angels and saints (chancel)
1928 3-light: Raising of Lazarus
1928 2 chapel windows: Virgin and Child (after Raphael's Sistine *Madonna*); St. Mildred
1930 1-light window: David (with harp)
1930 3-light window: Sermon on the Mount (cited in Hamilton as "Christ Blessing Children")[20]
1931 1-light window: St. Hilda (Lady Chapel)
1932 3-light window: Nativity
1935 3-light window: Christ in the Carpenter's Shop

Other Morris-style glass at All Saints by Duncan Dearle and by Lowndes and Drury dates from after 1940 and is outside the scope of this present study.[21]

ENDNOTES

1. *The Stained Glass of William Morris and his Circle* (New Haven and London, 1974), p. 20.
2. *Ibid.*, p. 16.
3. *Ibid.*, p. 43.
4. *Ibid.*, pl. 324.
5. *Ibid.*, pl. 568.
6. *Ibid.*, pl. 567.
7. *Ibid.*, pl. 624.
8. *Ibid.*, pl. 628.
9. *The Stained Glass of William Morris and his Circle: A Catalogue* (New Haven and London, 1975), p. 15.
10. *Ibid.*, p. 318.
11. *Ibid.*, p. 151.
12. *Ibid.*, pp. 15, 30.
13. "Morris and Company Stained Glass in North America", *The Journal of PreRaphaelite Studies* 5 (May 1985).
14. *The Stained Glass…A Catalogue*, pp. 53-4.
15. *Manitoba Stained Glass* (Winnipeg, 1970).
16. *The Stained Glass…A Catalogue*, pp. 214-17.
17. *Ibid.*, p. 216.
18. *William Morris & Company: Stained Glass in North America* (London, n.d.), p. 18.
19. *William Morris & Company…*, p. 13.
20. *Manitoba Stained Glass*, p. 182.
21. Glass formerly attributed to Morris & Co., in a private collection, Vancouver, at All Saints Anglican Church, Winnipeg (1932), and St. Luke's Anglican Church (c. 1921), although listed by Sewter and Ibach as authentic, has since been proven to be by other hands.

WALLPAPER

Katharine A. Lochnan

In its prospectus of 1861, Morris, Marshall, Faulkner & Co. stated its intention to undertake commissions for "any species of decoration, mural or otherwise, from pictures, properly so-called, down to the consideration of the smallest work susceptible of art beauty." After the Firm's display at the International Exhibition of 1862 created a demand for retail items, wallpaper was mentioned for the first time.

Throughout the previous decade, wallpaper had been the target of "design-reformers," led by A.W.N. Pugin and Owen Jones. The popular, highly naturalistic papers that had drawn their ire at the Great Exhibition of 1851 were rapidly supplanted by flat, abstract patterns deemed "morally superior."[1] One might well ask why, under the circumstances, Morris was drawn to wallpaper. The answer is to be found in the first pieces he designed in 1862. Employing motifs inspired by the Red House garden, and incorporating medieval and Japanese design ideas, *Daisy*, *Fruit* and *Trellis* (Nos. E: 6-8) were unapologetically naturalistic and three-dimensional, and constituted a revolt against the design-reformers themselves.

Because public taste was not yet ready for reorientation, the papers failed to sell. The business manager, Warington Taylor, who undertook to place Morris & Co. on a firm financial footing in 1865, dissuaded Morris from further experiments. It was only after Taylor's death in 1870 that Morris threw himself into wallpaper design, and it was during the 1870s that he produced the patterns that were to link his name inextricably to this medium. By this time, taste had shifted once again and Morris wallpaper found a ready market.

After trying unsuccessfully to print his first papers with zinc plates and transparent colours, Morris hired a block-cutter named Barret, from Bethnal Green. Tiring of supervising, he soon handed both block-cutting and printing over to the leading wallpaper manufacturer, Jeffrey and Co., of Islington. In consultation with Charles Eastlake, Metford Warner, the enlightened and

NO. E: 11. WILLIAM MORRIS, *Vine* (detail), 1874

sympathetic managing director of Jeffrey's, solicited wallpaper designs from artists. He was only too pleased to set up a special department to deal exclusively with Morris.

The artist began by making full-scale cartoons for the block-cutters using pencil, pen-and-ink and watercolour. He supervised the colour selection and continued to experiment with different combinations up to the last minute. Although the samples used by Morris as his reference-set are now in the Victoria and Albert Museum, it is far from easy to determine original colourways, as there are often several early variations. To complicate matters, successful patterns were issued intermittently in new colourways over a period of years. Early in this century, standards were evolved by Morris & Co. based on early colourways which are still referred to by Arthur Sanderson and Sons Ltd. Nonetheless, creative variations have been developed in response to changing tastes, most notably during the early 1970s when psychedelic colours were introduced.

NO. M: 20
FREDERICK HOLLYER,
Drawing Room, The Grange, 1887

NO. M: 21
FREDERICK HOLLYER,
*Margaret Burne-Jones's Bedroom,
The Grange,* 1887

Morris believed that, "the material being commonplace and the manufacture mechanical, the colour should above all things be modest."[2] He designed for the opaque body-colours then in use, making liberal use of his favourite "workaday green" and "holiday blue," and reserving touches of red and yellow for focal points. While tending toward grey tonalities in his papers, he had a horror of "muddy" or "dingy" colours. Brighter ones were used in light-toned papers.

While Morris saw wallpaper as a "makeshift" for the more desirable and expensive forms of wall-covering – murals, tapestry, and chintz (on a descending scale) – the market for wallpaper continued to expand as more and more properties, including Kelmscott Manor and The Grange, were held on a leasehold basis. Ford Madox Brown recalled how "[Burne-]Jones having moved into his new house gave a dance, a very swell affair, the house being newly decorated in the 'Firm' taste looked charming."[3] Burne-Jones selected *Jasmine* (1872) for use in the drawing-room (see No. M: 20), and *Lily* (1874) for Margaret's bedroom (see Nos. M: 21-22) at The Grange. After designing his first woven wool "tapestry" wall-covering in 1878, Morris used it in the drawing-room at Kelmscott House. Wallpaper was reserved for use in bedrooms.

To Morris, wall-treatments were the most important element in interior decoration, and he set out to educate public taste:

> Whatever you have in your rooms, think first of the walls; for they are that which makes your house and home; and if you don't make some sacrifice in their favour, you will find your chambers have a kind of makeshift lodging-house look about them, however rich and handsome your movables may be.[4]

Noting that "architectural effect depends upon a nice balance of horizontal, vertical and oblique lines in a room", Morris maintained that wallpaper should be selected based on "the character of the room to be decorated, on the extent of wall-space to be covered, on the amount and kind of light in the room, on the colour of the timber."[5] He believed that it was better to have "plain whitewashed walls" than to be tempted by "false economy" into buying cheap wallpaper, and viewed his own papers as a good long-term investment. Like all of Morris's productions, the paper was so expensive to produce by hand, and employed such high-quality materials, that it was priced beyond the pocket of the working man.

Walter Crane astutely observed that Morris's patterns were "decorative poems."[6] The poet in Morris believed that beauty, imagination and order were essential in successful pattern-designs.[7] Having reached the pinnacle of his achievement in the late 1870s, Morris spread his ideas through lectures addressed to artisans: "The Lesser Arts" (1877), "Making the Best of It" (1880), and "Some Hints on Pattern-Designing" (1881). His major themes were encapsulated in this statement:

> In all patterns which are meant to fill the eye and satisfy the mind, there should be a certain mystery. We should not be able to read the whole thing at once, nor desire to do so, nor be impelled by that desire to go on tracing line after line to find out how the pattern is made, and I think that the obvious presence of a geometrical order, if it be, as it should be, beautiful, tends toward this end, and prevents our feeling restless over a pattern.[8]

Morris believed that "any decoration is futile... when it does not remind you of something beyond itself, of something of which it is but a visible symbol."[9] Even when the motif or formal pattern-structure was suggested by another work of art, he returned to nature for inspiration. Seeking to "turn a room into a bower, a refuge," he returned to such touchstones as the English countryside, its hedgerows, and native field and garden flowers.

Morris did not hold with "vagueness" in drawing, believing that good designs required "definite form bounded by firm outline." He held that

"for the imagination to come in", nature must be conventionalized. His conventions were inspired by a variety of sources ranging from medieval tapestries and ancient herbals to Italian and Near-Eastern fabrics and Persian and Oriental carpets. He depicted plant forms in shallow relief with just enough hatching to suggest their existence in more. than one dimension, but not enough to create a tension between the pattern and the surface plane of the paper. He studied the growth patterns and structure of plants, trees and vines, and infused his vigorous designs with the quality he called "rational growth."[10]

Peter Floud has divided Morris wallpaper designs into four distinct groups. These are preceded by the three experimental papers of 1862-64 – *Daisy, Fruit* or *Pomegranate*, and *Trellis* (Nos. E: 6-8) – which are characterized by naturalism and clearly articulated pattern repeats. During the first period (1872-76), best represented by *Vine* (Nos. E: 10-11), Morris concealed the repeats among intricate and elaborate patterns. Following this period, in the mid-1870s, his style changed under the spell of historicism. To Morris scholars, this supposed loss of innocence and getting of wisdom is analogous to the Fall and Expulsion from Eden. Naturalism was greatly reduced and the structure of the design, including the repeat, was emphasized. The second period (1876-82), characterized by *Sunflower* (No. E: 14), saw the introduction of symmetrical ogee and oval "turnover" patterns adapted from woven textiles, which Morris studied in the South Kensington Museums

NO. E: 7. WILLIAM MORRIS, *Fruit* or *Pomegranate* (detail), 1864

(now the Victoria and Albert Museum). The designs of the third period (1883-90), especially *Wild Tulip* (No. E: 15), are said to reflect the diagonal pattern structure of a magnificent Italian Renaissance velvet acquired by the V & A in 1883. The eclectic fourth period (1890-96) saw a partial return to the naturalism of the early work.[11]

In all, Morris designed forty-one wallpapers and five ceiling-papers. Forty-one patterns were produced for the Firm by his pupils, John Henry Dearle (Nos. E: 19-20), Kate Faulkner (No. E: 18), Kathleen Kersey (No. E: 21), and May Morris, ten of them during his lifetime. Walter Crane, an associate of Morris & Co., also produced papers for Jeffrey and Co. (see No. A: 22).

The production of wallpaper is the only area of Morris's activity that survives to the present day, and it is for this that he is best-known. In 1930 Jeffrey and Co. closed down, and Morris & Co. transferred the wallpaper printing operation to the Perivale factory of Arthur Sanderson and Co. When Morris & Co. went into voluntary liquidation in 1940, Sanderson's purchased the blocks. Although many still remain in its possession, others were lost or discarded at critical junctures.

NO. E: 10
WILLIAM MORRIS,
Vine (detail), 1874

WOOD BLOCKS

No. E: 1

Block for the *St. James's Pattern* 1881
65.4 x 55.2 cm
Pearwood
Arthur Sanderson Canada Inc.

No. E: 2

Block for the *St. James's Pattern* 1881
Pearwood with metal strips
66.0 x 54.6 cm
Arthur Sanderson Canada Inc.

These are two of the sixty-eight blocks and four change-blocks required to produce the most ambitious of all patterns, the *St. James's* pattern (No. E: 3). Because the cost of production is prohibitive, the original blocks have never been reprinted, and remain in their original condition.

Morris's wallpaper blocks were made by professional block-cutters at Jeffrey and Co. from full-scale cartoons executed by Morris in pencil, ink, and watercolour wash.

Broad areas of pattern were printed from flat wooden plateaux standing in high relief above deeply chiselled valleys. Fine lines were printed from ridges of flat brass wire driven edgeways into the wood block. Brass pins were pounded into place to create a stippled effect.

Because larger blocks would be too heavy and unwieldy, they are always twenty-one inches square. Except in a few instances, each block contains one pattern-repeat and is used to print a single colour. Blocks used to print two colours are coloured by hand. Very large patterns require two or even three blocks to print each colour element of the pattern. These are referred to as "change blocks."

Morris's original wood-blocks remained in production for decades. Many were acquired by Sanderson's from Morris & Co. in 1940. Most of the ones used to print popular patterns have since been replaced with replicas. Block-making technology has changed over time. Made of highly absorptive pearwood, the original blocks swelled quickly when immersed in water and released paint easily during the printing process. When they became cracked and worn from the cycle of soaking, printing, and dehydration and could no longer be repaired, they were withdrawn from production. Blocks that contain metal inserts are more likely to become uneven over time than blocks made exclu-

NO. E: 1

NO. E: 2

sively of wood or of metal: moisture makes the wood swell while the copper remains unchanged.

The pearwood blocks were replaced initially with blocks made of wood laminates (including sycamore), which were somewhat less absorptive. Wood itself was ultimately replaced first with plastic compound on wood, then with laser-cut rubber compound blocks, which do not absorb moisture. Plastic and rubber do not have the same physical properties as wood; since their surfaces are hard and firm, they tend to push the paint toward the perimeter of the pattern-elements. Several generations of blocks are currently in use at Sanderson's, even in the printing of a single pattern.

The original printing process used by Jeffrey and Co. is very similar to the one used today at Sanderson's factory at Brook Mill, Lower Darwen, Lancashire. The colours were mixed with size and put in shallow trays or wells into which the blocks were dipped. The latter were suspended from above by a cord, and guided by the workman's hand from the well of colour to the paper which lay flat on a table before him. Each colour was allowed to dry before another was superimposed.[12] Today, one printer can print eight rolls of monochrome wallpaper a day.[13]

MATCHPIECE

No. E: 3
_____

WILLIAM MORRIS

St. James's 1881
Clark 28, Morris 126-7[14]
68 blocks and 4 change-blocks
Hand-block-printed matchpiece
10.6 m x 55.9 cm; repeat: 119.4 x 111.8 cm
Arthur Sanderson Canada Inc.

This is one of two *St. James's* broken-down matchpieces printed by Sanderson's from the original blocks. Intended as cartoons for the use of the printer, matchpieces begin with samples of each colour to be used and the number(s) of the block(s) required to print it. The blocks are then printed in sequence to demonstrate the cumulative build-up of colour and pattern. The block containing the outline is the last to be printed.

This pattern is composed of fifteen colours plus yellow and white (seventeen colours in all), printed from sixty-eight woodblocks and four change-blocks. Because of its large scale, two blocks are required for each vertical

NO. E: 3

repeat, which falls across two widths of paper.

The commission to work on a decorative scheme in St. James's Palace, London, begun in 1865, was the first non-ecclesiastical commission received by the Firm, and one of only two public commissions ever undertaken by it. The *St. James's* pattern was designed for use in the Wellington Room.

This flamboyant paper, with its rich, dotted acanthus meander, is closely related to Morris's designs for tapestry and embroidery (see No. F: 2). It employs the symmetrical "turnover" structure characteristic of the third period (No. E: 15). A net of ogees or ovals gives the pattern its stately and formal appearance.

WALLPAPER PATTERN BOOKS

No. E: 4
_____

Wallpaper Pattern book c. 1899-1916
Vol. A 16
183 sheets of wallpaper samples
82.5 x 65.1 x 4.4 cm
Each sheet identified on the *verso* in the centre with the
    name of the pattern, Log Book colourway number
    and price
Mid-green linen binding, cover printed in black letter-

ing: "Morris and Co. Ltd., 449 [Oxford] Street [London] N.W. W[ALLPAP]ERS", partly obscured by the superimposed white paper label printed in red: "New Address – Morris and Company, Ltd., 17 George Street, Hanover Square, London, W.1."
Private collection, Ottawa

No. E: 5

Wallpaper Pattern book c. 1899-1916
Vol. B 7
185 sheets of wallpaper samples
83.2 x 66.0 x 3.8 cm
Each sheet identified on the *verso* as above
Binding, lettering, and label same as above
Private collection, Ottawa

It is extremely difficult to date Morris & Co. wallpaper sample-books, as they were in use for many years, and do not bear publication dates. This set post-dates the production of *Myrtle*, which was added to the repertoire in

1899, and predates the move by Morris & Co. to George St. in 1917.

It corresponds to the earliest of three sets of pattern books housed in the library of the William Morris Gallery at Walthamstow, which were replaced following the move to George St., first by a set of similar proportions bound with glossy dark-green covers and bearing the new address in yellow, then by a much smaller, grey-cloth-bound set, the cover bearing the George St. address in black.

MORRIS WALLPAPER SAMPLES

THE PAPERS OF 1862-64

No. E: 6

WILLIAM MORRIS

Daisy 1864
Clark 1, Morris 3
11 blocks plus one old block

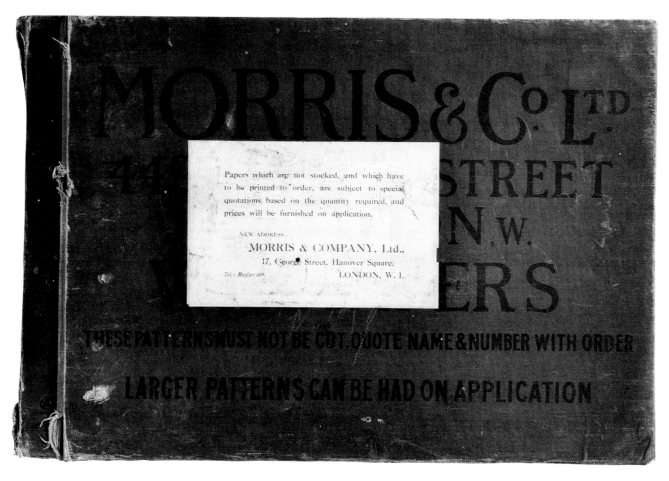

NO. E: 4

NO. E: 6

Hand-block-printed wallpaper
74.9 x 56.5 cm; repeat: 35.6 x 26.7 cm
Arthur Sanderson Canada Inc.

Although this was the first paper to appear on the market, it was the second to be designed in 1862. An inscription in the Log Book indicates that "one old block" was employed – no doubt a block cut by Mr. Barret of Bethnal Green before the transfer of this operation to Jeffrey and Co.

Like most early papers, *Daisy* was issued in three colourways in different tonal ranges, the pattern reversed in shallow relief out of a grey, white or pale-blue ground. The apportioning of colour demonstrates Morris's extensive use of "holiday" blue and "workaday" green; yellow and red, used sparingly, appear to jump out of the composition.

The conventionalized flower-forms used in the wallpaper recall the verdure of the medieval tapestries that Morris so greatly admired. The daisy motif is related to one designed by Morris for the *Daisy* hanging in 1860, the *Daisy* tiles of c. 1865 (No. H: 18), and numerous quarries for stained glass. Employing his knowledge of tile design, he brought order to bear on the pattern by evenly spacing

clumps of daisies, columbines, and two unidentifiable flowers[15] in alternating horizontal bands, which "punctuate the background," creating a "powdered" effect. While the pattern appears two-dimensional, a few lines of shading are used to suggest the three-dimensional nature of the sprightly plant-forms. A second plane is subtly indicated by touches of green which, by suggesting grass, heighten the naturalistic effect and facilitate the chromatic integration of pattern and ground.

This bold, heraldic pattern echoes Morris's love of the Middle Ages. It is very sophisticated, its so-called naivety fresh and deliberate. Based on four English field flowers, it could turn any room into a *hortus conclusus*. Not surprisingly, it headed the sales of Morris wallpaper practically without a break for fifty years.

This sheet (like Nos. E: 7-8) comes from the large floor-mounted stand-books which could be seen in the Morris & Co. shop.

No. E: 7

WILLIAM MORRIS

Fruit or *Pomegranate* 1864
Clark 2, Morris 6
12 blocks
Hand-block-printed wallpaper
74.9 x 56.5 cm; repeat: 53.5 x 53.5 cm
Arthur Sanderson Canada Inc.

This was the third paper to be designed in 1862, and the second to be issued in 1864. It appeared in three colourways nicknamed "dark," "light" and "No. 3" on grey, cream, and blue grounds, respectively. This variation was called "blue fruit" in the Log Book.

Morris identified "the branch formed on a diagonal line" as one of the underlying structures of Gothic design. While this pattern is based on the square grid used to design tiles, a staple of the Firm at this time, the division of each repeat into quadrants is masked by the way in which "a diagonal stem throws off leaf and fruit so as to present a fairly even distribution of forms."[16]

The pattern was conceived in three planes. All the fruits are shown in profile, with the exception of the pomegranate; seen from a variety of vantage-points, it appears almost to project from the surface of the paper. Dotting and hatching are used to give the fruit a naturalistic, three-dimensional quality. The network of branches, fruit and

flowers is superimposed over a delicate monochrome tracery composed of twigs and berries; this is reversed out of
a blue ground, giving the pattern a sense of infinite depth.

Peaches, oranges, lemons and pomegranates would not
have been found in the English country garden, but they
were to be seen in Victorian glass-houses and conservato-
ries. The style, execution and choice of colour bring to
mind medieval tapestries and manuscript illuminations.
Ripe fruits, especially pomegranates with their seeds revealed, are symbols of fertility, sexuality, and death. Morris was well aware of the symbolic meaning ascribed to
plants, flowers and fruits. In 1871 Rossetti began a series
of images of Jane Morris as *Proserpine* (see No. A: 44) holding a pomegranate in her hand.

This paper would have had the desired effect of turning any room into a bower. Similar motifs were used on
the walls and painted panels of the Green Dining Room
in the South Kensington Museums, which the Firm decorated in 1866.

No. E: 8

___

WILLIAM MORRIS

Trellis 1864
Clark 3, Morris 7
12 blocks
Hand-block-printed wallpaper
75.6 x 57.1 cm; repeat: 53.3 x 53.3 cm
Arthur Sanderson Canada Inc.

This was the first paper designed by Morris in November
1862 but, owing to delays in cutting the blocks, it was the
third one issued. Although Morris experimented with
light-green, dark-green and pink grounds in the cartoon,
the paper was issued on charcoal, light-grey, white, and
blue grounds.

This paper is said to have been inspired by the trellises
that bordered the central quadrangle at Red House; however, the rose trellis had long been a popular wallpaper
motif. Morris loved the simple wild rose which "grows in
every hedge...[,] nothing can be more beautiful than a
wayside bush of it, nor can any scent be as sweet and pure
as its scent."[17] It is rich in symbolism, being associated with
the Virgin Mary, Arthurian legend, the Tudor Renaissance,
and England itself.

Based on tile designs, each repeat is conceived as four
quadrants corresponding to the grid of the trellis, knit
together by the vigorously intertwining branch and diag-

NO. E: 8

onal stems of the old single rose. The flatness of pattern
and ground recalls the spatial structure of Japanese woodblock prints. The first major public display of Japanese
ukiyoe prints took place in London in April 1862 in the
"Japanese Court" of the International Exhibition. On
viewing it, William Burges came to the conclusion that

> to any student of our reviving arts of the thirteenth century an
> hour or even a day or two spent in the Japanese Department
> will by no means be lost time, for these hitherto unknown
> barbarians appear not only to know all that the middle ages
> knew but in some respects are beyond them and us as well.[18]

Along with Burges and Godwin, Rossetti purchased *ukiyoe*
prints from the display, which quickly became the rage
among his friends.[19]

The birds in the cartoon (and probably the dragonflies)
were added by Philip Webb, who supplied the animals in
the Firm's early stained glass. The motifs and style of execution recall the woodcut illustrations in the most famous
of all Japanese books, Hokusai's *Manga*, the bible of the
early *japonistes*. Although the birds are modelled on the
Tit, they are not ornithologically accurate.

No. E: 9

WILLIAM MORRIS

Lily 1874
Clark 13, Morris 367
8 blocks
Hand-block-printed wallpaper
55.2 x 33.6 cm; repeat: 30.5 x 53.3 cm
Provenance: Ian Hodgkins and Co. Ltd.
Private collection, Ottawa

In creating this variation on his best-selling paper, *Daisy*, Morris may have been motivated in part by financial considerations. It was produced in only one colourway.

The flowers are of the simple garden variety loved by Morris, and include lilies, bluebells and daisies. Although the compositional structure is based on that of *Daisy*, the motifs are more widely spaced, and the overall effect is lighter and airier. By replacing the grassy background with one of willow boughs, Morris broke with the naturalism of his early period. Removed from their natural setting, the flowers are transformed into formal motifs.

The same delicate willow background reappears in *Powdered* (No. E: 12), before being promoted to the status of a dominant motif in *Willow* (No. E: 13) and *Willow Boughs* (No. E: 17). The motif is thought to originate in the depiction of the osier in John Gerard's *Herball; or Generall Historie of Plantes*, published in 1633.

No. E: 10

WILLIAM MORRIS

Vine 1874
Clark 14, Morris 45
9 blocks
Hand-block-printed wallpaper
55.9 x 39.4 cm; repeat: 53.3 x 53.3 cm
Provenance: Ian Hodgkins and Co. Ltd.
Private collection, Ottawa

This pattern, one of the most beautiful of Morris's designs and the masterpiece of his first period (1872-76), was originally issued in two colourways nicknamed in the Log Book "olive vine" and "blue vine," the second of which is represented here. In colour and design it recalls medieval tapestries.

This paper demonstrates Morris's close observation of nature and illustrates to perfection the principle of "rational growth" outlined in his 1881 lecture, "Some Hints on Pattern-Designing", in which he maintained that "no stem should be so far from its parent stock as to look weak and wavering", and that "even where a line ends it should look as if it had plenty of capacity for more growth." The pattern "covers the ground equally and richly", a characteristic Morris believed was "the very test of capacity in a designer." He concealed the repeats through the use of an intricate meandering pattern (reminiscent of medieval scrollwork) that illustrates his maxim: "the more and the more mysteriously you interweave your sprays and stems the better."

This pattern has pagan and Christian associations which give it a sense of mystery. The vine hung with grapes was associated with the god Bacchus and jolly goings-on in the classical world; chiselled in stone on Romanesque and Gothic capitals, it symbolized the Christian mystery of transubstantiation. (Morris was very fond of the grape and good fellowship, and regularly emerged from his cellar brandishing bottles of wine.)

Vine was adapted by William De Morgan during the early Fulham period (1888-97) in the design of a tile (No. H: 36). It was one of Morris's favourite motifs in designing ornamental borders and panels for Kelmscott publications in the 1890s (see No. A: 29).

No. E: 11

WILLIAM MORRIS

Vine 1874
Clark 14, Morris 80
9 blocks
Hand-block-printed wallpaper
Complete roll: 57.1 cm (wide); repeat: 53.3 x 53.3 cm
Provenance: David A.P Watt; Edmund N. Parker
Maltwood Art Museum and Gallery, University of
    Victoria, British Columbia

Responding to the contemporary taste for rich surfaces that was fuelled by enthusiasm for Renaissance tooled and gilded Spanish-leather wall-hangings, Morris & Co. in the 1870s began to produce expensive gilt and lacquer versions of some papers of the 1870s, among them *Sunflower* (No. E: 15) and *Vine*.

This extraordinary colourway, nicknamed "gold lacquer" in the Log Book, was on the market by 1884, when

NO. E: 9

NO. E: 12

the first order was recorded.[20] It was printed using green and black paint and dark-brown lacquer on gold foil which was subtly embossed using a roller to create a crinkled effect, resembling the grain of leather. This fragile surface was backed with thick, fibrous yellow paper.

These expensive variations retained their popularity for some time. The Morris & Co. catalogue published c. 1913 indicates that "The *Vine, Sunflower, Acorn,* and *Lily and Pomegranate* designs can be had in various rich colourings with gold and lacquer in some cases with the design embossed." Although *Vine* was "frequently printed in gold and colours", it is unlikely that, at 25 to 40 shillings a piece, this was a stock item. A notice on the back of the sample in the pattern book for c. 1916 (No. E: 5) indicates that this variation was "printed to order."

By changing the colours of the pigments and incorporating metallic foils and lacquers, Morris was able to achieve completely different effects using the same woodblocks. The gilt version of *Vine* is closely related in concept to gold-ground painting and manuscript illumination, whereas the soft matte surface of "olive" and "blue" *Vine* gives the illusion of tapestry. Pale green over gold in "gold" *Vine* gives the fruit, leaves and tendrils the appearance of standing in high relief against a dark ground, whereas the much closer range of colours and tones used in "olive" and "blue" *Vine* makes all the design elements appear to exist in much the same plane.

Morris wallpapers were sold in rolls dubbed "English size," which were 11.0 m x 53.3 cm wide. Given the provenance of this exceptionally well-preserved roll and the similar roll of *Sunflower* (No. E: 15), it is likely that it was ordered by David A.P. Watt for his house in Montreal.

No. E: 12

WILLIAM MORRIS

Powdered 1874
Clark 15, Morris 234
7 blocks
Hand-block-printed wallpaper
55.9 x 36.8 cm; repeat: 26.7 x 52.1 cm
Provenance: Edward D. Nudelman, Seattle, 1992
Private collection, Ottawa

In *Powdered* – a variation on *Lily* (No. E: 9) – the flower motifs are reduced in scale from vigorous clumps to animated sprigs which punctuate the ground, giving the pattern a "powdered" appearance. They anticipate the

terracotta tiles used liberally during the late 1870s and 1880s to decorate the facades of the new red-brick Queen Anne buildings which were the architectural expression of the Aesthetic Movement. The delicate white willow pattern reversed out of the sunny yellow ground is very much in tune with the taste of the Movement, which was hitting its stride by the mid-1870s. This pattern was later produced as a chintz.

No. E: 13

WILLIAM MORRIS

Willow 1874
Clark 17, Morris 49
3 blocks
Hand-block-printed wallpaper
47.0 x 39.4 cm; repeat: 44.4 x 53.3 cm
Provenance: Ian Hodgkins and Co. Ltd.
Private collection, Ottawa

This light, airy pattern was extremely popular and very much in line with the taste of the Aesthetes. It was issued in at least eleven different colourways. Aymer Vallance notes that it is under-printed with hawthorn blossoms.[21]

While it continues to enjoy a traditional association with the English countryside and its riverbanks, *Willow* also appealed to the contemporary taste for things Japanese and for blue-and-white "willow pattern" china, which became the rage in artistic circles during the 1870s.

Similar motifs were to be found in Japanese prints and *objets d'art* of all kinds. When, in 1875, Arthur Lasenby Liberty opened his shop on Regent Street, which catered primarily to the Japanese taste, Morris, along with Rossetti and Burne-Jones, was among his first customers.

NO. E: 13

No. E: 14

WILLIAM MORRIS

Sunflower 1879
Clark 25, Morris 433
1 block
Hand-block-printed wallpaper
57.1 x 57.1 cm; repeat: 40.6 x 53.3 cm
Private collection, Ottawa

By 1879 the sunflower motif was closely associated with the Aesthetic Movement, but its use in the Morris circle can be traced back to the Oxford Union frescoes of 1857. There are few more magnificent patterns in Morris's repertoire.

This is the foremost example of the use of the vertical "turnover" pattern which Morris derived from his study of historic woven textiles at the South Kensington Museums, where he became an examiner of student work in 1876. It is in every way characteristic of the second period of his wallpaper production, in which the plant forms conform to symmetrical ogee and oval patterns, naturalism is greatly reduced, and the structure and framework of the design are emphasized.[22] In keeping with Morris's principles of design, the geometric structure of *Sunflower* limits the desire of the viewer to trace out the lines of this complex pattern.

Morris was to explore these design ideas in his woven textiles (No. F: 22). In this pattern, the monochromatic design is reversed out of a dark ground, creating what Morris referred to as a "damask effect."

No. E: 15

WILLIAM MORRIS

Sunflower 1879
Clark 25, Morris 132
1 block
Hand-block-printed wallpaper
Complete roll: 57.1 cm (wide); repeat: 40.6 x 53.3 cm
Lozenge-shaped registration mark indicates that this roll
    was printed 21 January 1879
Provenance: David A.P. Watt; Edmund N. Parker
Maltwood Art Museum and Gallery, University of
    Victoria, British Columbia, 1974

Originally ordered by David A.P. Watt for his house in Montreal, this is one of two rolls in the collection of the Maltwood Art Museum and Gallery.

NO. E: 16

A note in the Morris & Co. catalogue of c. 1913 reads: "probably the most popular of all William Morris designs for monochrome wallpaper[,] it is printed in a great variety of shades and can also be hand-embossed in gold and bronze colours."

This expensive variation was first issued during the 1880s, as the first order recorded in the Log Book is dated 1889.[23] The transparent brown lacquer prints unevenly on the gold foil, pooling and creating a rich effect, reminiscent of gilded Spanish leather. This was always an expensive variation; a notice on the back of the sample in the pattern book of c. 1916 (No. E: 5) indicates that it was "printed to order."

This paper was used in one of the smaller rooms of St. James's Palace (see No. E: 3).

THE THIRD PERIOD: 1883-90

No. E: 16

WILLIAM MORRIS

Wild Tulip 1884
Clark 32, Morris 162
18 change-blocks
Hand-block-printed wallpaper
55.2 x 43.2 cm; repeat: 64.8 x 26.7 cm
Provenance: Ian Hodgkins Co. Ltd.
Private collection, Ottawa

A variation on the pattern-structure known as "the branch formed on the diagonal line," this paper was produced in at least seven different colourways.

Peter Floud maintains that *Wild Tulip*, with its exotic conventionalized blossom, was directly inspired by a spectacular Italian Renaissance velvet acquired by the South Kensington Museums in 1883. By this time, Morris was considered such an authority by the museum that he was made an adviser on the acquisition of historic textiles. It is clear, however, that Morris's interest in the structure of Renaissance textile patterns began at a much earlier date. A related pattern may be seen in his cartoon for stained glass, *St. Agnes and St. Alban in Procession*, of c.1864 (No. A: 6).

No. E: 17

W I L L I A M   M O R R I S

Willow Boughs 1887
Clark 35, Morris 210
3 blocks
Hand-block-printed wallpaper
55.9 x 46.0 cm; repeat: 72.4 x 26.7 cm
Private collection, Ottawa

Willow (No. E: 13) was reworked into the slightly heavier pattern *Willow Boughs*, the most popular paper to appear between 1876 and 1892.

NO. E: 17

NO. E: 18

WALLPAPERS BY OTHER DESIGNERS

No. E: 18

K A T E   F A U L K N E R

Mallow 1879
Morris 425
1 block
Hand-block-printed wallpaper
33.0 x 53.3 cm
Private collection, Ottawa

The sister of Charles Faulkner, one of the original partners of the Morris firm, Kate Faulkner painted tiles with other members of the Firm in 1861. She also designed wallpapers for Jeffrey and Co. that drew on her experience in tile design.

This sample is taken from the end of a roll and shows the beginning of the pattern on the block.

No. E: 19

J O H N   H E N R Y   D E A R L E

Tom Tit 1897[24]
Morris 340
8 rollers
Machine-printed wallpaper
21.4 x 54.0 cm
Private collection, Ottawa

After Morris's death in 1896, Dearle became art director of the Firm and designed most of the new textiles and wall-

NO. E: 19

papers. Employing naturalistic motifs of birds on a rose bush, this paper recalls Morris's first wallpaper, *Trellis* (No. E: 8).

Morris objected to seeing his own papers printed by machine, believing that machine-printing brought with it both loss of quality and alienation of the worker.[25] However, he did agree to allow six designs by Dearle and Faulkner to be machine-printed. The Morris & Co. catalogue of c.1913 states that papers were "supplied to fill the need for cheap wall-hangings in unimportant parts of the house. They have not the body of colour or lasting quality of hand-blocked papers, and may fade where the others will not."

The process employed steam power. The design was reproduced by brass wire on rollers and all the tints were printed at once. According to Walter Crane, whose papers were frequently printed this way, the pattern was often imperfect and blurred.[26]

No. E: 20

JOHN HENRY DEARLE

Golden Lily 1899
Morris 360
11 blocks
Hand-block-printed wallpaper
80.0 x 55.2 cm
Private collection, Ottawa

Dearle was originally hired in 1878 to design backgrounds in tapestries at Merton Abbey. This pattern, with its rich acanthus meander, draws on his experience.

In *Golden Lily* Dearle demonstrates his ability to gen-erate patterns which are so close to Morris in style and colour that they have often been mistakenly attributed to him. Having absorbed the substance of Morris's lecture of 1881, "Some Hints on Pattern-Designing", Dearle has used green and blue liberally, while being sparing with his reds and yellows. Inspired by Morris's dramatic patterns of the 1880s, such as the *St. James's* pattern (No. E: 3), he gener-ally worked on an even larger scale than his mentor.

No. E: 21

KATHLEEN KERSEY

Arbutus 1903
Morris 493
8 blocks
Hand-block-printed wallpaper
63.5 x 55.9 cm
Private collection, Ottawa

This pattern, while demonstrating modernist *japoniste* tendencies, draws inspiration for its motif from Morris's wallpaper *Fruit* or *Pomegranate* (No. E: 7).

The pattern is based on Morris's concept of the "branch formed on the diagonal." The shallow space is given a sense of depth by superimposing the arbutus over a background of abstracted leaf-forms. The designer has taken Morris's advice to heart in giving prominence to green and blue, and reserving red for highlights.

NO. E: 21

NO. E: 20

ENDNOTES

1. Aymer Vallance, "The Decorative Art of Sir Edward Burne-Jones, Baronet", *The Easter Art Annual* (extra number of *The Art Journal*) (1900): 4.

2. "Some Hints on Pattern-Designing", first published 1881, reprinted in *The Collected Works of William Morris*, ed. May Morris, vol. 22 (London, 1914), pp. 191-92.

3. Quoted in William Waters, *Burne-Jones: An Illustrated Life of Sir Edward Burne-Jones, 1833-1898* (Aylesbury, Bucks.: Shire Publications Ltd., 1973), p. 22.

4. "The Lesser Arts of Life", a lecture delivered in 1882, published in *The Collected Works...*, vol. 22, p. 262.

5. *The Morris Exhibit at the Foreign Fair, Boston, 1883-84* (Boston: 1883), p. 18-20.

6. "William Morris and His Work", *William Morris to Whistler: Papers and Addresses in Art and Craft and the Commonweal* (London, 1911), p. 4.

7. "Some Hints on Pattern-Designing," pp. 180-84.

8. *Ibid.*, p. 177.

9. *Ibid.*

10. *Ibid.*, p. 199.

11. Peter Floud, "The Wallpaper Designs of William Morris", *The Penrose Annual*, vol. 54 (London, 1960), pp. 41-5.

12. Walter Crane, "Of Wallpapers" (London, 1893), p. 56.

13. For a description of the process used today, see Christine Woods, "Chip off the Old Block", *Traditional Interior Decoration* (April-May 1988): 84-92.

14. "Clark" refers to Fiona Clark, *William Morris: Wallpapers and Chintzes* (London, 1973); "Morris" is an abbreviation for Morris & Co. Printing Logs – manuscript log books housed in the Sanderson and Co. archives, Uxbridge, England, which contain small samples of each colourway and are organized chronologically.

15. Morris, for all that he consulted nature, used his imagination in the design of flowers and plants.

16. Ray Watkinson, *William Morris as a Designer* (New York, 1967), p. 45.

17. "Making the Best of It", c. 1879, *The Collected Works...*, vol. 22, p. 88.

18. Quoted in Elizabeth Aslin, *The Aesthetic Movement: Prelude to Art Nouveau* (New York, 1969), p. 81.

19. See *Le Japonisme* (Paris: La Réunion des musées nationaux, Musée d'Orsay, and La Fondation du Japon, Musée national d'art occidental, 1988), p. 74.

20. Morris and Co. Log Book.

21. Aymer Vallance, *The Life and Work of William Morris* (London, 1887; reprinted 1986), p. 89.

22. Floud, "The Wallpaper Designs of William Morris".

23. The order reads: "20 pces 26/1/89."

24. This is the earliest date inscribed in the Morris and Co. Log Book.

25. Surface roller-printing enabled the British wallpaper industry to produce 19,000,000 rolls per annum by 1860, but the products were not universally admired. In 1865, the year Morris produced his first papers, it was reported that "the conviction among all practical men, is that the anticipations, whether for good or evil, respecting the introduction of machinery into paper-staining are now fainter and feebler than at any period during the last 20 years." The paper used was thinner and of poorer quality, and the machine-process deposited less colour on the surface of the paper than hand-printing, frequently causing blurring and a loss of delicacy of line. Quoted in Greg Smith and Sarah Hyde, *Walter Crane: Artist, Designer and Socialist* (London, 1989), p. 60.

26. Crane, "Of Wallpapers", p. 59.

T E X T I L E S

Linda Parry

William Morris's interest in cloth as an important decorative accessory, as well as an important art form in itself, has always separated him from his peers. He was born of an enquiring generation that did much to improve the design of commercial manufacture, though he alone was fundamental in reviving traditional techniques, utilizing this knowledge as both designer and practitioner to produce new and original effects. He was by no means the first to advocate improvements or suggest that history had some of the answers. Before him, A.W.N. Pugin (1812-1852), Owen Jones (1809-1874) and Christopher Dresser (1834-1904) all wrote authoritative and discursive texts and produced designs to back up their theories. The designers, however, did not involve themselves in manufacture beyond a cursory knowledge of technique, so that, unlike Morris, they were unable fully to exploit the qualities of different fibres and of mixing texture, colour and weight. It is this innate ability to balance highly original design with innovative manufacture that makes Morris one of the most original designers of his or any other generation. As in most cases, however, success started from modest beginnings.

Lacking the equipment to weave and print textiles, Morris turned first to embroidery, a technique he was able to carry out simply with needle and cloth. His earliest examples are panels of haphazard layers of erratic stitches worked to produce thick, tapestry-like panels.[1] These show the type of idealized designs to be expected from a youth besotted with Arthurian legends and the concept of chivalry. Within a short time of his marriage, he had designed a series of embroideries for the decoration of his own home, the Red House, Bexleyheath.[2] These took the form of wall-hangings and were sewn by a group organized by Jane Morris and comprising friends and relatives. It is not known what Morris's initial, commercially worked domestic embroideries looked like, although it is probable that the first years of production concentrated on private commissions for friends and the decoration of the houses of the various members of the group.[3] Morris, Marshall,

NO. F: 1. WILLIAM MORRIS, *Embroidered curtain* (detail), probably designed and worked between 1870 and 1875

145

Faulkner & Co.'s début, at the 1862 London International Exhibition, included only church furnishings, despite an early circular from the firm boasting "embroidery of all kinds." It was not until the 1870s that commercial production began in earnest and from this time a very systematic development in both technique and design can be followed.

The three Morris embroideries now found in Canada (Nos. F: 1-3) represent significant periods in his output and cover a span from Morris's formative years as a designer to a time of high sophistication and commercial success enjoyed by Morris & Co. at the end of the nineteenth century. The example from the Maltwood Art Museum and Gallery, in Victoria, British Columbia – one of the earliest-known Morris embroidery designs – is both rare and important, despite its modest appearance. The stitching is rudi-

mentary but controlled and clearly dates from the period when the production of commercial embroidery was in its infancy. The colouring is stronger than in the only other known examples of this pattern (in the Victoria and Albert Museum) and, until this piece came to light, the London set, specially designed for the Ionides family, who were both clients and friends of Morris, was thought to be unique. Edmund N. Parker, who donated it, was also responsible for presenting the Museum with one of the earliest dateable printings of one of Morris's own patterns (No. F: 4). These textiles came originally from the David A.P. Watt Collection in Montreal.

At the outset, Morris selected existing early nineteenth-century blocks for the printing of the first textiles sold under his name. These came from the block stores of the Lancashire textile printing firm of Thomas Clarkson of Bannister Hall. Morris's choice was significant, as the 1830s witnessed the high-point of British production and Thomas Clarkson was the most celebrated and commercially successful printer of such "chintzes."[4] May Morris described the four patterns some years later: "These were on a white ground and … were copied from the pleasant old-fashioned shiny chintzes."[5] Only one other example of these early printings on fine wool is known today, apart from *Jasmine Trail* fragments (No. F: 4): a set of curtains of *Small Stem* design, one panel of which is now in the V & A. The recent discovery of *Jasmine Trail* in Canada is doubly significant, as the design shows clearly that it provided the inspiration for Morris's own first repeating tex-

tile design, *Jasmine Trellis*,[6] designed and printed between 1868 and 1870.

The collection in Canada clearly and succinctly illustrates important stages in Morris's design-development and shows the vital part that technique played in his work. Of the group of patterns designed before Morris had his own printing and weaving facilities, a preoccupation with flat wallpaper patterns can be seen in *Tulip, Iris* and *African Marigold* (Nos. F: 5-7, 9). Weaving of one form or another presented Morris with the technical problems on which he thrived. After a careful and informed study of historic patterns he was able to see that "turn-over" or mirror-imaged designs were the most successfully adapted to the loom. Similar "turn-over" devices appear in some of his earliest printed textile designs, such as *Bluebell* and *Honeysuckle* (Nos. F: 8, 10-12), and prove equally successful as surface-patterns. Early woven examples like *Tulip and Rose* (No. F: 19) show Morris's precocious understanding of the technique, and this particular pattern proved one of his most successful designs, despite being woven in a thick, rather unsubtle texture. Although Morris employed the services of a number of different contract weavers in the early years of production, the variety of technique that he required only became available to him in June 1881, when he set up his own weaving sheds at Merton Abbey.[7]

Morris's eventual move to Merton Abbey provided him with the means of successfully practising the various revived techniques of dyeing, block-printing, fabric- and tapestry-weaving and carpet-knotting that he longed to perfect. The early eighteenth-century buildings had previously been used by Huguenots for silk-throwing and, during the early part of the nineteenth century, as a textile printworks. They therefore needed little adaptation for use for textile manufacture. Three of Morris's patterns, drawn in anticipation of the move (see No. F: 14), were designed specifically to be printed by the indigo-discharge method, the successful application of which had eluded him and Thomas Wardle, the manufacturer who up to this time had printed all of Morris's own designs. The two men had worked together experimenting with dye recipes and printing methods at Wardle's factory at Leek, in Staffordshire, between 1875 and 1876.[8] Morris quickly perfected the discharge process at Merton Abbey and for the next few years produced a number of patterns specifically for this technique. The printing of cloth with indigo involves the total submersion of the fabric in a vat of indigo dye. The colour appears as the cloth is brought out and the dye oxidizes with the air. Patterns are then printed by block onto the blue cloth with a bleaching agent instead of the usual dye. The fabric is then washed and the bleached areas are cleared, producing a white pattern on a blue ground. Different shades of blue are made available by altering the strength of the dye or the length of time that the cloth stays in the vat. Variations in the pattern-colour can be made by using different strengths of bleach, so that

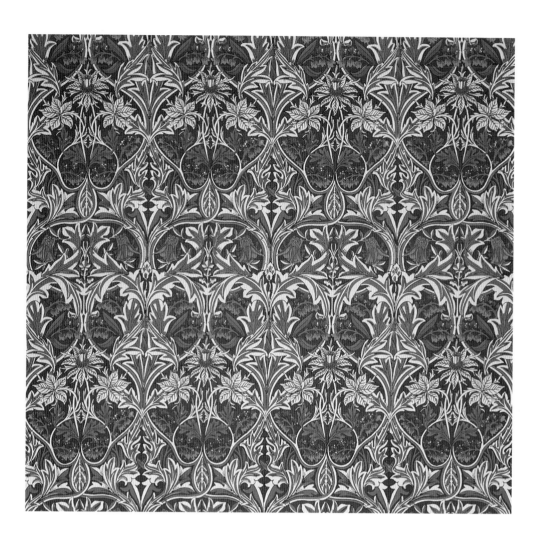

some areas are pale to mid-blue while others are white on a dark-blue ground. Once the blue and white areas are complete, other colours can be added, either by vat-dyeing with madder (red) or weld (yellow), or simply by overprinting the colours by block. Whereas Morris's early examples of indigo-dyeing were simple prints, generally using only two colours, later ones, such as *Evenlode* and *Rose* (Nos. F: 15, 17), were complex, having overprinted or discharged grounds and a number of colours. A vivid contrast between the two types of pattern is shown by the number of blocks used for each pattern.[9] Four blocks went into the printing of *Rose and Thistle*, whereas thirty-three and nineteen, respectively, were needed to complete *Evenlode* and *Rose*.

Complexities in later patterns are not only the direct result of Morris's increasing interest in technique. His fascination with historic design and his work as adviser on the acquisition of textiles to the authorities of the South Kensington Museums (now the V & A) had a marked effect on his work. Directional patterns like *Windrush* and *Cray* (Nos. F: 16, 18) have stylistic roots in Italian silks and velvets of the seventeenth century, and a number of Morris patterns (and later those of Dearle) have been compared with known, historic design-types, and even specific examples in the museum's collection.[10] After the move to Merton Abbey, Morris's patterns are titled after tributaries of the Thames – names more suitable than flowers for the later meandering stem-designs.

In line with contemporary British fashions at the end of the nineteenth century, later Morris & Co. textiles show a strong contemporary interest in Near and Middle Eastern design. Used at a time when both Morris and Dearle were producing patterns for the firm, this shows a considerable change of style by Morris, one so difficult to assess that, in at least two patterns (*Brocatel*, No. F: 24, and *Golden Bough*, No. F: 25), it is not possible to separate the two men's work. It is too simplistic to suggest that, as Morris was Dearle's mentor and greatest artistic influence, he should automatically have been the first to see the potential in Islamic patterns; the reverse is probably correct. The nineteenth-century European fashion for Eastern designs predates these patterns by some twenty years, and Morris had already flirted with the style much earlier in his career, in a few printed designs drawn while working at Leek with Wardle (see No. F: 7). Furthermore, despite an academic interest in historic textiles from Persia and Turkey, Morris always claimed that the main influence for his textile designs came from medieval Europe.[11] Dearle, on the other hand, always possessed a passion for Eastern design and both his commercial patterns and his private sketches[12] bear witness to this. His vastly underestimated abilities as a

designer are revealed at their best in these formal and precise patterns.

Dearle also used the more characteristically British motifs of spring and summer flowers in his work, perfecting these in a series of large embroidered wall-panels and portières (No. F: 2). These embroideries were worked under the close technical supervision of May Morris (1862-1938), William's second daughter, who took over direction of this side of Morris & Co.'s activities in 1885, when she was twenty-three years old. May was herself a formidable designer and craftswoman, producing goods not only for the firm but also for her own pleasure and that of her friends (see No. F: 3). Recent publications and a retrospective exhibition of her work[13] have helped to re-establish her as one of the most significant and original female designers of the nineteenth and twentieth centuries.

The manufacture of hand-knotted carpets and woven tapestries presented Morris with his greatest challenges as a textile manufacturer. Because he held both in such high esteem, and yearned for perfection in these tech-

NO. F: 19
WILLIAM MORRIS,
Tulip and Rose (woven curtain),
design registered 20 January
1876

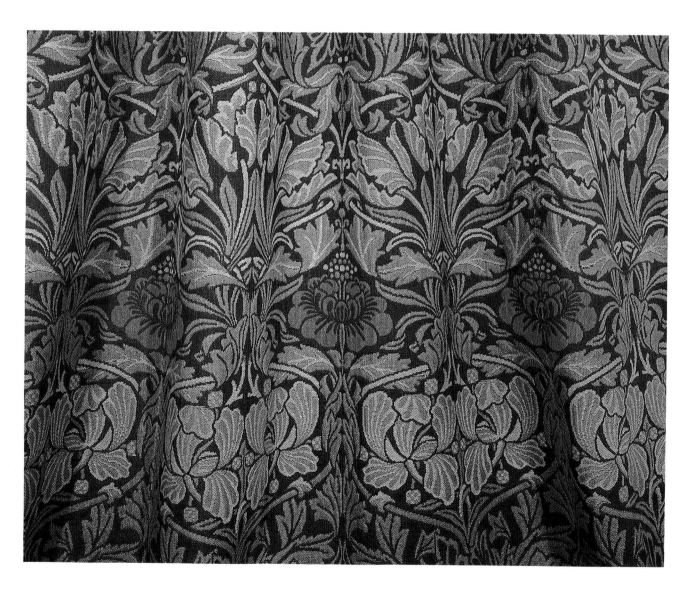

niques, production started comparatively late in his career. Only then did he have the confidence and experience to achieve the high standards he desired. Successful early experiments in carpet-knotting produced a series of small panels for use as decorative wall-hangings or bedroom mats (No. F: 29), and in 1879 Morris installed looms, each twelve feet wide, in the coach-house of his London residence, Kelmscott House, in Hammersmith, where the weaving of large carpets began. Production was transferred to Merton Abbey a few years later. Morris & Co. followed the style and technique of traditional Persian and Turkish manufacture, mixing these with Morris's and Dearle's very British floral designs (No. F: 30). By the 1880s, Morris had acquired a considerable following, and a series of specially commissioned "Hammersmith" carpets (named after their original place of manufacture) appeared over the next few years.

Tapestry was, without doubt, Morris's favourite textile technique. As a student he had seen early examples hanging in the medieval cathedrals of Northern France and these, in no small way, helped persuade him to "begin a life of art," as he was later to describe his conversion. His own production of tapestries consisted mostly of figurative panels, designed in collaboration with Walter Crane, Philip Webb and, most successfully of all, Edward

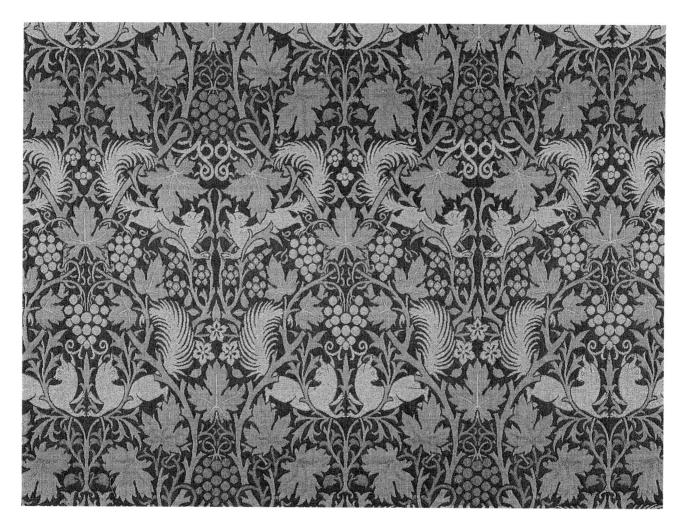

NO. F: 27
J.H. DEARLE,
Squirrel or *Fox and Grape*, c. 1898

Burne-Jones. Burne-Jones's figures established a fashionable style that was frequently copied and one that Henry Dearle was to emulate in his later designs for Morris & Co.. The church of St. Andrew and St. Paul in Montreal is fortunate in owning an example of this work, one of the last tapestries to have been woven at Merton Abbey (No. F: 31).

The collection of Morris textiles to be found in Canadian collections today presents a comprehensive microcosm of his life's work in this field and that of Morris & Co. Examples are not, however, simply restricted to the commercially produced woven and printed furnishings that were widely available through Morris & Co.'s London shop or W. Scott & Sons of Montreal. The Firm's more specialized hand-wrought skills of embroidery, tapestry weaving and carpet-knotting are also represented. In a number of cases it has not been possible to discover how and when these textiles found their way across the Atlantic, or how successfully such patterns were utilized in fashionable Canadian life. It is hoped that a renewed familiarity with such work may re-kindle memories and that this influential designer's work can at last be judged within a wider artistic context than has been possible before.

No. F: 1

WILLIAM MORRIS

Embroidered Curtain
Probably designed and worked between 1870 and 1875
Parry, p. 20 (illus. 24)[14]
Cotton twill ground, embroidered in crewel wools in
  various stitches including stem, back and herringbone
  with speckling; sections still show original braid
  and fringing
257.4 x 163.4 cm
Provenance: David A.P. Watt, Montreal; Edmund
  N. Parker
Maltwood Art Museum and Gallery, University of
  Victoria, British Columbia, gift of Edmund N. Parker
  (acc. no. U984.44.6)

A pair of curtains of this design, worked by Mrs. Alexander Ionides and members of her family, are now in the V & A. The Museum also owns a preparatory tracing of the design marked "Aglaia Coronio" – Mrs. Coronio being a member of the Ionides family and one of Morris's closest friends. This is one of Morris's earliest commercial designs, the traditional interlocking ogee forms showing the strong influence of historic textiles that Morris studied at the South Kensington Museums. He was to use this repeating device in many of his later woven textile designs.

No. F: 2

JOHN HENRY DEARLE

Partridge (embroidered panel)
Designed about 1890
Unfinished embroidery worked in silks on a ground of
  Oak silk damask; stitches used include stem, long
  and short, darning, detached buttonhole, laid and
  couched work, and French knots
295.0 x 156.0 cm
Morris & Co. catalogue, *Embroidery Work*, c. 1909
Provenance: bought in 1904 from Morris & Co.'s Oxford
  Street shop by Mrs. Cunliffe of Eaton Square,
  London, who gave it to Lady Margaret Ayre
Collection of the family of the late Margaret I. Ayre

One of a series of large embroidered wall-hangings showing birds in large-scale floral compositions. A pair, called *Pigeon* and *Owl*, which are known to have been commissioned from Morris & Co. about 1890, are now in the V & A. *Owl* is very similar to the *Partridge* design and shows the same curving acanthus leaf as its central motif with identical trailing honeysuckle, roses and large stylized flowerheads (see fig. F: 1). The lower section is different, however, and the symmetrical, curving leaves of the earlier piece have been changed to two small trees in the Canadian example. An additional bird can also be seen in the lower left-hand corner.

Whereas the original design is attributed to Henry Dearle, it is probable that the later changes were made by May Morris, the drawing being much closer to a series of inscribed *Tree* hangings designed by her about the same time.

This embroidery was bought from the Morris & Co. shop as a kit. The silk ground was marked with the design (this is still evident in small areas) and had a small section already embroidered in order to show the recommended technique. All the silks were supplied by the Firm. It would appear that the embroiderer, Mrs. Cunliffe, found changes in colour when she compared the colours of these embroidery silks to a Morris cushion-cover that she owned. An existing letter from Morris & Co., dated 25 August 1904, warns that silk yarns can appear "faded" when worked into an embroidery, but offers to rectify the matter if the cover is sent to them. We are left to guess the outcome of the complaint.

These wall-hangings proved to be a popular product of the Morris & Co. workshops. This is unusual, as the panels were comparatively expensive: £9 was charged for a panel embroidered in the workshops in 1893, at a time when £80 would have paid the annual rent on a large London house. However, a more appropriate comparison is with the cost of a Hammersmith carpet at £113 (see No. F: 30), which demonstrates the great value for money given by the Morris embroiderers.

A number of similar large embroideries are mentioned in the only existing records of this section of Morris & Co.'s activities: a notebook, now in the National Art Library, Victoria and Albert Museum, which lists orders made between 1892 and 1896. The firm offered a number of services for the collector, decorator or amateur embroiderer. Not only did they sell kits to be made at home, as in this example, but they also sold completed work. In addition, they ran a draughting service, drawing out embroidery designs onto background cloth, and would stretch and frame work done by clients.

May Morris became manager of the embroidery sec-

FIG. F: 1. J.H. DEARLE, *Owl* hanging, c. 1890. Embroidered in silks on a woven silk damask ground. Victoria and Albert Museum, London.

tion from 1885 and from this date all work was completed under her watchful eye. Many of the girls she employed were trained by her, and between 1890 and 1896 the embroiderers worked in the drawing-room of her home in Hammersmith Terrace, around the corner from Kelmscott House. After Morris's death, production moved to the shop at 449 Oxford Street.

No. F: 3

MAY MORRIS AND GEORGE JACK FOR MORRIS & CO. (?)

Three-fold screen
Designed between 1890 and 1900
Polished mahogany frame, partly veneered, inset with
    three embroidered panels on a ground of *Oak* woven-

silk damask; technique includes stem, long and short,
    and satin stitches
92.0 x 76.5 x 3.2 cm (each panel)
Provenance: Sotheby's London, 29 November 1984 (lot
    217); purchased at the sale
Private collection, Winnipeg

The embroidery panels of this screen are unusual and were probably designed by May Morris as a special commission and embroidered by her, or under her supervision, in the workshops of Morris & Co.. The three-fold wooden screen is similar to an example illustrated in the Morris & Co. catalogue *Embroidery Work*, published about 1909. This was available in a choice of walnut or mahogany at a cost of 12 guineas (£12.12s) for a two-fold and £17.10s for a three-fold screen.

The embroidered panels are unique in design, especially the centrally placed straight-stemmed lilies, but include meandering floral motifs similar to those in other Morris & Co. screen-panels. Comparisons in technique and colouring can be made between this example and embroideries designed by May Morris for her own personal use and for her friends. She often employed Morris & Co. silk damasks as the backgrounds for her own work, and her designs tend to be of a brighter, more individual colouring than the more tonally blended hues used in the firm's commercial work.

Other than a very brief formal education at Notting Hill High School between October 1874 and June 1877, May Morris's only artistic training came from attending the South Kensington School of Design (now the Royal College of Art in London). It was here that she perfected the skills of embroidery that she had learned at home from an early age. She could have had little time to devote to her own embroidery in the early years as manager of the embroidery section of Morris & Co., for she was preoccupied with supervision of the embroiderers and drawing new designs for the firm in the Morris style. Her later work, made to be exhibited under her own name at various contemporary exhibitions, or as presents or special commissions for friends, is all the more lovingly conceived and completed for this reason. She was a frequent exhibitor at the various London Arts and Crafts Exhibitions and became one of the leading craftswomen of her day. Her interest in embroidery technique led her to publish a number of articles, and her book *Decorative Needlework* (1893) is both a historic survey of the craft and a technical manual.

It is through May Morris's teaching that her influence is most strongly felt today. She offered private tuition in

NO. F:2
JOHN HENRY DEARLE,
Partridge (embroidered panel)
Designed about 1890

London as well as teaching in a number of the leading art schools of the day. Her influence was felt beyond Britain and she was looked on with great respect by some of the leading members of the American Arts and Crafts movement. From the winter of 1909 to the spring of 1910 she completed a very successful teaching tour in the United States and Canada.

The screen, along with other related eighteenth century-style pieces of furniture produced by Morris & Co., reflects the direction that the Firm had already taken by Morris's death in 1896, and also the current reawakened interest in the lighter, more elegant furnishings of that century that were an outgrowth of the so called "Queen Anne" style. The design vocabulary of the eighteenth century was certainly not foreign to the Firm from its inception, given Rossetti's and Taylor's particular enthusiasm for the period, as well as Webb's gradual appreciation of it. It was, however, W.A.S. Benson's succession to the chairmanship of the Firm in 1896, along with George Jack's role after 1890 as chief furniture-designer, and the contribution of furniture designs by Mervyn Macartney, that consolidated the emphasis on eighteenth-century furniture designs produced by the Firm. Thus, by the time of the 1910-12 catalogue, about eighty-eight of the approximately 106 designs shown therein were of eighteenth-century derivation as either high-styled or sophisticated veneered pieces of furniture, or more vernacular or "cottage furniture."

The form of the present piece has its eighteenth-century and earlier precedents. In France, folding screens were usually made with wooden frames and fabric coverings *ensuite* with the seating furniture of a particular room. In England, when not decorated with Oriental- or European-style lacquer, the leaves of folding screens were often painted on wood or leather with decorative or genre scenes, or were fitted with panels of tapestry or embroidery.

Throughout the nineteenth century, folding screens were still featured in pattern- and trade-books such as W. Smee and Sons' *Designs for Furniture of 1850.* Japanese screens enjoyed a great vogue during the 1870s and 1880s as quintessential elements in an "Aesthetic" interior. Another example of a Morris & Co. screen, this time with a turned wooden frame fitted with embroidered silk panels, can be seen in an illustration of the overly elaborate drawing-room of Stanmore Hall, which the Firm was called upon to decorate between 1888 and 1896. Hermann Muthesius, in his highly influential history of English domestic architecture and living habits, suggested that the folding screen

was an "almost indispensable piece of dining-room furniture", used as a protection against draughts. He stated as well, however, that in the drawing-room "the screen is a permanent furniture...[I]t...is rather lighter in character than that in the dining room. It is often covered in silk...."[15] – as was the present example.

– Linda Parry and Robert Little

PRINTED FABRICS

No. F: 4

WILLIAM MORRIS
(AFTER A TRADITIONAL DESIGN)

Jasmine Trail (printed wool) 1868-75
Fine woolen ground, block-printed for Morris by
    Thomas Clarkson, Bannister Hall
276.6 x 89.8 cm
Selvedge mark: *"Morris & Co., 26 Queen Square,
    Bloomsbury W.C."*
Provenance: David A.P. Watt, Montreal; Edmund
    N. Parker
Maltwood Art Museum and Gallery, University of
    Victoria, British Columbia, gift of Edmund N. Parker
    (acc. no. U984.44.5B)

This is the only known example of this design and is one of four 1830s' patterns chosen by Morris to reprint and sell under his name when he began to manufacture textiles. It was selected from the block store of the Lancashire printing firm of Thomas Clarkson of Bannister Hall, one of the foremost mid-nineteenth-century British printers of high-quality textile furnishings. The selvedge mark suggests a manufacturing date between 1868 and 1875.

No. F: 5

WILLIAM MORRIS

Tulip (printed cotton)
Design registered 15 April 1875
Parry cat. 7
Cotton ground, block-printed for Morris by Thomas
    Wardle, Leek
107.0 x 61.6 cm (approx.)
Selvedge mark: *"Morris & Company, 26 Queen Sqr
    Bloomsbury"*
Provenance: David A.P. Watt; Edmund N. Parker

Maltwood Art Museum and Art Gallery, University of
Victoria, British Columbia, gift of Edmund N. Parker
(acc. no. U984.44.3)

A preliminary design and the original printing blocks
for this textile are now in the William Morris Gallery,
Walthamstow. The Queen Square selvedge mark suggests
that this sample was one of the first of Morris's own designs
printed under the name of Morris & Co, which was registered on 25 March 1875.

No. F: 6
___

WILLIAM MORRIS

Tulip (printed cotton)
Design registered 15 April 1875
Parry cat. 7
Cotton ground, block-printed for Morris by Thomas
    Wardle, Leek
118.0 x 95.0 cm
Selvedge mark: *"Morris & Company, 449 Oxford Street"*
Block-edge has printed legend: *"Morris and Company,
    449 Oxford Street, London, Registered"*
Royal Ontario Museum, Toronto, purchase (acc. no.
    963.179.2)

A later version of the previous example, this cotton was
printed between 1877 and 1917, when Morris traded from
premises at Oxford Street in London. This design, with
gently waving stylized plant forms, reflects Morris's interest in wallpaper manufacture, for which he drew a number of designs about this time.

No. F: 7
___

WILLIAM MORRIS

Iris (fragment of printed cotton)
Design registered 25 April 1876
Parry cat. 16
Cotton ground block-printed for Morris by Thomas
    Wardle, Leek
94.0 x 94.0 cm (approx.)
The Museum for Textiles, Toronto, gift of Allan Suddon
    (acc. no. T90.0137)

There is a preliminary design for this textile, which shows
instructions for block-cutting, in the Helen and Sandford
Berger collection, Carmel, California. In a letter, Morris
referred to this pattern as "flower de luce," although this
name was never used commercially. The design dates from

NO. F: 7

the period when Morris was experimenting with dyes and
printing techniques at Leek. The hot sultry colouring is
reminiscent of the Eastern designs that Wardle both imported and copied in his own printing sheds.

No. F: 8
___

WILLIAM MORRIS

Bluebell or *Columbine* (printed cotton) 1876
Parry cat. 17 (see also p. 50)
Cotton ground block-printed for Morris by Thomas
    Wardle, Leek
99.0 x 89.0 cm
Selvedge mark: *"Regd Morris & Company"*
Attached is a Morris & Co. printed paper label which
    gives the name, pattern number 6693 and price of $4
The Montreal Museum of Fine Arts, gift of Mrs. J.
    Kippen (acc. no. 941.Dt. 7)

The original design for this textile is in the V & A.
    An entry in the Wardle pattern books (now in the
Whitworth Art Gallery, University of Manchester) indicates that the first trial printing of this textile took place in
Leek on 4 May 1876. This example was printed after 1917;
chemical dyestuffs almost certainly were used. Morris &
Co. experienced great difficulty in finding supplies of
natural dyestuffs during the First World War and by 1920
the majority of dyeing was with chemical-based artificial
colours.

WILLIAM MORRIS

African Marigold (printed cotton)
Design registered 7 October 1876
Morris & Co. catalogue, *Morris Chintzes, Silks,*
    Tapestries, etc., p. 5; Parry cat. 20
Cotton ground block-printed for Morris by Thomas
    Wardle, Leek
230.0 x 183.0 cm
The Museum for Textiles, Toronto, purchase (acc. no.
    T.91.0001)

The original design for this textile is at the William Morris,
Gallery, Walthamstow.

The problems that beset Morris and Wardle in their
attempts to dye with indigo successfully are highlighted
in this design. A five-month gap is documented between
the first attempts to print the design and its registration.
It is clear that Morris and Wardle failed to utilize the dye
with this example and Wardle, in desperation, used Prus-
sian Blue, an artificial dyestuff, the brightness of which

NO. F: 9

can be seen in this example. Wardle's action unleashed a
characteristic rebuke from Morris, but a more satisfactory
printing of this pattern was never achieved.

No. F: 10

WILLIAM MORRIS

Honeysuckle (printed linen bookbinding)
Textile registered 11 October 1876
Morris & Co. catalogue, *Morris Chintzes, Silks, Tapestries,*
    etc., p. 11; Parry cat. 21
Linen ground block-printed for Morris by Thomas
    Wardle, Leek
Private collection, Vancouver

This example represents a unique experiment by Morris,
in which a limited edition of *The Roots of the Mountains*
(published by Reeves and Turner in 1890) was bound with
Morris printed fabric. H. Buxton Forman refers to two
different patterns used, "a large pattern and the other of a
small."[16] Only examples showing *Honeysuckle* in its original size have been traced. Morris expressed his satisfaction
with the publication in typically self-deprecating fashion:
"I am so pleased with my book – typography, binding and
must I say it, literary matters – that I am any day to be seen
huggling it up, and am becoming a spectacle to Gods and
men because of it."[17]

A version of the book was exhibited at the 1890 Arts
and Crafts Exhibition (no. 604h).

This object also appears in the Books section of this
catalogue (see No. L: 14).

No. F: 11

WILLIAM MORRIS

Honeysuckle (printed linen)
Design registered 11 October 1876
Morris & Co. catalogue, *Morris Chintzes, Silks,*
    Tapestries, etc., p. 11; Parry cat. 21
Linen ground, block-printed for Morris by Thomas
    Wardle, Leek
69.5 x 96.5 cm
Selvedge mark: *"Regd Morris & Company"*
The Montreal Museum of Fine Arts, gift of Mrs. J.
    Kippen (acc. no. 941.Dt.5)

The original design for this textile is in the City Museum
and Art Gallery, Birmingham.

NO. F: 12

A printed silk version of this design was exhibited by Thomas Wardle under his name in the British India Section of the 1878 Paris Exhibition. This example and other early experimental patterns printed by Wardle onto imported Indian silk grounds are now in the V & A. This textile design was printed after 1917, when the Morris & Co. shop moved to George Street, Hanover Square.

No. F: 12

WILLIAM MORRIS

Honeysuckle (printed linen)
Design registered 11 October 1876
Morris & Co. catalogue, *Morris Chintzes, Silks, Tapestries, etc.*, p. 11; Parry cat. 21
Linen ground, block-printed for Morris by Thomas Wardle, Leek
90.0 x 97.5 cm
Selvedge mark: *"Regd Morris & Company"*
A printed Morris & Co. label attached gives the name, pattern number 1794 and price: "about one yard $4"
The Montreal Museum of Fine Arts, gift of Mrs. J. Kippen (acc. no. 941.Dt.6)

Like the previous example, this is a late printing and presumably (because of the dollar price-tag) was acquired through an unknown agent of Morris & Co. in North America.

WILLIAM MORRIS OR KATE FAULKNER

Peony (printed cotton)
Design registered 22 June 1877
Parry cat. 26
Cotton ground, block-printed for Morris by Thomas Wardle, Leek
68.5 x 98.0 cm
Selvedge mark: *"Regd Morris & Company"*
A printed Morris & Co. label gives the name, pattern number 9406 and the price: $2.
The Montreal Museum of Fine Arts, gift of Mrs. J. Kippen (acc. no. 941.Dt.4)

Kate Faulkner was the sister of Charles Faulkner, a founder member of Morris, Marshall, Faulkner & Co. and the Firm's first book-keeper. She was an accomplished commercial designer and produced wallpaper designs, painted tiles, pottery and gesso decoration for Morris & Co. and other manufacturers. As a close friend and neighbour of the Morris family when they were living in Queen Square, she also took part in embroidery groups initiated by Jane and May Morris. It is probable that some of Morris & Co.'s textiles were also designed by her, although attributions are based purely on stylistic comparisons.

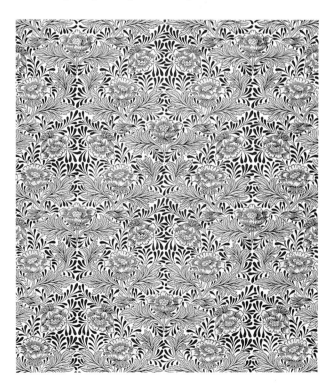

NO. F: 13

WILLIAM MORRIS

Rose and Thistle (curtain of printed cotton)
Designed before 1881
Parry cat. 40
Cotton ground block-printed at Merton Abbey
104.0 x 89.0 cm
Royal Ontario Museum, Toronto, purchased through
    the generosity of the Textile Endowment Fund
    Committee (acc. no. 988.234.1)

The original design for this textile is in the V & A; the
blocks are owned by the William Morris Gallery, Walthamstow.

One of three two-colour designs drawn by Morris a few
months before moving into his factory at Merton Abbey,
Rose and Thistle was designed in anticipation of setting up
and successfully using an indigo vat. These patterns were
designed specifically to be discharge block-printed after
indigo-dyeing. This example is surface-printed.

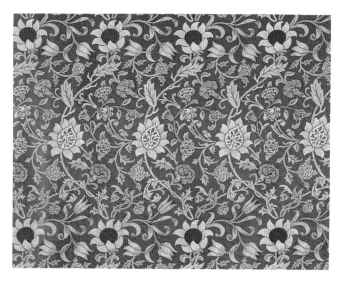

NO. F: 15

No. F: 15

WILLIAM MORRIS

Evenlode (printed cotton)
Design registered 2 September 1883
Morris & Co. catalogue, *Morris Chintzes, Silks,
    Tapestries, etc.*, p. 4; Parry cat. 47
Cotton ground indigo-discharged and block-printed at
    Merton Abbey
199.0 x 92.0 cm
Selvedge mark: *"Morris & Company, 449 Oxford Street,
    London S W"*
The Museum for Textiles, Toronto, purchase (acc. no.
    T.46/91)

The original design for this textile is in the V & A; the
blocks are in the William Morris Gallery, Walthamstow.

One of Morris's most complicated and extravagant
indigo-discharge patterns, *Evenlode* required thirty-three
blocks for printing. The first of Morris's designs to be
named after tributaries of the River Thames, it marks a
turning point in his patterns, which from this date show
bold meandering motifs. This example was printed between 1883 and 1917.

No. F: 16

WILLIAM MORRIS

Windrush (printed cotton)
Design registered 18 October 1883
Morris & Co. catalogue, *Morris Chintzes, Silks,
    Tapestries, etc.*, p. 8; Parry cat. 50

NO. F: 14

Cotton ground block-printed at Merton Abbey

58.6 x 48.7 cm

Selvedge mark: *"Morris & Company, 449 Oxford Street, London"*

An attached Morris & Co. printed paper label gives the later George Street, Hanover Square address

Royal Ontario Museum, Toronto, purchased through the generosity of the Textile Endowment Fund Committee (acc. no. 988.234.2)

The original design is in the collection of the William Morris Society, Kelmscott House, London; the original printing blocks are in the William Morris Gallery, Walthamstow.

Produced in seven different colourways, this piece was probably used as a sample to show clients in the Morris & Co. shop. A collection of similarly sized and labelled textiles used for this purpose was given by Morris & Co. to the V & A.

No. F: 17

WILLIAM MORRIS

Rose (printed cotton)

Design registered 8 December 1883

Morris & Co. catalogue, *Morris Chintzes, Silks, Tapestries, etc.*, p. 6; Parry cat. 53

Cotton ground indigo-discharged and block-printed at Merton Abbey

81.0 x 76.0 cm

NO. F: 17

NO. F: 18

Royal Ontario Museum, Toronto, purchased through the generosity of the Textile Endowment Fund Committee (acc. no. 988.234.2)

The original printing blocks for this textile are in the William Morris Gallery, Walthamstow.

For this design, Morris dyed the fabric blue in the indigo vat and then completely discharged the ground. This was a time-consuming and extravagant method of producing small areas of blue in the pattern but shows his fascination with the process and confidence in its use.

No. F: 18

WILLIAM MORRIS

Cray (printed cotton) 1884

Morris & Co. catalogue, *Morris Chintzes, Silks, Tapestries, etc.*, p. 9; Parry cat. 57

Cotton ground, block-printed at Merton Abbey

97.0 x 133.0 cm

Selvedge mark: *"Morris & Company"*
A printed Morris & Co. label gives the name, pattern
    number 2109 and price of $3.25
The Montreal Museum of Fine Arts, gift of Mrs. J.
    Kippen (acc. no. 941.Dt.8)

The original printing blocks for this textile are in the
William Morris Gallery, Walthamstow.

Morris's most complex design (and one of his most expensive), this fabric required thirty-four blocks for printing.
Produced in a number of different ground- and pattern-
colourings, it remained popular well into the twentieth
century, when it was printed onto a white ground to sat-
isfy Edwardian taste.

WOVEN FABRICS

No. F: 19
___

WILLIAM MORRIS

Tulip and Rose (pair of woven curtains)
Design registered 20 January 1876
Morris & Co. catalogue, *Morris Chintzes, Silks, Tapestries,*
    etc., p. 24; Parry cat. 12
Woolen triple cloth, woven for Morris by the
    Heckmondwike Manufacturing Company, Yorkshire
311.0 x 116.0 cm (each panel)
Provenance: Part of the furnishings of Alfred Baumgarten's
    residence at 3450 McTavish Street, Montreal
McCord Museum of Canadian History, Montreal

This fabric has the same technical structure as the three-ply
Kidderminster-type carpeting also woven by the Heckmondwike Manufacturing Company for Morris (see No.
F: 28). Despite this, there is no evidence to suggest that
this particular pattern was ever sold as a floor-covering
and it was registered specifically as a textile design. The
pattern was also used for finer fabrics woven with mixtures
of silk and linen and silk and cotton, although this heavier
woolen fabric proved to be the most popular. Described
as a "three-ply tapestry" in Morris & Co.'s catalogues (these
commercial titles have led to technical confusion in recent
years), the fabric's "rough bold texture of great durabil-
ity" is also commented on.

The Baumgarten House, built between 1885 and 1887
and enlarged in 1902, is now used as McGill University's
Faculty Club.

No. F: 20
___

WILLIAM MORRIS

Peacock and Dragon (woven woolen hanging) 1878
Morris & Co. catalogue, *Morris Chintzes, Silks,*
    Tapestries, etc., p. 27; Parry cat. 30
Wool, hand-loom jacquard-woven at Merton Abbey
233.5 x 166.0 cm
Howarth collection

This example, woven in a predominantly red colouring,
shows the use of a repeating woven design as a draped
wall-hanging. It has original woolen braid edging and was
almost certainly made up and trimmed in the Morris &
Co. workshops.

No. F: 21
___

WILLIAM MORRIS

Peacock and Dragon (woven woolen wall-covering) 1878
Morris & Co. catalogue, *Morris Chintzes, Silks,*
    Tapestries, etc., p. 27; Parry cat. 30
Wool, hand-loom jacquard-woven initially at Queen
    Square and later at Merton Abbey
206.0 x 881.0 cm
Private collection, on loan to the Beaverbrook Art
    Gallery, Fredericton, New Brunswick

This fabric covered the upper walls in the dining-room of
Charles Hosmer's residence on Drummond Street, Montreal, a building completed in 1901. Complete widths of
the fabric were seamed together and then battened to the
walls with braid trimming at ceiling and dado levels, providing a suitably "medieval" effect with the richly carved
antique panelling on the lower half of the walls.

This method of using fabric as a fixed wall-covering was one that Morris approved of but, because it was
extremely expensive, only a few schemes were completed.
Usually woven silk was used. One other commission, employing woven wool, survives at Ironmonger's Hall, London, the Board Room of which is decorated with Morris's
Bird fabric.

Peacock and Dragon was one of Morris's most popular
designs. This firmly structured and hard-wearing fabric
was used for curtaining, upholstery and wall-coverings,
both loosely hung and stretched on battens (see above).
Most often seen in the blue colouring used at the Hosmer
house, the predominately red scheme does seem to have
found favour across the Atlantic. It was also used in Charles

NO. F: 20

Glessner's house in Chicago, built for him by H.H. Richardson, who also advised on the furnishings.

The fabric formed part of the decorations in a number of notable British houses including the Hon. Percy Wyndham's country house, Clouds, near Salisbury in Wiltshire, and Morris's own Kelmscott House. It is clear that he was very fond of the pattern and believed that it came closest of all his repeating designs to his own ideal of a medieval hanging. Morris & Co.'s catalogue described it as "a perfect hanging for a mediaeval castle or mansion." The large pattern-repeat meant that the design was best seen in large quantities in vast interiors. At twenty-five shillings a yard, such hangings could only have been afforded by the wealthiest clients.

No. F: 22

WILLIAM MORRIS

Dove and Rose (woven curtain) 1879
Morris & Co. catalogue, *Morris Chintzes, Silks,
     Tapestries, etc.*, p. 25; Parry cat. 34
Jacquard-woven silk and wool, manufactured for Morris
     by Alexander Morton & Company, Darvel, Scotland
105.6 x 87.9 cm
Provenance: David A.P. Watt; Edmund N. Parker
Maltwood Art Museum and Gallery, University of
     Victoria, British Columbia, gift of Edmund N. Parker
     (acc. no. U984.44.1A)

The original design for this textile is in the City Museum and Art Gallery, Birmingham; a weaver's pointpaper is in

NO. F: 23

the William Morris Gallery, Walthamstow.

This technique, in which pockets of glimmering silk contrast with textured woolen areas, was one adopted by the Scottish manufacturer Alexander Morton for his own production some years later. An admirer of Morris who emulated his working practices in his own factory, Morton is now looked upon as one of the most outstanding figures in nineteenth-century British textile production.

No. F: 23

WILLIAM MORRIS

Oak (woven silk) 1881
Morris & Co. catalogue, *Morris Chintzes, Silks,
     Tapestries, etc.*, p. 25; Parry cat. 37
Jacquard-woven silk and wool damask
Originally manufactured on power looms for Morris by
     J.O. Nicholson of Macclesfield and later by hand-
     loom at Merton Abbey
124.0 x 153.0 cm
Royal Ontario Museum, Toronto, gift of Mrs. R.J. Mercur
     (acc. no. 941.14.1)

Designed for the furnishings of the Blue Room and Throne Room at St. James's Palace, London (see No. E: 3). This pattern, one of Morris's most conventional designs, proved to be one of their most commercially popular textiles and was used as a background for a number of the Firm's embroideries (see Nos. F: 2-3), as well as for upholstery, curtaining and wall-coverings.

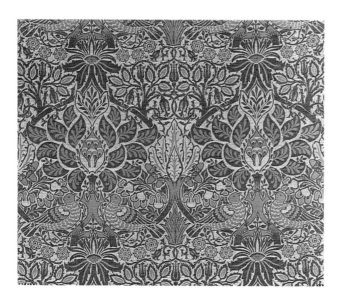

NO. F: 22

A strip in silk at the top of this sample suggests that the piece was a trial weaving completed at Merton Abbey. The design is usually woven in silk; a woolen weft, as in this example, is unusual.

No. F: 24

WILLIAM MORRIS OR
JOHN HENRY DEARLE

Brocatel (woven textile fragment) 1888
Parry cat. 65
Silk, hand-loom jacquard-woven at Merton Abbey
Irregular size: 71.7 x 134.6 cm (approx.)
Provenance: David A.P. Watt; Edmund N. Parker
Maltwood Art Museum and Art Gallery, University of
    Victoria, British Columbia, gift of Edmund N. Parker
    (acc. no. U984.44.4)

Probably the same design as two examples exhibited by Morris & Co. under the catalogue description "silk brocatelle" at the first Arts and Crafts Exhibition in 1888 (nos. 410, 438); it has been given a joint designer-attribution as it possesses stylistic elements characteristic of the work of

both Morris and Dearle. From 1888 on, Morris's preoccupations, particularly with book-production, politics and conservation matters, resulted in fewer designs being originated by him and more by Henry Dearle.

No. F: 25

WILLIAM MORRIS OR
JOHN HENRY DEARLE

Golden Bough (woven silk and linen tablecloth) 1888
Morris & Co. catalogue, *Morris Chintzes, Silks,
    Tapestries, etc.*, p. 26; Parry cat. 66
Silk and linen, hand-loom jacquard-woven at Merton
    Abbey
126.2 x 126.2 cm
Private collection, British Columbia

The original design for this textile is in the City Museum and Art Gallery, Birmingham.

Originally woven in four different colourways, this pattern proved very popular for church furnishings. It is known to have been used in a number of large schemes, including Stanmore Hall, Middlesex, a commission which

NO. F: 24

NO. F: 25

NO. F: 26

Morris & Co. completed between 1888 and 1896 for the Australian mining engineer William Knox D'Arcy.

No. F: 26

WILLIAM MORRIS

Ispahan (woven textile) 1889
Morris & Co. catalogue, *Morris Chintzes, Silks,*
    Tapestries, etc., p. 31; Parry cat. 64
Wool, hand-loom jacquard-woven at Merton Abbey
311.0 x 120.0 cm
Private collection, Winnipeg

Exhibited at the first Arts and Crafts Exhibition at the New Gallery, Regent Street, in 1888 (no. 404), where it is mistakenly catalogued as "Ispalian." This is, almost certainly, one of the three new designs for "stuffs" (along with *Brocatel* [No. F: 24] and *Golden Bough* [No. F: 25]) that Morris was pressed by one of his business managers to finish earlier in the year. Both the name of this pattern and its strong Islamic design elements indicate Morris's increasing interest in Near and Middle Eastern design.

No. F: 27

JOHN HENRY DEARLE

Squirrel or *Fox and Grape* (woven woolen curtain) c. 1898
Morris & Co. catalogue, *Morris Chintzes, Silks,*
    Tapestries, etc., p. 31; Parry cat. 94
Wool, hand-loom jacquard-woven double cloth manu-
    factured at Merton Abbey

181.5 x 129.5 cm
Private collection, Winnipeg

The original design and a working tracing are in the Helen and Sanford Berger collection.

The subject of this pattern is taken from one of *Aesop's Fables*. The textile was later marketed under the name *Squirrel*, as this presumably provided a more convincing description of the pattern. Although this is Henry Dearle's only repeating pattern illustrating animals, he produced a number of competent designs for verdure tapestries. Since Morris lacked confidence as a figure draughtsman, he often utilized the services of others for such work.

CARPETS

No. F: 28

WILLIAM MORRIS

Tulip and Lily (machine-woven carpeting) c. 1875
Parry cat. 140
Three-ply wool Kidderminster carpeting, woven for
    Morris by the Heckmondwike Manufacturing
    Company, Yorkshire
139.0 x 89.5 cm
Provenance: David Bindman, London
Enid MacLachlan

The type of durable, flat-weave technique illustrated here was employed for broadloom carpeting as well as for runners and smaller squares. It proved particularly popular for use on stairs and bedroom corridors when a matching

NO. F: 28

border was present, as in this example. Although Morris believed that machine-woven carpeting was inferior to hand-woven examples, he recommended its use in some of his grandest schemes. Subsequently, it was accepted in many fashionable homes. The Heckmondwike Manufacturing Company, although only established in 1873, soon acquired a reputation to rival many long-established British carpet manufacturers.

No. F: 29

WILLIAM MORRIS

Hammersmith Rug
Designed and made between 1878 and 1880
Hand-knotted carpet, worsted warps and woolen binding weft and knots; Ghiordes knots are used at a thickness of approximately 5 warp threads to the inch and 2 to the centimetre
66.0 x 111.8 cm
Hammersmith mark in top border of a hammer dissecting the letter *"M"* and wavy lines representing waves
Private collection, British Columbia

One of a series of small hand-woven rugs produced by Morris at Kelmscott House between 1878 and 1880. These are his earliest-known examples and this particular design, showing a vase of flowers, was used more than once. The pattern and format have strong similarities with other contemporary Morris work, including *Lily*, a machine-woven Wilton carpet of 1875, a set of designs for square embroidered cushion-covers or fire-screens (one is called *Flowerpot*), and his small-scale printed cotton *Flowerpot* or *Pots of Flowers*, which was registered in 1883. The source of the composition is a set of two seventeenth-century Italian lacis squares (lacis is a form of hand-knotted net in which the decoration is embroidered), acquired by the South Kensington Museums in 1875.

Though only early Morris carpets bear the Hammersmith mark, the name continued to be used to describe all carpets hand-knotted by Morris & Co., whether produced at Kelmscott House or, from 1881, at Merton Abbey.

It is likely that these small panels were woven primarily as experiments, with Morris testing techniques as well as formulating his ideas on carpet design. In August 1880 he wrote to his daughter to complain of the buckling that was appearing in the rugs, caused by using worsted warp threads, and from this time cotton was used. It is probable that these rugs served both as decorative wall-panels, because of their directional patterns, and as floor-coverings. Other similar panels are known, including three acquired from Morris by George Howard and used as bedroom mats in his houses, Naworth Castle, in Cumbria, and Castle Howard, near York. Howard was obviously charmed by these little panels, for in 1881 he asked Morris to design a large carpet for the Library at Naworth.

No. F: 30

WILLIAM MORRIS

Hammersmith Carpet
A version of the *Holland Park* design, originally woven
   in 1883
Hand-knotted carpet, cotton warps, jute binding wefts
   with woolen knots; Ghiordes knots are used at a
   thickness of 5 to the inch, 2 to the centimetre
504.3 x 412.0 cm
Provenance: purchased in London, c. 1972
Peter Tolliday Oriental Carpets, Vancouver

This carpet has the same field (centre) as that originally designed by Morris and woven in 1883 for the A.A. Ionides house at 1 Holland Park, in west London. The border comes from another important Morris carpet, the *Redcar*, designed by Morris between 1878 and 1882 for Red Barns, at Coatham, near Redcar, one of the residences of the Yorkshire ironmaster Sir Isaac Lowthian Bell.

It is difficult to determine the precise date that this carpet was woven. Four other full-sized versions of the *Holland Park* survive but only two are datable. The original, now in private ownership, was bought in the 1920s at Morris & Co.'s London shop by the aunt of the present owner. The second weaving, produced for the house Clouds about 1889, was sold at Sotheby's, London on 19 December 1986 (lot 381). Both of these weavings have Morris's most characteristic combination of a dark-blue indigo field with a madder-red border. This is also the colouring chosen for a late (possibly early twentieth-cen-

NO. F: 30

tury) weaving commissioned for the Combination Room of Cambridge University.

One other version, also in a private collection, has a light-coloured ground. However, this is cream rather than the apricot tinge of the Canadian carpet and is much closer in colouring to Morris's early rugs and carpets, such as the *Redcar*, which has a creamy-camel field and a green border, as in this example.

Two *Holland Park* carpets were exhibited by Morris & Co. at the London Arts and Crafts exhibitions of 1888 (no. 399) and 1899 (no. 398), respectively. As their catalogue entries are so brief, it is not possible even to hazard a guess as to which versions they refer.

Despite their high price, Morris & Co. produced a great many Hammersmith carpets in the late 1880s and '90s, when it is likely that this piece was woven. It is known that Alexander Ionides paid £113 for the original *Holland Park* (compare this with the price of supplying and laying machine-woven carpeting on all the stairs in the house for just over £85). Although Morris's design fee may have been part of this, subsequent weaving must have been of a similar high level.

Carpet-weaving was transferred from the coach-house at Kelmscott House to Merton Abbey in 1881. The roof was raised on the ground floor of the building, which enabled the installation of much larger looms than could be housed at Hammersmith. Carpet-weaving and embroidery were the only sections of the Works in which women were employed exclusively, Morris believing that they were capable of the best results in these techniques. Six girls were employed at any one time at the looms and two sets of sisters are listed as carpet weavers in the Arts and Crafts Exhibition catalogues. During the 1914-18 war, women were also employed for tapestry-weaving by Morris & Co.

TAPESTRIES

No. F: 31

EDWARD BURNE-JONES

Suffer Little Children to Come unto Me (tapestry)
Designed 1874 as a stained-glass panel, adapted for
    tapestry and woven 1934-35
Hand-woven tapestry with cotton warps and silk and
    wool weft threads: 12 warp threads to the inch
250.0 x 175.0 cm
This tapestry bears the bishop's-mitre symbol of the

NO. F: 31

Merton Abbey Tapestry Works and the weaver's
    initials: *"PS. SM. WS. AW."*
Provenance: commissioned by Lady Meredith, who
    presented it to the church
The Church of St. Andrew and St. Paul, Montreal

There is a preliminary drawing for the stained-glass design in Leeds City Art Gallery[18] and a pencil drawing of the composition by either Henry or Duncan Dearle in the Helen and Sanford Berger collection.

This tapestry was originally designed by Burne-Jones as part of a stained-glass window – one of four panels – for the nave of St. Mary the Virgin church at Speldhurst, in Kent. An entry dated 16 November 1874 in the artist's account book describes "4 small panels...Speldhurst nave ...Blessing children £10 ea....£40."

This stained-glass design appears to have been very popular and was used in twenty-four schemes after Speldhurst, thirteen of which were commissioned in the twentieth century. Later orders include windows for Bermuda (1907) and Isipingo, South Africa (1928). The tapestry is very close to the original stained glass but was re-drawn either by J.H. Dearle before his death in 1932 or shortly afterwards by his son Duncan (who took over as manager of the Works), presumably for use as a cartoon. The habit at Merton Abbey was to make a photographic enlargement of the preliminary drawing, onto which decorative details were added later. The full-sized cartoon was then used at the loom by the weavers.

One of the last-known tapestries to be woven by Morris & Co., it seems to have been specifically designed for St. Andrew and St. Paul's church in 1931-32 or soon afterwards. The side-chapel for which it was woven is dedicated to youth. Although too late to appear in H.C. Marillier's 1927 publication, *History of the Merton Abbey Tapestry Works*, this tapestry is mentioned in the author's amended typescript, the original of which is now in the Textiles and Dress Section of the V & A. This manuscript gives a precise date for the weaving. Morris & Co. tapestry weavers were particularly busy at the time of this commission. Between 1929 and 1933, two large tapestries were woven for Christ Church, Cranbrook, commissioned by George Booth, the Chicago newspaper magnate, for the community that he founded in Michigan Hills. In 1933 weaving started on a second panel for the chapel of Lancing College, a public school near Worthing, in Sussex. Two of the weavers employed on the *Suffer Little Children* tapestry, Mears and Wingate, were taken on especially for the Lancing College panel, so the Montreal panel must have followed soon afterwards.

Only Morris & Co.'s later tapestries have the identification marks of a bishop's mitre (to represent Merton Abbey), and weavers' initials, which are listed in the order of the weavers' seniority. This tapestry was woven by Percy Sheldrick, Sidney Mears, Wallace Stephens and Arthur Wingate. Percy Sheldrick joined Morris & Co. in 1921, having trained as a weaver at the Central School of Arts and Crafts following his demobilization from army service in the 1914-18 war. His college training was completed under Walter Taylor, who in turn had been taught to weave at Merton Abbey by Henry Dearle, Morris's first apprentice tapestry weaver. Sheldrick worked at Merton Abbey for nineteen years and was one of the last to leave in 1939, when he was the firm's master weaver. Duncan Dearle became Design Director and took over supervision of the Merton Abbey Works on the death of his father; he would certainly have been the supervisor of weaving at the time this panel was made. However, it is likely that Percy Sheldrick, being the most experienced hand employed, actually supervised the work.

Woven in the traditional "slit" technique, this tapestry shows the high level of technical expertise that was attained in the Morris workshops.

No. F: 32*

MAUD BEDDINGTON

The Maids of Elfenmere
Hand-woven tapestry
129.4 x 132.0 cm
Private collection, Vancouver

A second woven tapestry with strong Morris connections can be found in Canada today. This circular panel, *The Maids of Elfenmere*, was designed by Maud Beddington, a follower of Edward Burne-Jones, and almost certainly woven by William Sleath, one of the first tapestry apprentices at Morris & Co. under the tutelage of J.H. Dearle. A maverick character, he built up a busy freelance weaving and repairing business, in addition to continuing to work at Merton Abbey until 1920. At the Arts and Crafts Exhibition of 1906 he exhibited a tapestry panel designed by Maud Beddington called *The Watchman*. It is likely that *The Maids of Elfenmere* was woven about the same time.

The owner of this tapestry also possesses the original Beddington oil sketch of the composition and the preparatory cartoon, drawn onto a cotton ground. This shows a quite different technique than that used at Merton Abbey: the original drawings were photographed and then en-

NO. F: 32

larged prints were made to full size for direct use by the weavers at the looms.

ENDNOTES

1. Morris's *"Si Je Puis"* hanging is now at Kelmscott Manor, Oxfordshire. A second early piece, given by D.G. Rossetti to the painter William Bell Scott, has recently been brought to the author's attention.

2. Examples designed for the bedroom and drawing-room, and a large hanging showing a repeating sunflower pattern, can now be see at Kelmscott Manor.

3. In 1863 Edward Burne-Jones designed two sets of embroideries, one for his new home at 62 Great Russell Street, London and the other for John Ruskin. Examples for the former scheme, partially worked by Georgiana Burne-Jones, are now in the Victoria and Albert Museum, London.

4. During the late-eighteenth and nineteenth centuries, the term "chintz" was used to describe all glazed printed cottons. This was the most popular summer furnishing from the 1780s until the 1860s.

5. *William Morris: Artist, Writer, Socialist*, vol. 1 (London, 1936), p. 307.

6. See Linda Parry, *William Morris Textiles* (London, 1983), cat. 4, pp. 146-47.

   In the absence of any evidence of such a design, *Jasmine Trail* and *Jasmine Trellis* were thought to be the same pattern. It is hoped that this mistake will be corrected in a planned revision of my book.

7. Merton, Surrey, a village south of Wimbledon on the River Wandle, is the site of Merton Priory, built in 1115 by Gilbert, the Norman Sheriff of Surrey. Within the priory's walls a factory for printing calico was established in 1724, the chapel being utilized as the print-room. In 1752 a second mill was opened within the walls, and a third somewhat later.

8. Correspondence between Morris and Wardle, giving details of their experimental work together, is now in the National Art Library, V & A. Wardle's pattern-books, containing samples of Morris fabric trials, are part of the collection of the Whitworth Art Gallery, University of Manchester.

9. Many of Morris & Co.'s original pearwood printing-blocks have survived in public collections. A number are in the William Morris Gallery, Walthamstow, and one set, those for *Strawberry Thief*, is now in the V & A.

10. See Peter Floud, "Dating Morris Patterns", *The Architectural Review* (July 1959).

11. The term "medieval" in a British nineteenth-century context covered a much wider period than is acceptable today. Some textiles in the South Kensington Museums which Morris admired for their early qualities have been dated as late as the seventeenth century. Others have since been proved to be fake. See Parry, *William Morris Textiles* (London, 1983), p. 47.

12. A number of examples, including watercolour copies of Indian carpets and Persian silks from the South Kensington Museums Collection, are now in the Helen and Sanford Berger collection, Carmel, California.

13. Jan Marsh, *Jane and May Morris* (London, 1986); Linda Parry, *Textiles of the Arts and Crafts Movement* (London, 1988). The exhibition was mounted at the William Morris Gallery, Walthamstow in 1989.

14. Parry numbers refer to Linda Parry, *William Morris Textiles*.

15. *The English House* (Oxford, 1987), pp. 208, 218.

16. *The Books of William Morris* (London, 1897; reprinted 1968), no. 109, pp. 142-43.

17. Quoted in J.W. Mackail, *The Life of William Morris*, vol. 2 (London, 1899; reprinted New York, 1968), p. 227.

18. See A.C. Sewter, *The Stained Glass of William Morris and his Circle* (New Haven and London, 1974), fig. 449.

19. Sewter also lists a drawing "said to be for this window" in the Dundee Museum and Art Gallery, Dundee, Scotland (3/61).

FURNITURE

Robert Little

The "intensely medieval appearance"[1] of the earliest furniture designed by William Morris and Edward Burne-Jones, dating from 1856-57, for their Red Lion Square studio, placed their creators, perhaps unwittingly, in the camp of the more progressive designers and architects of the time. This group included William Butterfield, William Burges and G.E. Street, all of whom were devout Gothicists, much indebted to A.W.N. Pugin.[2] For nine months Morris had worked with Street, at whose office he met Philip Webb, destined to become the architectural mentor and principal furniture-designer for Morris & Co. until the late 1880s.[3] Webb was responsible for designing the elaborate, large-scale, commissioned pieces of furniture, especially those with painted decoration executed by artists associated with the firm (see No. G: 1). In addition, he developed a range of smaller, more portable, utilitarian furniture with no particular stylistic allusions but influenced nonetheless by the craft traditions of English regional or vernacular furniture.[4] These two types of furniture had been produced within a year or so of the firm's inception, for by 1862 it had exhibited at the International Exhibition examples of the fine painted Gothic-style furniture upon which rested so much of its subsequent reputation and public perception;[5] but it had also produced more day-to-day pieces, such as "a chest, a bookcase, a wardrobe, a sideboard, a washstand, a dressing table..." designed by Webb,[6] and made "by Mr. Curwen, a cabinet-maker in the neighborhood."[7] This broad range reflected Morris's own thinking with regard to furniture design, for in one of the few statements he ever made regarding furniture, he claimed,

> moreover I must needs think of furniture as two kinds...one part of it...the necessary workaday furniture...simple to the last degree....–But besides this...there is the other kind of what I shall call state furniture; I mean sideboards, cabinets and the like....[8]

NO. G: 6. WARINGTON TAYLOR and PHILIP WEBB for MORRIS & CO., *"Morris" reclining armchair*, 1866 and later

Ford Madox Brown also designed furniture for the Firm: very simple, low-cost, joiner-made cottage or vernacular furniture stripped of all extraneous ornamentation or veneer.[9] Morris himself owned bedroom furniture of this type.[10] One model of the *Sussex* chairs has been attributed to Madox Brown (No. G: 5).[11] Rossetti is also considered responsible for the design of another of the *Sussex* chairs.[12] His own particular tastes veered toward the late-seventeenth through early-nineteenth centuries, especially the elegantly scaled furniture of the Regency period, as reflected in his personal collection, and his own design for a settee of 1862-63.[13] The tendency to produce lighter, more portable furniture was encouraged by Warington Taylor, manager of the Firm from 1865 to 1870.[14] While steering Morris & Co. into lucrative custom-order commissions within an architectural framework designed in conjunction with Webb,[15] he promoted the design of readily saleable furnishings such as the *Sussex* chairs, which did not require extensive and costly designer-client consultations (Nos. G: 2-3). By this time, the Firm had acquired cabinet-making shops in Ormond Yard, in the Bloomsbury neighborhood near Queen Square.[16]

Morris himself became involved with the production of furniture when it had to be painted or gilded.[17] From 1870 the Firm was managed by George Wardle until he was succeeded by W.A.S. Benson in 1896.[18] In 1890 the Firm came under the control of F. and R. Smith,[19] and it acquired the extensive Pimlico workshops of one of the most prestigious cabinet-making establishments, Holland and Sons, who earlier in the century had made furniture to Pugin's designs.[20] In the 1880s and 1890s Morris & Co. furniture was increasingly designed by Philip Webb's architectural assistant, George Jack, along with Mervyn Macartney and W.A.S. Benson.[21] Their work reflected the current trends for furniture derived from the repertoire of English seventeenth- and eighteenth-century designs, the latter exemplified by the three-fold screen (No. F: 6). In this respect, Morris & Co. was not unlike many other top-flight decorating establishments that had to change with the times. By the early decades of the twentieth century, the Firm's catalogues still featured a few of the early-Gothic-style designs from the 1860s.[22] However, the majority of the designs reflected more conservative tastes, and by about 1926 the Firm's catalogue featured a small bookcase cabinet in a restrained "Art Déco" idiom.[23]

Thus, while the furniture designs developed by Morris & Co. evolved, and expanded from its initial Gothic Revival idiom to incorporate a much wider design vocabulary in its later, albeit more conservative products, it nonetheless maintained its high standards, its respect for truth to materials, and a sense of appropriateness of ornamentation. The painted narrative decoration of the early sideboard Burne-Jones executed for himself in 1860 (which later was part of his dining-room furniture at The Grange; see

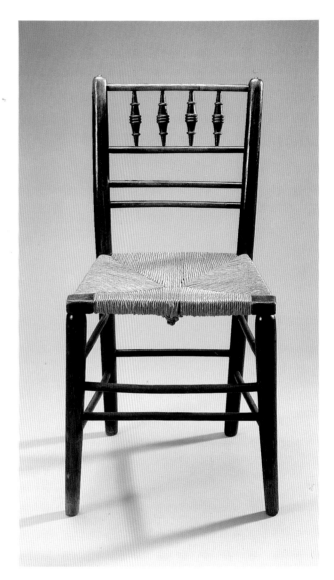

NO. G: 2
MORRIS & CO.,
Sussex arm chair, after 1865

NO. G: 3
MORRIS & CO.,
Sussex chair, after 1865

No. M: 19) gave way to Morris-like floral-patterned inlay, a technically more appropriate adornment for the later wooden piano-case George Jack designed in 1893 for the Sanderson family.[24] The structural integrity inherent in the architecture and furnishings of the Gothic style were perceived by Morris and his colleagues as surviving in the craft traditions of vernacular and more restrained high-style architecture and furnishings of the seventeenth and eighteenth centuries. This, on the one hand, reflected a nineteenth-century romantic attitude toward a more idealized and enriched cultural milieu that saw little positive in contemporary design. On the other hand, it reflected a concomitant concern for a national design aesthetic, for in the artifacts of these earlier periods was perceived a quintessentially English mode of expression.[25]

Yet, like many other objects sold by the Firm, even its most reasonably priced printed textiles, most of the furniture designs were beyond the purchasing power of all but the wealthy, a fact that intensely frustrated Morris. And while most items were made primarily by hand-crafted methods to exacting standards, they perhaps did not always bring as much joy to the maker as they did to the user. It was, significantly, in the *Sussex* chair design, more than any other product sold by the Firm, that the Morrisian dilemma was resolved. The turning and steam-shaping of most of the chair's parts, primarily by mechanically assisted methods, permitted a large production of good, integrally sound, functional design, at low cost.

No. G: 1*

PROBABLY BY PHILIP WEBB
FOR MORRIS & CO.

Library Bookcase c. 1865-77
Unidentified primary and secondary woods (possibly
    walnut or mahogany primary wood), painted, gilded
    and silvered decoration
glazed doors, brass(?) fittings
Width: 281.9 x 264.2 cm (approx.)
Painted and gilded decoration on two panel doors, one
    bearing a coat of arms: "Azure, a horse's head erased,
    argent between three horseshoes", the other panel
    bearing the script initial, *"T.R.M."*, a handwritten
    label inscribed *"Mr. W. Morris 26 Queen Square
    Bloomsbury London. Per L.N.W.R.* [*London and North-
    Western Railway*] *luggage Train"*, this label missing
    since about 1971
Provenance: originally made for Thomas R. Morris,
    brother of William Morris; Francis S. McNalty Esq.;
    sold, Christie, Manson, and Woods, London, 25 Feb-
    ruary, 1971, lot 170; R.H.V. Tee & Son, Vancouver
Private collection

NO. G: 1. Probably PHILIP WEBB for MORRIS & CO.,
  Library bookcase, c. 1865-77

The coat of arms painted on one of the door-panels of this
bookcase is that of William Morris's own family, and the
initials "T.R.M.", painted on the other panel, are those of
Morris's brother, Thomas. If the label bearing Morris's
Queen Street address, formerly attached to the bookcase
when it was sold in London in 1971, was original to the
piece, it suggests that the piece may have been made between
1865 and 1877, in the early period of the Firm's existence.

As such, it brings into focus a number of issues a young
design collaborative had to solve as it evolved from meeting the personal needs of its founding members, with their
very definite aesthetic and quality concerns, to a company
that must accommodate a new and varied clientèle, of presumably similar aesthetic persuasion, with different types
and styles of furniture.

As the Firm was increasingly called upon to provide
furnishings in varied media for many of Webb's architectural commissions, it broadened its scope to include works
executed in not only the revived Gothic design vocabulary
upon which the Firm was founded, but also high-style and
vernacular interpretations of seventeenth- and eighteenth-
century design traditions. Credit for initially guiding the
Firm in this direction has to be given to Rossetti, Madox
Brown, Taylor, and Webb. This willingness to look at
design sources other than Morris's beloved Gothic was
due, in part, to the fact that for many architects of his generation, including Webb, the Gothic Revival had run its
course. During the late-Stuart and throughout the subsequent Georgian period, many new types of domestic furniture evolved, one of these being the free-standing glazed
bookcase with central projecting cabinet, often fitted with
a drawer or desk. This achieved a synthesis of form in the
middle decades of the eighteenth century. Such a piece of
furniture, even by means of a later generic or vernacular
interpretation, must have served as a precedent for the
present bookcase.

Its details and decoration, however, are very much
within the range of the design vocabulary developed by
the Firm in the 1860s. Its parapet-like cornice, and mun-
tins with painted decoration of leaftips and flowerheads,
along with its Georgian vernacular or "Queen Anne"
form, betray the hand of Philip Webb. The door-panels,
with painted decoration of scrolling foliage surrounding
the initialled escutcheon and the coat of arms, suggest,
however, William Morris the textile designer, especially
his *Crown Imperial* design, registered in 1876.

No. G: 2

MORRIS & CO.

Sussex Arm-chair after 1865
Ebonized birch, rush seat
84.5 x 54.5 x 45.0 cm
Morris & Co. catalogue, c. 1910
Joan R. Randall

No. G: 3

MORRIS & CO.

Sussex chair after 1865
Ebonized birch, rush seat
83.5 x 42.0 x 41.0 cm
Morris & Co. catalogue, c. 1910
Joan R. Randall

No. G: 4

UNKNOWN DESIGNER

Settee in the "Sussex" style c. 1870s-80s
Ebonized birch, rush seat
93.5 x 117.5 cm x 57.0 cm
Joan R. Randall

Norah Gillow has proposed that this settee is derived from a Morris & Co. prototype.

No. G: 5

MORRIS & CO.

"Sussex" round-seat chair after 1865
Ebonized birch, rush seat
Height: 88.9 cm
Morris & Co. catalogue, c. 1910
Dennis Young, Halifax

The most significant contribution made by Morris & Co. to nineteenth-century furniture design was undoubtedly the range of seating furniture known as the "Sussex Rush Seated Chairs" (as they were published in the Firm's catalogues of about 1910-12). These designs, perhaps the most successful of the Firm's creations, were an extrapolation of several ideas.

Credit for the design of the chairs has been assigned variously to Ford Madox Brown and Dante Gabriel Rossetti. Madox Brown is said to have urged the Firm to make the chairs; indeed, one of the versions of these chairs, and

FIG. G: 1. Advertisement for *Sussex* rush-seated chairs, from a Morris & Co. sales catalogue, after 1899.

a related piano-stool with a circular rush seat and crossed back spindles, is often referred to as the *Madox Brown* chair.[26] Both Morris and Burne-Jones owned examples of this chair (see Nos. M: 19-20). Another arm-chair design with a lyre or wheatsheaf back-motif is entitled the *Rossetti* chair. Its form was derived from late eighteenth-century French regional chairs. An example of the *Rossetti* arm-chair graced the artist's sitting room at 16 Cheyne Walk. The *Sussex* model proper, available in side-chair, arm-chair, corner-chair, and settee versions, was distinguished by four turned spindles between the crest and lower rails of the back. The *Sussex* models were the least expensive chairs of the whole group. They were so successful that several rival firms offered their own versions (No. G: 4).

The *Sussex* name of the chair may, however, have been a misnomer, due possibly to the state of knowledge of vernacular furniture types in the 1860s. The turned elements of the chair, which are dowelled into one another to form a frame onto which a rush seat was woven, relate it to a tradition of chairmaking by members of the Turners' Guild that can be traced back at least to the Middle Ages. Recent research by Bernard Cotton has brought to light the existence, by the mid-eighteenth century, of English regional or vernacular chairmaking traditions that include turner-made chairs. Indeed, Cotton illustrates several types of vernacular chairs with turned elements and rush seats originating in several areas of England, including examples from East Anglia, dateable to about 1790 to 1830, from the West Midlands, dateable to about 1830 to 1840, and from the northwest region, dateable to about 1760 to 1870, but apparently none from the south-central or Sussex region.[27] While these chairs were supposedly made for regional consumption, one cannot preclude a wider dispersal into other areas of England by means of trade or individual dislocation. These above-noted chairs have features in common with an example depicted in an 1820 painting by C.R. Leslie called *Londoners Gypsying*.[28] All of these chairs have elements markedly like those found on the Morris & Co. *Sussex* chair. Thus, unwittingly, Mackail's comment about the chair may have been literally correct: "It was not his [Morris's] own invention but was copied with trifling improvements from an old chair of village manufacture *picked up* in Sussex",[29] although not necessarily made in Sussex.

Equally, the design precedents for the *Sussex* chair can also be seen in a type of seating furniture popular in England and America during the period 1790 to 1820 and known variously as "fancy" or "painted" furniture. Such furniture, so called because it was frequently "Japanned" or painted black, had details outlined in gilt and, when space permitted, was highlighted with small painted panels or details. A pair of arm-chairs of this type, similar to the *Sussex* arm-chair, has recently passed through London sales rooms.[30] Like the *Sussex* (and parenthetically the *Rossetti*) arm-chairs, it features in common the manner of attaching the arm supports through the seat rails on to the stretchers. Rossetti himself owned a Regency settee of this painted variety at least by 1863, by which time he had designed two settees. One model, shown at the 1862 International Exhibition, and known today only from a drawing, had a rectangular shape, fashioned of plain interconnected wooden elements – technically similar to the *Sussex* chair. He also designed a Regency-style settee intended for his bedroom, which is now in the Ashmolean Museum, Oxford. Thus at this early date in the career of Morris & Co., while Morris and Burne-Jones were still looking at the Middle Ages as a source for their work, Rossetti was already looking at the more recent past, at a type of furniture that was much lighter in scale.

So, too, was Warington Taylor, in his plea for the Firm to produce "movable furniture, light, something you can pull about with one hand."[31] It was Taylor after all who found the chair in Sussex around 1865. As the ablest manager of the Firm, he redirected it more effectively, secured imported commissions, and encouraged the fabrication and sale of ready-made items like the *Sussex* chair. Shortly after he joined the Firm as manager in 1865, his health broke, necessitating restorative retreats to his quarters in Hastings, in Sussex, where he directed the Firm's affairs by letter. Thus the *Sussex* chair synthesized elements derived from ancient and more recent vernacular craft traditions and had as well the lightness, elegance, and low price that appealed to an audience tiring of both the more commercially conservative and the ponderously progressive furniture then available. Models of these chairs sold for less than ten shillings each and were in constant production until at least 1914, if not later.

The *Sussex* range of chairs, much like the bentwood chairs developed in Austria by Michel Thonet (1796-1871) and the vernacular Chiavari chair popular in Italy, were

NO. G: 5

the most important forerunners of the low-cost, standardized furniture whose conception and production were to preoccupy many architects and designers in the early decades of the twentieth century. Morris, of course, would have been outraged at the notion of standardization, but his socialist side must have been pleased with such an attractive, inexpensive, basic piece of furniture. He used *Sussex* chairs in his dining-room and in his study, and Burne-Jones used them in his studio (see Nos. M: 17-18).

No. G: 6

WARINGTON TAYLOR AND
PHILIP WEBB FOR MORRIS & CO.

"Morris" Reclining Arm-chair 1866 and later
Ebonized wood, recently upholstered in Sanderson's
　Willow Boughs adapted for fabric, c. 1895
Height: 99.0 cm
Mary F. Williamson

Unlike much of the furniture sold by Morris & Co., the design of which is difficult to ascribe to one particular individual, the names of the collaborators involved in the design of the reclining chair sold by the Firm are known to us. A sketch by Warington Taylor for this chair, dated 1866, was sent to Philip Webb, apparently for approval, and the sketch was annotated by Taylor, "back and seat made with bars across to put cushions on, moving on a hinge, a chair model of which I saw with an old carpenter at Hurstmenceaux, Sussex by name Ephraim Colman."[32] Taylor, Webb and Colman thus should claim credit for the chair. Like the *Sussex* chairs, and so many other creations of the Firm, the *Morris* chair was a re-working, with some significant changes, of an existing idea.

Large-scale arm-chairs with adjustable backs were not an idea new to the nineteenth century. Among the earliest-known chairs of this form were examples recorded in Spain, France, and England by the third quarter of the seventeenth century, intended for use either as sleeping or as invalids' chairs. Such chairs were fitted with fixed seats and hinged backs, the inclination of which was adjustable by ratchets – much like the *Morris* chair. The few surviving examples suggest that, because of their inherent cost and the social customs of the time, they were made for persons of great wealth, and were intended for use in private chambers rather than in public or reception rooms. These were the precursors to the upholstered easy chairs developed during the eighteenth century in many varied forms, some of which still retained a hinged back. This form of chair is rarely seen in more vernacular interpretations. Changing social customs during the late-eighteenth and throughout the nineteenth century brought about a gradual easing as to the appropriateness and placement in particular rooms of various types of seating furniture. Thus, easy chairs of all types, mechanical and patented reclining chairs including the *Morris* chair, along with large, overstuffed seating furniture sold by Morris and other companies and formerly seen only in men's clubs, became more commonplace in the domestic drawing-room. However, they were still intended primarily for men, as the strictures of women's daytime dress precluded lounging in an easy chair. It would however be hard to imagine Jane Burden Morris bound by such social conventions. The *Morris* reclining chair was the survivor of an earlier chair-type within a more liberated social context for its use.

Stylistically, the *Morris* chair was likewise a synthesis of diverse design elements. Its square tapered front legs with brass shoe castors, its upswept arms, and tall, slightly tapered back, relate to the design vocabulary of chairs popular toward the end of the eighteenth century, but whose basic forms remained within the chairmakers' repertoire and were known by means of pattern-books. Toward the mid-1830s, turning reached a zenith of popularity as a means of embellishing furniture. This was especially so with regard to chair design, where spool-turning was often used to shape most structural members. Spool-turned easy chairs became a sub-style or type of furniture that remained popular throughout the nineteenth and into the twentieth century. Morris & Co. adopted this style not only for its reclining chair but also for a settee and a chaise-longue of related design. This nineteenth-century interpretation of an earlier seventeenth-century decorative device was synthesized with what was basically an underlying form of eighteenth-century derivation.

The reclining chair was apparently very popular; both Morris himself and Burne-Jones owned examples upholstered in velvet (see also No. M: 20). Supposedly copied by other English suppliers, it was also fashionable in the United States. In Philadelphia, Allan and Brothers made at least two versions, very close to the Morris original, but with slight variations to the back and arm terminals. The American designer Gustav Stickley also made his own very rectilinear version of the reclining chair but, apart from its cushioned upholstery and adjustable back, it had little in common with the Morris version.

ENDNOTES

1. J.W. Mackail, *The Life of William Morris*, vol. 1 (London, 1899; reprinted New York, 1968), p. 116.

2. N. Cromey-Hawke, "William Morris and Victorian Painted Furniture", *The Connoisseur* 191 (January 1976): 34-38; and Charles Handley-Read, "Progressive Design, Reformers and Innovators", *World Furniture*, ed. Helena Hayward (London, New York, Sydney, Toronto, 1965), pp. 216-20.

3. Jeremy Cooper, *Victorian and Edwardian Furniture and Interiors: From the Gothic Revival to Art Nouveau* (London, 1987), p. 157.

4. Mark Girouard, *Sweetness and Light: The Queen Anne Movement, 1860-1900* (New Haven and London, 1977), pp. 16-19.

5. Philip Henderson, *William Morris: His Life, Work and Friends* (London, 1986), p. 10.

6. Mackail, *The Life of William Morris*, vol. 1, p. 159.

7. *Ibid.*, p. 154.

8. Quoted in Elizabeth Aslin, *Nineteenth-Century English Furniture* (London, 1962), p. 56.

9. Gillian Naylor, *The Arts and Crafts Movement*, 2nd ed. (London, 1990), pl. 17.

10. Cooper, *Victorian and Edwardian Furniture...*, p. 155.

11. Charlotte Gere and J. Mordaunt Crook, *Morris and Company* (London, 1979), p. 9, cat. 12; and Simon Jervis, "Sussex Chairs in 1820", *Furniture History* (1974): 99.

12. Jervis, "Sussex Chairs in 1820": 99.

13. Charlotte Gere, *Nineteenth Century Decoration: The Art of the Interior* (New York, 1989), pp. 14-15, pl. 6-7; p. 331, pl. 397.

14. Duncan Robinson and Stephen Wildman, *Morris and Company in Cambridge* (Cambridge, 1980), p. 69, cat. 85.

15. Henderson, *William Morris...*, pp. 80-6.

16. Girouard, *Sweetness and Light...*, p. 19.

17. Mackail, *The Life of William Morris*, vol. 1, pp. 179-80; and Aslin, *Nineteenth-Century English Furniture*, p. 58.

18. Mackail, *The Life of William Morris*, vol. 2, p. 46.

19. Henderson, *William Morris...*, p. 86; and Cooper, *Victorian and Edwardian Furniture...*, p. 160.

20. Cooper, *Victorian and Edwardian Furniture...*, p. 165.

21. Pauline Agius, *British Furniture: 1880-1915* (Woodbridge, Suffolk, 1978), p. 24; Aslin, *Nineteenth-Century English Furniture*, p. 58; and Cooper, *Victorian and Edwardian Furniture...*, p. 165.

22. Cooper, *Victorian and Edwardian Furniture...*, p. 165.

23. Morris & Co. catalogue, c. 1910-12, frontispiece and p. 23, no. 519.

24. Morris & Co. catalogue, n.d. (after 1926), p. 6; Cooper, *Victorian and Edwardian Furniture*, plate 453.

25. This fact was central to Hermann Muthesius's thinking; see *The English House*, abridged translation of *Das Englische Haus*, 2nd ed. (Berlin, 1908-11; Oxford, 1987), pp. 15-18.

26. Gere and Crook, *Morris and Company*, p. 8.

27. Bernard D. Cotton, *The English Regional Chair* (Woodbridge, Suffolk, 1990), pp. 13, 236, 292-96, 314-15, and 328-29.

28. See Jervis, "Sussex Chairs in 1820": 99.

29. Mackail, *The Life of William Morris*, vol. 2, p. 46. Italics mine.

30. Christie, London, 12 July 1990, lot 104, ill.

31. Quoted in Naylor, *The Arts and Crafts Movement*, p. 107.

32. Quoted in Aslin, *Nineteenth-Century Furniture*, p. 55.

C E R A M I C S

Essay by Elizabeth Collard

Entries by Meredith Chilton

William Frend De Morgan, the potter closest to William Morris, was both of his time and apart from it. The preoccupation with decorative design that rapidly gathered momentum in Victorian days, sweeping potters along with it, dictated the direction of his inventiveness. Yet his work, marked as it was by what his sister-in-law and biographer, Mrs. A.M.W. Stirling, called "the stamp of his individual genius," set him apart and denied success to copyists.

There was no potting tradition in this Londoner's background. There were, however, pronounced versatility and a spirit of innovation. He counted among his forbears adventurous military men; a grandfather, who came to Quebec to be trained in mercantile pursuits, returned to England to become a clergyman, and was later an actuary (an emerging profession). His father, Augustus De Morgan, belonged to a new breed of mathematicians revitalizing the discipline in England and developing the abstract approach to algebra. His mother, Sophia Frend, supported advanced causes, including women's suffrage. Even as an octogenarian, her enthusiasm for new ideas was evident. William grew up in a home where innovation was an inheritance as well as the intellectual climate. He was himself to be an innovator, enthusiasm characterizing his spirited approach to every venture.

Significantly, De Morgan's associates remembered him almost as much for his scientific investigations as for his artistic accomplishments. "There was hardly anything that he was not prepared to improve upon," said Reginald Blunt, his pottery manager.[1] Halsey Ricardo, his partner, called him "a scientific enthusiast," every subject he took up vivified by his imagination.[2] Initially, he planned a career in the fine arts, enrolling in the Royal Academy Schools in 1859. Though he was soon disillusioned (with his talent and the teaching), those few years, scarcely four in all, were crucial, for it was then that De Morgan formed the great fortunate friendships of his life – friendships that drew him into the decorative arts.

NO. H: 13. WILLIAM DE MORGAN, painted by Charles Passenger, *Dish*, 1888-97

One friend was Henry Holiday (1839-1927), an artist and worker in stained glass. It was Holiday who, in 1863, took De Morgan to Red Lion Square and introduced him to William Morris. De Morgan came to regard Morris as "the most wonderful genius I ever knew."[3] His own sense of fun, his humour (often seen in his ceramic designs), the ease with which he slipped into the feigned and theatrical cockney speech affected by the Pre-Raphael-ites, his ready wit (inherited from both parents), all made him at once at home in the Morris circle.

For both De Morgan and Morris, their association enriched creativity and sheer enjoyment of life. Blunt remembered Morris, "keen to discuss some new project," bounding up the stairs shouting "Bill!" at the top of his voice.[4] William Bale, one of De Morgan's painters, recorded that Morris "was always coming round to get ideas."[5] De Morgan liked to recall expeditions when the two of them never stopped laughing.[6] They had aims and ideals in com-mon, although De Morgan did not share all Morris's convictions. Over poli-tics they "battled" happily until De Morgan found such chats "less and less possible."[7] De Morgan was not a member of the Art Workers' Guild, though he was of its off-shoot, the Arts and Crafts Exhibition Society. He was a friend and ally of Morris, not a disciple. Morris sold De Morgan's work and used it in decorative schemes, but De Morgan remained independent. "A common error," he once said, "is to suppose that I was a partner in Morris's firm. I was never connected with his business beyond the fact that, on his own initiative, he exhibited and sold my work, and that subsequently he employed my tiles in his schemes of decoration.... I never could work except by myself and in my own manner."[8]

Though De Morgan's independence was never in question, Morris did have a profound effect upon his career. Soon after they met he urged him to experiment with stained glass. De Morgan dabbled (his word) in glass and began tile-painting, doing some designs for Morris. By 1872, when he was

NO. H: 18
WILLIAM MORRIS,
Daisy, c. 1865

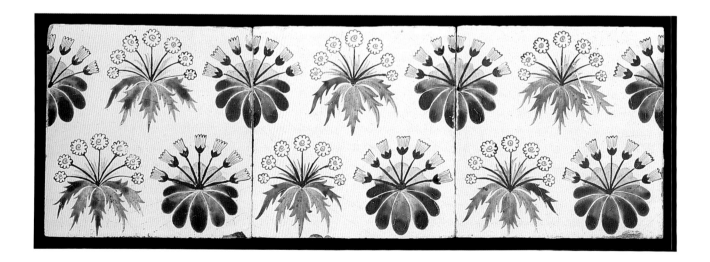

NO. H: 23
WILLIAM DE MORGAN,
Boa Constrictor, 1872-81

ready to expand his activities, tiles were in the ascendant, a turn of events that had its own effect on Morris & Co.

Morris's involvement with tiles had begun before the meeting with De Morgan. It started when he wanted tiles for a fireplace surround in the Red House. Dissatisfied with what he could find in England, Morris had imported tile-blanks from Holland, experimented with painting on them, and fired them in a kiln for stained glass.[9] From that time on (1862), tile-decorating became one of the activities of Morris, Marshall, Faulkner & Co. (later reorganized as Morris & Co.). Many of the early tiles were painted by Kate and Lucy Faulkner and Georgiana Burne-Jones.[10] By the time De Morgan entered the Morris circle, this work was already under way, but as his tile-production gradually increased, the need for the Firm to engage in it lessened. J.W. Mackail noted that tile-painting at Morris & Co. "had… almost ceased" by 1881. Certain of Morris's patterns were carried on to the end of the century, but these, as Mackail said, were "chiefly for use in fire-places" and their production was limited.[11] De Morgan had become a major influence, even though, as he made clear, he was never a partner in the Firm. De Morgan and Morris worked together while working separately.

All De Morgan's work was carried on in London or its vicinity: in Fitzroy Square (prior to 1872); in Cheyne Row, Chelsea (1872-81); at Merton Abbey, near Morris's workshops (1882-88); and in Townmead Road, Fulham (1888-1907). In 1888, with the move to Sands End Pottery, he entered into a partnership with Halsey Ricardo that was dissolved in 1898 when he formed a new partnership with Charles and Fred Passenger and Frank Iles. At first he, too, purchased blanks on which his designs were painted, not by himself but by those employed for this work (painters' initials frequently appear on De Morgan wares). But that driving need to improve, noted by Blunt, made De Morgan explore potting, with the result that tiles were later made at his own premises, and pots were hand-thrown, using his own earthenware body.

The nature of their repetitive use put tiles in the mass-production category. For reproducing patterns, in any number required, De Morgan devised an ingenious method. As normally carried out, it involved an outline drawing (on translucent paper) affixed to a sheet of glass, with tissue-paper on the other side, and the whole set against the light. A painter traced the design onto the tissue, adding colours by reference to a master drawing. Completed, the tissue was laid face down on a tile covered with a white slip (made into a paste with sodium silicate), sodium silicate was brushed over it, and powdered glaze sprinkled on "like sugar from a sugar-castor."[12] In the firing the pigments combined chemically with the slip, the paper burned away, and the tile emerged with colours glowing. Every tile was, in this way, a hand-painted effort.

For hollow-wares, designs might be painted directly on the pieces, or stencils used. Notations on some of the more than 2,000 sketches and designs preserved at the Victoria and Albert Museum, London, indicate that painters were occasionally allowed initiative, but in essence De Morgan exerted tight factory discipline. When Bale once added an ornament, De Morgan spotted it at once and demanded an explanation. "I thought it wouldn't matter...", Bale answered. "*I thought!*" De Morgan repeated. "Please understand I don't pay you to think! If you think again, you must think elsewhere!"[13]

Colour, a potent means of making an impact, occupied De Morgan's scientific enthusiasm for years, in particular lustre (metallic) colour. In an 1892 lecture before the Society of Arts, he outlined his long research, from the day he set the roof afire (prompting his landlord to hasten his departure) to the successes, when his lustred wares burst forth in a blaze of red, gold, ruby, or a haunting yellow-grey that in certain lights flashed suddenly with azure.

Morris's urging to try stained glass had actually led De Morgan to lustre. It was his noting the iridescence that occasionally developed from the "yellow stain of silver" on overfired glass that prompted him to search out "the lost Art of Moorish or Gubbio lustre" (already re-discovered in Italy, though De Morgan did not know it at the time).[14] Lustre is notoriously difficult to control in firing. Depending on technique, it can result in a dazzling metallic sheen or shimmering iridescence. Because De Morgan's work was experimental – and progressive – his lustre might vary in intensity or fail altogether in spots, but even when he ran into obvious difficulties results could be impressive. Subtle effects were achieved with varying tones of the same colour.

NO. H: 1. WILLIAM DE MORGAN, painted by Fred Passenger, *Covered Vase*, 1880-97

Not only his lustre glowed brilliantly; De Morgan's "Persian" colours (rich blues, turquoise, puce, green) were attracting attention by the 1870s. "Persian" was a word in all art-conscious potters' and designers' vocabularies. Owen Jones had endorsed it in 1856. *The Art Journal* praised "Persian design" tiles in 1871.[15] Christopher Dresser wrote in 1873 that no ornament was more "intricately beautiful."[16] De Morgan was of his time and at one with Morris in being inspired by Islamic art, loosely defined as Persian. His own designs were often derived from the work of Turkish potters who had been active near Iznik three centuries earlier.

De Morgan did not limit himself to Islamic sources: he drew upon classical mythology, medieval art, the Renaissance, and natural history. His humour found expression in grotesques and fantasies; impossible creatures sprang exuberantly into life when his imagination played over them. Heraldic beasts decorated tiles, ships of the ancient world sailed lustre seas, sinuous serpents gave rhythm and movement to flat patterns. What May Morris called his "winding beast-forms and great sweeping lines" were his special bent.[17] Blunt wrote of "the perfectly adapted pattern...of limb and fin and wing."[18] Flowers were favourites on tiles, from the exotic to the familiar, from "Persian" to the ubiquitous sunflower of Victorian decoration. To each he gave his own interpretation. The occasional floral tile (a water-lily pattern is one) shows Japanese influence, but the cult of Japan and the blue-and-white craze that saw Edward Burne-Jones and his wife dining off Japanese porcelain and Dante Gabriel Rossetti excitedly turning over an oriental dish of "splendid blue" at a dinner party (and thereby depositing a large salmon on the tablecloth)[19] never gripped De Morgan to the extent that Islamic sources did.

Like Morris, De Morgan was not a copyist. His sources inspired him but he made them his own; what he borrowed he recreated. His wife, the artist Evelyn Pickering, summed up the power of his designs when she said, "the secret is – William himself."[20]

All De Morgan's ceramic work was in earthenware. He disliked most porcelain and had "an incurable aversion" to Sèvres, which, he said, set his teeth on edge.[21] A preference for earthenware was a feature of artistic taste of the day. It was noted by *The Art Journal* after the 1871 International Exhibition in London, when "bold and artistic earthenware" overshadowed the "less demonstrative" porcelain.[22] Tiles were part of this resurgence of earthenware. Their Victorian revival for interior decoration amounted almost to a mania. One North American writer suggested single tiles could rank as ornaments, "like vases or other pottery,"[23] and framed De Morgan tiles were used in this manner, although usually they were set in walls or around fireplaces.

Tiles were De Morgan's staple output, an economic dependability, but

NO. H: 15. WILLIAM DE MORGAN, painted by Fred Passenger, *Vase*, 1888-97

after the move to Merton Abbey he gave increasing attention to decorative pots (vases, bowls, dishes). At every level of fashionable society it was accepted that art pottery was a necessity. No home could be without it, Canada's *New Dominion Monthly* told its readers in January 1878. De Morgan's pottery catered to the informed, intellectual segment of this pottery-buying public. Princess Louise, Queen Victoria's artist-daughter, whose Rideau Hall drawing room in Ottawa was crowded with "costly" art objects,[24] purchased De Morgan lustre in the form of bowls and flat dishes.[25]

De Morgan achieved for earthenware what Morris was doing for textiles and wallpapers. He received important commissions for tiles, and his pots were admired by the discerning. Such examples as can be traced to Canadian ownership in these years were in the hands of the art-loving affluent.[26] As an artist-potter, De Morgan was an artistic success and a financial failure. Never an astute businessman, he discarded pots he might have sold, advised customers to go elsewhere for cheaper tiles, was always without enough working capital. When, in 1892, he began spending winters abroad for health reasons, leaving employees to guide an already shaky enterprise for half the year without his all-presiding presence, the end, though not rapid, was inevitable. Tastes, too, began to change. *House Beautiful*, reviewing the Chicago Arts and Crafts Exhibition in May 1898, paid tribute to what Morris had done to revive craftsmanship, but deplored making a fetish of what was past and looked forward to new designers and new ideas.

In 1907 De Morgan sadly closed his business. To Blunt he had written in despair, "Who would be an art potter?" and to his friend C.R. Ashbee he admitted, "It costs me so much money every year to make pots that I can't make pots any more."[27] For four years two of his painters, Charles and Fred Passenger, and his kiln-master, Frank Iles, worked on from an address in Brompton Road, using De Morgan's designs (with his permission) on purchased blanks. But in 1911 it all came to an end. De Morgan himself, with that versatility that was an inheritance, had turned to a new career: almost overnight he became a best-selling novelist. *Joseph Vance*, published in 1906,

NO. H: 7
Back of dish

NO. H: 7. WILLIAM DE MORGAN, *Dish*, 1882-88

was hailed by the literary critic Lewis Melville as "the first great English novel that has appeared in the twentieth century."[28] A perceptible link connects De Morgan's work as a ceramic designer and a novelist: to both creative expressions he brought a characteristic attention to detail handled with a skill that concealed the painstaking effort behind it.

De Morgan was a potter, in that tiles and pots were eventually made at his own premises, under his close supervision, but it was the designs that were his real interest. For this reason his work is sometimes disliked by potters, as the twentieth-century expert in lustre, Alan Caiger-Smith, has pointed out: "This is not strange, for De Morgan was not much interested in the pots themselves; they were simply forms for which he made designs."[29] It was, however, the designs, arresting, compelling, unforgettable, that gave De Morgan lasting fame. Certain of the early ones show the influence of William Morris (according to De Morgan, Morris did three tile designs for his execution),[30] and associates (Ricardo, for example) contributed a number, but any assistance of others pales before his fecundity.

Elements found in De Morgan's designs appeared in the work of contemporaries. Ships with billowing sails – classical, medieval, Viking – were frequent favourites, not only with ceramic designers but with metalworkers. John Pearson, who may have worked for De Morgan as a tile-painter before joining Ashbee's Guild of Handicraft, and who later set up on his own, produced copper chargers embossed with sailing ships and cavorting fish.[31] The versatile designer Walter Crane (1845-1915),[32] a friend of Morris and De Morgan, had his own versions of mythical ships – for instance, a galley and mermaids for Maw & Co. in the 1880s,[33] a classical maiden sailing the waves on Pilkington vases.[34] It was an eclectic age, in which the past was ransacked for ideas and no one had exclusive rights to the sources, but copyists failed then and have failed since to capture the elusive charisma that was "William himself." He did not carry the craftsman's work through from conception of design to finished article. His painters copied his designs onto tiles and pots, but his was what a modern ceramic designer, Martin Hunt, has called "the passion" that underlies all effective ceramic design,[35] whether for industry (as in Hunt's case) or the work of "a few" designing "for the few" (as *The Studio* wrote of the fourth Arts and Crafts Exhibition in London).[36] De Morgan belonged to his day, yet at the same time the extraordinary resourcefulness of his talent set him apart.

His novels are no longer widely read but his pottery is regarded as among the important artistic expressions of the period. C.R. Ashbee had the foresight to look ahead and predict of this highly individualistic De Morgan ware: "After his death we shall for great sums collect it into cabinets."[37]

"PERSIAN" DECORATED WARES

No. H: 1

WILLIAM DE MORGAN
PAINTED BY FRED PASSENGER

Covered Vase 1880-97
Earthenware with a white slip and underglaze "Persian"
  decoration in turquoise, blue, green and purple
Height: 40.4 cm
Inscriptions: *W. DE MORGAN*; *FULHAM F.P* painted
  in black
Provenance: the estate of Fred Cowans, Montreal, 1982
Private collection, Ottawa

William De Morgan's "Persian" decoration was inspired
by the brilliantly coloured pottery of Iznik, in Turkey –
one of his most profound artistic influences. Pottery was
made at the royal kilns in Iznik from the end of the fifteenth-century. Iznik wares closely mirrored themes and
motifs used in Ottoman manuscript illumination. By
c. 1551 a vibrant four-colour palette of blue, turquoise,
green and purple was introduced, painted on a white slip
and covered with a thin, clear glaze.

The first European attempts to reproduce Iznik pottery in the nineteenth century were in France, by Joseph-
Theodore Deck (1823-1891), whose wares were exhibited
in Paris in 1867 and in London in 1871. The V & A purchased a mosque lamp with "Persian" decoration by Deck
at the Paris Exhibition in 1867. Minton also made "Persian"
wares and tiles, and the Art Pottery Studio copied pieces
from the South Kensington Museums in the 1870s. De
Morgan was doubtless aware of both Deck's and Minton's
work in this area.

Like Morris, De Morgan was an ardent admirer of
Islamic design. He had access to the extensive collections
of Turkish, Syrian and Persian wares in the V & A, which
were published in a fully illustrated catalogue by C.D.E.
Fortnum, *Maiolica, Hispano-Moresque, Persian, Damascus
and Rhodian Wares*, in 1873. He was also able to use Owen
Jones's *Grammar of Ornament* (1856), in which the principles of Islamic decoration are discussed and illustrated.

De Morgan developed his "Persian" colours in c. 1875-
76 and continued to use them until the pottery closed in
1907. The success of the palette depended in part upon
a brilliant white ground which added luminosity to the
translucent colours. This vase is an excellent example of the
rich blues De Morgan developed, and of how he adapted
Iznik designs to new shapes. Here, two imaginary and

hybrid palmette blossoms spring forth from a dense clus-
ter of "Persian" leaves.

William Bale, one of De Morgan's painters, recorded
that, "Every Persian vase, or nearly so, turned out in his
pottery had a starting by his own hand.... [H]e would
begin a design, say with a flower or a bit of ornament,
and then tell us to put so many around."[38]

No. H: 2

WILLIAM DE MORGAN

Vase 1888-97
Earthenware with a white slip and underglaze "Persian"
  decoration in green, turquoise, blue and purple
Height: 10.0 cm
Marks: impressed tulip
Provenance: Chadwick Shand Gallery, Toronto, 1986
Private collection, Ottawa

NO. H: 2

No. H: 3

WILLIAM DE MORGAN
PAINTED BY CHARLES PASSENGER

Rice Dish 1888-97
Earthenware with a white slip and underglaze "Persian"
    decoration in turquoise, blue, green, purple and black
Diameter: 23.0 cm
Inscriptions: *CP* painted in black
Provenance: Richard Dennis, London, 1970
Private collection, Ottawa

The rice dish, a shallow dish with a central boss and a wide,
flat rim, was a shape first used by De Morgan at Merton
Abbey between 1882 and 1888. Initially, undecorated rice
dishes were acquired from J.H. Davis of Hanley, Staffordshire; Davis produced fine earthenwares as much for export
as for domestic use between 1881 and 1891. De Morgan
also made his own wares, some of which, as this dish, were
based on the shapes of dishes produced by other manufacturers. The rice dish became one of De Morgan's standard
forms and adapted well to both "Persian" and lustre decoration. The distinctive shape enabled the artist to divide
the dish into two separate areas of decoration. Here, De
Morgan framed an abstract floral motif with a repeating
pattern of six lotus flowers.

No. H: 4

WILLIAM DE MORGAN
PAINTED BY JAMES OR
JOHN HERSEY

Bowl 1888-97
Earthenware with a white slip and underglaze "Persian"
    decoration in turquoise, blue, green, pink, purple
    and black
Diameter: 14.3 cm
Inscriptions: *W. DE.MORGAN & CO J.H.* painted in
    black
Provenance: Richard Dennis, London, c. 1989
Private collection, Ottawa

Although the colours on the interior of this small bowl
have run under the glaze during firing, it is easy to discern the exterior alternating panels of blue and turquoise
enclosing small carnations. Carnations first appeared on
Iznik pottery between 1550 and 1560, where they became
a favoured floral motif with other flowers such as tulips
and roses. A larger, footed bowl with a matching dish is
in the V & A; it was painted by Joe Juster with exactly the
same pattern.

WILLIAM DE MORGAN

Vase 1888-97

Earthenware with a white slip and underglaze "Persian" decoration in turquoise and blue

Height: 28.0 cm

Marks: impressed Tudor rose encircled with *WM DE MORGAN & CO – SANDS END POTTERY – FULHAM*

Provenance: gift to the collector by the late Fred Cowans, Montreal

Private collection, Montreal, lent in memory of the late Fred Cowans

The late Fred Cowans was the proprietor of The China Shop in Montreal, which opened in 1942. The shop specialised in fine English porcelain and pottery, initially pre-dating 1840. Some furniture, silver, glass and papier maché were also sold. Mr. Cowans and his manager, Miss Betty Ramsay, had a significant influence on many post-war Canadian ceramic collections. The shop flourished until 1985, when it was closed, four years after Fred Cowans' death in 1981. This vase, which had been made into a lamp, was part of Mr. Cowans' private collection, and had originally belonged to his parents.

NO. H: 5

NO. H: 6

LUSTRE WARES

No. H: 6

WILLIAM DE MORGAN

Goblet 1882-88

Earthenware with alkaline glaze, copper lustre decoration

Height: 10.0 cm

Marks: impressed oval *DE MORGAN MERTON ABBEY*

Provenance: Christie's, London, 17 March 1980, lot 30

Private collection, Ottawa

No. H: 7

WILLIAM DE MORGAN

Dish 1882-88

Glazed pottery, copper lustre decoration

Diameter: 30.5 cm

Marks: impressed *H*

Provenance: Richard Dennis, London

Private collection

This exuberant and fanciful hippocamp, a mythical creature, part horse and part fish, has been whimsically transformed by William De Morgan. Instead of hooves, the hippocamp has flippers. In this instance, it was inspired by classical and Renaissance motifs. Traditionally, *hippocampi* draw the chariot of Neptune and Galatea.

A slightly different version of this design was used for tiles. One appeared in a fireplace designed by Norman Shaw in 1879.[39] The pricked blue design for this tile, with the Chelsea-period serial number 283, is in the V & A.[40] As De Morgan's Chelsea productions appeared to have consisted chiefly of tiles, this dish was tentatively ascribed to the Merton Abbey period. *Hippocampi* continued to appear in De Morgan's menagerie from time to time. They were featured on one of the Livadia jars made at Fulham.[41]

The design was painted on a commercial blank. The uneven quality of the lustre was due to imperfect firing.

No. H: 8

WILLIAM DE MORGAN
PAINTED BY FRED PASSENGER

Dish c. 1880-90
Staffordshire pottery blank; glazed pottery, decorated
    with copper lustre on front and back, some silver
    lustre on front alone
Diameter: 37.0 cm
Marks: impressed *20*
Inscriptions: *FP* in lustre
Provenance: Sidney Carter, Montreal; Mrs. D.C.
    MacCallum, Montreal; gift to collector, 1972
Private collection, Ottawa

Imperious peacocks on display were among De Morgan's best-known designs and were used many times. No two

NO. H: 9

peacock dishes are alike; each shows variety in decoration or background. The design on this large example appears to have been developed in about 1880 and, as was often the case, there is no mark to indicate a precise date. Therefore, a general date encompassing the approximate period when the design was most popular has been ascribed.

Mrs. D.C. MacCallum (1888-1974) was a noted Montreal collector of eighteenth-century English porcelain, but not actively of nineteenth-century pottery. Her collection was sold in 1967 by Donald McLeish of The Chelsea Shop, Toronto. Pieces bearing her printed label may be found in many Canadian public and private collections. This dish was displayed for years in her china-room in Montreal before being given to the collector in 1972.

No. H: 9

WILLIAM DE MORGAN
PAINTED BY B. OR F. SIROCCHI

Vase 1888-97
Earthenware with alkaline glaze, copper lustre decoration
Height: 24.5 cm
Inscription: *Not. S* painted in lustre
Provenance: Fred Cowans, Montreal; The China Shop,
    Montreal, 1982
Private collection, Ottawa

NO. H: 8

The uneven quality of the decoration on this vase illustrates the difficulties of firing lustre.

De Morgan described the lustres he used in an address given to the Society of Arts on 31 May 1892: "The pigment consists simply of white clay, mixed with copper scale or oxide of silver, in proportions varying according to the strength of colour we desire to get."[42] These pigments were painted on the surface of a fired glaze, preferably with a high alkaline content. The decorated pottery was fired again in order to soften the glaze. The kiln was then starved of oxygen, altering the metallic compounds painted decoratively on the surface of the pottery. The length and the intensity of the reduction firing had a marked effect on the range of colours.

No. H: 10

WILLIAM DE MORGAN

Vase 1888-97
Earthenware with alkaline glaze, copper lustre decoration
Height: 10.0 cm
Mark: impressed tulip
Provenance: Christie's, London, 17 March 1980, lot 32
Private collection, Ottawa

NO. H: 10

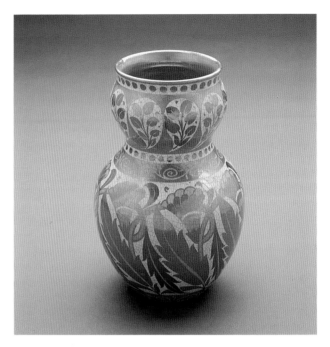

NO. H: 11

No. H: 11

WILLIAM DE MORGAN
PAINTED BY JOE JUSTER

Vase 1888-97
Earthenware with alkaline glaze, decorated in yellow,
    lustred with silver and touches of copper
Height: 18.5 cm
Marks: impressed within a circle of dots enclosing
    W.DE MORGAN & CO SANDS END POTTERY
Inscriptions: *J.J. 2345 5* painted in blue
Provenance: Richard Dennis, London, c. 1987
Private collection, Ottawa

The floral design gracefully repeated around the lower part of this vase is reminiscent of designs created by De Morgan for tiles. It was painted by Joe Juster, who has been credited as the most able of all De Morgan's artists.[43]

No. H: 12

WILLIAM DE MORGAN
PAINTED BY JOE JUSTER

Vase early Fulham period, 1888-97
Earthenware with alkaline glaze, red lustre decoration
Height: 28.3 cm
Inscription: *JJ* painted in lustre
Provenance: Mrs. Graham Drinkwater, Montreal

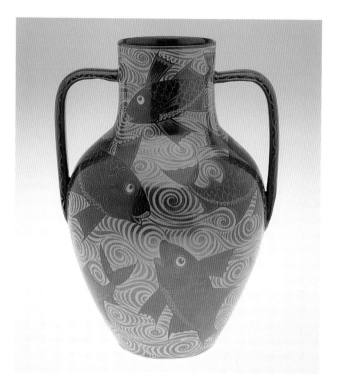

McCord Museum of Canadian History, Montreal, gift
of the estate of Mrs. Graham Drinkwater, 1964
(acc. no. M977X.55)

One of De Morgan's favourite motifs was the fish. Several
vases painted in a similar manner to the McCord vase are
known, in both lustre and "Persian" colours (see No. H: 5).
Here, the fish have been painted with spontaneity, and
appear to be darting about, giving the illusion of movement. De Morgan's graphic abilities, as well as his sense of
humour, are well illustrated.

No. H: 13

WILLIAM DE MORGAN
PAINTED BY CHARLES PASSENGER

Dish 1888-97
Glazed pottery, copper and silver lustre decoration
Diameter: 26.4 cm
Marks: impressed *WEDGWOOD // DVB* and *DVB T*
Inscriptions: *CP* in red lustre within two concentric
    circles, bordered by *W.D.M – FULHAM*
Provenance: Graham Drinkwater, Montreal
The Montreal Museum of Fine Arts, gift of Graham
    Drinkwater, 1921 (acc. no. Dp.4)

In 1917 Evelyn De Morgan, William De Morgan's widow,
gave the V & A twenty-two packages containing her hus-

band's designs and books of receipts, including 1,248 sheets
of watercolour drawings. It is possible to refer much, but
not all, of De Morgan's pottery to these designs. De Morgan's design of an eagle grasping a pike, or a lizard, is in
the V & A.[44] Although the design was only for the well of
a dish, the Montreal Museum of Fine Arts' example shows
the powerful image completely filling the dish. Close
examination reveals that Charles Passenger executed the
design faithfully; only the eagle's feathers have been embellished, and a few leafy sprays added to the sides of the dish.

No. H: 14

WILLIAM DE MORGAN
PAINTED BY CHARLES PASSENGER

Dish 1888-97
Wedgwood blank; glazed pottery, decorated with
    copper lustre
Diameter: 23.5 cm
Marks: impressed *Wedgwood*
Inscriptions: *W.D.M. FULHAM CP* painted in lustre
Provenance: E.B. Greenshields; Mrs. Graham Drinkwater;
    Fraser Brothers, Montreal, 1962
Private collection, Ottawa

E.B. Greenshields (b. 1850), a prominent Montreal businessman and president of the Montreal Art Association,
was associated with several important pieces of De Morgan
pottery which are still in Canadian collections. He purchased the pottery when new, possibly from William Scott
& Son of Montreal. Several of his De Morgan pieces,

including this saucer-shaped dish, were inherited by his daughter, Mrs. Graham Drinkwater. Both Mr. and Mrs. Drinkwater gave pieces to the MMFA (No. H: 13) and to the McCord Museum (No. H: 12). This dish was acquired by the collector during the sale of items from Mrs. Drinkwater's estate in 1962.

The interplay of the fish and duck motifs is an excellent example of the rhythm and movement that characterize many of De Morgan's designs.

No. H: 15

WILLIAM DE MORGAN
PAINTED BY FRED PASSENGER

Vase 1888-97
Earthenware with alkaline glaze; decoration outlined in
    cobalt blue and lustred in different tones of silver
    and copper
Height: 45.0 cm
Marks: impressed circle of dots enclosing *W. DE*
    MORGAN & CO. SANDS END POTTERY
Inscriptions: *FP* painted in black
Provenance: Lyons Gallery, London, 1976; MacMillan
    and Perrin, London
Private collection, Winnipeg

The gourd-shape of this vase was adapted by De Morgan from Persian pottery. It was decorated with an unusual combination of different tones of copper and silver lustres, which give the vase a soft and subtle finish. De Morgan has grouped fantastic animals together in a manner reminiscent of a medieval bestiary and embellished them with swirling plant motifs.

No. H: 16

WILLIAM DE MORGAN
PAINTED BY FRED PASSENGER

Bowl 1907-11
Earthenware with silver lustre on a cobalt blue tinted
    alkaline glaze; produced by Passenger and Iles,
    Brompton Road, London
Diameter: 12.2 cm
Inscriptions: *FP* in lustre; printed adhesive label:
    Guaranteed designed by Wm. De Morgan and executed by
    his original [craftsmen].
Provenance: the Estate of Mrs. T.A. Crerar; Mr. and
    Mrs. Bernard Naylor
Winnipeg Art Gallery, gift of Mr. and Mrs. Bernard

Naylor, in memory of her mother, Mrs. T.A. Crerar, 1968 (acc. no. CR-67-34)

William De Morgan actively retired from pottery manufacturing in 1905 and Sands End Pottery closed two years later. The artists Fred and Charles Passenger and the kilnmaster Frank Iles moved to Brompton Road, London, where, together with F.L. Ewbank, the sales manager, they started a new business using De Morgan's designs. This enterprise was in operation between 1907 and 1911. Pottery decorated at Brompton Road was identified by an adhesive label, such as the one on the Winnipeg bowl.

The bowl was formerly owned by Mrs. Jessie H. Crerar (1876-1975). Her husband, Senator Crerar, was president and a founding member of United Grain Growers, and served as a federal cabinet minister under Sir Robert Borden and William Lyon MacKenzie King. The bowl was given to the Winnipeg Art Gallery in 1968 by Mrs. Crerar's daughter, Dorothy Anna Naylor, as part of a substantial gift from the Crerar estate.

No. H: 17

WALTER CRANE
PAINTED BY WILLIAM S. MYCOCK

Vase 1911
Earthenware with silver lustre decoration on a cobalt
    blue glaze, green lustre interior; produced by
    Pilkington's Royal Lancastrian Pottery
Height: 26.0 cm
Marks: base impressed *2472 P England X1*
Inscriptions: lustre monogram of Walter Crane and *DES*
    monogram of Wm S. Mycock and a dove
Provenance: purchased from Pilkington Brothers, after
    1911
Royal Ontario Museum, Toronto, 1915
    (acc. no. 915.29.20)

Walter Crane's association with the ceramic industry began after 1866 when he supplied Wedgwood with several designs. He also designed tiles, particularly for the nursery, and ornamental vases for Maw and Company. In 1880 he became art superintendent of the London Decorating Company, which specialized in encaustic tiles.

The Pilkington brothers, known for their glasshouses and coal mines, established the Royal Lancastrian Pottery near Manchester in 1892. Initially, tiles were produced, though vases were exhibited at the Paris Exhibition of 1900. William and Joseph Burton developed a new glaze

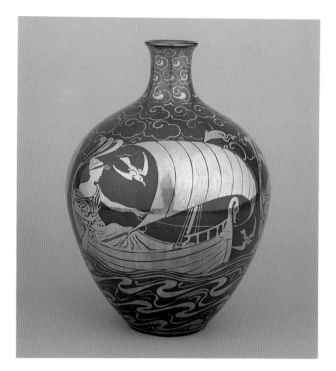

NO. H: 17

and a process of decorating in lustre which went into large-scale production after 1903. The Burton's deep silver-ruby and red-blue lustres were particularly notable. Besides Walter Crane, Lewis F. Day (1845-1910) and Charles Voysey (1857-1941) contributed designs to Pilkington's.

Crane's earliest work for Pilkington's was in 1900 when he produced two sets of designs for tiles. Between 1904 and 1906 Crane produced a series of designs both for tiles and wares which took advantage of the new glaze and lustres. He visited the factory to discuss the painting of his designs. William Mycock, the painter of the vase, was one of three Pilkington artists involved in this work.

This vase was acquired by the Royal Ontario Museum directly from Pilkington's and became part of the collection in 1915. It was the first example of Arts and Crafts pottery to be collected by a Canadian institution.

TILES

No. H: 18

WILLIAM MORRIS

Daisy c. 1865
(?) Dutch blank, painted by Morris & Co.; glazed earthenware, overglaze decoration in blue-green and yellow
15.2 x 15.2 cm (each); 3 examples

Provenance: Richard Dennis, London, 1988
Private collection, Ottawa

Ornamental tiles had become an increasingly popular element of interior decoration in the 1860s. William Morris first decorated tiles for the Red House in 1862. Unable to find hand-made tiles in England, Morris and his friends turned to Holland and used glazed earthenware tile blanks for their lyrical designs.

Daisy was one of Morris' earliest tile designs. It is closely associated with a crewel-embroidered wall-hanging designed by Morris for the Red House in 1860 which is now in Kelmscott Manor. Morris later adapted the design for wallpaper (see No. E: 6).

No. H: 19

WILLIAM MORRIS

Scroll c. 1865
Dutch blank, decorated by Morris & Co. (?) or by a Dutch firm; glazed earthenware, overglaze decoration in cobalt blue
12.7 x 12.7 cm
Provenance: Richard Dennis, London, 1988
Private collection, Ottawa

Early tiles decorated by Morris & Co. were fired in the same kiln as the stained glass. There were also aesthetic connections between the Firm's tiles and stained glass. Here, the tile has been divided into small squares and dec-

NO. H: 19

NO. H: 20

orated with a simple, repetitive design, reminiscent of stained-glass quarries.

Scroll and derivatives of this design were also produced in Holland, particularly by Ravestyn, Van Hulst, and other tile factories.

No. H: 20

EDWARD BURNE-JONES

Sleeping Beauty c. 1865
Dutch blank, designed in 1864, painted by Morris & Co.; glazed earthenware decorated in overglaze polychromes
15.2 x 15.2 cm
Provenance: Richard Dennis, London
Private collection, Ottawa

This tile was part of a series designed by Burne-Jones which was composed of nine two-tile scenes recounting the story of Sleeping Beauty. It is the second tile in the third set. The princess is shown hesitating on the threshold of the room where the Wicked Fairy awaits with her spindle.

Burne-Jones acknowledged the inspiration of Ludwig Richter's drawings for his fairy-tale tiles. He is known to have made three series: *Sleeping Beauty*, *Cinderella*, and *The Beauty and the Beast*. A surviving panel of tiles now in the William Morris Gallery, Walthamstow, but formerly in Birket Foster's house, was signed by Lucy Faulkner. Both Lucy and her sister Kate were associated with the decoration of Morris & Co.'s tiles.

No. H: 21

WILLIAM MORRIS

Tulip and Trellis c. 1872-81
(?) Dutch blank, probably produced by William De Morgan; glazed earthenware, overglaze decoration in cobalt blue and green
15.2 x 15.2 cm
Provenance: Haslam and Whiteway, London, 1990
Private collection, Ottawa

A few of Morris's designs for tiles were produced by both Morris & Co. and De Morgan. De Morgan appears to have disclaimed this role and was reported to have said, "Morris never made but three designs for my execution – the Trellis and Tulip, the Poppy and another – I forgot the name. I never could work except by myself and in my own manner."[45] However, Morris had a strong influence on De Morgan's early work, and he was a close friend.

As this design was executed at both workshops, its attribution to De Morgan is tentative.

No. H: 22

WILLIAM DE MORGAN

Flowers and Vase 1872-81
Earthenware with white slip, underglaze decoration in black and blue
15.2 x 15.2 cm (each); two-tile panel
Mark: one tile unmarked, the other: impressed hemisphere with three dots and *W D E/MORGAN*
Provenance: Kathy Brunner, Antiquarius, London, 1984
Private collection, Winnipeg

May Morris described De Morgan's early work at Chelsea as "simple and occasionally naive."[46] This two-tile panel, with an experimental and badly crazed glaze, is stamped with one of De Morgan's Chelsea-period marks and is distinguished by its simplicity. A working drawing on tracing paper of this design is in the V & A's collection of De Morgan's work.

No. H: 23

WILLIAM DE MORGAN

Boa Constrictor 1872-81
Earthenware with white slip, underglaze decoration in yellow, blue, green and black
19.3 x 19.8 cm; 19.5 x 20.3 cm; two-tile panel

NO. H: 22

Mark: impressed *W. DE MORGAN* within a rectangle

Provenance: purchased from Haslam and Whiteway, London, 1975

The Montreal Museum of Fine Arts, Gilman Cheney Bequest, 1975 (acc. no. Dp. 84-85)

A watercolour of this design, painted in orange, green and black, is in the V & A (E.597-1917). The drawing was executed at Chelsea.

No. H: 24

WILLIAM DE MORGAN

Stork and Frog 1872-81

Wedgwood blank; glazed earthenware, decorated with copper lustre

15.0 x 15.0 cm

Provenance: Richard Dennis, London, 1990

Private collection, Ottawa

The *Stork and Frog* tile was intended to be placed with other fanciful birds and mythical creatures (such as No. H: 27) in an alternating arrangement with tiles decorated with a spray of foliage. The design, an early one, illustrates De Morgan's delight in comical renditions of animals and birds. Two different versions of this design, one in brown, yellow and green, and the other in blue, are in collection of De Morgan's original drawings at the V & A.

No. H: 25

WILLIAM DE MORGAN

Peacock and Robin 1872-81

Architectural Pottery blanks; glazed pottery, copper lustre decoration

10.2 x 10.2 cm (each); four examples

Mark: impressed within raised horizontal bands *ARCHITECTURAL / POTTERY CO / POOLE . DORSET*

Provenance: Richard Dennis, London, 1990

Private collection, Ottawa

Most of De Morgan's bird tiles were boldly decorated with a single specimen. They were often designed to be placed in an alternating arrangement with less visually striking tiles, ornamented with foliage or scrolls (see No. H: 26). These tiles are unusual, as the basic concept has been much reduced in scale.

No. H: 26

WILLIAM DE MORGAN

Scrolled Foliage 1872-81 or later

Wedgwood blank; glazed pottery, copper lustre decoration

15.3 x 15.3 cm

NO. H: 24

NO. H: 27

Mark: impressed *L*
Provenance: Kathy Brunner, Antiquarius, London, 1980
Private collection, Winnipeg

De Morgan is known to have used blank glazed tiles made in Holland, as well as tiles made by Minton, Hollins and Co., the Architectural Pottery Co., Craven, Dunhill and Co., and particularly by Wedgwood, which was noted for its lustre decoration. In his 1892 address to the Society of Arts, De Morgan recounted that "The best of the first lustres I made on Staffordshire ware was on ironstone or granite. The body was repellant in colour, but the glaze particularly good. Latterly, we have used the common white made with tin...."[47] He continued to use commercially produced tiles for some lustre decoration, even after he developed his own clay body.

No. H: 27

WILLIAM DE MORGAN

Fantastic Bird 1882-88
Earthenware with alkaline glaze, copper lustre decoration
15.0 x 15.0 cm
Marks: impressed oval *DE MORGAN . MERTON ABBEY*
Provenance: Richard Dennis, London, 1990
Private collection, Ottawa

Animals and birds were De Morgan's favourite subjects during his Chelsea period. He was well acquainted with engravings of birds. His mother, Sophia De Morgan, recalled that as a child he was engrossed with Thomas Bewick's *History of English Birds*: "The little fellow looks through the book, and can now tell the name of almost every bird."[48] Though many of De Morgan's birds are easily identified, this one was a creative fancy.

No. H: 28

WILLIAM DE MORGAN

Fantastic Ducks 1882-88
Wedgwood blank; glazed pottery, decorated with copper lustre
15.3 x 15.3 cm
Mark: impressed *C*
Provenance: Kathy Brunner, Antiquarius, London, 1983
Private collection, Winnipeg

De Morgan developed at least five different designs with repeating patterns of birds. Most of these designs appear to have been made at Chelsea. *Fantastic Ducks* remained in production until the late Fulham period (see No. H: 45). As with many of De Morgan's designs for tiles, they were produced in both lustre and underglaze polychromes. This permitted a design to be interpreted creatively and resulted in many different versions of the same design.

NO. H: 28

NO. H: 29

NO. H: 30

NO. H: 31

No. H: 29

WILLIAM DE MORGAN

New Persian No. 1 1882-88
Earthenware with white slip, underglaze decoration in
    cobalt blue, turquoise, light green, dark green
    and black
15.2 x 15.2 cm (each); four examples
Mark: impressed square with an image of an abbey
    church and *W DE MERTON ABBEY*
Provenance: Richard Dennis, London, 1978
Private collection, Ottawa

After De Morgan had developed his "Persian" colours in
c. 1875-76, he was commissioned by Frederic Lord Leighton to assist with the completion of the Arab Hall, an
Islamic-inspired annex to the painter's house in Holland
Park Road. De Morgan was set the task of organizing the
tiles Leighton had collected during his travels in the Near
East, and also created replacements for broken or missing
tiles. De Morgan was involved with the project from 1877
until 1881.

The tiles created for Lord Leighton were the only true
copies of Iznik and Damascene tiles made by De Morgan.
All his other "Persian" decorated tiles, such as *New Persian
No. 1*, owed their inspiration to Islam but were his own
creative inventions. However, De Morgan greatly benefitted from his association with Lord Leighton and from the

opportunity to handle and closely examine Leighton's
collection of tiles. De Morgan used "Persian" decoration
continuously throughout his artistic career.

No. H: 30

WILLIAM DE MORGAN

Single Rose 1882-88
Earthenware with white slip, underglaze decoration in
    cobalt blue, turquoise and green
15.2 x 15.2 cm (each); four examples
Marks: impressed oval *DE MORGAN . MERTON
    ABBEY*
Provenance: P.J. Reeves, London, 1989
Private collection, Ottawa

No. H: 31

WILLIAM DE MORGAN

Carnation 1882-88
Earthenware with white slip, underglaze decoration in
    green and manganese
15.2 x 15.2 cm
Mark: impressed square with an abbey church
    W DE MERTON ABBEY
Provenance: Paddy Frost Antiques, Antiquarius,
    London, 1989
Private collection, Winnipeg

Carnations were a flower beloved by Morris and De Morgan. Catleugh points out the affinity between this tile design and Morris's chintz, *Carnation*, designed in 1875.[49] Developed by De Morgan early in his Chelsea period, *Carnation* was advertised in the 1880 catalogue, *Painted Tiles to be had of William De Morgan at Orange House Pottery*. Four *Carnation* tiles also appeared on an updated broadsheet illustrating De Morgan tiles available through Morris & Co.

No. H: 32

WILLIAM DE MORGAN

Moffatt 1882-88
Earthenware with white slip, underglaze decoration in
    turquoise, green and black
15.2 x 15.2 cm
Marks: Impressed rectangle with an abbey church
    MERTON DM ABBEY
Provenance: Thomas Sutton, London, 1927
Royal Ontario Museum, Toronto, 1927 (acc.
    no. 927.96.8d)

This simple and bold design appears in De Morgan's collection of tile designs now in the V & A. The design was

painted in watercolours in purple, brown, green and blue.

Eight single tiles and tile-panels were purchased by the Royal Ontario Museum from Thomas Sutton in 1927 – the first significant collection of De Morgan tiles to be acquired by a Canadian institution.

No. H: 33

WILLIAM DE MORGAN

B.B.B 1882-88
Earthenware with white slip, underglaze decoration in
    green, yellow, blue, manganese and black
15.6 x 15.6 cm (each); two examples
Marks: impressed within an oval *W. DE MORGAN
    MERTON ABBEY*
Provenance: W.S. Maxwell, Montreal
The Montreal Museum of Fine Arts, gift of W.S.
    Maxwell, 1926 (acc. no. Dp.4-5)

B.B.B was named for a Norwich fireplace manufacturer and tile merchant, Barnard, Bishop and Barnard. Featured in the 1880 catalogue, *Painted Tiles to be had of William De Morgan at Orange House Pottery*, it became De Morgan's most popular and well-known design.

NO. H: 32

NO. H: 34

NO. H: 33

No. H: 34

WILLIAM DE MORGAN

Chicago 1888-97
Earthenware with white slip, underglaze decoration in
    blue, turquoise, green, manganese and black
20.2 x 20.2 cm (each); three examples
Mark: impressed Tudor rose encircled by *Wm DE*
    MORGAN – SAND'S END POTTERY – FULHAM
Conrad Biernacki

The dark-blue ground of these tiles gives a rich contrast
to the vibrantly coloured, alternating floral design. The
1887 stock list of De Morgan's tiles lists *Chicago* – one of
his most expensive – as costing 7s 6d per tile.

No. H: 35

WILLIAM DE MORGAN

New Persian No. 2 1888-97
Earthenware with white slip, underglaze decoration in
    blue, turquoise and green
15.5 x 15.5 cm
Marks: impressed Tudor rose with blue enamelled flower
    centre, encircled by *W. DE MORGAN & CO –*
    SAND'S END POTTERY – FULHAM
Provenance: F.B. Locker
The Montreal Museum of Fine Arts, gift of F.B. Locker,
    1918 (acc. no. Dp.19)

This tile – the first De Morgan tile to be given to a Canadian institution – was donated to the Montreal Museum of
Fine Arts in 1918, two years after its decorative arts collections were established by F. Cleveland Morgan. Unfortunately, nothing is known about the donor, F.B. Locker.

No. H: 36

WILLIAM DE MORGAN

Vine 1888-97
Earthenware with white slip, underglaze decoration in
    green and purple
20.3 x 20.3 cm
Provenance: Richard Dennis, London, c. 1989
Private collection, Ottawa

Several De Morgan designs echo ones made by William
Morris for wallpaper. Such is the case with *Single Rose* (No.

NO. H: 36

H: 30) and this tile, the title of which is inscribed on the
drawing for the design, made previous to 1888 (V & A).[50]
It is reminiscent of Morris's *Vine* wallpaper, produced in
1874 (see Nos. E: 10-11).

No. H: 37

WILLIAM DE MORGAN

Galleon 1888-97
Earthenware with white slip, underglaze decoration
    in green
20.3 x 20.3 cm
Mark: Impressed Tudor rose encircled by *Wm DE*
    MORGAN & CO – SAND'S END POTTERY –
    FULHAM
Provenance: Richard Dennis, London, 1989
Private collection, Ottawa

Ships with billowing sails were an important motif of Iznik
pottery of the second half of the sixteenth century. De
Morgan was probably inspired by this Ottoman pottery
when he developed his designs for ships both for wares
and tiles. His ship designs, of which he developed eighteen different designs for single tiles, are sumptuous and
full of movement and graceful lines. His imaginary galle-
ons sailing in brisk winds over choppy seas were frequently
accompanied by sea monsters, fishes and dolphins.

No. H: 38

WILLIAM DE MORGAN

Sailing Ship 1888-97
Earthenware with white ship, underglaze decoration
   in green
15.0 x 15.0 cm
Mark: impressed Tudor rose encircled by *Wm DE*
   MORGAN & CO – SAND'S END POTTERY –
   FULHAM
Provenance: Richard Dennis, London, c. 1976
Private collection, Ottawa

No. H: 39

WILLIAM DE MORGAN

Mouse amid Flowering Plants 1888-97
Earthenware with white slip, underglaze decoration in
   green and brown
15.3 x 15.3 cm
Mark: impressed circle of dots enclosing *W. DE*
   MORGAN & CO SAND'S END POTTERY
Provenance: Kathy Brunner, Antiquarius, London, 1987
Private collection, Winnipeg

Part of a tile panel, this little mouse scampering through
dense foliage is a good example of the over sixty individual animal designs created by De Morgan. Catleugh has
estimated that these were manufactured in as many as 6,320

ways, including different background-colours and designs,
lustres and coloured details.[51]

No. H: 40

WILLIAM DE MORGAN

Raised Lion 1888-97
Earthenware with white slip, relief lions in yellow, glazed
   in "teapot-brown" manganese glaze
14.0 x 14.0 cm
Mark: impressed circle of dots enclosing *W. DE*
   MORGAN & CO SAND'S END POTTERY
Provenance: Richard Dennis, London, c. 1970
Private collection, Ottawa

Catleugh attributes this design to De Morgan's Chelsea
period.[52] The relief version, possibly moulded by Halsey
Ricardo, was decorated in a variety of ways (see No. H:
41) and was evidently a popular tile, as a slightly different
version was created in 1898.

No. H: 41

WILLIAM DE MORGAN

Raised Lion 1888-97
Earthenware with white slip, relief lions in ochre and
   black on turquoise ground
15.3 x 15.3 cm

NO. H: 37

NO. H: 38

Mark: impressed Tudor rose encircled by *W. DE MORGAN & CO – SAND'S END POTTERY – FULHAM*
Provenance: Richard Dennis, London, 1990
Private collection, Ottawa

No. H: 42

HALSEY RICARDO FOR
WILLIAM DE MORGAN

Fabulous Beast 1888-97
Craven Dunhill blank; glazed pottery, copper lustre decoration
20.4 x 20.4 cm
Mark: impressed within vertical and horizontal grid of raised bands *CRAVEN / DUNHILL / & CO / JACKFIELD / SALOP*
Provenance: Haslam and Whiteway, London, 1990
Private collection, Ottawa

Halsey Ricardo entered into partnership with De Morgan in 1888, when the Sand's End Pottery was established in Fulham. Many relief tiles are attributed to Ricardo (see Nos. H: 40-41), as are a small number of lustred tiles with fabulous beasts.

NO. H: 40

No. H: 43

WILLIAM DE MORGAN

Grebe 1888-97
Earthenware with alkaline glaze, copper lustre decoration
15.0 x 15.0 cm
Mark: impressed Tudor rose encircled by *Wm DE MORGAN & CO – SAND'S END POTTERY – FULHAM*
Provenance: Richard Dennis, London, 1990
Private collection, Ottawa

No. H: 44

WILLIAM DE MORGAN

Small B 1898
Earthenware with white slip, underglaze decoration in green, yellow and brown
15.2 x 15.2 cm
Marks: impressed circle enclosing *DM/98*
Provenance: Thomas Sutton, London, 1927
Royal Ontario Museum, Toronto (acc. no. 927.96.4)

Small B was one of De Morgan's first designs for tiles, having been developed shortly before or after his move to Chelsea, in c. 1870-72. A version of the design, numbered 8, is in the collection of De Morgan drawings in the

NO. H: 39

NO. H: 42

NO. H: 45

NO. H: 43

NO. H: 46

V & A. The inspiration for the tile may have come from one named *Bough*, designed by William Morris.[53]

Once De Morgan developed a successful design, he had no hesitation about keeping it in production. This pattern was still being made up to eighteen years after its inception. Many of the more than 300 tile designs De Morgan produced at Chelsea were still in production at the end of his artistic career.

No. H: 45

WILLIAM DE MORGAN

Fantastic Ducks 1898
Earthenware with alkaline glaze, underglaze blue and
   silver lustre decoration
15.3 x 15.3 cm
Mark: impressed circle enclosing *DM/98*
Provenance: P.J. Reeves, London, 1989
Private collection, Ottawa

For a description, see No. H: 28.

No. H: 46

WILLIAM DE MORGAN

Carnations and Primroses 1898
Earthenware with white slip, underglaze decoration in
   blue, turquoise, green and purple
15.2 x 15.2 cm
Marks: impressed circle enclosing *DM/98*
Provenance: Thomas Sutton, London, 1927
Royal Ontario Museum, Ontario (acc. no. 927.96.5)

ENDNOTES

1. *The Cheyne Book of Chelsea China and Pottery* (London, 1924; reprinted 1973), p. vii.
2. *Ibid.*, p. 115.
3. Quoted in A.M.W. Stirling, *William De Morgan and His Wife* (New York, 1922), p. 75.
4. *The Wonderful Village* (London, 1918), p. 174.
5. Bale's reminiscences are found in Stirling, *William De Morgan and His Wife*, pp. 92-4.
6. J.W. Mackail, *The Life of William Morris*, vol. 2 (London, 1899; reprinted New York, 1968), pp. 16.
7. Stirling, *William De Morgan and His Wife*, p. 116.
8. Quoted in *Ibid.*, p. 78.
9. Julian Barnard, *Victorian Ceramic Tiles* (London, 1972), pp. 117-18.
10. Richard and Hilary Myers, "Morris & Company Ceramic Tiles," *Journal of the Tiles and Architectural Ceramics Society* 1 (1982): 19.
11. Mackail, *The Life of William Morris*, vol. 2, pp. 42-3.
12. Ricardo's account, given in Blunt, *The Cheyne Book…*, p. 117.
    Martin Greenwood, in *The Designs of William De Morgan* (London, 1989), p. 17, says a stencil-method was used on tiles painted in copper lustre.
13. Quoted in Stirling, *William De Morgan and His Wife*, pp. 92-3.
14. W.J. Furnival, *Leadless Decorative Tiles* (Stone, Staffordshire, 1904), p. 743.
15. *Art Journal Catalogue of the International Exhibition 1871*, p. 48.
16. *Principles of Decorative Design* (London, 1873; reprinted 1973), p. 11.
17. *Burlington Magazine* (September 1917); and Stirling, *William De Morgan and His Wife*, p. 99.
18. *The Wonderful Village*, p. 190.
19. A.M.W. Stirling, *Life's Little Day* (New York, 1924), p. 214.
20. Stirling, *William De Morgan and His Wife*, p. 101.
21. Stirling, *Life's Little Day*, p. 232.
22. *The Art Journal* (April 1872).
23. E.C. Gardner, *Home Interiors* (Boston, 1878), p. 173.
24. *The Gazette* (Montreal), 12 June 1880.
25. Princess Louise lent four De Morgan items to the 1924 Chelsea exhibition. See Blunt, *The Cheyne Book*, p. 81 and pl. 31.
26. Elizabeth Collard, *Nineteenth-Century Pottery and Porcelain in Canada* (Montreal, 1967), pp. 157-58.
27. Quoted in Fiona MacCarthy, *The Simple Life* (London, 1981), p. 103.
28. See excerpts from reviews printed at the back of another De Morgan novel, *Somehow Good* (London, 1913).
29. *Lustre Pottery* (London, 1985), pp. 168-69.
30. In later years, he remembered the names of two (*Trellis and Tulip* and *Poppy*) but could not recall the third. Stirling, *William De Morgan and His Wife*, p. 78.
31. They were sold by Liberty's in the 1890s; see Barbara Morris, *Liberty Design* (London, 1989), pp. 77-8.
32. Crane's ceramic designing began in the 1860s (for Wedgwood). See Walter Crane, *An Artist's Reminiscences* (London, 1907; reprinted Detroit, 1968), p. 93.

33. Illustrated in Hugh Wakefield, *Victorian Pottery* (London, 1962), pl. 85.

34. Pilkington offered this design in various colours. It is illustrated in red in Lynne Thornton, "Pilkington's 'Royal Lancastrian' lustre pottery", *Connoisseur* (May 1970): 11. A latecomer to the art pottery field, the Pilkington firm achieved its own reputation for notable lustreware after the turn of the century.

35. Lecture delivered before the Royal Society of Arts, London, 27 November 1990.

36. *The Studio* (October 1893).

37. MacCarthy, *The Simple Life*, p. 103.

38. Greenwood, *The Designs of William De Morgan*, p. 17.

39. See Jon Catleugh, *William De Morgan Tiles* (New York, 1983), pl. 205.

40. See Greenwood, *The Designs of William De Morgan*, pl. 867, p. 141.

41. See William Gaunt and M.D.E. Clayton-Stamn, *William De Morgan* (London, 1971), pl. 114, p. 122.

42. *Journal of the Society of Arts*, 1892.

43. Gaunt and Clayton-Stamn, *William De Morgan*, p. 21.

44. See Greenwood, *The Designs of William De Morgan*, no. 1,263, p. 43.

45. Catleugh, *William De Morgan Tiles*, p. 47.

46. "Reminiscences of William De Morgan", *Burlington Magazine* (August and September 1917).

47. "A Paper on Lustre Ware", *Journal of the Society of Arts* (July 1892).

48. Quoted in Stirling, *William De Morgan and His Wife*, p. 41.

49. Catleugh, *William De Morgan Tiles*, p. 58.

50. Greenwood, *The Designs of William De Morgan*, p. 136.

51. Catleugh, *William De Morgan Tiles*, pp. 86-7.

52. *Ibid.*, p. 98.

53. *Ibid.*, pp. 48-9.

JEWELLERY

Katharine A. Lochnan

Surveying the state of jewellery design and manufacture in Britain in the early 1860s, William Burges concluded that it was "defective in taste." He despaired of significant change until "the modern tradesman is content to transform himself or his apprentices into artists by giving them the same sort of education that Cellini had."[1] At war with the division of labour, Morris, Marshall, Faulkner & Co. set out in 1861 to rectify this situation. The Firm announced in its prospectus that it would undertake commissions in "Metal Work in all its branches, including Jewellery."[2]

Morris and his friends believed that good design and craftsmanship were inseparable from a knowledge of the history of the medium in question. It is not surprising, in this regard, that they were interested in antique jewellery, as well as in contemporary jewellery that employed ancient methods or represented the continuation of an unbroken tradition. The Pre-Raphaelites were among the first to collect antique, sentimental, folk, and exotic jewellery. Attracted by colour, light, and symbolism, with a sensibility conditioned by a love of things medieval, they favoured enamel, pearl, ivory, amber, coral, turquoise and semi-precious stones, and much preferred handmade to machine-made jewellery, however much it lacked precision.

Dante Gabriel Rossetti was drawn primarily to traditional and folk jewellery of European and Eastern origin with little intrinsic value. His "mania for buying bricabrac" to "stick" in his pictures led him to junk shops in Leicester Square and Hammersmith.[3] This "secondary" jewellery was completely antithetical to middle-class Victorian taste, which gravitated toward "primary" jewellery made of precious stones and metals set in the latest style. In 1861 Rossetti began to paint single-figure subjects of women sporting colourful and exotic jewellery, none of it imaginary. Clad in artistic dress, his sitters, especially Jane Morris, inspired imitation and gave rise to "the fashion among aesthetes for unusual oriental or antique jewels" (see No. M: 27).[4] When the Aesthetic Movement took hold around 1880, the

NO. I: 1. *Pendant*, English, c. 1860

217

wearing of jewellery went out of fashion, and for a time "a plain string of amber beads was the only acceptable ornament" (see No. M: 10).[5]

In 1861, Burne-Jones mentioned jewellery in a letter to Cormell Price as one of five areas in which Morris & Co. intended to work.[6] His maternal grandfather, Benjamin Coley, was a Birmingham jeweller, which may help to account for his special interest in this area. Following in Rossetti's footsteps, he hunted for antique jewels, being so carried away by enthusiasm on one occasion that he spent his last eight pounds on a watch for his wife.

Georgiana Burne-Jones, conditioned somewhat by her strict Methodist upbringing, was modest in her use of personal ornament. Her granddaughter Angela Thirkell described her in old age as wearing on her head "swathes of soft lace, pinned here and there with an old paste brooch".[7] Some of the jewellery that survives in the family was probably given to her early in her married life, between 1860 and 1866 (Nos. I: 1-3), after which a prolonged affair with Maria Zambaco diverted her husband's attentions. Deeply devoted to his daughter Margaret, Burne-Jones enjoyed giving her jewellery in the 1880s and 1890s, when she was old enough to wear it. In addition to

NO. M: 10
FREDERICK HOLLYER,
Portrait of Margaret Burne-Jones,
October 1882

NO. M: 27
HARRY F. PHILIPS,
Jane Morris in Old Age, c. 1913

NO. I: 5
Necklace, Indian, possibly
19th-century

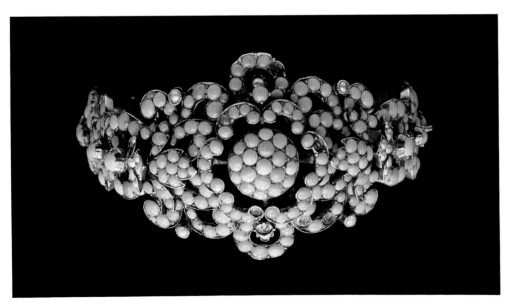

NO. I: 6
Bracelet, Anglo-Indian,
19th-century

antique jewels (No. I: 4), Margaret Burne-Jones owned Indian (Nos. I: 5-6) and peasant jewellery.

Despite the announcement in the Morris & Co. prospectus, very little jewellery can firmly be attributed to members of the Firm. Rossetti and Webb designed and had made a very small number of items between 1861-64, and in 1861 Morris wrote to Arthur Hughes soliciting a jewellery design.[8] Burne-Jones made drawings for jewels "annotated with notes regarding the use of enamel and stones" in a sketchbook provisionally dated 1861-65, but they appear never to have seen the light of day.[9] Pieces of jewellery were displayed by Morris & Co. in the Mediaeval Court of the International Exhibition in 1862. Charlotte Gere has observed that

> only two commissions for jewellery are documented in Webb's accounts. It has been assumed in the absence of evidence that these and the jewellery exhibited by the firm in 1862 were made up by Hill and Mosely, jewellers, who occupied the ground floor in the house where Morris had the firm. In 1865 the Morris enterprise was moved to Queen Square and the link with Hill and Mosely would have been broken.[10]

The fact that no reference to jewellery appears to post-date the mid-1860s has led to speculation that the Firm ceased to receive commissions after that date.[11] Burne-Jones continued to make designs independent of Morris & Co., some of them based on antique prototypes (Nos. I: 2-3). Lady Burne-Jones claimed in the *Memorials* that her late husband became interested in jewellery design only when he accepted the commission for the 1883 Whitelands cross from John Ruskin, and that he "carefully and completely designed and saw executed" only one brooch in the form of a dove.[12] He is nonetheless known to have had several other pieces made to his specifications, includ-

NO. I: 8
EDWARD BURNE-JONES,
Gentleman's Ring, English, 1890s

ing the pearl ring he wore habitually on his little finger late in life (No. I: 8).

In 1862 the Roman jeweller Castellani made his public début in Britain in the "Italian Court" of the International Exhibition. Based on antique prototypes, and employing ancient methods, his "archaeological jewellery" immediately attracted the admiration of the Pre-Raphaelites. William Burges (who was responsible for the Ecclesiological Society stand in the "Mediaeval Court," two bays of which were occupied by Morris & Co.) promoted Castellani in an article that appeared in the *Gentleman's Magazine* in 1863, in which he wrote that he had "at last given the 19th century some jewellery that an artist or architect could see buying and which no-one need be ashamed to wear."[13]

Castellani's protégé, Carlo Giuliano, established his London workshop on Frith St. in 1860, worked to the same high standard (No. I: 9), and espoused the same ideals as Morris & Co. It was to Giuliano that Burne-Jones entrusted the execution of his most important commission, the bird brooch, probably at the request of his patron. He gave less demanding work to Child and Child of Kensington (No. I: 8). Other pieces of jewellery designed by these establishments reflect Burne-Jones's influence, and appear to have been derived from his designs.

Burne-Jones was not the only jewellery designer in the Morris circle. At the turn of the century May Morris made jewellery, some of it inspired by pieces that Rossetti had given her mother. These were bequeathed to the Victoria and Albert Museum. Much of the jewellery designed by May Morris is now in Cardiff.

Despite the fact that so little jewellery was designed by members of the Morris circle, their love of the antique, the naïve, and the exotic, their respect for hand craftsmanship, and their affection for semi-precious stones with symbolic significance, contributed to the evolution of Art Nouveau jewellery design.

No. I: 1

Pendant
English, c. 1860
Heart-shaped lapis-lazuli pendant and chain in an
    engraved gold mount set with pearls
Width: 3.5 cm
Provenance: Georgiana Burne-Jones; Margaret
    Burne-Jones
Private collection

Heart-shaped pendants were popular in Britain in the seventeenth and eighteenth centuries. With its traditional, sentimental association, the heart was a favourite symbolic device in the Morris circle. Rossetti owned a pendant in the form of a pierced heart below a crown (possibly eighteenth century, Spanish), and was particularly fond of a heart-shaped jewel worn by his mistress and housekeeper, Fanny Cornforth, in *The Blue Bower*, which he later gave to Jane Morris.

Burne-Jones was "fascinated by the iconography of hearts."[14] The heart appears in several of his designs for jewellery in the "Secret Book of Designs" in the British Museum and in his "Thoughts of Designs for the Book of Flowers" in the Victoria and Albert Museum.

This jewel was probably given to Georgiana Burne-Jones by her husband early in their marriage. It is either the pendant worn in the 1870 portrait by Sir Edward

Poynter, or closely related to it.[15] Burne-Jones evolved his own colour symbolism, making it difficult to determine the significance of the choice of lapis, traditionally associated with the virgin's robe. He ascribed colours to the days of the week: blue was associated with Wednesday.[16]

No. I: 2

Brooch
Spanish or Portuguese, late 18th c.
Oval, silver, closed-back, pavé-set with yellow
    chrysoberyls; no marks
Width: 35.0 mm
Provenance: Georgiana Burne-Jones (?); Margaret
    Burne-Jones
Heather Maclachlan

This large antique jewel was originally made as a man's hat-, egret- or sleeve-ornament. In the eighteenth century it would have been worn vertically; during the Victorian era it was turned into a brooch and worn horizontally. The silver setting appears to be Georgian and the pin-post Victorian.[17]

Burne-Jones may have acquired the brooch for Georgiana to wear with the antique pocket watch, purchased in 1862-64, which she always wore at her waist. From the Poynter portrait of 1870 the watch appears to be pavé-set with chrysoberyls in much the same way as the brooch.

No. I: 3

Brooch
Possibly Iranian, 18th c.
Hand-painted enamel with mother-of-pearl centre, set in
    silver; no marks
Width: 37.0 mm
Provenance: Georgiana Burne-Jones (?); Margaret
    Burne-Jones
Heather Maclachlan

After the Gothic Revival gave rise to the taste for enamel jewellery, "a passion for enamelling swept through late 19th c. artistic society."[18] Burne-Jones would have been drawn to this brooch in part because it was made of enamel and pearl.

The charm and naivety of the sunflower motif, a favourite symbol for the Aesthetic Movement, would also

NO. I: 2

NO. I: 3

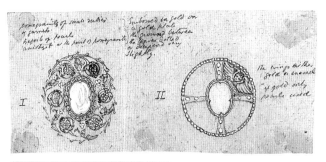

FIG. I: 1. EDWARD BURNE-JONES, Design for a brooch in
Byzantine style
Pierpont Morgan Library, New York

have appealed to him. He was very fond of sunflowers, as
can be seen from a letter he wrote to Frances Horner:

> Do you know the face of sunflowers? How they peep at you
> and look brazen sometimes and proud – and others look shy
> and some so modest that up go their hands to hide their brown
> blushes, and some have bees for brooches in most admirable
> taste... – I could draw them forever, and should love to sit
> for days drawing them.[19]

While the origin of this brooch cannot be identified
with certainty, Susan Stronge observes that there is "definitely an oriental influence", and has proposed that it may
be Iranian.[20] This opinion is endorsed by Gere and Munn,
who also believe that it may once have formed part of a
necklace. Given the state of knowledge at that time, Burne-
Jones may have believed this jewel to be seventeenth-century and of European origin.

The brooch could well have been one of Burne-Jones's
early acquisitions for Georgiana, as the artist was interested in enamelwork in the 1860s. It could have inspired
his design for a jewel "in Byzantine style" in a sketchbook
now in the Pierpont Morgan Library (fig. I: 1),[21] which
in turn may be based on a sheet in the Wightwick Manor
sketchbook, dated c. 1861-65, bearing annotations regarding the use of enamel and stones. The leaves, which are
later, may have been added at this time.[22]

The contemporary enthusiasm for the Byzantine style
finds its origin in the writings of John Ruskin. Castellani
displayed three brooches in the Byzantine and medieval
styles at the International Exhibition of 1862.

No. I: 4

Brooch
English, c. 1850-60
Bird in silver, pavé-set with turquoises, a few seed pearls,
    and a ruby for the eye
Width: 5.5 cm
Provenance: Margaret Burne-Jones
Private collection

Bird-shaped brooches, representing doves sacred to Venus,
pavé-set with turquoises symbolizing "forget-me-nots,"
were often given as presents to bridesmaids or friends of
the bride.

This brooch is of particular interest because it appears
to be the prototype for the jewel executed to Burne-Jones's
specifications by Giuliano around 1890: a brooch in the
shape of a bird set against a background of foliage, with
translucent green and red enamel, and pavé-set with coral,
turquoise, pearls and a ruby. Three were made, one of
which belonged to Margaret Burne-Jones (fig. I: 2).

Similar designs for brooches in the shape of doves,

NO. I: 4

FIG. I: 2. EDWARD BURNE-JONES (design) and
    CARLO GIULIANO (jeweller)
An openwork gold brooch pendant in the form of a bird on an olive
    branch, decorated with translucent green and red enamel and set
    with turquoise and coral cabochons, pearls and a single ruby
Private collection

FIG. I: 3. EDWARD BURNE-JONES
Designs for brooches in the shape of doves
Victoria and Albert Museum, London

with and without foliage, are to be found in Burne-Jones's
1885-98 sketchbook, in the British Museum, and in his
"Thoughts of Designs for the Book of Flowers: Designs for
Jewellery", in the Victoria and Albert Museum (fig. I: 3).

No. I: 5

Necklace
Indian, possibly 19th c.
Triple-fringed, turquoises and seed pearls, kundan
    setting, suspended on gold chains
Width: 21.5 cm
Provenance: Margaret Burne-Jones
Heather Maclachlan

As early as 1851, Indian jewellery attracted the attention
of design reformers, and the "irregularly shaped stones and
lack of mechanical precision appealed instantly to the pub-

lic tired of ornate, geometrical pieces."[23] Being "the absolute antithesis of mid-Victorian taste", it was considered
suitably artistic.[24] Rossetti and Holman Hunt amassed collections of Indian jewellery, and Giuliano was inspired to
create necklaces in the Indian taste.

Susan Strong maintains that the simple style of this
necklace points to "village" rather than "court" origin.
It would originally have been fastened with silk threads
wound around conical cores where the three strands come
together, but appears to have been restrung in England on
wires attached to gold chains of British manufacture.[25]

The necklace was undoubtedly acquired in London. It
is typical of the kind of Indian jewellery sold by Liberty's
and Child and Child. Even Morris & Co. sold Indian
wares. Margaret had at least one other nineteenth-century
Indian turquoise-and-gold necklace which was purchased
from Child and Child.

Bracelet
Anglo-Indian, 19th c.
Silver bangle with pavé-set turquoises and a few seed
    pearls, with a hinged clasp
Height: 37.0 mm
Provenance: Margaret Burne-Jones
Heather Maclachlan

Turquoise jewellery of this type was popular in Victorian England. Turquoises symbolize "forget-me-nots" and were popular in sentimental jewellery. Forget-me-not motifs can be detected among the complex interlaced patterns making up this piece. It appears to have been made in India, in imitation of contemporary British jewellery, possibly by Hamilton, a Scottish jewellery firm in Calcutta, which employed native craftsmen to make jewellery for the Anglo-Indian and British markets. The construction is fairly rudimentary, and may be the work of a student.[26]

Georgiana Burne-Jones's sister Alice married the British art teacher John Lockwood Kipling, who for many years ran the government art school in Calcutta and curated the Lahore museum. He did much to promote traditional Indian arts and crafts, and in 1881 organized an exhibition of Punjab native arts and manufactures. Their son Rudyard, who had been sent to boarding school in England, developed a deep attachment to "aunt Georgie" and "cousin Margaret." The Kipling family could well have been the source of this bracelet. According to family tradition, it was worn by Margaret Burne-Jones with the Indian necklace (No. I: 5). Its scale and style, however, would suggest that it might have been worn with a more elaborate Indian necklace in her possession, purchased from Child and Child.[27]

No. I: 7

Engagement Ring
British, c. 1885-86
Sri Lankan sapphire mounted as a ring in yellow gold
    with pearl shoulders, the shank engraved *"Facti:
    Sumus:Sicut:Consolati"*, each word separated by a heart
Height of bezel: 4.0 mm
Provenance: J.W. Mackail; Margaret Burne-Jones
Heather Maclachlan

This ring was given by the classical scholar Prof. J.W. Mackail (see No. M: 12) to Margaret Burne-Jones before their marriage in 1886. Burne-Jones probably had mixed feelings about this event, for he wrote to Frances Horner, "I got her a moonstone that she might never know love and stay with me. It did no good, but it was wonderful to look at."[28]

Munn points out that rings of this type were commercially available and very popular at that time, and that its choice is consistent with Pre-Raphaelite taste. Burne-Jones had his own personal symbolism for the sapphire, with which the couple were undoubtedly familiar. He proclaimed it the "crown of stones," saying "sapphire is truth, and I am never without it," and declaring "Sapphires I make my totem of!"[29] This stone was associated by Burne-Jones with Friday.[30]

The ring is more remarkable for the engraved inscription inside the shank, which is in the tradition of English "posy rings." Derived from a corruption of the French word *"poésie,"* these love-tokens go back to the middle ages. Inscriptions were generally in English or Old French, the language of courtly love; the Latin inscription on this ring reflects Prof. Mackail's classical bent, and may be loosely translated as "We are made for each other's consolation." Mackail was then a rising star in the literary scene at Oxford. In 1899 he published his two-volume biography of William Morris.

The separation of each word by a heart recalls the frequent use of this device by Burne-Jones (see Nos. I: 1, 8). The sapphire and pearls are held in place with ornamental trefoils, which echo Gothic ornament.

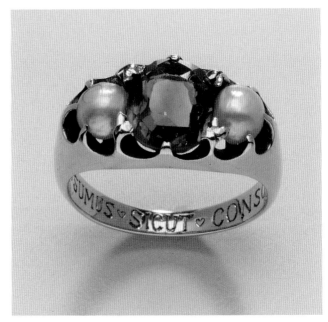

NO. I: 7

No. I: 8

EDWARD BURNE-JONES

Gentleman's Ring
English, 1890s
Silver ring set with a heart-shaped piece of pearl
Child and Child, Kensington
Height: 2.0 cm
Provenance: Edward Burne-Jones
Private collection, Ottawa

This ring is one of the few pieces of jewellery designed by Burne-Jones that was actually executed. It bears the impressed mark which Child and Child used for jewellery, a sunflower between two "C"s. Harold Child believed in the medieval tradition of craftsmanship which involved apprenticeship, a *wanderjahre*, and a *meisterjahre*.[31] In this he shared the opinions of Morris and Giuliano.

Burne-Jones was a frequent visitor at the shop where he bought and commissioned pieces after his designs. Munn has pointed out that the work he entrusted to Child and Child was of "an intensely personal and romantic nature."[32] His designs influenced much of the production of this jewellery firm. The symbolism of the pearl heart was undoubtedly personal. In later life the artist wore this ring on the little finger of his left hand;[33] it is visible in a photograph by H. and R. Stiles, dated 1895.[34]

No. I: 9

CARLO GIULIANO

Brooch c.1880
Gold, blue and black hand-painted enamel, set with
    a pearl
Signed *"C.G."* beneath the pin
1.8 x 4.1 cm
Private collection, Toronto

Born in Naples, Giuliano is thought to have trained under Castellani in Rome, and to have come to London to set up a business under his aegis around 1860. He quickly established a reputation for his superb enamel work and granulation, and catered to the taste for "archaeological jewellery," drawing on many sources of inspiration. Some of his work was in the Gothic Revival style made popular by A.W.N. Pugin during the 1850s.

This pin, with its *fleur-de-lis* finials, recalls French Gothic ornament, and is typical of the delicate polychrome enamel jewels made by Giuliano in the 1880s. The lozenge-

shaped central motif is decorated front and back, and closely resembles the elements which make up a larger, lozenge-shaped pendant executed in a revival of English seventeenth-century enamel work.[35]

By 1874 Giuliano was so successful that he was able to open retail premises at 115 Piccadilly, where he was patronized by artists and aesthetes. Burne-Jones commissioned him to make one of his two most important pieces of jewellery, a brooch in the form of a dove. Although a number of other jewels bearing Giuliano's mark demonstrate the influence of Burne-Jones, their designs cannot be firmly attributed to him.

Echoing the views of Morris, in 1889 Giuliano gave a paper to the Society of Arts entitled "The Art of the Jeweller" in which he maintained that a jeweller needed fourteen years of apprenticeship and should be accomplished in life drawing and have a good knowledge of earlier works of art.

ENDNOTES

1. "Antique Jewellery and its Revival", *Gentleman's Magazine* 14 (1863): 402.

2. I could not have written this section without the generous assistance of Charlotte Gere and Geoffrey Munn. While the introduction is rooted in their pioneering books and articles on this subject, the identification of the pieces of jewellery, and the notes which accompany them, depend heavily on information they supplied in the course of conversations with me in London on 5 and 11 November 1991. Charlotte Gere generously vetted this section, adding important fragments of information and saving me from the inevitable pitfall of jumping to conclusions in an area about which so much still remains to be discovered.

3. Shirley Bury, "Rossetti and His Jewellery", *Burlington Magazine* 118 (February 1976): 102.

4. Charlotte Gere, *Victorian Jewellery Design* (London, 1972), p. 145.

5. Margaret Flower, *Jewellery: 1837-1901* (New York, 1951), p. 10.

6. Gere, *Victorian Jewellery Design*, p. 145.

7. Quoted in Charlotte Gere and Geoffrey Munn, *Artist's Jewellery: PreRaphaelite to Arts and Crafts* (Woodbridge, Suffolk, 1989), p. 141.

8. Apparently his request crossed a letter in the post from Hughes announcing his resignation from Morris and

Co. I am grateful to Douglas Schoenherr for bringing this to my attention.

9. Gere and Munn, *Artists' Jewellery...*, p. 139.

10. Charlotte Gere to Katharine Lochnan, 24 March 1992, Art Gallery of Ontario, Toronto.

11. *Ibid.*

    Gere writes that "Nobody seems to know the exact reason why jewellery was given up" by Morris & Co.

12. Georgiana Burne-Jones, *Memorials of Edward Burne-Jones*, vol. 2 (London, 1904), p. 132.

13. Quoted in Geoffrey Munn, *Castellani and Giuliano: Revivalist Jewellers of the Nineteenth Century* (London, 1983), p. 19.

14. *Ibid.*, p. 68.

15. Gere and Munn, *Artists' Jewellery...*, repro. p. 140.

    Georgiana wears a related pendant in a portrait by her brother-in-law Sir Edward Poynter, dated 1870 (*Ibid.*, p. 140). Rosalind Howard, one of Georgiana's closest friends, commissioned Poynter to make the portrait at a time when Georgiana was deeply distressed by her husband's affair with Maria Zambaco. She had given her a locket described as a "heart-shaped pendant of pearls surrounding a lock of brown hair and inscribed 'Georgie Burne-Jones from Rosalind Howard.'" Georgiana wrote to Rosalind, "I have stipulated that your little locket shall be distinctly visible in it, and though no one else shall know what that means when we are dead and gone, you and I shall while we live" (Ina Turner, *Victorian Sisters: The Remarkable Macdonald Women and the Great Men they Inspired* [Bethesda, Md.,

1987], pp. 124-25).

16. Frances Horner, *Time Remembered* (London, 1933), p. 120.

17. These observations were made by Ronald Fraleigh of Fraleigh Jewellers Gemologists, Toronto.

18. Gere, *Victorian Jewellery Design*, p. 163.

19. Quoted in *Time Remembered*, p. 119.

20. In conversation with Katharine Lochnan, London, November 1991.

21. Munn to Lochnan, 3 October 1991. Art Gallery of Ontario, Toronto.

22. This observation was made by Ronald Fraleigh.

23. Flower, *Jewellery...*, p. 47.

24. Gere, *Victorian Jewellery*, p. 144.

25. Susan Stronge, in conversation with the author, London, November 1991, and observations by Ronald Fraleigh.

26. This observation was made by Ronald Fraleigh.

27. Gere and Munn, *Artists' Jewellery...*, pp. 150-51.

28. Quoted in Horner, *Time Remembered*, p. 120.

29. *Ibid.*, pp. 121-22.

30. *Ibid.*, p. 120.

31. Geoffrey Munn, "Child and Child and their Artistic Patronage", *The International Silver and Jewellery Fair and Seminar* (London, 1987), p. 32.

32. *Ibid.*, p. 35.

33. There is another ring with a heart-shaped sapphire, also worn regularly by Burne-Jones, in a private collection.

34. See Jeremy Maas, *The Victorian Art World in Photographs* (London, 1984), no. 181.

35. See Munn, *Castellani and Giuliano...*, pl. 167-8.

METALWORK

Brian Musselwhite

Ralph Nicholson Wornum (1812-1877), of *The Art Journal*, observed that the metals on exhibit at the Great Exhibition of 1851 were uninspired: "There is no great variety of choice of taste; the Louis Quinze prevailing."[1] Even the popular displays of the "Mediaeval Court," which included metals, had no "application of a peculiar taste to modern and ordinary wants or purposes, but simply the copy of an old idea; old things in an old taste."[2]

Writing on the subject of gold and silver forty-two years later, in 1893, W.A.S. Benson could still state that

> Unhappily there is little original English work being done in these metals. The more ordinary wares have all life and feeling taken out of them by mechanical finish, an abrasive process being employed to remove every sign of tool-marks. The all-important surface is thus obliterated. As to design, fashion oscillates between copies of one past period and another.[3]

Morris and the other founder-members of the Firm had originally been optimistic by including metals in the prospectus of 1861. "Metal work in all its branches, including Jewellery" was listed below mural decoration, carving and stained glass but above furniture. In placement, this was premature, as the real relationship of metal to the overall production of Morris, Marshall, Faulkner & Co. was more accurately positioned in the shorter prospectus of the same year. Potential customers were informed that the company employed "Fine Art Workmen in Painting, Carving, Furniture and the Metals." Of the five categories, the founder-members were least successful with the metal category. The pair of brass candlesticks designed for the Red House by Philip Webb was, sadly, a rarity.

It must have been quickly realized by the founder-members that the category of metal could prove problematic. Even when supplied with designs, individual silversmiths were rare. By the mid-nineteenth century, out of

NO. J: 1. W.A.S. BENSON, *Kettle-on-Stand*, c. 1900

economic necessity, they usually worked for larger firms of manufacturing silversmiths which had their own standards of design. To compound the problem, the intrinsic value of the precious metals added greatly to the cost of the finished item. Morris, Marshall, Faulkner & Co. would have to be supplied with silver from outside the Firm. After 1895, their steady source of domestic silver came from the Birmingham Guild. The clean lines and hammered finishes fitted the Morris & Co. concept. After 1880, William Arthur Smith Benson (1854-1924) produced much silverplated work for Morris & Co. but he produced almost nothing in sterling. In the end, all the metalwork sold by the Firm was from outside the company.

The most important contribution by the English Arts and Crafts Movement to the art of metalwork was the elevation of non-precious metals to new levels of artistic and social acceptability. Although numerous metals and their alloys, including brass, bronze, lead, pewter, cast iron, wrought iron and steel, were frequently mentioned in the artistic publications of the time, it was copper especially that was ideally suited to the dictates of the movement and the guilds. Traditionally used for utilitarian objects, its glowing red tint and low cost helped make it the metal of choice; but it was its malleability that made it so appealing to the craftsman. The hand-hammered copper surface treatment soon became synonymous with the Arts and Crafts look, so much so that competing manufacturers, wishing to create the same effect, used machines that stamped out the hand-hammered finish. By the end of the Arts and Crafts Movement, even objects of precious metals were given this surface treatment.

The void of a metal supplier was not filled until the arrival of W.A.S. Benson in the 1880s. He had became an adherent of Morris's aesthetic philosophies early in life. However, unlike Morris, Benson was not opposed to the use of mass-production machinery, and all his life he championed the potentialities of machine manufacture through his designs.

During the 1880s he was actively involved with Morris & Co. As well as selling his metalwork and light-fixtures in their showrooms, he also designed furniture and wallpaper. Benson became director of Morris & Co., Decorators Ltd. when Morris died and continued with his own firm until he retired in 1923.

The Artificers' Guild produced wrought iron ideally suited to Morris & Co. requirements. The silversmith and metalworker Nelson Dawson and the designer Edward Spencer revived the art of the blacksmith in London through their guild. Spencer (1872-1938) designed a wide range of wrought-iron implements, including candlesticks, sconces and firedogs. The Artificers' Guild exhibited in Montague Fordham's gallery in Maddox Street, London, which also displayed the work of May Morris.

NO. J: 2
W.A.S. BENSON,
Lamp-on-Stand, c. 1900

No. J: 1

W.A.S. BENSON
DESIGNED FOR W.A.S. BENSON & COMPANY

Kettle-on-Stand c. 1900
Electro-plated; squat "curling stone" copper kettle with
    brass handle, spout and lid, on a matching brass
    tripod stand with copper alcohol-burner; stationary
    woven cane bail-handle and ivory finial; may be miss-
    ing the alcohol-burner extinguisher
Height: 24.9 cm; width: 20.8 cm
Base of kettle impressed with shield of three hammering
    tools, separated by the letters *W A S B*; impressed *B*
    and *V* outside of shield: one foot impressed with *L 1*
Royal Ontario Museum, gift of Bernard and Sylvia Ostry
    (acc. no. 989.313.14.1-4)

Although much of Benson's output is now considered part
of the mainstream Arts and Crafts Movement, his boy-
hood introduction to lathes and other machinery led to his
lifelong acknowledgement of the machine. This method
of production was at odds with that of William Morris,
and therefore Morris must be credited with recognizing
the important contribution Benson made to the Arts and
Crafts Movement.

    The design of this kettle and stand seems to have been
a favourite of Benson's and appears in different finishes
in the Benson catalogue of 1899-1900. In combination
with different stands, it was still being produced as late as
1907-10.[4]

No. J: 2

W.A.S. BENSON
DESIGNED FOR W.A.S. BENSON & COMPANY

Lamp-on-Stand c. 1900
Copper and brass
Height: 144.0; width of base: 35.0 cm
Private collection, British Columbia

Although his kettle-on-stand proved to be popular with
the general public, Benson was primarily a designer and
manufacturer of light-fixtures. Working mainly in brass
and copper or a combination of the two, he created standardized parts that could be made into numerous lamps. An
innovative feature in his illustrated catalogues was the
specific information on the lighting needs of different areas
of the house.

NO. J: 3

The copper flanges forming the leaves of the plant are
especially typical of his designs during the 1890s.

    Although not now viewed as an Art Nouveau designer,
Benson sold his work through Siegfried Bing's Maison
de L'Art Nouveau in Paris. His lamps were illustrated in
English and continental periodicals, and one magazine
described his work as "palpitatingly modern."[5]

No. J: 3

EDWARD SPENCER
DESIGNED FOR THE ARTIFICERS' GUILD LTD.

Six-Branch Candelabrum c. 1919
Wrought iron
Height: 74.7 cm, width: 36.5 cm
One foot impressed: *2508*
Royal Ontario Museum, purchased from the Artificers'
    Guild Ltd., London, 1920 (acc. no. 920.94.1)

Candelabra such as this example were a specialty of the Artificers' Guild. Typical of the best of the Guild's work, the candelabrum emphasizes the qualities so admired by followers of the English Arts and Crafts Movement, showing the influence of English medieval ironwork without slavishly copying it. It appears at first to be only a strong, massive, hammered form but on closer inspection reveals the delicate twisting and curling of the branches and the engraved decoration around the candle-nozzles. The candle-branches seem to have greater strength with their counterweighted branches.

During the late nineteenth century there was a renewed interest in medieval ironwork. Publishers issued numerous books on the subject, and the large and important collection of wrought iron at the Victoria and Albert Museum appeared in 1892. The Victorians were very interested in the early stages of this material and were the first to push iron to its limits, using it in the manufacture of ships, trains, and the frameworks of bridges and buildings.

No. J: 4

E D W A R D   S P E N C E R
DESIGNED FOR THE ARTIFICERS' GUILD LTD.

Two-Branch Candelabrum c. 1919
Wrought iron with lead-weighted base
Height: 50.0 cm; width: 31.5 cm
Royal Ontario Museum, purchased from the Artificers' Guild Ltd., London, 1920 (acc. no. 920.94.2)

This two-branched example demonstrates the clever design of these candelabra. The branches are actually extensions of the trunk which then loop to form a heart. From there they continue to develop into a tulip-like plant which curls one "leaf" back around the curve of the heart. The simple raising of the edge of the foot perfectly balances the upper part. Although this twisting of the branches can be found in early examples of metal-smithing, it is to the credit of the designer that it is not a slavish copy.

Along with the silversmith and metalworker Nelson Dawson and his wife, Edith, who specialized in enamel-work, Spencer founded the Artificers' Guild in 1901. Later, after Dawson left the Guild, Spencer was appointed head designer.

This candelabrum and the previous example were purchased by the Royal Ontario Museum in 1920, and are therefore among the earliest examples of the English Arts and Crafts Movement to enter a Canadian public collection.

NO. J: 4

ENDNOTES

1. "The Exhibition as a Lesson in Taste", *The Crystal Palace Exhibition Illustrated Catalogue* (London, 1851), p. viii.
2. *Ibid.*, p. v.
3. "Metal Work", *Arts and Crafts Essays by Members of the Arts and Crafts Exhibition Society* (London, 1893), p. 79.
4. A similar example is illustrated in *Reflections: Arts & Crafts Metalwork in England and the United States* (New York, 1991, ill.13) and mentioned in *Victorian and Edwardian Decorative Art: The Handley-Read Collection* (London, 1971, E70).
5. Alastair Duncan, *Art Nouveau and Art Deco Lighting* (New York, 1978), p. 65.

"Buy from us with a golden curl"

PRINTS

Brenda Rix

William Morris's dream of creating a well-designed, beautiful book was not realized until the founding of the Kelmscott Press in 1890, but it was while a student in the 1850s that he developed a lifelong fascination with the art of the book. During his time at Oxford, Morris studied medieval manuscripts in the Bodleian Library, and by 1856 he was producing his own hand-painted or illuminated books. His interest in early printing also began in the 1850s and there is evidence that he made his first attempt at wood-engraving in 1855.

In the realm of printmaking, the name of Albrecht Dürer held particular sway over the youthful Morris and Edward Burne-Jones. Dürer's work was praised by John Ruskin in *Modern Painters*, of which they were devoted readers, and the two young students spent hours poring over a woodcut copy of the engraving of *Knight, Death and the Devil*, found in the front of H. de la Motte Fouqué's *Sintram and His Companions* (see No. M: 21).[1] Morris also collected Dürer prints or photographs of them.[2] Although Dürer's work epitomized the Northern Renaissance, a period which Morris came to loathe, he would later justify his continued admiration for the German master by saying that Dürer's "figure works...were Gothic in essence."[3] Most of the Dürer prints that Morris is known to have studied in the 1850s were engravings rather than woodcuts, and it was apparently not Dürer who inspired him to take up the wood-engraving tools for the first time.

In the autumn of 1855 Morris and Burne-Jones became ecstatic over a wood-engraved illustration by the Dalziel Brothers of *The Maids of Elfen-mere* (No. K: 2) after a drawing by Dante Gabriel Rossetti. J.W. Mackail records that Morris immediately began to draw on wood and cut his own designs.[4] Although none of these early prints is known to have survived, Morris was evidently inspired by the wood-engraving technique of the Dalziels, admiring what he considered to be a faithful recording of Rossetti's drawing. He would later write that wood-engraving "is a difficult art, but there is noth-

NO. K: 3. CHARLES JAMES FAULKNER after DANTE GABRIEL ROSSETTI, *Buy from us with a Golden Curl*, 1862

ing to *teach* that a man cannot learn in half a day, though it would take a man long practice to do it well. There *are* manufacturers of wood-engraving e.g. the Dalziells [*sic*] as big humbugs as any within the narrow seas."[5]

Morris's plans to include illustrations in his first publishing venture did not come to fruition. A prospectus was sent out in 1855 for *The Oxford and Cambridge Magazine*, but the journal lasted only one year, from January to December 1856, and expense prohibited including wood-engravings. One of Morris's articles for the journal praised "two wonderful wood Engravings" by the German artist Alfred Rethel (1816-1859).[6] Rethel was seen as a modern Holbein, and Morris enthusiastically describes the subject matter of *Death the Avenger* and *Death the Friend* (fig. K: 1). He must also have been attracted to the simple linear treatment and strong silhouettes of the figures, which showed, according to Morris's way of thinking, that the wood-engraver understood the limitations of the woodblock.

The period from 1855 to 1870 has been called the "golden age" of Victorian book illustration and, as the demand grew for wood-engravings in popular books and magazines, the Dalziel Brothers became the merchant

Der Tod als Freund.

Herausgegeben aus der Matrize der Holzschneidekunst von H. Bürkner in Dresden.

Erschienen bei Ed. Schulte (J. Buddeus'sche Buch- und Kunsthandl.) in Düsseldorf.

FIG. K:1
ALFRED RETHEL
(German, 1816-1859)
Death the Friend, 1851
    (wood-engraving)
Art Gallery of Ontario, Toronto,
    gift of the Trier-Fodor
    Foundation, 1982

princes of the trade. Morris and Burne-Jones were particularly irked by what they considered to be the inappropriate use of the woodblock by such firms. In 1862 Burne-Jones was critical of the kind of "scribble" and senseless "scrawl" which he felt made up the bulk of their work, saying that the only way to engrave on wood is "very simply, with little or no cross-hatching, and no useless cleverness."[7] Many years later, Morris reiterated that it "is quite pitiable to see the patience and ingenuity of such clever workmen, as some modern wood-cutters are, thrown away on the literal reproduction of mere meaningless scrawl."[8]

To Morris, the Victorian desire for prints that were facsimiles of drawings left no room for the wood-engraver to translate or interpret artists' drawings and little possibility that the woodblock was being used properly. In his lecture on "Woodcuts of Gothic Books", delivered in 1892, he stated that the sketch provided to the wood-engraver should be "as slight as possible i.e., as much as possible should be left to the executant". The drawn design thus provided only a guide for the executant, and the resulting product, whether it was "pottery, or glass, or wood-cutting," should to some extent express the executant's individuality and, more to the point, should have qualities that were uniquely suited to that material. Successful wood-engravings, for example, should have the clarity and simplicity which characterized the Gothic woodcuts of the fifteenth century when artists were true to the materials and "true to themselves."[9]

When Morris, Marshall, Faulkner & Co. was set up in 1861, printmaking was not listed among the services which the firm claimed to be able to provide. Nevertheless, in 1862 a wood-engraving after an illustration by Rossetti for his sister Christina's *Goblin Market* (No. K: 3) was executed by the firm's book-keeper, Charles Faulkner, and is the only print which carries the "MMF & Co" signature. In contrast to contemporary illustration, the manner of cutting the block is broad and lively and obviously met with Morris's approval.

When Morris himself began to cut the blocks for a mammoth publication to illustrate his poem *The Earthly Paradise* in 1864 or 1865, he first enlisted several people connected with the firm to help (No. K: 7). He then "became possessed with the idea of cutting the blocks himself"[10] and took as his models fifteenth-century woodcuts, possibly from the early printed books in his own newly begun collection (see Nos. L: 1-12). The project represented his first major attempt to control the design and publication of one of his own writings, and in size (folio), format (double column) and ornament (woodcut) it emulated fifteenth-century prototypes.

The sketches, by Burne-Jones, were inspired by the graceful Venetian prints in his copy of Francesco Colonna's *Hypnerotomachia Poliphili* (1499).

NO. K: 7
ELIZABETH BURDEN after
EDWARD BURNE-JONES,
Cupid Going Away, printed in
1974 from block cut, c. 1865

Morris's woodcut interpretations of his friend's work are darker and more detailed, making use, for example, of strong parallel lines for shading, which are closer in appearance to those of German prints and possibly even to those of Dürer. Following the technique that would be employed in the later Kelmscott Press books, Morris used the hard end-grain of the woodblock, a standard procedure in contemporary wood-engraving, but cut the lines broadly in order to approximate the effects of early woodcuts.

Unfortunately, the unavailability of an appropriate typeface to balance the illustrations resulted in the poem's publication in a commercial edition with only one woodcut in 1868 (No. K: 5). Morris did not personally take up printmaking in any concentrated way again, and the only other woodcut from the series which was published in the nineteenth century appeared after Morris's death in the last Kelmscott book, *A Note by William Morris on his Aims in Founding the Kelmscott Press* (No. L: 38), published in 1898.

In 1871 Morris made another abortive attempt at combining illustration and text for his poem *Love is Enough* (No. L: 13). This time, he designed and cut two initials and several borders. Again, available typefaces proved to be unequal to the task and, at this stage in his career, Morris lacked the time and the technical know-how to design his own typeface. Almost twenty years would pass before he was able to achieve this control, with the establishment of his own press.

To Morris, most illustrated books dating after the fifteenth century, and certainly those of the nineteenth century, were poorly designed and made no attempt to integrate text, decoration and illustration. In contrast, when the Kelmscott Press was founded in 1890, wood-engraved illustrations were intended to be part of the "harmonious whole." Although he maintained that illustrations should have two functions – story-telling and ornamentation – the emphasis was placed on the latter "decorative" function, as Morris apparently believed that illustration and decoration served the same ornamental purpose.

The illustrator whom Morris found to be most sympathetic to these aims was Burne-Jones, who provided illustrations for twelve Kelmscott publications, including eighty-seven drawings for their one lavishly illustrated book, *The Works of Geoffrey Chaucer* (No. L: 30). Burne-Jones wrote to Charles Eliot Norton about the *Chaucer*: "I am making the designs as much to fit the ornament and the printing as they are made to fit the little pictures – and I love to be snugly cased in the borders and buttressed up by the vast initials...."[11]

Burne-Jones's images for the Kelmscott Press borrow much from his earlier work. Although his designs for paintings, tapestries and stained glass were completely reworked, graceful female figures, who float through medievalized, dreamlike environments, are characteristic motifs. The shallow, compressed space adds to the emotional intensity of the scenes and also translates well into flat, decorative wood-engraving.

Other artists who worked for the Kelmscott Press provided illustrations for only one book each: Charles M. Gere (1869-1957), *News from Nowhere*, 1893 (No. L: 21); Walter Crane (1845-1915), *The Story of the Glittering Plain*, 1894 (No. L: 23); and Arthur J. Gaskin (1862-1928), *The Shepheardes Calender*, 1896 (No. L: 33). In Morris's opinion, none of their contributions was particularly successful. Walter Crane's use of white-line images on heavy black backgrounds, which were reproduced in the most lifeless fashion by the wood-engraver, A. Leverett, helps to justify Morris's criticism.

The majority of the Kelmscott illustrations were engraved by William Harcourt Hooper (1834-1912), a Hammersmith neighbour of Morris's who had been a successful wood-engraver during the 1860s. He was brought out of retirement by Morris and encouraged to forget about the fine-line, facsimile engravings upon which his reputation was based, and to think in terms of the simple, broadly drawn German woodcuts of the fifteenth century. The subtle tones of Burne-Jones's sketches made his task more difficult. Hooper was aided on occasion by photography and by such technicians as Robert Catterson-Smith, who helped transfer the drawings to the blocks for the *Chaucer*, a long, complicated process (see Richard Landon's essay in this book).

In 1893 Morris wrote that a "book ornamented with pictures that are suitable for that, and that only, may become a work of art second to none, save a fine building duly ornamented, or a fine piece of literature."[12] With the founding of the Kelmscott Press, and particularly with the creation of the Kelmscott *Chaucer*, Morris was finally able to integrate text, decoration and illustration and to focus on the book as an entity to be completely moulded to his ideal of beauty.

No. K:1

WILLIAM HOLMAN HUNT

My Beautiful Lady and Of My Lady in Death 1850
Etching on *chine collé*
20.5 x 12.2 cm (imp.)
Art Gallery of Ontario, Toronto, purchase, 1978 (acc.
    no. 78/101)

In 1848 the painter William Holman Hunt became a found-ing member of the Pre-Raphaelite Brotherhood (PRB). His etching *My Beautiful Lady and Of My Lady in Death* ap-peared as the frontispiece in the first issue of *The Germ: Thoughts towards Nature in Poetry, Literature, and Art*, a peri-odical begun by the PRB in January 1850. Proofs, such as the one exhibited, were printed and sold separately. The

NO. K:1

print illustrates two poems by Thomas Woolner (1825-1892), a sculptor, occasional poet and another member of the PRB. Although *The Germ* went bankrupt after only four issues, it was much admired by Morris and Burne-Jones and inspired their *Oxford and Cambridge Magazine* in 1856.

In an unusual format that is reminiscent of a medieval altarpiece and predella, Holman Hunt's plate combines two images, one over the other. The top etching illustrates "My Beautiful Lady", in which Woolner describes how nature comes alive in the presence of his lover. The lower etching is for "Of My Lady in Death", a poem that appears a few pages later in the journal. The image captures a young man's grief at the time of his lover's death.

The emotion-charged scenes with figures dressed in medieval costumes struck a responsive chord in Burne-Jones and Morris. Burne-Jones praised the etching in the opening issue of *The Oxford and Cambridge Magazine*, call-ing it "truly a song without words."[13]

No. K:2

DALZIEL BROTHERS AFTER
DANTE GABRIEL ROSSETTI

The Maids of Elfen-mere
In William Allingham, *The Music Master* (1855)
Wood-engraving
12.6 x 7.6 cm (image)
Edward P. Taylor Reference Library, Garrow Collection,
    1954, Art Gallery of Ontario, Toronto

The Irish poet William Allingham (1824-1889) was well-known to the Pre-Raphaelite artists and apparently per-suaded his publisher, Routledge, to include his friends' illustrations in a book of his poems in 1855. *The Music Master, A Love Story and Two Series of Day and Night Songs*, with nine prints executed by the major wood-engraving firm of Dalziel Brothers, has been credited with initiating the "golden age" of Victorian book illustration.

In the book's preface, Allingham thanks "those excel-lent painters who on my behalf have submitted their gen-ius to the risks of wood-engraving" (p. ix). Rossetti, who had never drawn on the wood-block before, drew *The Maids of Elfen-mere* in pencil, ink, and red chalk directly onto the whitened block with an intricacy of line and shad-ing that the Dalziels found difficult to reproduce. When the book was published, Rossetti apparently tore the illus-tration out of his copy and complained that it was "as hard as nail, and yet flabby and vapid to the last degree."[14]

The Maids of Elfen-mere records the tragedy of a pastor's son who longs to possess three supernatural maidens (see also No. F: 32). When Morris and Burne-Jones saw the illustration, they found immediate confirmation of their developing ideas about art. Burne-Jones wrote that it was "the most beautiful drawing for an illustration I have ever seen, the weird faces of the maids of Elfen-mere, the musical timed movements of their arms together as they sing, the face of the man, above all, are such as only a great artist could conceive."[15]

No. K: 3

CHARLES JAMES FAULKNER AFTER
DANTE GABRIEL ROSSETTI

Buy from us with a Golden Curl
Frontispiece in Christina Rossetti, *Goblin Market and
    Other Poems*, 1862
Wood-engraving
10.5 x 9.1 cm (image)
Thomas Fisher Rare Book Library, Norman J. Endicott
    Collection, University of Toronto

In an attempt to avoid the grief caused by his previous association with Dalziel (No. K: 2), Rossetti enlisted the help of Morris, Marshall, Faulkner & Co. in 1862 to launch a book of poems by his sister, Christina Rossetti (1830-1894). His illustration, *Buy from us with Golden Curl*, for the "Goblin Market", shows a group of evil goblins begging a curl from Laura in exchange for baskets of fruit (representing sensual pleasures), which she craves. In the distance, her sister Lizzie flees temptation.

Charles Faulkner was a member of Morris's circle at Oxford and became a lifelong friend. In 1857 he assisted Rossetti and Morris in painting the murals in the Oxford Union Debating Society building, and in 1860 he helped to paint patterns on walls and ceilings at Red House. He became the book-keeper and one of the founders of the Firm in 1861. He and his two sisters subsequently painted tiles for Morris, and in 1862 he made his first wood-engraving, *Buy from us with a Golden Curl*. Burne-Jones described the event in a letter to his sister-in-law: "Rossetti, in despair, gave a very careful block to Faulkner the other day, and that ingenious man's first attempt is a regular triumph."[16] Faulkner's technique is remarkable for an amateur printmaker; the image is full of rich patterning and is cut with a bold, animated line.

Faulkner's print was one of two wood-engravings after Rossetti drawings that appear at the front of the book; the

other, engraved by Joseph Swain, was executed in a similarly robust style. The richness of the illustrations contrasts sharply with the mundane appearance of the typeface and printing in the rest of the book.

No. K: 4

DALZIEL BROTHERS AFTER
EDWARD BURNE-JONES

King Sigurd
In *Good Words* (1862)
Wood-engraving
15.2 x 11.4 cm (image)
Edward P. Taylor Reference Library, Garrow Collection,
    1954, Art Gallery of Ontario, Toronto

As the demand for illustrations in popular books and magazines grew during the 1850s and 1860s, the Dalziel Brothers came to dominate the wood-engraving trade. Burne-Jones's *King Sigurd* appeared in 1862 in the journal *Good Words*, as an illustration to a poem by William Forsyth. His female figures have the graceful beauty that was inspired by Rossetti, but they have been engraved using a sophisti-

NO. K: 4

cated system of patterning and line that creates a smooth, lifeless surface. *King Sigurd* was one of the few drawings that Burne-Jones allowed to be subjected to the vagaries of commercial wood-engraving.

The publication of William Forsyth's poetic version of the Norse saga in 1862 is evidence that the romantic, medieval qualities of the story had an appeal for Victorian audiences long before the publication of Morris's important *Story of Sigurd the Volsung and the Fall of the Niblungs* in 1876. Morris himself included Norse themes in several of his writings in the 1850s and 1860s.

No. K:5

WILLIAM MORRIS AFTER
EDWARD BURNE-JONES

Three Female Musicians
From *The Earthly Paradise*, Part 1, first ed., 1868
Buxton Forman 17
Wood-engraving
7.0 x 6.2 cm (image)
Provenance: presentation copy from the author to
    Edward D. J. Wilson
Thomas Fisher Rare Book Library, Norman J. Endicott
    Collection, University of Toronto

With the publication of *The Earthly Paradise* in three volumes between 1868 and 1870, Morris's literary fame was assured. Set in the fourteenth century, the Prologue describes how three travellers from Norway search for an earthly paradise and discover a remote island in the Atlantic. Upon meeting up with the island's Greek inhabitants, they begin to exchange folktales. The resulting twenty-four stories run to 42,000 lines of poetry.

The only embellishment in early editions of the poem was a wood-engraving of female musicians, which was printed on the title-page and again at the end of each book.[17] The image, engraved on wood by Morris after a drawing by Burne-Jones, shows three maidens standing against a garden wall and playing lutes and a rebec.[18] The figures are posed like the classical Three Graces, but their medieval costumes, sweet facial expressions, and positioning in a shallow picture space are all characteristics of the Pre-Raphaelite aesthetic. Morris's wood-engraving technique reflects his study of German and Italian fifteenth-century prints.

For the first edition of *The Earthly Paradise*, Morris may have felt that a small print, executed in a simple, highly

NO. K:5

decorative manner, would best harmonize with available typefaces. His use of flat, ornamental foliage also relates to his study of medieval art, and a similar approach can be found in Morris's stained-glass designs (Nos. A: 6, D: 2-3).

No. K:6

WILLIAM MORRIS AFTER
EDWARD BURNE-JONES

Cupid's First Sight of Psyche
From "The Story of Cupid and Psyche"
Wood-engraving on hand-made wove paper
Printed in 1974 from block cut c. 1865
11.1 x 8.0 cm (image)
Private collection, Ottawa

No. K:7

ELIZABETH BURDEN AFTER
EDWARD BURNE-JONES

Cupid Going Away
From "The Story of Cupid and Psyche"
Wood-engraving on hand-made wove paper
Printed in 1974 from block cut c. 1865
10.5 x 15.8 cm (image)
Private collection, Ottawa

NO. K: 6

No. K: 8

WILLIAM MORRIS AFTER
EDWARD BURNE-JONES

Charon's Fee
From "The Story of Cupid and Psyche"
Wood-engraving on hand-made wove paper
Printed in 1974 from block cut c. 1865
10.7 x 15.7 cm (image)
Private collection, Ottawa

According to his daughter May, "Morris always had a
yearning for illustrations to his poems; he saw the stories
in brilliantly-defined pictures and desired that other people should do so, too. 'There is nobody but Burne-Jones
who can do them,' he often said."[19]

Burne-Jones probably began to draw the illustrations
for *The Earthly Paradise* in 1864. Georgiana Burne-Jones
wrote of their final trip to Red House: "The last visit we
paid to Upton was in September, 1865.... Indoors the talk
of the men was much about The Earthly Paradise, which
was to be illustrated by two or three hundred woodcuts,
many of them already designed and some even drawn on

the block."[20] The project absorbed much of Morris and
Burne-Jones's creative energy until it was laid aside in 1868,
and the book was published in a commercial edition with
only one illustration (No. K: 5).

The first block of *The Earthly Paradise* was cut by the
commercial wood-engraver Joseph Swain, but Morris was
unhappy with the result, and after several other blocks
were cut by his sister-in-law, Elizabeth Burden (1842-1924),
the Firm's foreman, George Wardle (1836-1910), and others, he apparently took the rest of the blocks "all in hand
and carried them through, not without some lively scenes
in Queen Square. He cut with great ardour and with much
knowledge, but the work did not always go to his mind.
It was necessarily slow and he was constitutionally quick:
there were then quarrels between them."[21] In the end, forty-
six blocks were cut, of which Morris completed thirty-six
or thirty-seven. All were for "The Story of Cupid and
Psyche", one of the stories for the month of May.

May Morris later remembered evenings spent watching
her father busily working under the brilliant light of the
lace-maker's lamp (fig. K: 2):

> In the evenings – what delight! there sometimes appeared a
> gloriously, mysteriously shining object, behind which he
> would work with bright cutting tools on a little block of
> wood, which sat on a plump leather cushion. The beautiful
> edition of "The Earthly Paradise" that he and Burne-Jones
> had at heart had not yet been given up, and these were the
> wood blocks for one of its stories, the "Cupid and Psyche"
> illustrations, most of which my father cut himself.[22]

Burne-Jones's drawings for "The Story of Cupid and
Psyche" provided a reservoir of images which he reused
in later paintings, such as the *Cupid and Psyche* frieze in
George Howard's morning-room in Palace Green.[23] Morris,
too, gained much from this attempt at book production.
He developed an inventive wood-engraving technique that
owed stylistically to German and Italian fifteenth-century
prints, and he also began to form the principles of book
design that would not be fully developed until he established the Kelmscott Press some twenty years later.

The book was to have been a folio edition in double
columns. Specimen pages were put into Basel and Caslon
type by the Chiswick Press, but neither type was deemed
strong enough to balance the illustrations. Although the
lack of an appropriate typeface appears to have dealt the
final blow to the project, the overwhelming magnitude
of the venture, as well as the successful publication of
The Life and Death of Jason in 1867, may have encouraged

NO. K: 8

Morris to have *The Earthly Paradise* published sooner than planned in a trade edition.

In 1874 Morris was considering starting an illuminated version of "Cupid and Psyche", in which he would transcribe some of Burne-Jones's drawings to accompany his calligraphy. He never forgot his original vision of *The Earthly Paradise*, but an illustrated Kelmscott edition did not appear in his lifetime and Burne-Jones's proposal to publish it in 1897 was also abandoned with his death in 1898.[24]

No. K: 9

W I L L I A M   S T R A N G

Emery Walker 1906
Binyon 473[25]
Drypoint with plate-tone on laid paper
51.4 x 37.6 cm (imp.)
Signed by the artist, in graphite, l.r.: *Wm Strang*
Inscribed, in graphite, l.r.: *Emery Walker*
National Gallery of Canada, purchase, 1922 (acc. no. 2215)

Emery Walker (1851-1933) was by trade a photogravure and collotype printer and a typographical expert. His high standards of design and workmanship had a significant impact on printing in his own day and into the twentieth century. Morris and Walker first became acquainted in 1883 or 1884 at a Socialist meeting in Bethnal Green. The two lived near each other and shared many interests, not the least of which was a fascination with fifteenth-century printed books.

In November 1888, at the first exhibition of the Arts and Crafts Society, Walker gave his famous lecture on letterpress printing, using lantern-slides. Morris had been pondering how to design a new typeface for some time and was particularly inspired when he saw the enlarged details. A year or two later, as Morris established the Kelmscott Press, Walker's expertise provided him with invaluable direction and assistance.

William Strang produced more than 700 prints using a wide range of techniques, and also had a distinguished career as a book illustrator and portrait etcher. This drypoint portrait of Walker is in the style of Strang's teacher,

NO. K: 9

Alphonse Legros (1837-1911), with its detailed drawing of the head and sketchy treatment of the torso area. This format in turn looks back to the seventeenth-century *Iconography* series of famous men by Anthony Van Dyck.

No. K: 10

MALCOLM OSBORNE AFTER
GEORGE FREDERICK WATTS

William Morris 1913
Mezzotint on wove paper
31.7 x 22.5 cm (imp.)
Art Gallery of Ontario, Toronto, gift of the C.N.E.,
    1966 (acc. no. 124)
For illustration see page xvi.

George F. Watts (1817-1904) is often remembered today for his large allegorical paintings executed in the "grand manner," but until the 1880s he was known chiefly for his portraits. In 1852 he began a series of likenesses of friends and

famous contemporaries, a kind of pantheon of great Victorians. Morris and Burne-Jones both sat for Watts in 1870.[26] Morris wrote to his wife, Jane, on 15 April 1870 that "I am going to sit to Watts this afternoon, though I have got a devil of a cold-in-the-head, which don't make it very suitable."[27] Watts's portrait of Morris has been much reproduced, and May Morris observed in 1910 that the painting remained "the truly great and sympathetic representation of my father at this time."[28] Watts has focused attention on the sitter's sensitive, intelligent face by spotlighting it against a dark background.

A member of the Royal Academy, Malcolm Osborne was proficient in a variety of printmaking techniques, including etching, mezzotint and aquatint. He was also prolific, and provided plates for many popular art periodicals. This mezzotint was exhibited at the Royal Academy in 1913.

ENDNOTES

1. A framed impression of Dürer's engraving appears on the wall in a bedroom in Burne-Jones's house, The Grange, Fulham (see M: 21). This may be the one given to him in 1865 by John Ruskin.
2. Morris to Cormell Price, 6 July 1855, in *The Collected Letters of William Morris*, ed. Norman Kelvin, vol. 1 (Princeton, N.J., 1984), no. 7, pp. 13-14.
3. "The Woodcuts of Gothic Books" (lecture delivered 26 January 1892), quoted in *William Morris: Artist, Writer, Socialist*, ed. May Morris, vol. 1 (Oxford, 1936; New York, 1966), p. 319.
4. *The Life of William Morris*, vol. 1 (London, 1899; reprinted New York, 1968), p. 87.
5. Morris to Thomas Wardle, 14 November 1877, *The Collected Letters...*, vol. 1, no. 454, p. 410.
6. "'Death the Avenger' and 'Death the Friend'", *The Oxford and Cambridge Magazine* (August 1856): 477.
7. Georgiana Burne-Jones, *Memorials of Edward Burne-Jones*, vol. 1 (London, 1904; reprinted New York, 1971), pp. 254-5.
8. "The Woodcuts of Gothic Books", p. 333.
9. *Ibid.*, p. 334-38.
10. Mackail, *The Life of William Morris*, vol. 1, p. 190.
11. Letter dated 20 December 1894, Pierpont Morgan Library, New York, gift of John M. Crawford. Quoted in Susan Casteras, *et. al.*, *Pocket Cathedrals: Pre-Raphaelite Book Illustration* (New Haven, 1991), p. 38.

12. "The Ideal Book" (lecture delivered 19 June 1893), quoted in May Morris, *William Morris...*, vol. 1, p. 318.

13. "Essay on 'The Newcombes'", *The Oxford and Cambridge Magazine* (January 7 1856): 60.

14. Quoted in Forrest Reid, *Illustrators of the Sixties* (London, 1928; reprinted New York, 1975), p. 32.

15. "Essay on 'The Newcombes'", 60.

16. G. Burne-Jones, *Memorials...*, vol. 1, p. 254.

17. Morris's block was burned in a fire at Strangeways, the printers, in 1877, and a new block was engraved by George Campfield for subsequent editions.

18. The poses of the three female figures and the location of the wall behind are reminiscent of Burne-Jones's drawing *Going to Battle* (1858-59; Fitzwilliam Museum), illustrated in D. Robinson and S. Wildman, *Morris & Co. in Cambridge* (Cambridge, 1980), pl. 10, cat. 12.

19. *William Morris...*, vol. 1, p. 402.

20. G. Burne-Jones, *Memorials...*, vol. 1, p. 294.

21. Quoted in Mackail, *The Life of William Morris*, vol. 1, p. 190.

22. May Morris, *The Collected Works of William Morris*, vol. 3 (London: Longmans, 1910-15), p. xxv.

23. Morris may have intended that *The Earthly Paradise* include as many as 500 wood-engravings. Large groups of Burne-Jones's drawings for the project exist in the Ashmolean Museum, Oxford, the City Museum and Art Gallery, Birmingham, the Pierpont Morgan Library, New York, and the collection of Mr. and Mrs. Sanford L. Berger, Carmel, California.

24. Only about ten sets of proofs were pulled during Morris's lifetime. In 1974 Rampant Lions Press and Clover Hill Editions printed and published an edition from the forty-four original blocks owned by the Society of Antiquaries, London. Four hundred sets were printed with the text using the "Troy" type invented by Morris for the Kelmscott Press. Another 100 sets of proofs of the engravings were also issued; the three prints included in this publication come from the set numbered 88/100. For full discussions of the history of *The Earthly Paradise* project, see A.R. Dufty, *The Story of Cupid and Psyche* (Cambridge, 1974) and Joseph R. Dunlap, *The Book that Never Was* (New York, 1971).

25. Binyon number refers to Laurence Binyon, *William Strang: A Catalogue of his Etched Work, 1882-1912* (Glasgow, 1912).

26. Watts's portrait of Morris is now in the National Portrait Gallery, London, and the portrait of Burne-Jones, dated 1870, is in the City Museum and Art Gallery, Birmingham.

27. *The Collected Letters...*, vol. 1, no. 110, p. 115.

28. *The Collected Works...*, vol. 3, p. xxviii.

BOOKS

Richard Landon

Right at the end of his career, William Morris succinctly summarized what he had learned about the production of beautiful books in the opening paragraph of his *A Note…on his Aims in Founding the Kelmscott Press*:

> I began printing books with the hope of producing some which would have a definite claim to beauty, while at the same time they should be easy to read and should not dazzle the eye, or trouble the intellect of the reader by eccentricity of form in the letters. I have always been a great admirer of the calligraphy of the Middle Ages, and of the earlier printing which took its place. As to the fifteenth-century books, I had noticed that they were always beautiful by force of the mere typography, even without the added ornament, with which many of them are so lavishly supplied. And it was the essence of my undertaking to produce books which it would be a pleasure to look upon as pieces of printing and arrangements of type. Looking at my adventure from this point of view then, I found I had to consider chiefly the following things: the paper, the form of the type, the relative spacing of the letters, the words, and the lines; and lastly the position of the printed matter on the page.[1]

What Morris was able to achieve with the Kelmscott Press[2] in a span of time not much longer than five years seems remarkable, for, however one might regard the books as pieces of design, they are consistent and instantly recognizable. Apart from his level of energy and powers of concentration and his many years' work as a designer of glass, fabric and ceramics, Morris had, from the 1850s, pursued the design of his own literary output without notable success, but with ambitious plans, and some practical experience. His study of medieval manuscripts and early printed books, his experiments in calligraphy, and his attempts to produce an illustrated edition of *The Earthly Paradise* can be viewed as part of a long, circuitous apprenticeship for the "typographic experiment" at Kelmscott House. During this period he was also, of course, a voluminous writer, the manager of a large firm, and

NO. L: 30. GEOFFREY CHAUCER, *The Works of Geoffrey Chaucer*, copy 1,
Hammersmith: Kelmscott Press, 26 June 1896

249

an active participant in many causes, from Socialism, in which he played a major role, to architectural conservation.

The Earthly Paradise, published between 1868 and 1870, and *The Life and Death of Jason* (1867), which was originally conceived as part of it, were planned by Morris and Edward Burne-Jones to provide the vehicle for a big book "with lots of stories and pictures."[3] The emphasis was definitely on the word "lots." The first edition of *The Earthly Paradise*, with no original illustrations (save for one repeated decoration; see No. K: 5), contains over 1,200 pages and, according to the various surviving lists, over 300 (and perhaps as many as 500) wood-engraved illustrations were envisaged. In 1865 Burne-Jones began to draw designs and Morris (and others) began to engrave them, but it was slow work. Morris completed about forty of the blocks but the project was abandoned in 1868; it has been called "the book that never was." (See Nos. K: 5-8, for a more detailed discussion of this book and its posthumous fate.)

One of Morris's engravings appeared in the last Kelmscott Press book (No. L: 38), with a Morris border to frame it in the style he preferred. In 1872, just after he had written *Love is Enough*, he and Burne-Jones again turned their attention to book design, Morris designing borders and initials and Burne-Jones at least one illustration and a border. Trial pages were pulled, but again the project came to naught and the book was published, in 1873, without decoration but with an attractive Morris-designed binding (No. L: 13). *Love is Enough* did eventually appear in a Kelmscott Press edition, with two Burne-Jones illustrations and Morris borders, but Morris was dead by that time.

In the 1870s Morris took up calligraphy and manuscript ornamentation and produced a series of manuscripts on paper and vellum, in several styles, some with paintings by Burne-Jones (see No. A: 26). In the 1850s he had written a few in Gothic script but, beginning in 1869, and with the assistance of four Renaissance Italian writing manuals he had purchased, his calligraphy became more varied and sophisticated and the decoration more elaborate. His *Aeneid* of 1875 was written in a strong Roman script on vellum and decorated with initials that presage those designed for the Kelmscott Press. It was left unfinished by Morris after page 177, but later completed by Graily Hewitt and others. Morris's experiments with calligraphy and decoration were important because of the feeling for letter-forms he developed and his concept of the "full page," which is so characteristic of many Kelmscott books.

Just before the foundation of the Kelmscott Press, Morris again attempted to design three of his own books, using the Chiswick Press, to achieve something of the typographical effect of books of the fifteenth century. Of the few old-face types available he chose Basle Roman for *The House of the Wolfings* (1889) and *The Roots of the Mountains* (1890) (No: L: 14). For *The*

Story of Gunnlaug the Worm-Tongue (1891) he experimented with a replica of William Caxton's fourth type, but its appearance was consciously antiquarian and it was never offered for sale.

Although Morris lived during an age of great book collectors, his own library was not a vast general assemblage of rare books and manuscripts like those of the Earl of Crawford, Henry Huth or Lord Amherst, nor a small cabinet of high spots like the Rowfant Library of Frederick Locker-Lampson.[4] Rather, it consisted of carefully chosen examples of early European printing, with an emphasis on the illustrated books of Germany and France. He also collected medieval illuminated manuscripts, the best examples of which were bought in the last few years of his life. The final collection contained about 800 early printed books and 100 or so manuscripts. That Morris was acknowledged as an important collector is demonstrated by his inclusion in the large woodcut, *A Book-Sale at Sotheby's Auction-Room*, which appeared in *The Graphic* on 26 May 1888.

Around 1864 Morris was introduced to Frederick S. Ellis,[5] an antiquarian bookseller in Covent Garden, who became his publisher, Kelmscott Press editor, and close friend. According to Ellis, the first great book purchased by Morris was the 1473 Ulm edition of Boccaccio's *De Claris Mulieribus*, for which he paid £26. At about this time he also acquired copies of the 1493 *Nuremberg Chronicle* (No. L: 10) and Brant's 1497 *Ship of Fools* (No. L: 11). In 1876 a catalogue of the library was drawn up and among its approximately 300 books, thirteen incunabula are listed, together with some forty sixteenth-century continental books, many of them illustrated with woodcuts.[6] At this time he apparently owned only six manuscripts. In 1880 Morris sold part of his collection to Ellis and White because of, according to his daughter May, "the cares of a house and of business."[7] J.W. Mackail, his first biographer, claimed, however, that he "had sold the greater part of his valuable library, in order to devote the proceeds to the furtherance of Socialism."[8] At a Socialist meeting, around 1884, Morris met Emery Walker and invited him to visit the library at Kelmscott House. Here the books were put to practical use as Walker explained to him the techniques of early printers, based on his years of work in the printing trades. After the famous lecture by Walker at the Arts and Crafts exhibition in November 1888, when Morris decided to design a new font of type, he began systematically to buy examples of early printing, both Gothic and Roman.

In 1890 another catalogue of the library was begun by Jenny Morris and continued by Morris and Sydney Cockerell.[9] It reveals the increased pace of acquisition as does a surviving invoice from Quaritch.[10] Once the Kelmscott Press was under way, Morris continued to add books and manuscripts steadily to his library, and his acquisition can partially be traced through reference to Cockerell's detailed diaries.[11] Cockerell became Morris's librarian in October 1892 and secretary of the Kelmscott Press in July 1894, and was thus very closely involved during the most active period of collecting.

Morris was a careful buyer and concerned about how much he had to pay, particularly for manuscripts. However, once he had seen something that really appealed to him, he would inevitably succumb, even though the process might take a long time. He first saw the Huntingfield Psalter (now in the Pierpont Morgan Library, New York) in August 1892, when Quaritch sent it on approval at £800. It was returned but appeared in a Quaritch catalogue the following year, when Morris still found himself able to resist. In July 1894, however, he had it on approval again, but Cockerell was instructed to return it. In April 1895 it was offered again, and Cockerell wrote to

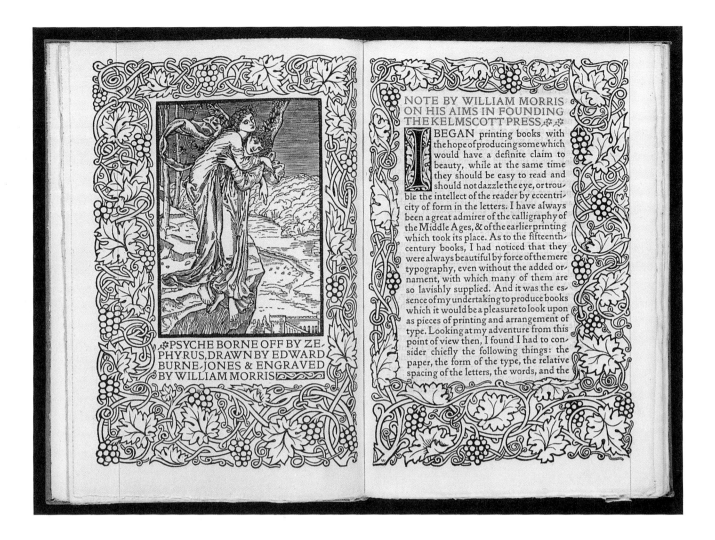

Quaritch on the 29th "to express his regret that he does not feel able to become the purchaser of the book." The end of indecision was in sight, however, for only three days later Cockerell recorded in his diary, "W.M. went to Quaritch's with F.S. Ellis and bought the Huntingfield Psalter." Having broken the ice, he shortly after plunged in and bought the Tiptoft Missal for £900; it is also now in the Morgan Library. A receipt of 7 October 1892 reveals that, of the £1,350 owed to Morris by Quaritch for the Kelmscott Golden Legend, £1,237 7s. 5d. was taken up "by books bought on various occasions."[12] The Kelmscott Press and Morris's library were inextricably intertwined.

Morris's books were used for inspiration and amusement as well as for the solution of practical design problems. He made lantern-slides from them for his lecture "The Woodcuts of Gothic Books" and used them to illustrate his article "On the Artistic Qualities of the Woodcut Books of Ulm and Augsburg in the Fifteenth Century", published in *Bibliographica* in 1895. The grand illustrated catalogue planned by Morris and Cockerell, and

NO. L: 38
WILLIAM MORRIS,
*A Note by William Morris on
   his Aims in Founding the
   Kelmscott Press*, Hammersmith: Kelmscott Press,
24 March 1898

announced as a forthcoming Kelmscott Press book in 1894, was never completed, although Cockerell used some of the reproductions, for which lineblocks had been made, in one of the last Kelmscott books: *Some German Woodcuts of the Fifteenth Century* (No. L: 36).

After Morris's death in October 1896, the library was purchased *en bloc* for £18,000 by Richard Bennett, an obscure and eccentric collector from Lancashire who disliked large folios. Bennett kept only thirty-one manuscripts and 389 printed books. The rest were disposed of by Sotheby's at an auction held from 5 to 10 December 1898, where they fetched almost £11,000. In 1902 Bennett sold his library to Pierpont Morgan, and thus the cream of Morris's bibliophilic exertions went to New York. Morris was a passionate man whose boundless energies were expended in many different ways and on many different things. He was a genuine bibliophile but with marked differences from others of that breed, and the passion he expended on his library clearly gave him great satisfaction.

Emery Walker, a largely self-educated printer who established his own engraving business in 1886, became virtually a partner in the Kelmscott Press. His technical expertise and his contacts in the printing trades were indispensable to Morris, and to almost every other private press proprietor in England and Germany until his death in 1933. On the evening of 15 November 1888 he gave a lecture, illustrated with lantern slides, some of which had been taken from books in Morris's library, and the sight of the early type and illustrations blown up triggered in Morris an immediate reaction. On the way back to Hammersmith, Morris turned to Walker and said simply, "Let's make a new font of type." Immediately his zest and energy were focused on the new project and on the foundation of the Kelmscott Press. Walker's lecture also received a favourable review in the *Pall Mall Gazette* of 16 November 1888, written by Oscar Wilde.

Morris began by designing the Golden type, based on the face used by Nicolas Jenson in his Italian Pliny of 1476 and, more directly, on the *Historia Fiorentina Populi*, also printed in Venice in 1476 by Jacobus Rubeus in a similar type. Morris also owned Jenson's 1472 Latin Pliny (No. L: 1), which used the same face. Walker made photographic enlargements of pages from the books, and Morris traced them until he felt confident in his feeling for the forms of the letters. He then drew them free-hand and Walker reduced them photographically. After many revisions they were given to Edward Prince, a type punch-engraver, and the punches were cut, the matrices formed and the type cast. Prince made smoke-proofs at each step of the engraving so that small adjustments in the design could be made. Golden type, a fourteen-point (or "English") Roman, was ready for use by January 1891 and the first Kelmscott book, *The Story of the Glittering Plain* (No. L: 15), was finished on 4 April.

Morris preferred Gothic typefaces and set about designing one as soon as Golden was finished. Using the same techniques, but no specific models, he began designing Troy. It bears a close resemblance to a face used by Peter Schoeffer in Mainz and to Günther Zainer's of Augsberg (see No. L: 6). Troy was cast in Great Primer (eighteen-point) size and was referred to by Morris as a "semi-Gothic type designed...with special regard to legibility."[13] For the long-planned edition of Chaucer it became evident that Troy would be too large and, reluctantly, Morris had a twelve-point version cut, which was called Chaucer. All the Kelmscott books were printed with these three faces. Eventually the types, punches, and matrices were acquired by the Cambridge University Press, where they remain in that institution's collection of private-press types.

Walker introduced Morris to Joseph Batchelor, the hand-papermaker in Little Chart, Kent, in October 1890. From his firm Morris ordered paper modeled on Italian paper of the 1470s and watermarked with a flower he had designed. The first batch of Flower was found to be too small and was used only for the earliest Kelmscott books. In April 1891 the second size of Flower was delivered and used for *The Golden Legend* (No. L: 19). In 1893 a slightly larger size was ordered, watermarked with a perch. Perch was used for the second Kelmscott edition of *The Story of the Glittering Plain* (No. L: 23) and for the *Chaucer* (No. L: 30). The fourth paper supplied by Batchelor's was Apple, a paper of unusual dimensions, first used for *The Earthly Paradise* (No. L: 31).

Morris detested "large-paper" copies of books, which were very popular with collectors in the 1890s, because they spoiled his carefully calculated margins. As a kind of substitute most Kelmscott Press books appeared, in a few copies, printed on vellum. For *The Story of the Glittering Plain* (No. L: 15), a supply of Roman vellum was left over from the calligraphic experiments (enough to print six copies), but no more could be obtained from Italy because of the Vatican's needs, and Morris was supplied by the English firms of Henry Band of Brentford and William J. Turney of Stourbridge.

The printers' ink for the Kelmscott Press was initially supplied by Shackell, Edwards & Co. of London, although Walker had suggested using one manufactured in Hannover, Germany by Jänecke. It proved to be very stiff and the pressmen objected, so the Shackell, Edwards brand was used until the Spring of 1895, when yellow stains began to appear on some pages of the *Chaucer*. They were eventually removed by bleaching in the sun, but Morris got Jänecke to supply a slightly softer version of his ink, and all the gatherings from T onwards of the *Chaucer* were printed with it, as were all other Kelmscott books. Morris required a very black ink for most of the printing. For red and blue inks he also experimented; the blue was supplied by Winsor and Newton, according to specifications supplied by him, and several different reds were used, mostly from Shackell, Edwards.

The illustration and decoration of most Kelmscott Press books was a collaboration between Morris and Burne-Jones, but other people were involved as well. Morris's borders and initials were engraved primarily by William Hooper, a Hammersmith neighbour, who could work directly from his drawings, which had been photographically reproduced on the blocks. The translation of Burne-Jones's pencil sketches into woodblocks required a more elaborate procedure, and the help of Robert Catterson-Smith, an art teacher, was enlisted. A photographic print of the sketch was made by Walker and covered with a thin wash of Chinese white. Catterson-Smith then traced over the lines, which were faintly visible, with a sharp pencil, using the original drawing as a guide. He next used a sable brush and very black Chinese ink to go over the print again, which thickened the lines, and he would consult Burne-Jones about difficult bits. The drawing was then transferred photographically to the surface of a woodblock and engraved by Hooper.[14] The illustrations and borders were printed directly from the blocks, but electrotypes were made of the initials and ornaments after Walker

NO. L: 8
EUCLID,
Elementa Geometria, Venice:
Erhard Ratdolt, 1482

NO. L: 15
WILLIAM MORRIS,
The Story of the Glittering Plain,
Hammersmith: Kelmscott
Press, 8 May 1891

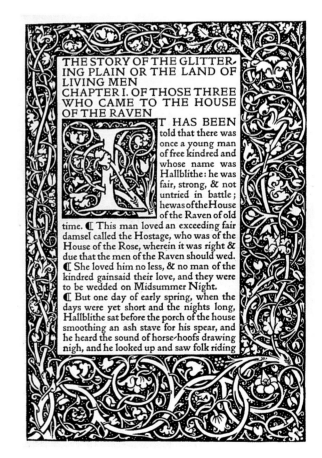

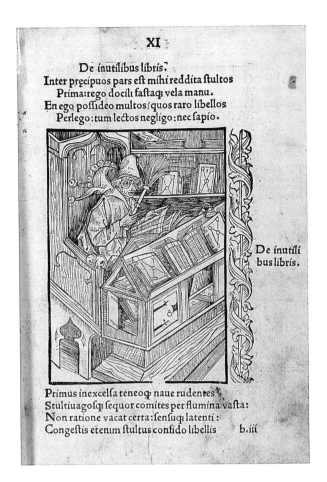

was able to persuade Morris that the impression from an electrotyped initial was indistinguishable from that of the original block.

All the bindings on Kelmscott books were done by J. and J. Leighton of London (apart from the special pigskin binding done for the *Chaucer* by the Doves Bindery (see No. L: 30, copy 1). There were only two kinds: a quarter-linen back with blue boards and a printed paper label, and full limp vellum with silk ties and Golden or Troy lettering on the spine. Morris thought of the quarter-linen bindings as temporary, to be replaced with a more permanent binding of the collector's choice, but most copies have remained in their original boards. He does not seem to have been specially interested in bindings, although there were some very fine ones in his library (see No. L: 4).

The Kelmscott Press was located in a series of buildings in Hammersmith near Kelmscott House, the main one being Sussex Cottage, no. 14 Upper Mall. The size of the staff of the press varied somewhat, according to how many books were in production and how large they were, but in

NO. L: 11
SEBASTIAN BRANT,
Stultifera Navis, Basel: Johann
Bergmann de Olpe, 1497

NO. L: 23
WILLIAM MORRIS,
The Story of the Glittering Plain,
Hammersmith: Kelmscott
Press, 17 February 1894

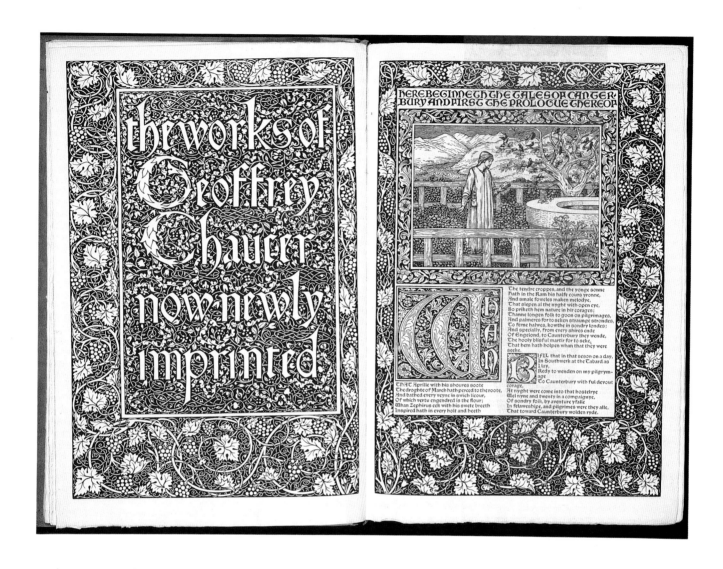

NO. L: 30
GEOFFREY CHAUCER,
The Works of Geoffrey Chaucer,
copy 2, Hammersmith:
Kelmscott Press, 26 June 1896

1895, when work on the *Chaucer* was at its busiest, there were eleven. Each year a "wayzegoose" was held and the printers and their friends would repair with Morris to a hotel or inn, eat a large dinner with a good supply of wine, port and cigars, and celebrate with toasts, songs and recitations. Morris's printers were well paid, but the quality of the work expected from them was very high. The Kelmscott Press owned three Albion presses and a proofing press, the third Albion being large and specially reinforced with steel bands. It was purchased late in 1894 to cope with the great pressure required to print the decorated pages of the *Chaucer.*

While a great deal has been written about the Kelmscott Press as part of the history of printing and book design, very little attention has been paid to the texts that were published. Most of them fell into one of three categories: Morris's own works, medieval English texts, and English literary classics. Occasionally a book would be produced by special arrangement, such as Wilfrid Scawen Blunt's *Love Lyrics* (No. L: 16). The small books, which were popular and sold quickly, in effect subsidized the large books, particularly the *Chaucer*. Eleven Kelmscott books were published by Reeves and Turner, but the colophons emphasized that they were merely distributors. "I don't mind having a publisher, so long as he has nothing whatever to do with any question except purely business ones",[15] said Morris, and this statement summed up his attitude. This applied as well to Bernard Quaritch, who published four Kelmscott books and with whom Morris had many misunderstandings. Editing and proof-reading presented continuous difficulties, particularly for the medieval texts, as Morris was not inclined to take very seriously the minutiae of scholarship. Most of the editing was done by Ellis, and both he and Morris did go to some trouble to procure decent copytexts, especially for the *Chaucer* (see No. L: 30). The proof-reading for the early books was done by Halliday Sparling, but Cockerell, among his other talents, was an excellent proof-reader, and all this work eventually was done by him.

About twenty books went through various stages of planning and production but were never completed. The most notable of these was an edition of Froissart's *Chronicles*, which was envisaged as a kind of companion to the *Chaucer*. It got as far as a two-leaf specimen, printed on vellum and issued in 160 copies on 7 October 1897, and a sixteen-page gathering, printed in thirty-two copies on paper and privately distributed to Morris's friends in December 1896.

It is now very difficult to determine whether or not the Kelmscott Press made any profit, because of the confusion in the early financial records. This question did not seem to bother Morris very much, as he did not charge the Press for his own services, a major consideration. Discounting that, it seems likely that a small profit was made overall, the smaller books subsidizing the larger ones. The Kelmscott Press was, after all, something of a Utopian experiment.

Morris is generally regarded as the father of the modern private press movement, and the Kelmscott Press books have had a considerable influence on design and printing in many parts of the world, both positive and negative. In the United States they were being imitated while they were still being produced, the imitations generally falling short of the originals because of a lack of taste and technique. It proved very difficult to imitate the production methods of the Kelmscott Press.

Kelmscott books were eagerly collected as they came off the press and have continued to exercise a particular fascination for book collectors. All but four Kelmscott publications displayed are to be found in this country and vividly demonstrate the continuing influence of William Morris and his Kelmscott Press in Canada.

No. L:1

PLINIUS SECUNDUS

Historia Naturalis
Venice: Nicolas Jenson, 1472
Goff P788[16]
Fo. 358 leaves
Provenance: John Shelly; Georgius Klebs; William
    Morris (Sotheby no. 954)[17]
Department of Rare Books and Special Collections,
    McGill University Libraries, Montreal

> I have got on my shelves now a Jenson's Latin Pliny, which,
> in spite of its beautiful type and handsome painted ornaments,
> I dare scarcely look at, because the binder (adjectives fail me
> here) has chopped off two-thirds of the tail margin: such stu-
> pidities are like a man with his coat buttoned up behind, or a
> lady with her bonnet put on hind-side foremost.

This rather severe reference to this copy of the 1472 Pliny,
in a lecture delivered by Morris to the Bibliographical
Society in 1893, obscures his obvious delight in the type,
lay-out and decoration of Jenson's first edition (the third
printed edition of the text). Morris had purchased in 1889,
according to Cockerell, the 1476 Jenson Italian edition of
Pliny (Morris's copy is now in the Huntington Library),
together with Jacobus Rubeus's 1476 edition of Aretino's
Historia Fiorentina, printed with Jenson types. Photographic enlargements from the Italian Pliny, which had
also been used by Emery Walker as lantern slides for his
1888 lecture, provided the direct models for the design of
Golden type, although the details of each letter were con-
siderably modified by Morris when he re-drew them. The
type (115 R)[18] is the same in both the Latin and Italian editions, and possibly Morris, attracted by the decorated pen-
work initials, purchased this copy between 1889 and 1893.
The painted initial at the beginning of the text shows Pliny
presenting a copy of his work to the Emperor Vespasian.

No. L:2

SAINT BERNARD OF CLAIRVEAUX

Flores
[Nuremberg: Johann Sensenschmidt and Heinrich Kefer
    for Heinrich Rummel, not after 1470]
Goff B388
Fo. 162 leaves

Provenance: William Morris (Sotheby no. 164); Douglas
    Cockerell; William Inglis Morse
Dalhousie University Libraries, Halifax, Nova Scotia,
    William Inglis Morse Collection, Cockerell Collec-
    tion no. 3

Sensenschmidt produced the first printed books in Nuremberg, beginning in 1470, in partnership with Heinrich
Kefer, who had been an associate of Johann Gutenberg in
Mainz. The *Flores* of Saint Bernard of Clairveaux is not
dated, but its type (114G) is the same as that used in two
other books dated 1470, and thus is from the first stage of
Sensenschmidt's press. He later moved to Bamberg. This
copy, from Morris's library, has been rubricated, with some
of the initials delicately flourished. The type, set in double columns with forty lines to the page, is a large round
face with the typical Gothic qualities that most appealed
to Morris. This is a large copy, with the marginal proportions of the two-page opening that became a standard feature of Kelmscott Press books. It is bound in contemporary
calf-skin, with an elaborate pattern of blind-tooling, and
was purchased by Douglas Cockerell for that reason at the
Morris sale.

No. L:3

JACOBUS PHILIPPUS
FORESTI BERGOMENSIS

Supplementum Chronicarum
Brescia: Boninus de Boninis de Ragusa, 1485
Goff J209
Fo. 359 leaves
Provenance: William Morris (Sotheby no. 161); Douglas
    Cockerell; William Inglis Morse
Dalhousie University Libraries, Halifax, Nova Scotia,
    William Inglis Morse Collection, Cockerell Collec-
    tion no. 4

This popular Chronicle of world history, both religious
and secular, provided one of the models for Schedel's more
famous *Nuremberg Chronicle* but continued to be re-edited
and expanded well into the sixteenth century. It was first
printed in 1483 in Venice and this Brescia edition was produced by the peripatetic printer Boninus of Ragusa, who
worked there from 1483 to 1491. The smaller text type
(93G) was cast on a larger body, giving the impression of
leading between lines, and harmonizes well with the larger
heading type (150G) found at the beginning of each chapter. The ornamented capitals in this copy, as well as the

layout of the text, would have caught Morris's eye, but his purchase of it was also probably influenced by its striking binding: fifteenth-century German calf with metal bosses and clasps and elaborately tooled floral motifs on both covers. Douglas Cockerell reproduced this binding in his *Bookbinding, and the Care of Books*, 1901 (pl. II).

No. L: 4

HUGO DE PRATO FLORIDO

Sermones de Sanctis
Heidelberg: [Printer of Lindelbach?] 1485
Goff H513
Fo. 299 leaves
Provenance: William Morris (Sotheby no. 712); Douglas
    Cockerell; William Inglis Morse
Dalhousie University Libraries, Halifax, Nova Scotia,
    William Inglis Morse Collection, Cockerell Collec-
    tion no. 6

NO. L: 4

This is the first book printed in Heidelberg, its printers being either Johann and Conrad Hist from Speier or Heinrich Knoblochtzer, who continued to print in Heidelberg. Its text-type (90G) is the usual rounded Gothic used at Strassburg, which was, about this time, mixed with the newly introduced Schwabacher types. The titling type is Gothic 180, also used very widely. This copy, number 712 in the Morris catalogue, is bound in full pigskin, very elaborately tooled, with quite different designs on the upper and lower covers. The title-label on the upper cover appears to be contemporary, but the clasps are modern reproductions. The cover design contains in its borders the plant motifs which appear in the printed borders of Kelmscott Press books. A mistake was evidently made in the stamping of the lower right corner of the panel which has been patched with parchment.

No. L: 5

JUSTINUS AND LUCIUS FLORUS

Historici viri clarissimi; Gestorum Romanorum
Bologna: Bendictus Hectoris, 1505
Fo. 100 leaves; woodcut initials
bound with

PAULUS OROSIUS

Historiarum Adversos Raganos Libri VII
Venice: Christophorus de Pensis de Mandello for
    Octavianus Scoti, 1499
Goff O100
Fo. 72 leaves
Provenance: William Morris (Sotheby no. 739); Douglas
    Cockerell; William Inglis Morse
Dalhousie University Libraries, Halifax, Nova Scotia,
    William Inglis Morse Collection, Cockerell Collec-
    tion no. 28

The binding on this volume is described in the Morris sale catalogue (no. 739) as "contemporary Venetian brown morocco" and by Cockerell in *Bookbinding...* as merely "Italian sixteenth century goatskin." The text by Orosius is set in a conventional late fifteenth-century Roman type (109R) in a single column, but is interspersed with striking woodcut initials of several sizes. The swirling vines and leaves of the "N" on the *verso* of leaf b3 recall the style of Morris's initial letters, even though the form of the letter is Roman, whereas Morris preferred Gothic.

NO. L: 6

EARLY PRINTED BOOKS WHICH
INFLUENCED MORRIS

No. L: 6

Speculum Humanae Salvationis
Augsburg: Monastery of SS. Ulrich and Afra, not after
    1473
Goff S670
Fo. 270 leaves; 176/192 woodcuts[19]
Thomas Fisher Rare Book Library, Schoenborn Collec-
    tion, University of Toronto

This edition of the popular collection of biblical stories was
printed in the monastery of SS. Ulrich and Afra, using the
types and woodcuts of Günther Zainer. It has been called
a "manual for poor preachers", and the German translations were, according to a note in the Charles Fairfax
Murray copy, "for nuns and other religious persons who
do not understand Latin." It was, however, the woodcuts
that especially attracted Morris and this is one of a group of
illustrated books of the 1470s and 1480s that he described
in lectures and articles and which influenced the design
of his own books. Morris's copy of this book, now in the
Pierpont Morgan Library, was probably acquired by him
between 1889 and 1892, when he mentioned it in his lecture "The Woodcuts of Gothic Books" and illustrated some
of the woodcuts with lantern slides: "all these books have
great merit as works of art; it would be difficult to find
more direct or more poetical rendering of the events given
than those of the *Speculum Humanae Salvationis*...."

In his description of the book for his projected but
uncompleted catalogue of his library, begun in May 1894,
he says that the woodcuts "are rude, but have much character though they are not so decorative as some others of the
Augsburg & Ulm books." His emphasis on the illustration
of a text (the telling of a story) as well as the decoration
of a page echoes his concern for the use of woodcut illustration and decoration in the books of the Kelmscott Press.

CONRAD VON MEGENBURG

Das Buch der Natur
Goff C843
Augsburg: Johann Bämler, 1478
Fo. 292 leaves; 12 woodcuts
Blacker-Wood Library of Biology, McGill University,
    Montreal

Another favourite printer of Morris's, well-represented in
his collection of German illustrated books, was Johann
Bämler, whose long career at Augsburg spanned the years
1472 to 1495. In his essay "On the Artistic Qualities of the
Woodcut Books of Ulm and Augsburg in the Fifteenth
Century", written for the journal *Bibliographica* in 1895,
Morris says, "of the other contemporary, or nearly contemporary, printers Bämler comes first in interest.... His
Buch der Natur has full-page cuts of animals, herbs, and
human figures exceedingly quaint, but very well designed
for the most part. A half-figure of a bishop 'in pontificali-
bus' is particularly bold and happy." Bämler printed three
editions of von Megenburg's natural history, the first in
1475 and a third in 1481. It is the first printed book to contain figures of animals and only appeared in German, being
one of the earliest scientific texts in that language.

EUCLID

Elementa Geometria
Venice: Erhard Ratdolt, 1482
Goff E113
Fo. 138 leaves; woodcut diagrams, borders and initials
Thomas Fisher Rare Book Library, University of Toronto

Among the models used by Morris for the decorative
woodcut borders and initials in Kelmscott Press books
were the books printed in Venice and Augsberg by Erhard
Ratdolt. Ratdolt worked in Venice with other German
printers from 1476 to 1486, when he returned to his native
Augsburg. His large woodcut borders of intricate foliage
patterns on a black or red background and *entrelac* initials
fitted perfectly with the kind of ornamentation Morris
espoused as an integral part of book design. Morris owned
a copy of the Ratdolt edition of Appian's *Libri De Bellis
Civilibus Romanis* (1477), which has two magnificent borders. He may have used a copy of Ratdolt's most famous
book, the 1482 Euclid, in which one of the borders was

repeated, along with fifteen large white-on-black initials
and over 600 woodcut and type-rule diagrams. In a letter
of 1892 to Gilbert Redgrave, the expert on Ratdolt's work,
Morris cautioned, "I do not profess merely to follow precedent, or to imitate Ratdolt." The resemblances are, however, striking.

ULRICH VON RICHENTAL

Concilium zu Constencz
Augsburg: Anton Sorg, 1483
Goff R196
Fo. 249 leaves; 39 full-page and 1,161 small coloured
    woodcuts
Provenance: Richard Morawetz
Thomas Fisher Rare Book Library, University of Toronto

Anton Sorg, a printer who flourished in Augsburg from
1475 to 1493, produced two books that especially appealed
to Morris, who wrote:

> The two really noteworthy works of Sorg (who...was some-
> what a plagiaristic publisher) are, first the *Seusse*, which is
> illustrated with bold and highly decorative cuts full of mean-
> ing and dignity, and next, the *Council of Constance*, which is
> the first heraldic woodcut work (it has besides the coats-of-
> arms, several fine full-page cuts, of which the burning of Huss
> is one). These armorial cuts, which are full of interest as giv-
> ing a vast number of curious and strange bearings, are no less
> so as showing what admirable decoration can be got out of
> heraldry when it is simply and well drawn.[20]

This vivid vernacular account of the Council of Constance (1414 to 1418) was the only edition to be published
during the fifteenth century. Because it is so extensively
illustrated, the relationships between the large text-type
(118G), the titling type (140G) and the woodcuts demonstrate many different aspects of page design. The illustration that particularly caught Morris's attention, the
burning of Huss (which took place in Constance on 6 July
1415), has under it another woodcut of his ashes being
shovelled into a cart for disposal in the Rhine.

HARTMANN SCHEDEL

Liber Chronicarum
Nuremberg: Anton Koberger, 1493

Goff S307
Fo. 226 leaves; 645/1,809 woodcuts
Thomas Fisher Rare Book Library, University of Toronto

The *Nuremberg Chronicle* is the best-known illustrated book of the fifteenth century. Its 645 woodcuts (used a total of 1,809 times) depict the history of the world from the creation to 1493. Although the scholarship of its compiler, Schedel, is derivative, the book is a *tour de force* of design, the woodcuts by Wolgemut and Pleydenwurff, and possibly the young Dürer, being placed within the type of the text to create complex patterns for single-page and double-page openings. Morris bought his first copy of the *Chronicle* around 1864 from F.S. Ellis, and gave it as a wedding present to William Michael and Lucy Rossetti in 1874. Some time before 1890 he bought another copy, the one used by Sydney Cockerell to provide a census of the woodcuts (Sotheby no. 353). It took him a very long time to count the repetitions and the operation has never been performed again. Morris used the *Chronicle* as a particular example to illustrate the sudden development of neoclassical styles in Germany, which he, of course, deplored: "the later books published by the great Nuremberg printer, Koberger, in the fourteen-nineties, books like the *Nuremberg Chronicle* and the *Schatzbehalter*, show no sign of the coming change, but ten years worn, and hey, presto, not a particle of Gothic ornament can be found in any German printed book."21

No. L: 11

SEBASTIAN BRANT

Stultifera Navis
Basel: Johann Bergmann de Olpe, 1497
Goff B1086
Qto. 148 leaves; 111/113 woodcuts
Provenance: John Eliot Hodgkin; Louis Melzack
Thomas Fisher Rare Book Library, University of Toronto

Morris purchased his copy of the first Latin edition of Brant's great satire (now in the Pierpont Morgan Library) before 1865. Its series of woodcuts, some of which may be by Dürer, directly illustrate the verses, and leafy borders decorate the pages. *The Ship of Fools* was written in German and published by Brant's friend, Bergmann de Olpe, in 1494. His pupil Jacob Locher rendered it into Latin for the 1497 edition and it quickly appeared in several European languages. Morris also owned a copy of the 1570 English edition, translated by Alexander Barclay and first issued in 1509. For bibliophiles,

the book's most evocative image is "Of Useless Books": the be-spectacled collector, with his duster saying, "of splendid books I own no end; but few that I can comprehend."

No. L: 12

JACOBUS DE VORAGINE

The Golden Legend
London: Wynkyn de Worde, 1527
STC 24880
Fo. 384 leaves; 67/87 woodcuts
Thomas Fisher Rare Book Library, University of Toronto

On 21 July 1890 Morris purchased a copy of the 1527 Wynkyn de Worde edition of *The Golden Legend* with the specific objective of reprinting the text. He planned to use Caxton's first edition of 1483 as the basis for his text and eventually borrowed the Cambridge University Library copy for that purpose, so presumably wished to have the later de Worde reprint to read. It is the last of the Caxton/de Worde series and is described as "extremely rare" in the Sotheby's 1898 catalogue of Morris's books. The woodcuts are mostly small and rather crude, somewhat overwhelmed by the dense black type.

MORRIS PRE-KELMSCOTT EXPERIMENTS

No. L: 13

WILLIAM MORRIS

Love is Enough or the Freeing of Pharamond
London: Ellis & White, 1873
Octo. [6] 134 pages
Thomas Fisher Rare Book Library, University of Toronto

Morris's poetic romance *Love is Enough* was begun after his first trip to Iceland in 1871 and, like the elaborate plans for *The Earthly Paradise*, he envisioned an illustrated and decorated edition. Both he and Burne-Jones designed floral border-decorations and initials and they were cut in wood. Two trial leaves survive (in the Pierpont Morgan Library) and demonstrate vividly the design problems. Although the border designs are closer to Morris's calligraphic style and more delicate than his later Kelmscott borders, they overwhelm the conventional type-face. *Love is Enough* appeared in 1873 (early copies in late 1872) without decoration or illustration. Its binding, however, has an attractive willow and myrtle block in gilt, reminiscent of Morris's designs for manuscripts done at this time. The Kelmscott Press edition, with two Burne-Jones illustrations and Morris borders and initials, did not appear until 1898.

No. L: 14

WILLIAM MORRIS

The Roots of the Mountains...
London: Reeves and Turner, 1890
Qto. [8] 424 pages
Private collection, Vancouver

Morris's final attempt to use the commercially available type of the Chiswick Press to achieve a medieval look, in the design for his long prose saga *The Roots of the Mountains*, pleased him but was not ultimately satisfactory. The Basle Roman type was set more closely, head-lines were abandoned in favour of side-notes, and the title-page was designed so that it was filled with text, creating the marginal proportions Morris preferred. Two hundred and fifty copies were printed on special Whatman paper and bound in specially calendered Morris & Co. chintz. Although he declared himself to be "so pleased with my book – typography, binding and must I say it, literary matter – that I am any day to be seen huggling it up, and am become a spectacle to Gods and men because of it",22 he was ready to found the Kelmscott Press and gain total control over the design of his books.

   This book also appears in the Textiles section of this catalogue (see No. F: 10).

THE KELMSCOTT PRESS

No. L: 15

WILLIAM MORRIS

The Story of the Glittering Plain
Hammersmith: Kelmscott Press, 8 May 1891
Peterson A1 23
Qto. 96 leaves; wood-engraved border and initials
Private collection, Ottawa

Morris had planned to issue *The Golden Legend* as the first Kelmscott Press book, but the first batch of paper supplied by Batchelor was not large enough and he turned instead to one of his own stories. In the autumn of 1890 he contracted with his friend Walter Crane to supply illustrations

to be cut on wood but became impatient, and the book appeared decorated with Morris's border and initials. The border design bears a striking resemblance to Ratdolt's borders in his Appian of 1477 and Euclid of 1482 (No. L: 8). Crane's illustrations were used in the second Kelmscott version in 1894. The first sheet was printed in the new Golden type on 2 March and the colophon is dated 4 April. On 7 May Wilfrid Scawen Blunt was lunching with Morris when the first bound copy was brought in and Blunt asked him what he meant to do with these books. "Sell them of course," replied Morris and Blunt paid him a pound for the first copy of the first Kelmscott book. It was bound in stiff vellum with wash leather ties (the only time they were used). Two hundred copies were printed on paper and six on vellum. This copy contains a presentation inscription from Morris to Kate Faulkner, the sister of his old friend and partner Charles Faulkner. She worked for the Morris firm for many years. It is cited in Peterson as copy A1u.

No. L: 16

WILFRID SCAWEN BLUNT

Love-Lyrics & Songs of Proteus
Hammersmith: Kelmscott Press, 27 February 1892
Peterson A3
Qto. 132 leaves; wood-engraved border and initials
Special Collections Room, Metropolitan Toronto
   Reference Library

The simple design and decoration of this edition of Wilfrid Scawen Blunt's love poems, the third Kelmscott Press book, conceal the considerable complexities of its production. On 19 November 1890 Morris wrote to Blunt, an old friend, "I shall of course be very pleased to print your book, if I may have my own way about the get up – which, I take it is what you want."24 However, Blunt asked that the initials be printed in red, and it is some measure of Morris's attitude towards this experiment that no other Kelmscott book was printed in this way. Typesetting and the printing of proofs proceeded slowly throughout 1891, but at the end of September eighteen pages had to be cancelled because of the protest of Margaret Talbot, the wife of a British Embassy official in Paris, over a series of sonnets called "Natalie's resurrection", which she felt alluded to their recently concluded love affair. This episode must have held a certain poignancy for Morris, as Blunt had been carrying on an affair with Jane Morris for some time and

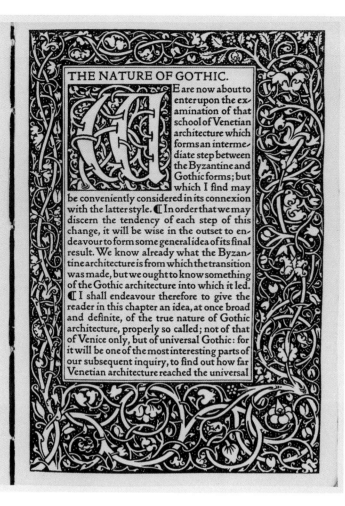

most enduring and beneficent effect on his contemporaries, and will have through them on succeeding generations. ❡ John Ruskin the critic of art has not only given the keenest pleasure to thousands of readers by his life-like descriptions, and the ingenuity and delicacy of his analysis of works of art, but he has let a flood of daylight into the cloud of sham-technical twaddle which was once the whole substance of "art-criticism," and is still its staple, and that is much. But it is far more that John Ruskin the teacher of morals and politics (I do not use this word in the newspaper sense), has done serious and solid work towards that new-birth of Society, without which genuine art, the expression of man's pleasure in his handiwork, must inevitably cease altogether, and with it the hopes of the happiness of mankind.

WILLIAM MORRIS,
Kelmscott House, Hammersmith.
Feb 15th, 1892.

THE NATURE OF GOTHIC.

WE are now about to enter upon the examination of that school of Venetian architecture which forms an intermediate step between the Byzantine and Gothic forms; but which I find may be conveniently considered in its connexion with the latter style. ❡ In order that we may discern the tendency of each step of this change, it will be wise in the outset to endeavour to form some general idea of its final result. We know already what the Byzantine architecture is from which the transition was made, but we ought to know something of the Gothic architecture into which it led. ❡ I shall endeavour therefore to give the reader in this chapter an idea, at once broad and definite, of the true nature of Gothic architecture, properly so called; not of that of Venice only, but of universal Gothic: for it will be one of the most interesting parts of our subsequent inquiry, to find out how far Venetian architecture reached the universal

NO. L: 17

she read the proofs of *Love-Lyrics*, the only Kelmscott Press book with which she was intimately involved. The proofs were also corrected by Lady Gregory, another former mistress of Blunt, who also (anonymously) wrote the twelve-poem sequence "A Woman's Sonnets." The book was finally finished on 26 January 1892 and issued on 27 February. Three hundred copies on paper (none on vellum) were printed and 220 were sold quickly at two guineas. A small profit was made by Blunt, who had financed the project.

No. L: 17

JOHN RUSKIN

The Nature of Gothic
Hammersmith: Kelmscott Press, 22 March 1892
Peterson A4
Qto. 68 leaves; wood-engraved border and initials
Special Collections Room, Metropolitan Toronto
    Reference Library

Morris read Ruskin's *The Stones of Venice* in 1853, while a student at Exeter College, Oxford, and its influence on

his life and work was profound. Ruskin was a "master", and thus it was natural that Morris should take up Sydney Cockerell's suggestion, made in June 1891, that he should reprint its central chapter "The Nature of Gothic." George Allen acted as publisher and 500 copies (none on vellum), printed with Golden type and with a border and initials by Morris, were issued at thirty shillings on 22 March 1892. Morris also wrote a preface for this fourth Kelmscott book. He regarded Ruskin's essay as "one of the very few necessary and inevitable utterances of the century"; and from Ruskin Morris derived one of his central principles, that "art is the expression of man's pleasure in labour."

No. L: 18

WILLIAM MORRIS

A Dream of John Ball and A King's Lesson
Hammersmith: Kelmscott Press, 24 September 1892
Peterson A6
Qto. 66 leaves; wood-engraved frontispiece, wood-
    engraved borders and initials
Provenance: Bertrand Russell

The Bertrand Russell Archives, McMaster University Library, Hamilton

The first illustration to appear in a Kelmscott book (the sixth) was, appropriately, by Edward Burne-Jones. The two texts, first published in the *Commonweal* in 1886 and 1887, had been published as a book by Reeves & Turner in 1888, with a gravure frontispiece based on the same design by Burne-Jones. Morris designed a full border and the lettering to accompany the illustration and the whole was engraved by W.H. Hooper onto a single block. For the rather odd Roman lettering, Morris used his copy of Arrighi's *Il Modo* (1526) as a model, but greatly modified Arrighi's graceful letters. The book was set in Golden type and printed quickly in April and May of 1892, but had to wait for the frontispiece to be completed. The 300 copies on paper and eleven on vellum were issued on 24 September. This copy was presented by T.J. Cobden-Sanderson to Bertrand Russell on 13 December 1894.

No. L: 19

JACOBUS DE VORAGINE

The Golden Legend
Hammersmith: Kelmscott Press, 3 November 1892
Peterson A7
Qto. 3 volumes; 2 wood-engravings, wood-engraved title, borders and initials
Special Collections Room, Metropolitan Toronto Reference Library

The Golden Legend was among Morris's favourite books, and his library held many editions of it. As F.S. Ellis, the editor of the Kelmscott Press edition, expressed it in his "Memoranda, Bibliographical & Explanatory", at the end of volume 3: "Among the books which serve to illustrate the religious life and mode of thought that prevailed in the middle ages, none holds a more important place than the Legenda Aurea." As early as the summer of 1890, when he bought his copy of the 1527 edition (No. L: 12), Morris was planning to print *The Golden Legend* as the first Kelmscott book. Although it was the seventh, it was the first large production of the press, the first to have a wood-engraved title, the first to have original illustrations by Burne-Jones, and the first medieval text.

The publisher was Bernard Quaritch, the famous antiquarian bookseller, and the contract (11 September 1890) specified that Morris was "to have absolute and sole control over choice of paper, choice of type, size of the reprint and selection of the printer." The first Caxton edition

(1483), borrowed from Cambridge University Library and transcribed by Phyllis Ellis so that the inky fingers of the printers would not come into contact with the book, was used as copy-text, and proofs were read against the original. *The Golden Legend* presented Morris with his first large-scale practical problem of design and typography: how to use Roman type to achieve the proper "feeling" for a medieval text. He chose a single-column page, recognizing that "our book is to be a *reprint* not a facsimile," and paid close attention to the proportions of the margins. The first sheet was printed in May 1891, and the first volume was finished by October. The title and the illustrations were not, however, engraved until June and August 1892, when all three volumes were almost complete, and thus were inserted as separate leaves. Quarter holland, with blue paper boards, was used as a binding for the first time and the 500 paper copies (none on vellum) were delivered to Quaritch by 4 October. On 28 October a celebratory dinner was held at the Blue Posts Restaurant, and Morris declared himself "proud" of the book.

No. L: 20

WILLIAM CAXTON (trans.)

The History of Reynard the Foxe
Hammersmith: Kelmscott Press, 25 January 1893
Peterson A10
Qto. 106 leaves; wood-engraved borders
Special Collections Room, Metropolitan Toronto Reference Library

By early 1892 Morris had designed and had cast his Troy type and its smaller version, Chaucer. They were first used for *The Recuycell of the Historyes of Troye* (24 November 1892) and again for *Reynard the Foxe*. This is a translation by Caxton from the Dutch, first published by him in 1481, and to Morris "one of the very best of his works as to style." It was edited for the Kelmscott edition by Henry Halliday Sparling, who had married Morris's daughter May in June 1890, and sold by Quaritch, with whom Morris had a contract. Three hundred copies were printed on paper and ten on vellum, of which Quaritch took 275 paper and six vellum. Two of Morris's full borders and several partial borders and initials were used for decoration, and a touch of colour was added through the use of a red chapter-title and *explicit*. The printing began in early September and the colophon is dated 15 December 1892. By 6 March 1893 this copy was in Toronto, that being its date of accession by the Toronto Public Library.

WILLIAM MORRIS

News from Nowhere
Hammersmith: Kelmscott Press, 24 March 1893
Peterson A12
Octo. 160 leaves; wood-engraved frontispiece, wood-
    engraved borders and initials
Bruce Peel Special Collections Library, University of
    Alberta, Edmonton
For illustration see page 17.

News from Nowhere, Morris's Utopian novel, was first
printed in *Commonweal* from 11 January to 4 October 1890.
Its first English book edition was published by Reeves &
Turner in 1891, but it was one of the first to be planned by
Morris for the Kelmscott Press. It was being printed in June
1892, but publication was delayed by the lack of a suitable
frontispiece. In October Cockerell suggested a picture of
Kelmscott Manor should be used as a frontispiece for *News
from Nowhere*, and Morris agreed to engage Charles M.
Gere, a young artist from Birmingham. His drawing was
engraved by Hooper within a Morris border, and printing
of it was completed on 7 March 1893. Three hundred paper
copies and ten vellum were printed in Golden type; it was
published and sold by Reeves & Turner. Kelmscott Manor
still looks as it did in Gere's illustration.

No. L: 22

WILLIAM MORRIS

Gothic Architecture
Peterson A18
Hammersmith: Kelmscott Press, 21 October 1893
Sixtmo. 37 leaves; vellum copy; wood-engraved initials
Private collection, Toronto

This is one of forty-five copies on vellum of the only
Kelmscott Press book not to be printed in Hammersmith.
During October and November of 1893 the annual Arts
and Crafts Exhibition was held at the New Gallery, and a
press was moved there so that *Gothic Architecture* could be
printed in public. The crowds were large and, according
to Halliday Sparling, their "presence imposed a severe
strain upon the pressman Collins's Celtic modesty." It is a
small book, the first sexidecimo printed by Kelmscott, and
there were three impressions of 500 copies each, with two
corrections made between the first and second. The text
was taken from a lecture by Morris given to the Arts and
Crafts Exhibition Society in 1889. The four-line initials
by Morris appear in this book for the first time.

WILLIAM MORRIS

The Story of the Glittering Plain
Hammersmith: Kelmscott Press, 17 February 1894
Peterson A22
Qto. 96 leaves; 23 wood-engravings, wood-engraved
    borders and initials
Department of Archives and Special Collections,
    University of Manitoba Libraries, Winnipeg

This second Kelmscott edition of *Glittering Plain* was the
one Kelmscott Press book Morris considered to have been
a failure. In the autumn of 1890 he had formally engaged
his friend Walter Crane to supply illustrations for his fantasy prose romance, first published in the *English Illustrated
Magazine* in 1890, but was too impatient to wait for them,
and the first Kelmscott book (No. L: 15) appeared unil-
lustrated. He had offered to split the profits with Crane,
and the project was taken up again in late 1892. Crane produced twenty-three drawings, which were cut on wood
by A. Leverett, and Morris designed borders and frames
for them, all but one of which were never used again.
Although Morris wrote to Crane, "I think your woodcuts
look delightful",[25] he was clearly not satisfied, and Crane
himself observed that he doubted "if I was ever quite Gothic
enough in feeling to suit his taste."[26] The engraved title
was cut by Hooper. Two hundred and fifty paper and seven
vellum copies were printed in Troy type and published by
the Press itself on 17 February 1894.

No. L: 24

WILLIAM MORRIS

The Wood Beyond the World
Hammersmith: Kelmscott Press, 16 October 1894
Peterson A27
Qto. 136 leaves; wood-engraved frontispiece, wood-
    engraved borders and initials
Special Collections Room, Metropolitan Toronto
    Reference Library

The Wood Beyond the World, a heroic romance, was written
by Morris for the Kelmscott Press, and it is thus a Morris
first edition (a cheap edition was published by Lawrence
& Bullen in 1895). It was printed in Chaucer type during
the spring of 1894 (the colophon is dated 30 May) but not
issued until October because of a delay in completing the
Burne-Jones frontispiece. The two borders by Morris are
first used in this book, along with ten new half-borders.

NO. L: 24

The chapter-titles and shoulder-notes were printed in red. The 350 paper and eight vellum copies were almost all sold, by the Press itself, by the publication date at two guineas for paper copies and ten for vellum.

No. L: 25

Psalmi Penitentiales
Hammersmith: Kelmscott Press, 10 December 1894
Peterson A30
Octo. 36 leaves; wood-engraved borders and initials
Thomas Fisher Rare Book Library, University of Toronto

This text of the *Penitential Psalms* is based on an English metrical version found in a fifteenth-century Book of Hours belonging to Morris (now in the Pierpont Morgan Library). It was transcribed and edited by F.S. Ellis and, as often, he and Morris disagreed about editorial notes and the glossary, which Morris felt should be kept to a minimum. Ellis did extensively edit the text of the *Psalms*, but

at one point wrote to Morris, "I cannot make very much sense of this line, but it is exactly to MS. & I dare say the old boy who wrote it knew what it meant?" The book is printed in Chaucer type, with seven three-quarter engraved borders and initials. Most effectively, the English verses are printed in black, while the Latin texts are in red. Although issued on 10 December, the entire edition of 300 paper and twelve vellum copies had been subscribed for by 4 October.

No. L: 26

Syr Perecyvelle of Gales
Hammersmith: Kelmscott Press, 2 May 1895
Peterson A33
Octo. 56 leaves; wood-engraved frontispiece, wood-
    engraved borders and initials
Thomas Fisher Rare Book Library, University of Toronto

Syr Perecyvelle of Gales was based on a text from *The Thornton Romances*, edited by James O. Halliwell for the Camden

Society in 1844 and one of Morris's favourite books. The Kelmscott edition was again edited by F.S. Ellis and is an almost exact reprint. It was appropriately printed in Chaucer type, with two full borders, initials of two sizes and a wood engraved frontispiece by Burne-Jones (for which he was paid £20). The titles were printed in red. The printing was completed on 16 February but, as so often happened, publication was delayed because of the illustration. By 2 May, the date of publication, virtually all the 350 paper and eight vellum copies had been sold.

No. L: 27

WILLIAM MORRIS

The Life and Death of Jason
Hammersmith: Kelmscott Press, 5 July 1895
Peterson A34
Qto. 184 leaves; 2 wood-engravings, wood-engraved
    borders and initials
Bruce Peel Special Collections Library, University of
    Alberta, Edmonton

The Life and Death of Jason, Morris's long poem, was first published in 1867 and revised for subsequent editions in 1868, 1882 and 1895. The Kelmscott Press edition, printed in a large quarto format with Troy type, was begun in March 1894 and set in type by October. Burne-Jones did not, however, deliver his two designs until 21 January 1895, and it was finally finished on 25 May. Morris re-used, for the only time, the two full borders he had designed for *The Tale of Beowulf* (1895), as well as a number of partial borders and initials. "Line-fillings," as they were called by Cockerell, were cast in metal and used for the first time in *Jason* to fill in even more of the white spaces on pages. More red than usual was used. Only 200 paper and six vellum copies were issued at five guineas and twenty guineas, and Morris attributed its slow sale to its high price. The production cost was £338 15s. 6d., and Burne-Jones was paid £40 for his two illustrations.

No. L: 28

DANTE GABRIEL ROSSETTI

Hand and Soul
Hammersmith: Kelmscott Press, 12 December 1895
Peterson A36
Sixtmo. 33 leaves; wood-engraved borders and initials
York University Archives and Special Collections,
    Downsview, Ontario

This was the only Kelmscott Press book published in the United States. Irving Way, of Way and Williams (Chicago), proposed the joint venture to Morris in April 1895 and, because it was a small book with no illustrations, Morris agreed. Thus 225 paper and ten vellum copies were printed for England and 300 paper and eleven vellum for America. Rossetti's symbolic tale of the artist was written for the first number of the *Germ* in 1849 and reprinted twice, in 1869 and 1870. Morris was, of course, an old friend and associate of Rossetti and remained an admirer of his work, despite Rossetti's relationship with Jane Morris. Three of Rossetti's books were printed by the Kelmscott Press.

No. L: 29

WILLIAM MORRIS

The Well at the World's End
Hammersmith: Kelmscott Press, 4 June 1896
Peterson A39
Qto. 252 leaves; 4 wood-engravings, wood-engraved
    borders and initials
Provenance: W.H. Hooper
Private collection, Ottawa

The longest of the Morris prose romances, *The Well at the World's End* took longer to produce than any other Kelmscott book. The earliest reference to it (by Cockerell) is dated 21 April 1892, when he examined some proofs. Illustrations for it were first to be done by Charles Fairfax Murray; however, in the spring of 1893 Morris offered the job to Arthur J. Gaskin, another of the Birmingham artists. Gaskin eventually contributed nineteen designs, some of which were engraved by Hooper and printed in proof, but Morris was dissatisfied and finally, in February 1895, he turned to Burne-Jones. His four illustrations, engraved as usual by Hooper, with eight new borders by Morris, finally appeared on 4 June 1896.

This is a presentation copy from Morris to W.H. Hooper and contains four original drawings by Morris for the border decorations (see No. A: 29).

No. L: 30

GEOFFREY CHAUCER

The Works of Geoffrey Chaucer
Hammersmith: Kelmscott Press, 26 June 1896
Peterson A40
Fo. 282 leaves; 87 wood-engravings, wood-engraved
    borders and initials

Provenance: T.E. Lawrence, C.L. Burton (copy 1)
Copy 1: Special Collections, Douglas Library, Queen's
   University, Kingston
Copy 2: Rare Book Collection, National Library of
   Canada, Ottawa

The crowning achievement of the Kelmscott Press and, to
many, the "most beautiful of all printed books" (as Yeats
expressed it), the Kelmscott Chaucer took five years to
complete. The principal collaborators, Morris and Burne-
Jones, who had begun to read Chaucer to each other while
students at Oxford, first began to discuss their projected
new edition in 1891. The difficulties were formidable: the
length of the text and the problems of editing it, choos-
ing a type and format that would accommodate the text
and the large number of Burne-Jones illustrations (eventually there were eighty-seven), the sheer effort required
to print it (a new press had to be acquired), the creation
of special bindings, and, finally, financing and marketing
an expensive book (the edition size was increased and it
almost broke even). F.S. Ellis was the editor, and he and
Morris, with difficulty, persuaded Oxford University Press
to allow them to use "a limited number of readings" from
Walter W. Skeat's great edition, then in preparation. In
fact, they adopted Skeat's text almost verbatim, eliminat-
ing his textual apparatus and notes.

   In January 1892 the Troy type was delivered and trial
pages were set. The type proved too large, and its reduced
size, called Chaucer, was ready by July, when the folio
format with the type set in double columns of fifty-eight
lines each was adopted. Printing began on 8 August 1894
and was finished on 8 May 1896. Morris began to design
the borders early in 1893 and eventually completed fourteen large borders (see No. A: 28), eighteen different
frames for the illustrations, twenty-six initial words, and
the title-page. Burne-Jones began his illustrations late in
1892, working primarily on Sundays, when Morris would
visit and talk with him. At the beginning, forty-eight
illustrations were planned, rising to sixty, and, finally,
to eighty-seven as he added to those parts of the text
that most appealed to him. Burne-Jones was concerned to
break away from the long tradition of Chaucer illustration, which went back to the earliest manuscripts, and his
view of Chaucer was certainly different than that of Morris, as is revealed in a letter to Swinburne: "Morris has been
urgent with me that I should by no means exclude these
stories from our scheme of adornment – especially he had
hopes of my treatment of the Miller's Tale, but he ever
had more robust and daring parts than I could assume."[27]

The binding of the *Chaucer* was, as usual, blue holland
boards with a linen spine, but in February 1896 Morris
announced plans for four special bindings. Although very
ill, he completed an intricate design based on a fifteenth-
century binding from his own library, and forty-eight
copies (three on vellum) were bound in full white pigskin
by the Doves Bindery. One of the copies displayed, which
belonged to T.E. Lawrence (of Arabia), is in the special
binding.

   The total production cost for the *Chaucer* was £7,217 11d.,
and although the 425 paper and thirteen vellum copies sold
quickly, Morris had a long row with Bernard Quaritch,
his former publisher, about discounts and the book was,
in effect, subsidized by the other Kelmscott books. The
first two bound copies were delivered to Morris and Burne-
Jones on 2 June, and on 24 June Douglas Cockerell took a
copy in the Doves binding to Folkstone, where Morris was
convalescing: "very satisfactory", he wrote in his diary.
On 3 October he died at Kelmscott House.

No. L: 31

WILLIAM MORRIS

The Earthly Paradise
Hammersmith: Kelmscott Press, 24 July 1896–
   27 September 1897
Peterson A41
Qto. 8 volumes; wood-engraved borders and initials
Thomas Fisher Rare Book Library, University of Toronto

When Morris died, three volumes of *The Earthly Paradise*
had been published and the remaining five appeared at
intervals until the autumn of 1897. This long poem had
first been published in 1868-70 and was supposed to have
been illustrated. The Kelmscott edition was not illustrated,
but he had designed ten new borders and four half-borders
which were never used again (for designs for decorated initials, see No. A: 26 a-d). The new Apple paper (46.3 x 32.4
cm) was first used for this book and resulted in an odd
format (as Morris expressed it, "a sort of mild quarto, and
yet looking like an octavo."). Two hundred and twenty-
five paper and six vellum sets were printed.

No. L: 32

Laudes Beatae Mariae Virginis
Hammersmith: Kelmscott Press, 7 August 1896
Peterson A42

Qto. 24 leaves; wood-engraved borders and initials
Department of Rare Books and Special Collections,
    McGill University Libraries, Montreal

On 25 May 1893 Morris bought, for £115, a thirteenth-century English psalter which he named the Nottingham Psalter (now in the Pierpont Morgan Library). From it he extracted the *Laudes Beatae Mariae Virginis*, and it was issued by the Kelmscott Press on 7 August 1896, printed in three colours with Troy type. An inserted slip, dated 28 December 1896, was sent to subscribers, as a clergyman had written to say that the text had been printed in 1579 and ascribed to Stephen Langton. In fact, it appears in several other manuscripts as well. It was decorated with half-borders and initials, some printed in blue, while the texts of the Psalms are printed in red.

No. L: 33

EDMUND SPENSER

The Shepheardes Calender
Hammersmith: Kelmscott Press, 26 November 1896
Peterson A44
Qto. 56 leaves; 12 process block illustrations, wood-engraved initials
Private collection, Ottawa

A.J. Gaskin (1862-1928), whose illustrations for *The Well at the World's End* (No. L: 29) had been rejected by Morris, provided twelve designs for *The Shepheardes Calender*, one for each month. They were printed from process blocks made by Emery Walker's firm and are considered by some critics the most successful of the Kelmscott Press illustrations. The book, a medium quarto, was set in Golden type, with Morris initials and a bit of red printing. The printing was completed shortly after his death when Walker and Cockerell were attempting to finish all the Kelmscott Press projects and wind up Morris's affairs.

No. L: 34

Sire Degrevaunt
Hammersmith: Kelmscott Press, 12 November 1897
Peterson A47
Octo. 48 leaves; wood-engraved frontispiece, wood-engraved borders and initials
Private collection, Toronto

This was a favourite story of Morris's, drawn from the Halliwell edition of *The Thornton Romances*, and the draw-

ing-room of Red House, his early home, had a wall-painting by Burne-Jones based on it (see No. A: 2, for a watercolour study). The book was finished on 14 March 1896, but the Burne-Jones frontispiece was not printed until October 1897, when it had to be rushed through the press and the Leighton bindery so that it could be issued with its companion volume, *Syr Isambrace* (No. L: 35). Thus, because the ink was not quite dry, a flimsy was inserted between the frontispiece and the first page of text, the only Kelmscott Press book to have one, and a clear violation of Morris's principle that both pages of an opening should be seen together.

No. L: 35

Syr Isambrace
Hammersmith: Kelmscott Press, 11 November 1897
Peterson A48
Octo. 26 leaves; vellum copy; wood-engraved frontispiece, wood-engraved borders and initials
Private collection, Toronto

The text of *Syr Isambrace*, like that of *Syr Perecyvelle* (No. L: 26) and *Sire Degrevaunt* (No. L: 34), was taken from *The Thornton Romances*. It was partly printed by June 1896 but not finished until 14 July 1897 and not actually issued until 11 November, to coincide with *Sire Degrevaunt*. It also contains a Burne-Jones frontispiece and Morris borders and initials. This copy is one of eight printed on vellum, which originally cost four guineas.

No. L: 36

SYDNEY COCKERELL (ed.)

Some German Woodcuts of the Fifteenth Century
Hammersmith: Kelmscott Press, 6 January 1898
Peterson A49
Octo. 36 leaves; 35 line-block illustrations, wood-engraved initial
Department of Archives and Special Collections,
    University of Manitoba, Winnipeg

At various times during his career Morris had attempted to make a catalogue of his library and, having discovered in 1892 that Sydney Cockerell was a very good cataloguer, he evolved a project to publish an extensively illustrated book based on their joint efforts. "This will be largely illustrated with facsimiles of the plates and pages of the books themselves", he told an interviewer in 1895. This

APRIL.

Thenot. Hobbinoll.

Thenot   ELL me, good Hobbinoll,
what garres thee greete?
What? hath some wolfe
thy tender lambes ytorne?
Or is thy bagpype broke,
that soundes so sweete?
Or art thou of thy loved
lasse forlorne?
Or bene thine eyes attem-
pred to the yeare,
Quenching the gasping furrowes thirst with rayne?
Like April shoure so stremes the trickling teares
Adowne thy cheeke, to quenche thy thristye payne.

Hobbin. Nor thys, nor that, so muche doeth make me mourne,
But for the ladde, whome long I lovd so deare,
Nowe loves a lasse that all his love doth scorne.
He, plongd in payne, his tressed locks dooth teare.

Shepheards delights he dooth them all forsweare;
Hys pleasaunt pipe, whych made us meriment,
He wylfully hath broke, and doth forbeare
His wonted songs, wherein he all outwent.

Thenot What is he for a ladde you so lament?
Ys love such pinching payne to them that prove?
And hath he skill to make so excellent,
Yet hath so little skill to brydle love?

Hobbin. Colin thou kenst, the southerne shepheardes boye:
c 3   21

NO. L: 33

grand plan was abandoned after his death, but Cockerell was able to combine illustrations of woodcuts for which line-blocks had already been made with part of Morris's 1895 article "On the Artistic Qualities of the Woodcut Books of Ulm and Augsburg in the Fifteenth Century." Thirty-five illustrations were used and the book was finished on 15 December 1897 and issued in 225 paper and eight vellum copies. They had all sold before late November, the eagerness caused by the announcement that the Kelmscott Press was going to close.

No. L: 37

WILLIAM MORRIS

The Story of Sigurd the Volsung…
Hammersmith: Kelmscott Press, 25 February 1898
Peterson A50
Fo. 110 leaves; 2 wood-engravings, wood-engraved
    borders and initials

Bruce Peel Special Collections Library, University of
    Alberta, Edmonton

Morris had long planned an elaborate edition of *Sigurd the Volsung*, which had first been published in 1877. Burne-Jones was to provide about twenty-five illustrations, but, as he had no artistic sympathy with the work and only agreed to participate to "pacify and please Morris", his progress was very slow and Morris's death caused the abandonment of the full project. Cockerell, however, persuaded Burne-Jones to do two illustrations for a more modest undertaking and they were used together with two full borders designed by Morris for an edition of *The Hill of Venus* and based on the ornament in two of his psalters. It is believed that one of these was the Windmill Psalter, his last acquisition, and one of his greatest (now in the Pierpont Morgan Library). Only 160 copies on paper and six on vellum were printed.

WILLIAM MORRIS

A Note by William Morris on his Aims in Founding the Kelmscott Press
Hammersmith: Kelmscott Press, 24 March 1898
Peterson A53
Octo. 40 leaves; wood-engraved frontispiece, wood-engraved borders and initials
Private collection, Toronto

"This was the last book printed at the Kelmscott Press", reads the colophon of Morris's *Note... on his Aims*. He had written the short essay for publication in an American magazine, *Modern Art*, in 1896, and it served to introduce Cockerell's longer "A Short History and Description of the Kelmscott Press" and his "Annotated List" of all the Kelmscott books. It also brought together again, for a final time, the Press and Burne-Jones, whose frontispiece had originally been designed for an edition of *The Earthly Paradise*, which was engraved by Morris in the mid-1860s and was here "touched up" by Catterson-Smith. A large edition of 525 paper and twelve vellum copies was printed, finishing on 4 March 1898. It was officially published on 24 March, and on 31 March Cockerell wrote *"explicit"* to the Kelmscott Press.

ENDNOTES

1. *A Note by William Morris on his Aims in Founding the Kelmscott Press* (Hammersmith, 1898), p. 1.
2. The literature concerning Morris and the Kelmscott Press is vast. I am particularly indebted to William S. Peterson's *The Kelmscott Press: A History...* (1991) and his *Bibliography of the Kelmscott Press* (1984). The catalogue of the Pierpont Morgan Library exhibition in 1976 has also been of special assistance and, in particular, the essay by Paul Needham, "William Morris: Book Collector", the only sustained account of Morris's library. A useful list of sources, including unpublished ones, is given by Peterson in *The Kelmscott Press*, pp. 355-7. Nos. L: 1-5 in this section are Morris's own copies of incunables. Nos. L: 6-12 are other copies of books owned by him or specifically mentioned by him.
3. William Allingham, *A Diary* (London, 1907), p. 137.
4. The library of Alexander William, 25th Earl of Crawford and 8th Earl of Balcarres (1812-1880) has been admirably described by Nicolas Barker in *Bibliotheca Lindesiana* (London, 1977). That of Henry Huth (1815-1878) was sold by Sotheby's between 1911 and 1920. That of William Amhurst Tyssen-Amherst, 1st Baron Amherst of Hackney (1835-1909) was sold by Sotheby's in 1908 and 1909. The Rowfant Library of Frederick Locker-Lampson (1821-1895), named after his house, was sold *en bloc* to an American collector in 1905.
5. Frederick Startridge Ellis (1830-1901), antiquarian book-seller, publisher and Kelmscott Press editor.
6. The manuscript of this catalogue is in a private collection in the United States. It was exhibited at the Morgan Library in its 1976 exhibition.
7. May Morris, *The Collected Works of William Morris*, vol. 24 (London, 1915), p. xv.
8. J.W. Mackail, *The Life of William Morris*, vol. 2 (London, 1899; reprinted New York, 1968), p. 87.
9. This manuscript catalogue is also in a private collection in the United States. It was exhibited at the Morgan Library in its 1976 exhibition.
10. Bernard Quaritch (1819-1899) was the foremost anti-quarian bookseller of his time and one of Morris's pub-lishers. After 1890 Morris purchased many books and manuscripts from him.
11. Cockerell's diaries are in the Department of Manu-scripts of the British Library, London.
12. Quoted from *The Kelmscott Press Golden Legend: A Documentary History...* (College Park, Maryland, and Council Bluffs, Iowa, 1990), p. 24.
    The original is in the Bodleian Library.
13. Morris to Bernard Quaritch, 1 June 1892; quoted in Peterson, *The Kelmscott Press*, p. 92.
14. This account of the process is based on Catterson-Smith's own description, written in 1917 and published in the Pierpont Morgan Library Morris catalogue (no. 96). Walker also described the process in a 1922 letter to May Morris (now in the British Library), which is cited by Peterson in *A Bibliography of the Kelmscott Press*, p. xxix.
15. Mackail, *The Life of William Morris*, vol. 2, p. 249.
16. Goff numbers refer to Frederick R. Goff, *Incunabula in American Libraries: A Third Census...* (Millwood, N.Y., 1973).
17. Sotheby numbers refer to *Catalogue of a Portion of the Valuable Collection of Manuscripts, Early Printed Books, &c, of the Late William Morris*, the catalogue of the auction held by Sotheby, Wilkinson and Hodge, Wellington St., London, 5-10 December 1898.
18. This and subsequent numerical designations refer to a

method of differentiating the body-size of type in early printed books. Twenty lines of type, set solid, are measured vertically in millimetres; thus "115R" means that the type is a Roman face and twenty lines measure 115 mm. 114G (see No. L: 2) means that the type-face is Gothic and twenty lines measure 114 mm.

19. Woodcut illustrations in early printed books were often used more than once in the same book. Thus the repeats are indicated as part of the collation for this and the other illustrated incunables in this section: "176/192" means that 176 woodcuts are used a total of 192 times.

20. "On the Artistic Qualities of the Woodcut Books of Ulm and Augsburg in the Fifteenth Century", *Bibliographica*, vol. 1 (London, 1895-97), p. 452.

21. *The Ideal Book*, ed. William S. Peterson (Berkeley, 1982), p. 25.

22. Mackail, *The Life of William Morris*, vol. 2, p. 227.

23. Peterson numbers refer to W.S. Peterson, *A Bibliography of the Kelmscott Press* (see endnote 2).

24. Morris to Blunt, 19 November 1890, quoted from Peterson, *The Kelmscott Press...*, p. 221.

25. Cited in Peterson, *A Bibliography of the Kelmscott Press* (p. 60), from the original, owned by William P. Barlow, Jr., and privately printed by him in 1975.

26. "The Work of Walter Crane", *The Art Journal*, "Easter Annual" (London: 1898), p. 10.

27. Quoted in Duncan Robinson, *A Companion Volume to the Kelmscott Chaucer* (London, 1975), p. 27.

PHOTOGRAPHY

Maia-Mari Sutnik

No unified school of photography emerged from the Arts and Crafts movement that has the distinctiveness of William Morris's designs and illustrations. Nonetheless, a group of photographers is linked to Morris by attitudes and ideals shared with the Pre-Raphaelites. Potentially, photography could have been effective in facilitating Morris's sense of mission, both as an artist and as a socialist and visionary, for Morris struggled to revolutionize the values and correct the inequities of Victorian industrial society. One can speculate that Morris was not inspired by photographically illustrated books and folios produced by the many evolving high-quality photomechanical processes, and possibly saw photography as simply the outcome of scientific and mechanical progress.[1] But if photography lacked the humanity Morris sought in art, he clearly recognized its utility. His Oxford Street Shop offered photographs and sketches of designs for his clients, and it was a process-engraver and photographer, Emery Walker, whose photographically illustrated lecture on typography influenced Morris's eventual commitment to printing. It was also Walker who became responsible for the photographic archive of Morris's work, now at St. Bride's Printing Library and the National Portrait Gallery Archives, London.[2]

It may be telling that Morris broke his silence on the subject of photography only to express some alarm at the prospect of being photographed: "I have never mustered courage enough to get my photograph taken; I suppose I shall soon; Mrs. Cameron threatened me with the operation.... I don't suppose I shall escape long."[3]

The separation between the process and the product was a deeper problem for many others besides Morris, especially whenever photography sought to cross the boundaries of the established arts. Morris's contact with John Ruskin would certainly have had some effect on his thoughts about photography. Ruskin, once fascinated by the properties of the Daguerreotype, now considered the camera too secular and deficient; true art, he felt, must be

---

NO. M: 4. JOHN R. PARSONS, photographer, posed by DANTE GABRIEL ROSSETTI, *Jane Morris (seated)*, July 1865

made by hand to convey a higher order of feeling and inspiration.

The broad issues of mid-Victorian photography – realism, naturalism, capacity for pictorial truth, reproduction of minutiae, and the medium's purpose and value – had embroiled artists and photographers for some time. On the one hand, the efficacy of the camera was praised for capturing images that transmitted prints of tonal equivalence and for its measure of exactitude in recording objects. On the other hand, artists and critics feared its competitiveness with the fine arts and criticized photography for displacing cherished values. Ruskin called for his "chemical friends to throw their vials and washers down the gutter-trap,"[4] as he believed that true art was achieved by devotion to the observation and interpretation of nature. Photographers responded adversely, feeling that attempts to imitate nature with photographic precision by any other medium than their own was futile.

FIG. M: 1
JOHN R. PARSONS
Portrait of Alexa Wilding, c. 1865
(albumen, cabinet card)
Private collection

Neither Ruskin's condemnation of the camera nor the conservative reaction of the arts community discouraged its popularity. The Pre-Raphaelites, like so many of their contemporaries, also employed photography surreptitiously to avoid the stigma attached to its use. The painters Ford Madox Brown (No. M: 2), John Everett Millais, Arthur Hughes, William Holman Hunt, and Dante Gabriel Rossetti (No. M: 1) all relied on photography at one time or another.[5] And the desire by photographers to become integrated into the fine arts contributed to the cross-over of ideas between photography and painting. The composite fabrications of Oscar Gustave Rejlander and Henry Peach Robinson, and the spiriting away of Julia Margaret Cameron's portrait subjects from ordinary circumstances to the romanticized world of legends and allegories, were attempts to re-define aesthetics. Cameron's calls for "Art" in photography were then seen as indulgent, yet the force of the personalities portrayed in her pantheon of celebrated sitters could only have been conveyed by the particular visual properties of photography.

No event, however, has come to dominate the concept of Pre-Raphaelite photographic representation more than Rossetti's request of 5 July 1865 for Jane Morris to come to his residence in Cheyne Walk, Chelsea, at eleven a.m. on a Wednesday, to be photographed.[6] Rossetti was to direct the photography of the studio professional, John R. Parsons. When one compares the somewhat prosaic Parson studio-posed model (fig. M: 1) with Rossetti's dynamic spacing and languid arrangements of Jane, the extent of the latter's involvement in creating hauntingly evocative and enigmatically charged images is revealed (Nos. M: 3-4). Rossetti's vantage may have been his infatuation with Jane, and his creative impulse to transform the wife of William Morris from "an ordinary woman"[7] to his pictorial muse. The inward tension of Rossetti's moral dilemma is released in his many idealized paintings of Jane as an archetypal Pre-Raphaelite "stunner"[8] – an otherworldly figure with loose, flowing hair, large, dark eyes, elongated neck and full, sullen lips,

NO. M: 6. FREDERICK HOLLYER, *The Burne-Jones and Morris Families at The Grange*, 1874

NO. M: 5. LEWIS CARROLL (Rev. Charles Lutwidge Dodgson), *The Rossetti Family in the Cheyne Walk Garden*, October 1863

FIG. M: 2
LEWIS CARROLL
Rossetti Playing Chess with his Mother, 1863 (albumen)
Private collection

FIG. M: 3
LEWIS CARROLL
Christina Rossetti with her Mother, 1863 (albumen, cabinet card)
Private collection

and possessing a self-contained grace and mystery (see No. A: 43). Clearly preoccupied with his adoration for Jane, Rossetti nevertheless perceived her as serving his artistic as well as his amorous purposes. Fascinating as the photographs are in themselves, they do not correspond to conditions of actuality. Rather, they express creative ideas and camera-knowledge, demonstrating how well both were manipulated and thereby arguing the case for photography being no less interpretive than a painting of the same subject. Nine years later, Jane Morris, photographed by Frederick Hollyer in the Burne-Jones and Morris family group (No. M: 6), appears trapped and dispirited by the conflicts that plagued her life, a representation closer to the truth of her experiences. It is tempting to state that Rossetti's vision of Jane revealed more about Rossetti than about his subject.

Two years earlier, in 1863, the Rev. Charles Lutwidge Dodgson (Lewis Carroll) spent three days at Cheyne Walk, making several intimate photographic portraits of the Rossetti family. He posed the Rossettis by the steps leading from the house to the garden, depicting them with an overall grace and naturalism. His arrangements revive classic poses: reading books, playing games of chess, and "conversation" pieces (figs. M: 2-3). While these photographs are sensitive studies of great simplicity and humanity, the Rossettis appear emotionally enclosed and internalized, as if Carroll has taken into account Rossetti's loss of his wife (and favourite model) Elizabeth Siddal not long before. Although, technically, Carroll was very accomplished, the nineteenth-century photographer was at the mercy of the unexpected elements that could thwart his or her best efforts. Christina Rossetti reveals: "It was our aim to appear in the full family group of five, but whilst various others succeeded, that particular negative was spoilt by a shower and I possess a solitary print taken from it in which we appear as if splashed by ink"[9] (No. M: 5).

As an amateur, Carroll relied on his intuitive eye for capturing visual form and harmony, and saw his work as being primarily for his own enjoyment and that of his circle of friends, of which the painter Arthur Hughes was a member (see No. B: 3). Frederick Hollyer (1837-1933), on the other hand, achieved public recognition for himself and his celebrated friends through photography. Hollyer, very much a central figure in the art and literary scene, took up photography about 1860 to establish a business making fine reproductions of paintings, exhibitions and studio installations, and doing photographic portraiture. His Pembroke Square studio was a vibrant setting for the stylish recording of Pre-Raphaelite taste and trends.

Even the "cabinet" card, a popular commercial-studio format, received very distinctive treatment by Hollyer; his are recognizable by their sub-

NO. M: 8
FREDERICK HOLLYER,
Portrait of Edward Burne-Jones,
c. 1882

NO. M: 11
FREDERICK HOLLYER,
Portrait of Margaret Burne-Jones,
October 1884

tle platinum-print quality, enhanced by handpainted gold borders on the mount. Burne-Jones and William Morris and assorted members of their families (No. M: 6) served as Hollyer's subjects many times. In his formal portraits, women shun the camera and are portrayed with gentle and delicate beauty, a quality clearly possessed by Margaret Burne-Jones (Nos. M: 10-11); Edward Burne-Jones also looks away from the camera, thus emphasizing a well-shaped head, a brow that was "extraordinary", and a "forehead wide, and rather high and calm", which Georgiana Burne-Jones noted with admiration.[10] Hollyer's exterior photographs of Burne-Jones and Morris are seemingly more casual. One feels that these are not meant for the public eye but to capture the experience of immediacy and the spirit of their long-standing friendship (Nos. M: 7, 15).

Hollyer's commercial work was straightforward and unadulterated. His views of The Grange, Burne-Jones's 1717 house on North End Road in Fulham (Nos. M: 16-22), do not pretend to be anything but documentary

NO. M: 19
FREDERICK HOLLYER,
Dining Room, The Grange, 1887

NO. M: 22
FREDERICK HOLLYER,
*Margaret Burne-Jones's Bedroom,
The Grange*, 1887

records. One finds these studies interesting in their honest revelation of present conditions and their attempt to bring the viewer closer to the artist. Burne-Jones did not live in a sterile environment, but one that was rich in the aesthetic taste of the period, as exemplified by the designs for the interior by Morris & Co. Hollyer's camera has succeeded in bringing direct insight into the professional and personal sides of a much-celebrated artist. During the last decade of the century, Hollyer became a member of The Linked Ring, a secret society not unlike the "brotherhood" of the Pre-Raphaelites, which had formed in opposition to the Photographic Society of Great Britain. At Ring meetings he would have held company with Frederick H. Evans (1853-1943), the photographer of the most magnificent view of Morris's Kelmscott Manor, *The Attic*, taken in 1896 (No. M: 26).

   Evans's love of architecture was shared by Morris, who also expressed his appreciation of the complete and logical style of Gothic cathedrals, which they both felt served the intellect as well as the imagination of man. In an

address to the Royal Photographic Society in 1900, Evans said,

> If we valued our great architecture as we ought, we should not only have photographic records of scale of all the important details,...but we should also have every aspect of our great buildings in general, in particular, from the point of view of beauty.... [This would be] an inestimable joy for our descendants, when these architectural treasures are gone forever.[11]

A talented amateur photographer and a well-known and highly regarded bookseller, Evans retired from literary commerce in 1898 to dedicate himself to photography, thereby locating himself at the centre of aesthetic debate on the merits of this medium as fine art. In opposition to manipulated and soft-focus gum-print images, Evans extolled the value of the "pure" photograph – a camera art without artifice, retouching or manipulation. For Evans, this quality of expression was creativity on a par with other fine arts. He made platinum prints that are exquisite in their careful handling of light and tone, space and atmosphere, which lend the images their emotive substance. It was at Kelmscott Manor (Nos. M: 23-26) that Morris felt the joy of retreat, an abiding record of which is preserved in Evans's studies.

By the time of Morris's death in 1896, photography had neither made revolutionary victories nor sustained heavy losses. The lines between the camera and the hand became increasingly blurred as new innovations and technical advances were accepted with excitement. While changes inspired new modes and new ideas of photographic thought, it was the product of these that best reflected the struggle and significantly opened the medium to serious analysis and discussion. No longer the handmaiden of painting, photography came to artistic and social fruition by means of its flexibility, by the widespread recognition of its visual properties, and by its ability to redefine its role as the medium demystified and aligned itself with progressive ideas in the following decades. Within these values, photography could also aspire to become as egalitarian a form of expression as those which earlier had inspired the art of William Morris.

NO. M: 23
FREDERICK H. EVANS,
Kelmscott Manor: From the Meadows, 1895

W. & D. DOWNEY, LONDON

*John Ruskin and Dante Gabriel Rossetti in Cheyne Walk
Garden* June 1863
Albumen print on mount (cabinet card)
14.4 x 10.0 cm (image); 16.5 x 11.0 cm (mount)
Provenance: Helen Rossetti Angeli
Private collection, Vancouver
For illustration see page 5.

No. M: 2

ELLIOT & FRY, LONDON

Portrait of Ford Madox Brown c. 1878
Albumen print on mount (*carte-de-visite*)
9.2 x 6.0 cm (image); 10.6 x 6.4 cm (mount)
Provenance: Helen Rossetti Angeli
Private collection, Vancouver
For illustration see page 3.

No. M: 3

JOHN R. PARSONS, POSED BY
DANTE GABRIEL ROSSETTI

Jane Morris (standing) July 1865
Silver bromide print (from original collodion negative)
24.5 x 19.5 cm
Provenance: Helen Rossetti Angeli
Private collection, Vancouver
For illustration see page 8.

No. M: 4

JOHN R. PARSONS, POSED BY
DANTE GABRIEL ROSSETTI

Jane Morris (seated) July 1865
Silver bromide print (from original collodion negative)
24.5 x 19.5 cm
Provenance: Helen Rossetti Angeli
Private collection, Vancouver

Research on the Parsons-Rossetti negatives, to be published
at a later date, has been undertaken by Janet Dewan. It is
possible that the prints in this exhibition were made from
the original collodion plates. Correspondence in the Victoria and Albert Museum Library, London, suggests that
Helen Rossetti Angeli still had the original plates in her
possession in 1943. A bound album in Morris fabric, containing nineteenth-century albumen prints and corresponding modern prints, is in the collection of the V & A.
This album was assembled before 1933 by Dr. Gordon
Bottomley for May Morris, from ineptly framed prints
owned by her father, William Morris. Copy negatives were
also made by Emery Walker sometime before 1930 and are
now in the St. Bride's Printing Library, London. Copy-
prints exist in the archives of the National Portrait Gallery, London.

No. M: 5

LEWIS CARROLL (REV. CHARLES
LUTWIDGE DODGSON)

The Rossetti Family in the Cheyne Walk Garden
October 1863
Albumen print
17.0 x 21.0 cm
Provenance: Helen Rossetti Angeli
Private collection, Vancouver

NO. M: 9

Christina (on steps), Dante Gabriel (standing), mother Frances Rossetti, William Michael, and Maria Francesca Rossetti (around table).

No. M: 6

FREDERICK HOLLYER

The Burne-Jones and Morris Families at The Grange 1874
Albumen print on mount (cabinet card)
10.1 x 14.0 cm (image); 10.8 x 16.4 cm (mount)
Provenance: Helen Rossetti Angeli
Private collection, Vancouver

No. M: 7

FREDERICK HOLLYER

Burne-Jones and Morris 1874
Platinum print
13.5 x 9.5 cm
Provenance: Sir Edward Coley Burne-Jones, Bt.
Private collection
For illustration see page ii.

No. M: 8

FREDERICK HOLLYER

Portrait of Edward Burne-Jones c. 1882
Platinum print on mount (cabinet card)
14.7 x 9.0 cm (image); 16.5 x 11.0 cm (mount)
Provenance: Sir Edward Coley Burne-Jones, Bt.
Private collection, Ottawa

No. M: 9

FREDERICK HOLLYER

Portrait of Georgiana Burne-Jones c. 1882
Platinum print on mount (cabinet card)
14.0 x 9.0 cm (image); 16.6 x 10.8 cm (mount)
Provenance: Sir Edward Coley Burne-Jones, Bt.
Private collection, Ottawa

No. M: 10

FREDERICK HOLLYER

Portrait of Margaret Burne-Jones October 1882
Platinum print on mount (cabinet card)
14.3 x 9.1 cm (image); 16.5 x 10.8 cm (mount)
Provenance: Sir Edward Coley Burne-Jones, Bt.
Private collection, Ottawa
For illustration see page 218.

NO. M: 12

No. M: 11

FREDERICK HOLLYER

Portrait of Margaret Burne-Jones October 1884
Platinum print on mount (cabinet card)
14.6 x 9.0 cm (image); 16.7 x 10.9 cm (mount)
Provenance: Sir Edward Coley Burne-Jones, Bt.
Private collection, Ottawa

No. M: 12

FREDERICK HOLLYER

Bowyer Nichols, J.W. Mackail, H.C. Beeding c. 1882
Platinum print on mount (cabinet card)
9.8 x 15.0 cm (image); 10.8 x 16.5 cm (mount)
Provenance: Sir Edward Coley Burne-Jones, Bt.
Private collection, Ottawa

No. M: 13

H. & R. STILES, LONDON

Edward Burne-Jones with Grand-Daughter, Angela Mackail
   May 1892
Platinum print on mount
14.6 x 10.3 cm (image); 14.5 x 10.0 cm (mount)
Provenance: Sir Edward Coley Burne-Jones, Bt.
Private collection, Ottawa

Angela Mackail, the daughter of Morris's biographer J.W. Mackail (see No. M: 12), later gained fame as the novelist Angela Thirkell. Her first marriage, to the singer and journalist James Campbell McInnes (which ended in divorce in 1917), produced two writer sons: the London-based novelist Colin McInnes, and the diplomat, critic and autobiographer Graham McInnes (1912-1970), who after

NO. M: 13

graduation emigrated to Canada from Australia and subsequently published two books on Canadian art, in 1939 and 1950 respectively, and three volumes of autobiography.

No. M: 14

UNKNOWN, BRITISH (20th c.)

Portrait of Lady Burne-Jones
Bromide print
20.0 x 14.9 cm
Provenance: Sir Edward Coley Burne-Jones, Bt.
Private collection, Ottawa

No. M: 15

FREDERICK HOLLYER

Burne-Jones and Morris, Sunday Morning, The Grange Garden 27 July 1890
Platinum print on mount
8.5 x 7.0 cm (image); 10.6 x 7.5 cm (mount)

Provenance: Sir Edward Coley Burne-Jones, Bt.
Private collection
For illustration see page 295.

No. M: 16

FREDERICK HOLLYER

The Grange, North End Road, London 1887
Albumen print on mount
22.6 x 27.9 cm (image); 25.4 x 30.5 cm (mount)
Provenance: Sir Edward Coley Burne-Jones, Bt.
Private collection

No. M: 17

FREDERICK HOLLYER

Garden Studio, The Grange 1887
Albumen print on mount
23.0 x 28.0 cm (image); 25.4 x 30.5 cm (mount)
Provenance: Sir Edward Coley Burne-Jones, Bt.
Private collection

No. M: 18

FREDERICK HOLLYER

Garden Studio, The Grange 1887
Albumen print on mount
22.5 x 28.1 cm (image); 25.4 x 30.5 cm (mount)
Provenance: Sir Edward Coley Burne-Jones, Bt.
Private collection

Two views of Burne-Jones's very practical studio, hung with his works, amid which are garden benches and West

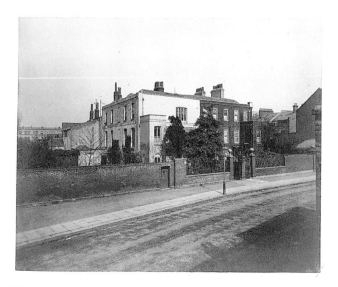

NO. M: 16

NO. M: 17

Country ladder-back church chairs, along with examples of the Firm's popular *Sussex* arm-chairs.

– Robert Little

No. M: 19

FREDERICK HOLLYER

Dining Room, The Grange 1887
Albumen print on mount
22.4 x 28.2 cm (image); 25.4 x 30.5 cm (mount)
Provenance: Sir Edward Coley Burne-Jones, Bt.
Private collection

View into the dining room showing the sideboard with depictions of *Ladies and Animals*, painted by Burne-Jones just before his marriage in June 1860. Dating from the same year is the oak trestle-table designed by Philip Webb, who also possibly designed the fitted china-cabinet. The vernacular Windsor arm-chair of c. 1840-60 was probably from Buckinghamshire and is a fitting complement to the Burne-Jones sideboard, which is set out with late-Georgian silverware. Over the fireplace is a Regency convex glass mirror. The adjustable chandelier in the Georgian Revival style is probably by W.A.S. Benson.

– Robert Little

No. M: 20

FREDERICK HOLLYER

Drawing Room, The Grange 1887
Albumen print on mount
22.9 x 28.2 cm (image); 25.4 x 30.5 cm (mount)
Provenance: Sir Edward Coley Burne-Jones, Bt.
Private collection
For illustration see page 126.

The drawing room of The Grange, suitably furnished with Morris & Co. *Jasmine* wallpaper, a *Morris* reclining arm-chair in Utrecht velvet, two corner sofas, a small settee covered in *Rose and Thistle* fabric, and bookcases, probably by W.A.S. Benson. Over the Regency mantel, flanking William Blake Richmond's portrait of Margaret Burne-Jones, are two reduced casts after Michelangelo. Also on the fireplace, as well as on the bookshelf, are brasswares from the Middle East, the source of the unusual ceiling-lantern. To the right of the late-Gothic cupboard, over the corner sofa, are some of Burne-Jones's collection of Dürer engravings.

– Robert Little

No. M: 21

FREDERICK HOLLYER

Margaret Burne-Jones's Bedroom, The Grange 1887
Albumen print on mount
22.9 x 28.2 cm (image); 25.4 x 30.5 cm (mount)
Provenance: Sir Edward Coley Burne-Jones, Bt.
Private collection
For illustration see page 127.

Visible on the walls are framed graphic works by Dürer and Burne-Jones, hung on Morris & Co. *Lily* paper. Toward the back, beyond the simple fireplace, is the bed with its hangings in the Firm's *Bird* woven fabric, along with an embroidered bed-cover. Near the bed is a small West Coun-

NO. M: 18

try church chair of c. 1860, probably from Holcombe Rogus in Devon, of which there were examples everywhere in the house. Tucked between books and flowers on the mantelpiece are two Japanese fans.

– Robert Little

No. M: 22

FREDERICK HOLLYER

Margaret Burne-Jones's Bedroom, The Grange 1887
Albumen print on mount
22.4 x 28.1 cm (image); 25.4 x 30.5 cm (mount)

Provenance: Sir Edward Coley Burne-Jones, Bt.
Private collection

A view into the bedroom, showing a writing-desk – most probably by Philip Webb. Above a miniature version after Michelangelo's *Slave* and framed works by Burne-Jones and his colleagues is a hanging bookcase with oriental porcelains. Over the wash-stand, to the left and partially hidden by the *japonaiserie* reeded screen, is a fragment of the Firm's *Honeysuckle* fabric protecting the *Lily* wallpaper.

– Robert Little

No. M: 23

FREDERICK H. EVANS

Kelmscott Manor: From the Meadows 1895
Platinum print mounted on wove paper
9.6 x 20.4 cm (image); 37.6 x 51.2 cm (mount)
National Gallery of Canada, Ottawa (acc. no. 21709)

No. M: 24

FREDERICK H. EVANS

View from the Tapestry Room, Kelmscott Manor,
    Oxfordshire 1896
Platinum print on mount
18.6 x 9.8 cm (image); 22.7 x 12.1 cm (mount)
Centre Canadien d'Architecture/Canadian Centre for
    Architecture, Montreal

No. M: 25

FREDERICK H. EVANS

View from the Orchard, Kelmscott Manor, Oxfordshire 1897
Platinum print on mount
14.3 x 20.1 cm (image); 26.5 x 32.9 cm (mount)
Centre Canadien d'Architecture/Canadian Centre for
    Architecture, Montreal
For illustration see page 10.

No. M: 26

FREDERICK H. EVANS

Kelmscott Manor: The Attic 1896
Platinum print on mount
15.6 x 20.2 cm
Provenance: Gordon Conn, Toronto
International Museum of Photography, George Eastman
    House, Rochester, N.Y., purchase, 1953

Gordon Conn, a Canadian painter, collector and art dealer who served as executor of such artists as G.A. Reid, Mary Wrinch Reid and Marion Long, formed a friendship with Evans during the mid-1920s in London. Conn posed for Evans in 1928 and began to collect his work. In 1950 he offered his collection of some sixty Evans prints to the Art Museum of Toronto (now the Art Gallery of Ontario), but the donation was turned down. Three years later the collection was acquired by George Eastman House, Rochester, New York, and in 1964 became the nucleus of Beaumont Newhall's Evans retrospective. In 1979 Mrs. Rheta Conn donated to the AGO five Evans prints, including portraits of Gordon Conn and *A Souvenir of Aubrey Beardsley*.[12]

No. M: 27

HARRY F. PHILIPS

Jane Morris in Old Age c. 1913
Gelatin silver print
13.8 x 8.6 cm
Provenance: Ian Hodgkins Co. Ltd.
Private collection, Ottawa
For illustration see page 218.

This portrait of Jane Morris was taken by Harry F. Philips of Leek, apparently during one of her visits to Morris's old friend and colleague, Thomas Wardle, whose textile printing works were located in that city. Another pose from the same sitting, showing Jane in full-length seated in a garden, is in the V & A. The mottled texture of the photograph indicates that this vignetted head was enlarged from a negative. One recognizes her abundant hair, now white, and the same sad eyes that gazed out in photographs from her youth. Having succeeded in purchasing Kelmscott Manor only in December 1913, Jane died in Bath at the end of the following January at the age of seventy-four.

– Douglas E. Schoenherr

ENDNOTES

1. Morris opposed the materialism and artifice of Victorian values. His response to the 1851 Great Exhibition, at which photography was on substantial display, was one of outright rejection. The work of some calotypists was presented in the Fine Arts section, but photography was also exhibited with "Philosophical Instruments" – musical, horological, and surgical – as well as being shown with telescopes and the electric telegraph.

2. Helen Wodzicka, "The Emery Walker Photographs at St. Bride's", *The Journal of the William Morris Society* 11 (1970): 13-27.

3. Norman Kelvin, ed., *The Collected Letters of William Morris* 1 (Princeton, Princeton University Press, 1983), p. 87.

4. Michael Bartram, *The Pre-Raphaelite Camera* (Boston, 1985), p. 35.

5. Aaron Scharf, *Art and Photography* (Harmondsworth, Middlesex, 1974), pp. 107-8.

6. Victoria and Albert Museum Library, London.

7. Bartram, *The Pre-Raphaelite Camera*, p. 136.

8. Jan Marsh, *Pre-Raphaelite Woman* (London, 1987), p. 17.

9. Helmut Gernsheim, *Lewis Carroll Photographer*, revised ed. (New York, 1969), p. 56.

10. Bevis Hillier, *Victorian Studio Photographers* (Boston, 1975) p. 84.

11. Beaumont Newhall, ed., *Photography: Essays and Images* (Boston, 1980), p. 179.

12. See Maia-Mari Sutnik, "Photographs of Frederick H. Evans", *AGO News* (December 1990): 3.

GENERAL INDEX

INDEX TO EXHIBITS

Carlo Catenazzi, Glenn Reichwein, Art Gallery of Ontario: Nos. A: 6, A: 7, A: 16, A: 19, A: 27c.-d., A: 30, A: 38, A: 44, B: 2-3, F: 3, F: 7, F: 9, F: 15, F: 20, F: 28, F: 30, G: 2-4, G: 6, H: 34, I: 1-7, I: 9, K: 1-5, K: 10, L: 6, L: 11, L: 22, L: 25-26, L: 31, L: 34-35, L: 38, M: 7-8, M: 10-13, M: 16-22, fig. K: 1, fig. 5 on p. 32; T. Beasley: Nos. E: 1-3, E: 6-8; Beaverbrook Art Gallery: Nos. A: 4, A: 7, A: 20a.; B. Boyle, Royal Ontario Museum: Nos. A: 13, A: 20b., A: 25, C: 1-2, F: 6, F: 14, F: 17, F: 23, H: 17, H: 32, H: 46, J: 1, J: 3-4; Bruce Peel Special Collections Library, University of Alberta: No. L: 21; Centre Canadien d'Architecture / Canadian Centre for Architecture: Nos. M: 24-25; Dalhousie University Library: No. L: 4; Edmonton Art Gallery: No. A: 24; George Eastman House: No. M: 26; J. Gorman, Vancouver Art Gallery: No. A: 14; C. Guest, The Montreal Museum of Fine Arts: Nos. F: 8, F: 11-13, F: 18, H: 13, H: 23, H: 33; G. Kernan, AK Photos: Nos. A: 2, A: 10, A: 12, A: 26, A: 33, A: 37; R. Keziere: Nos. A: 35, A: 40-41, D: 2, D: 4, E: 11, E: 15, F: 1, F: 4-5, F: 22, F: 24-25, F: 27, F: 29, F: 32, J: 2, M: 1-6, figs. M: 1-3; E. Mayer: Nos. F: 2, F: 26, H: 15-16, H: 22, H: 28, H: 31, H: 39; McCord Museum of Canadian History: Nos. F: 19, H: 12; McLennan Library, McGill University: Nos. A: 27a.-b., L: 1; Media IV, Queen's University: No. L: 30 (copy 2); B. Merrett: Nos. D: 3, F: 31, fig. 3 on p. 18; Metropolitan Toronto Reference Library: Nos. L: 17, L: 24; D. Miller: No. G: 5; K. Minchin: No. F: 21; Peter Nahum: fig. A: 5; National Gallery of Canada: Nos. A: 1, A: 22-23, A: 28, A: 31-32, A: 34, A: 36, A: 43, B: 4, K: 9, M: 23; National Library of Canada: No. L: 30 (copy 1); L. Ostrom, Christie Lake Studios: Nos. A: 3, A: 5, A: 8-9, A: 17, A: 29, D: 1, E: 4, E: 9-10, E: 12-13, E: 16-21, H: 1-4, H: 6, H: 8-11, H: 19-20, H: 29-30, H: 36, H: 38, H: 42-43, H: 45, I: 8, K: 6-8, L: 15, L: 33, M: 27; *Private Eye*: Nos. A: 15, B: 1; R.H.V. Tee and Sons Ltd.: No. G: 1; R.M. Tremblay: No. H: 5; University of Manitoba: No. L: 23; S. Zwerling Photo Ltd.: No. A: 18.

Fig. A: 8 reproduced by permission of the Birmingham Museum and Art Gallery; fig. K: 2 courtesy of the Trustees of the British Museum; fig. 1 on p. 23 courtesy of Harvard University Art Museums; fig. 2 on p. 25 courtesy of The Montreal Museum of Fine Arts; fig. 4 on p. 29 and fig. B: 1 courtesy of the National Gallery of Canada; fig. I: 1 courtesy of the Pierpont Morgan Library; figs. F: 1, I: 2-3 courtesy of the V & A; fig. 1 on p. 11 courtesy of the William Morris Gallery; fig. D: 1 courtesy of Wilmot United Church, Fredericton.